HARD TRUTH

ALSO BY NEVADA BARR

HARD TRUTH

Nevada Barr

DOUBLEDAY LARGE PRINT
HOME LIBRARY EDITION

G. P. PUTNAM'S SONS NEW YORK

This Large Print Edition, prepared especially for Doubleday Large Print Home Library, contains the complete, unabridged text of the original Publisher's Edition.

G. P. PUTNAM'S SONS
Publishers Since 1838
Published by the Penguin Group
Penguin Group (USA) Inc., 375 Hudson Street, New York, New York 10014, USA • Penguin Group (Canada), 10 Alcorn Avenue, Toronto, Ontario M4V 3B2, Canada (a division of Pearson Penguin Canada Inc.) • Penguin Books Ltd, 80 Strand, London WC2R 0RL, England • Penguin Ireland, 25 St Stephen's Green, Dublin 2, Ireland (a division of Penguin Books Ltd) • Penguin Group (Australia), 250 Camberwell Road, Camberwell, Victoria 3124, Australia (a division of Pearson Australia Group Pty Ltd) • Penguin Books India Pvt Ltd, 11 Community Centre, Panchsheel Park, New Delhi—110 017, India • Penguin Group (NZ), Cnr Airborne and Rosedale Roads, Albany, Auckland 1310, New Zealand (a division of Pearson New Zealand Ltd) • Penguin Books (South Africa) (Pty) Ltd, 24 Sturdee Avenue, Rosebank, Johannesburg 2196, South Africa • Penguin Books Ltd, Registered Offices: 80 Strand, London WC2R 0RL, England

ISBN 0-7394-5262-2

Printed in the United States of America

ENDPAPER MAP BY JACKIE AHER

This is a work of fiction. Names, characters, places, and incidents either are the product of the author's imagination or are used fictitiously, and any resemblance to actual persons, living or dead, businesses, companies, events, or locales is entirely coincidental.

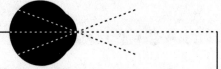

This Large Print Book carries the
Seal of Approval of N.A.V.H.

*For Linda. A true Southern gentlewoman,
she wouldn't dream of coming to dinner
without a hostess gift.*

Nor would she flinch from the necessary murder.

acknowledgements

This book was not only made possible but turned into an absolute joy by the rangers at Rocky Mountain National Park, most especially Superintendent Vaughn Baker, District Ranger Patty Shafer, Exceptional Child Sierra Shafer, Backcountry Rangers Lisa Hendy and Ryan Schuster, Frontcountry Ranger Shannon Olmstead, Chief of Interpretation Larry Frederick, Research Administrator Terry Terrell and Assistant Superintendent Tony Schetzle.

Thanks must also go to Dr. Alexis Hallock, who helped me through the fascinating vagaries of the spinal cord.

HARD TRUTH

one

"Jiminy Christmas!" Heath resisted the call of stronger language out of respect for her aunt's southern sensibilities. "Cross them or fold them or something. Don't just leave them laying there like a couple of dead carp." Heath looked away from her legs. Though they were tidily covered in denim trousers and, to all intents and purposes, looked like the legs of any seated, trim, forty-one-year-old woman, she couldn't bear the sight of them.

"How about I pretzel them?" Gwen said, turning from the campground's specially designed picnic table where she was setting out a plate on the specially designed end so Heath's specially designed wheelchair would roll under oh-so-specially. "Why don't you get Wiley to do it? He's a highly trained helper."

Heath looked to where the dog lay under the table watching a momma mallard and her three late-season ducklings with an evil glint in his eyes. He was originally named Prince Theo III but she and her aunt called him Wiley because of an uncanny resemblance he bore to the cartoon coyote after a run-in with roadrunners and sticks of TNT.

"Wiley's off duty."

"Wiley's always off duty."

Heath leaned over, her belly pressed against the wheelchair's safety belt: an indignity the doctors had promised she could forgo when she got used to her "altered circumstances" and quit pitching face forward every time she leaned too far. With hands as angry and curved as talons, she grabbed her right ankle and jerked upward. She could feel the leg in her hands but not her hands on her leg. It reminded her of a creepy childhood trick. Her best friend Sylvia would hold her palm to hers, then, feeling the backs of the fingers, one her own, one Heath's, she'd intone: "This is what dead people feel like," and the two of them would squeal in horrific delight.

"This is what dead people feel like," Heath said.

Gwen ignored her.

Wiley watched the baby ducks picking at crumbs with a fluff of ducky butts and murmurs of ducky glee.

Heath set her ankle on the opposite knee, like stacking firewood, and wondered if she'd cut off her circulation or done any other damage to her insensate lower half. At least the plastic tubes were gone. The modern-day Frankensteins who had reworked her lower half had cheerfully told her that regaining control of her bowels and bladder was a "positive sign." She tried to be grateful for this small shred of autonomy—and dignity—left to her.

For a couple months after the fall, she'd played Christopher Reeve, pretending to be as optimistic, as cheerful, but she was a lousy actor and when the doctors told her, with a crushed third lumbar vertebra, she had the chance of the proverbial snowball in hell of climbing again, she'd rung down the curtain. The first of many curtains.

Little light now came into her spiritual house.

"Shit," she said, for no other reason than it seemed to express the gestalt of the moment.

Gwen turned, leaned on the prosthetically elongated end of the picnic table. Gwendolyn Littleton was Heath's aunt. She was seventy-one, thin and in superb condition. Her hair was eternally and determinedly red. She swore she would go to the grave clutching a bottle of Lady Clairol in one hand and a bottle of hormone replacement pills in the other. She wore her naturally frizzy hair up in a wild bird's nest she referred to as a neo–Gibson Girl. Her face wasn't youthful or even pretty, but Heath loved it. Every wrinkle turned up at the end, forced against gravity and life's myriad evils by Gwen's tendency to laugh at that which did not kill. She wasn't laughing now. The hurt Heath had caused showed around Gwen's mouth and eyes. A flinching as if from a physical blow.

"Maybe a camping trip was a rotten idea."

"Not camping, *handi*camping," Heath retorted, and was sorry when the pinch of pain on her aunt's face deepened.

"Got to call it something, sugar," Gwen

said gently, her southern drawl making "sugar" the sweetest of words.

Heath said nothing. Shame clogged her throat. Shame and self-pity and shame at the self-pity. "Hey, Wiley," she called the dog. He heaved himself to his paws with a gusty sigh and ambled over in his loose-jointed way. It had been said that every cloud had a silver lining. For Heath this bedraggled, smart, ugly dog was it, the one thin flicker in the great dark firmament, like low summer lightning beneath a midwestern tornado sky.

"Hey dog," she said, and scratched his ratty ears.

On December twenty-third, Heath had fallen from an ice chute up by the Keyhole on Longs Peak. Rotten ice had dropped her sixty-eight feet to a helicopter ride and her new life as a cripple. Sixty-eight feet. Lucky to be alive, everyone said. The hospital had been her world through March. Physical therapy, Prozac. More physical therapy, Effexor. Pool therapy, Xanax; lots of Xanax. Watching people in gaily colored scrubs, prattling in gaily banal conversation, manipulating chunks of flesh and bone she could no longer feel gave Heath the creeps.

On the ides of March she'd given up, quit. The antidepressants she flushed down the john. She wasn't depressed because her brain didn't work. She was depressed because her life no longer worked. The wheelchair came in April. Wiley in June. The dog and Gwen kept Heath from folding like a cheap kite in a windstorm.

"Lucky to be alive," Heath said, to see if it sounded true yet.

It didn't.

"Lucky for *me*," Gwen replied, and again Heath felt guilty.

The late summer day had eased seamlessly into night. Stars appeared and disappeared as the last of the monsoons—the northern edge of them—visited Rocky, and thunder cells racketed around the mountains. Lightning flickered over Longs Peak and Flattop. Thunder rolled down the canyons from the high places, bringing the ineffable perfume of rain on pines, an elixir that made even Heath feel alive. The feeling was followed immediately by the memory of A Life.

"What is it, darlin'?" Gwen asked as she tidied away the ends of their meal, whisking the crumbs from the hot dog buns onto the ground for the ducklings.

"You're feeding the wildlife," Heath accused to avoid the question.

"The crumbs just fell off." Gwen sat on the picnic table, feet on the bench. "You look so down. Mountain air is supposed to lift the spirits, make the heart sing."

"Yeah," Heath agreed. Then the wine said: *It might work if I wasn't a fucking cripple.* She smiled because Gwen wanted her to, but she could feel the riptide of alcohol and despair dragging her down to the cold dark bottom of the sea where one day she could drown in booze or bitterness. She tried to think of heroes, of Lance Armstrong, of the man who cut his arm off with a pocketknife rather than die in the wilderness, of those people who'd overcome and triumphed. But they could walk. An arm was nothing. A few toes. A foot. Even one leg. From where she sat, those looked like a cakewalk. They, the lucky, the one-armed, the one-legged, the three-toed, were not helpless. It was the helplessness as much as the loss of her old life—her old self—that scared Heath witless. Scared her so bad she'd told no one. Not even Gwen. Bears could eat her, fires burn her, criminals mug her, little boys torment her, and there was nothing she could do about it but rail pathetically.

Or die.

"Stop it," she said.

"What?" Gwen roused from contemplation of an ember in the barbeque grate, a poor understudy for a campfire but all that was allowed in the park during fire season.

"Wiley was licking my hand," Heath lied.

Gwen looked at the relatively innocent dog lying some yards from the wheelchair but said nothing. "I'm for bed—not to sleep, to read," she assured her niece, and Heath wondered if the stab of fear she'd felt at being left alone had shown on her face.

"I'm going for a walk—a roll," Heath announced, to prove fear wasn't what Gwen had seen.

The older woman stopped, one foot in the tent, one out, the rain fly in her hand.

Heath waited to be told not to go or for Gwen to pretend she wanted to come along. After too long a silence, Gwen said, "Don't run over anybody," and ducked out of sight into the orange toadstool she was calling home for three nights. Heath would sleep in the back of the RV. It had been fitted out for her special needs.

"Fucking special Olympian," she muttered to herself and unlocked the brakes on her chair so Gwen would hear her rolling away and know she wasn't bluffing about the walk.

Though she could afford a mechanized chair, she'd opted for the hand-powered variety. Rolling her own weight around was a small thing, but it mattered. Not much, but she had fallen from the realm of choosers into the realm of beggars, and she clung to it.

The paths—Heath was enough of a snob she couldn't bring herself to call them trails—throughout the Sprague Lake Handicamp were wide and graveled. Like the picnic tables and toilets, they were designed to accommodate people with disabilities. The one she chose headed toward the lake, an exquisite shallow jewel of water, dammed in the early part of the twentieth century to form a fishing lake for a lodge, long-since dismantled. Having rolled a few yards, Heath stopped. The crunching of wheels on crushed rock should have convinced Gwen she'd really gone. And Gwen would be listening, worrying, waiting. Knowledge of this protective love grated on Heath's nerves. To be helpless was either to be alone or without privacy. The former was terrifying, the latter intolerable. With a determined push, she sent herself, not on the level boardwalk spanning a lobe of the lake, but up the "steep" path that wound into a forest of lodgepole and ponderosa.

A grade she once wouldn't have deigned to call a bunny slope now taxed her back and shoulder muscles. The vertebra she'd smashed was low enough she still had some motor control in her hips and butt. The doctors said that made her stronger. *Stronger than what?* She sweated and puffed. Effort filled the mind. Fear was not gone, only pushed back, just out of sight. It followed her, chasing her into the thicker darkness beneath the evergreens.

Heath drove blind but she didn't slow down. Knuckles brushed fur. Wiley had come unbidden. The dog stayed close but he was not a seeing-eye dog. Her right wheel crashed into a branch or rock; the chair twisted, throwing Heath to one side. A flash of old wisdom spun through her mind: Steer into the skid. But this was not ice, it was gravity, and she went down. Three seconds in darkness and not-so-free fall took a long time and ended abruptly. Her elbow struck something soft. She had the decency to hope it wasn't Wiley.

Above ear level she could hear the spinning of a wheel. Only a few months had passed since she'd taken this seat that was to be hers for life, yet already she knew the wheelchair like liars claimed to know the backs of their hands. Each click and slip and groan spoke to her. By the clean whir of the hub, she knew the wheel had not been damaged.

For half a minute, she gave in to the rattle and hum of wheel and brain waves sloshing against her reoriented skull. When her thoughts cleared, she took stock. Nothing hurt. But then half of her could be gashed and bleeding and, in the dark, she'd never know it.

"The hell with you, then," she muttered to her legs and focused on that which was still sensate.

The arm of the chair beneath her dug into her side. She could feel where the belt pulled across her abdomen. Because of the crazy-quilt wiring of nerves and sensations she retained, the medical wizards assured her she had the capacity to enjoy a "fairly normal" sex life—whatever that was. As a consolation prize, sex didn't cut it. Asked to choose between sex and a 5–13 pitch, Heath would have climbed.

For a while she lay still. The wheel spun. Mosquitoes whined in her ear. Strong in her nostrils, the smell of dirt and loam comforted her. Wiley licked her hands and face. Lying alone in the dark, a wreck of bone and metal, suited her.

Till she heard the snuffling. Then the fear she'd been running from caught up to her.

Even fear had changed. When she was a real person, a whole person, *herself*, fear tingled and burned through her veins like lightning, electrifying brain and muscle till she felt as if she could think her way through solid stone, outrun jaguars. Now it was a sick cold thing that spread like poison, shutting her down, reeking out through her pores in a chill sweat.

A whuff. A piggy grunt.

Bear. There were no grizzly bears in Rocky but, for the most part, grizzlies weren't interested in eating people. They wanted to scare them away. Black bears,

usually shy, when they came, came to dine.
A year before, a black bear had bitten into
the skulls of two young men up at Fern
Lake. They'd been sleeping in their tents.
Surely, even sleeping, two young men were
more formidable than one middle-aged
paraplegic strapped to an overturned chair.

*Sprague Lake Handicamp would be just
the place for a hungry bear: human snacks
arranged on metal and plastic trays. The
Park Service should have named the place*
Cantina de los osos. Heath snorted at the
thought and the snuffling came again.
Louder, closer this time.

Wiley began to growl, low in his throat, the
kind of growl that raised his hackles and
hers. Primal in its intensity, fear ran through
Heath like black ice. Even the quiescent
flesh of her lower body seemed to thrum
with it. Every cell demanded flight, and for
one brief second she believed she would
rise up from the dirt and run from the
woods.

The adrenaline rush jerked her shoulders
but her legs remained dead weight. Wiley
left her side, no longer growling but rum-
bling deep in his chest. The bear would kill
him, snap his scrawny neck with one swipe.

The loss of the mangy-looking dog was more than Heath could stand. A modicum of courage returned. She could move.

Fumbling at her waist, she undid the safety belt with more luck than dexterity. The weight of her legs pulled her over onto the dirt. She could feel it under both hands, beneath her chin.

"Wiley," she said. "Come here, boy. Now. Come. Now!" Though she'd meant to shout, pushed with lungs and diaphragm, her voice was a tiny thread of air, like screams in a nightmare.

The chair had saddlebags filled with the necessary things of life: magazines, dog biscuits, cigarettes and, because she was roughing it in the special wilderness, a flash-light.

Maybe light would frighten away the bear. Maybe it would only let her see who was coming to dinner. However humble, a goal gave her strength. She wriggled and pawed at the leather flap. The ends of her fingers felt numb. For one horrible moment she thought her crash had broken another verte-bra, one higher in her back, and the swelling was robbing her of sensation in the half-body that remained to her.

The buckle gave way and the contents of the pouch fell out, striking wrists and dirt. Fingers scrabbled. The barrel of the flashlight came under her hand and she grabbed it. Wiley's rumble escalated to a high-pitched whine that penetrated the enamel of Heath's teeth and made her skull reverberate. Dragging her weight on her elbows, legs trailing behind, she crawled toward the dog.

"Quiet, Wiley. Come here."

The hand without the flashlight struck something furry. Hoping it was part of Wiley and not the bear, she closed her fingers around a bony ankle. Wiley let out a bark that ripped the darkness.

Still holding onto the dog, she thumbed the flashlight on. She held it backward and the light blasted her retinas. Startled, she dropped it. Found it. Pointed it in the right direction. "Holy shit," she whispered.

Then the screaming began.

two

Anna looked at her left hand for the umpteenth time. The band of gold on her ring finger was so new it was mirror-bright from jeweler's polish and there was hardly a scratch on it. The band was plain: no twining leaves, no gems, no patterned etching. No words were engraved inside. When Paul had brought her the rings to ask if they might be used, he'd told her their story. In 1945, after being mustered out of the army, his father bought them from a jewelry store in New York City, then brought them back to Natchez in hopes he would one day wed. Four years later he'd met the woman who would be Paul's mother and they'd set the date. When the day came, Paul's father went to the chest in his bedroom where they'd been kept. A hole was gnawed through the corner of the chest, and the back of the cardboard box that had contained the rings was eaten away. Inside the box, where the rings had waited so long, were two dried-up acorns.

On the way to the church, the groom picked up two tin rings at the five-and-dime. A year later, on their first anniversary, he'd replaced them with gold.

In 1952, with the first child due, Mrs. Davidson was sewing a tiny layette while Mr. Davidson knocked out the back wall of the bedroom to build a nursery onto the house. Amid the debris and dirt from the wall of the ninety-three-year-old house was the detritus of a long-dead packrat's nest. Pride of place among the screws and bolts and hairpins were the wedding rings.

It had been decided that they would be set aside for the baby to bring to his or her mate for their wedding. Paul's first wife wanted diamonds. Knowing that, he had never shown her the rings or told her the story.

"Our union was prophesied by a rat," Anna had said, but she loved the rat, the ring, the man and the tale. She even loved the former Mrs. Paul Davidson for being too greedy to want the gold and too ambitious to keep the man.

From the wooden balcony of her honeymoon cabin, Anna watched the rat's gold catch the candlelight. The cabin was of logs, new and neatly fit together, red-brown with polyurethane finish. The balcony was on the second floor with French doors that let into a pleasant bedroom. From where she sat, she could see the mountains of Colorado, sparked tonight by lightning, and smell the sweetness of pine.

The place was ideal. The ring ideal. If Anna had only had a husband to share it with, the honeymoon would have been close to perfect.

She stared at the cell phone Paul had given her, a phone with free long distance and more minutes than it had taken the Hebrew god to create the world. Cell phones were annoying. They were too small, made odd noises, cut in and out. Mostly Anna hated them because they were, by nature, intrusive. They broadcast civilization's blather and fuss into places it was never meant to be; their shrill insistence and one-sided shout sullied the myriad blessings of the out-of-doors. Despite this antithetical relationship, she considered using it, calling Paul just to tell him how sweet the air, how bright the stars. It was an hour later in Port Gibson, Mississippi, than it was in Estes Park, Colorado, nearly eleven o'clock. Paul would probably have been in bed for an hour. He wouldn't mind her waking him, not on their honeymoon. What self-respecting bridegroom would?

As she reached for the phone, the radio in the bedroom demanded her attention.

"Two-oh-one, ROMO. Two-oh-one, ROMO." ROMO: ROcky MOuntain, the park's designating letters. Anna had never worked anyplace where dispatch went by a name. She thought it rather endearing. And she welcomed the interruption. Ruining some visitor's evening was preferable to staring at the phone.

"This is two-oh-one." There was a momentary pause. Anna was not only the first woman ever to be a district ranger in Rocky Mountain National Park but had only been the Thompson River District Ranger for two days. ROMO was not yet accustomed to hearing her voice.

She grabbed notebook and pen. "Go ahead, ROMO."

The night dispatcher was a seasonal employee but she'd been with the park for seven seasons and knew her business. She laid out what facts were known in a voice better suited to soothing crying infants than spelling out law enforcement horrors. Anna loved it. There was no situation that couldn't be improved with a little maternal calm.

"We've had a garbled report from a gas station owner just outside the park. An RV pulled in several minutes ago requesting an ambulance at Sprague Lake Handicamp. The RV's driver was agitated. Apparently he'd tried to call from Sprague, but couldn't get a signal."

"Any indication of who was injured?"

"Two women, evidently. I got all this from the gas station attendant. The RV man drove off before giving any other information. An ambulance has been dispatched."

"Where's two-oh-two?" Anna gave the number of the law enforcement ranger who was on duty in the frontcountry from four till midnight, when the park's problem calls were turned over to the local sheriff's department.

"Tied up with an elk/Toyota collision by Bear Lake."

"I should be at Sprague in ten to fifteen minutes," Anna said and broke contact.

The cabin she rented from the NPS was on the outskirts of the park across from the Visitors' Center. She was so new to the place, she had yet to unpack, and cardboard boxes took the place of furnishings. Most of her things had not been moved, only as much as could be loaded into a small U-Haul in a hurry. This proof of the unsettled nature of her life was sufficiently depressing, she was grateful when she could leave it.

Out alone at night, the dark mountains around her, Moraine Meadow rolling out gray and silver to the west, the scent of rain and pine and dust gentle on the air blowing in through the car's window, Anna was reassured she'd made the right decision in leaving Mississippi . . . leaving Paul. District ranger in Rocky Mountain was a pay grade higher on the government service scale, and the park itself considerably up the food chain as far as glamour, adventure and political clout went, than her old duty station, the Natchez Trace Parkway. It was an opportunity that wouldn't knock often. The plum had only fallen to Anna by way of a series of fortuitous events.

Lorraine Knight, the chief ranger at Yosemite, with whom Anna had worked in the past, had taken the deputy superintendent's position at Rocky. When one of her district rangers, a thirty-five-year veteran of the NPS, had retired, Lorraine contacted Anna and helped shepherd her application through the inevitable jungles of red tape at the regional personnel office.

Two days before they were to be married, Anna and her husband-to-be, Paul Davidson, sat down to discuss the job offer. Paul had recently been reelected sheriff of Claiborne County. Anna had been offered the position of a lifetime, thirteen hundred miles west.

They loved their jobs.

They loved one another.

But they'd been at their jobs many more years than they'd been sweethearts.

One year, they'd decided. For one calendar year, they would carry on a long-distance marriage. At the end of that year, one would give up a job and make a home in the other's shadow.

Or they wouldn't.

The "wouldn't" was unspoken but Anna, if not Paul, heard it loud and clear.

Three days after the wedding, she moved to Rocky. Customarily the NPS wasn't so heartless, but Rocky had been too much in the news that summer. The park needed normalcy. The rangers, particularly in Thompson River District, needed reassurance, routine. Even more so than most corporate cultures, that of a national park was vulnerable to epidemics of mass insanity. Perhaps because of the isolation and the high adrenaline aspects, park personnel bonded quickly and tightly. When something disrupted those bonds, the reverberations could shudder on for years. Anna had seen litigious employees divide a park. In the case of Rocky it had been the search for missing children. For four weeks ROMO searched. The children were never found. After the search was discontinued, the Thompson River District Ranger retired. The rangers involved intimately with the search had been left with the weight of three lifetimes of unfinished business to carry on their shoulders.

At the edge of Moraine Meadow, just before the ragged black line of trees swallowed the road, two coyotes trotted across in front of Anna's car. Though western Colorado suffered a drought, the glacier-carved meadow was rich with grass. Mice, picas, squirrels and other small denizens raised big broods on the wealth of forage. As a consequence these Rocky Mountain coyotes were fat, their fur thick and glossy in the moonlight. The two of them could have understudied for Rin and Mrs. Tin Tin.

Where Anna had grown up, on the edge of Smoke Creek Desert, the coyotes looked like starving mangy hounds. It was good to see at least some of the park's critters looking so prosperous. Balance was impossible to maintain when the depredations of man smashed so many links from the food chain. The bigger carnivores—grizzlies, wolves and, ever increasingly, mountain lions—had been killed off. Coyotes weren't fearsome enough to thin the herds of elk. Once in a while they'd get a newborn or the old and sickly, but not often enough. The elk were rapidly eating themselves into a food shortage that would bring on starvation and its attendant diseases. Assuredly this would thin the herds, but it wasn't the sort of spectacle John Q. Public liked to bring the kiddies camping to see.

In Yellowstone National Park in Wyoming, wolves had been successfully reintroduced. So successfully, occasionally a wolf was seen outside the park. Not a month before, a rancher up near Jackson had shot a nursing female. Resource managers from Yellowstone searched but she'd hidden her den too well, and her pups weren't found. Colorado used this and other wolf-as-evil-predator stories to justify the state resolution that these four-legged, livestock-eating varmints would never be brought back to Rocky.

Wyoming's wolves were only one day's long walk north. There were those hoping a few would take it into their heads to cross state lines. If the wolves came on their own, they'd fall under the protection of the endangered species act.

The black shadows of the trees took the coyotes, then Anna's patrol car. She caught up with the park's ambulance at the Big Thompson River Bridge and trailed it to

Sprague Lake Handicamp. The ambulance ran dark. At this hour, with little or no traffic to hinder it, the rangers had rightly chosen not to break the peace of the park and run with lights and siren.

Sprague Camp's toilets were on a center island in the middle of a large parking lot with spaces radiating out like spokes. The rim of this ovate wheel was where the sites were located, all of them with easy access by graveled path to the asphalt. The ambulance and Anna circled the lot slowly. There was none of the light and babble of a hair-raising event to clue them in to which campers had placed the call.

When they'd completed half the circle, the ambulance's headlights cut an angular woman from the surrounding night. She had wild red hair, was clad in a blue sweatshirt and khaki shorts and was waving them to the curb.

She introduced herself as Doctor Gwen Littleton, OB-GYN, retired. Anna's favorite sort of emergency hostess, she was calm, sensible and informative.

The only aspect of her demeanor that suggested all was not well was the blood smeared down the front of her shorts.

three

"No, no," Heath was crying, but the screaming wouldn't stop. Her mind jumped to its
feet and ran to them. The need and the
response to it were so great, it startled her
to find she still lay on the ground, less
ambulatory than a beached whale.

With sudden inspiration she turned the
light back on herself. "See," she said. "A
lady. Just a crippled lady. See my chair? I
crashed. I can't hurt you. Look." She shone
the light down at her legs. "I can't walk.
You're okay. Hush now. Hush."

They couldn't have been more than
twelve years old. Both were thin to the point

bones stuck out at pelvis and collarbone. Heath could see this because they wore nothing but filthy underwear. One had on panties that once had been pink and a matching camisole, ripped at one shoulder exposing a breast so scratched and muddied, at first Heath hadn't differentiated fabric from skin. The other girl wore white cotton panties and a bra, intact but filthy. Mud, feces, blood: Heath couldn't tell. From the smell it was probably all three. They had nothing else: no shoes, no socks, no water, nothing. Scratches, cuts and bruises discolored their legs and feet.

"It's over now. I'm here. You're okay." *I'm here. Jesus.* Helplessness washed over Heath till she was nauseated with it. There wasn't a damn thing she could do, not even yell for Gwen. The girls had quieted to whimpers, the low pitiful kind that puppies make when they have nightmares, but they looked ready to bolt back into the woods if she made any loud noises. That couldn't happen. Heath couldn't carry that around with her. *Not in a fucking wheelchair.*

"Could you please help me?" she said finally, her voice as soft and kind as if she lured bunnies from their burrow. "See, I'm paralyzed and my chair fell over and I can't get myself up." In all the months since the accident, Heath had never once asked for help. Now that she did, she felt as if she were lying. The fact that it was true and that she asked it of two little girls who could not even help themselves struck her as horrifically funny and she laughed.

The sound struck the girls like a blow and they skittered, ready to run.

"Oh my god. Please," Heath cried, terrified they'd run back into whatever hell they'd just found their way out of. "I'm hurt. Please help me, I'm hurting." This last was a lie. Not only was there no feeling in half of Heath's body but there was enough adrenaline in her veins she doubted she'd have felt pain even if she'd crashed in a nest of yellow jackets.

The girls stopped. One of them—the one with the bared breast—took a step closer.

"I'm all tangled up. See?" Again Heath shone the flashlight on her legs and the overturned wheelchair.

"We thought you were a bear," the girl said in a voice years too young for the body it emanated from, the voice of a three-year-old.

"I thought *you* guys were bears," Heath told her. "I got scared and tried to get back to camp but my wheelchair fell over."

"Heath! Heath!" A sharp-edged cry came through the darkness. Before the girls could run, Heath hurried on. "That's my aunt. She's an old lady." Mentally she apologized to Gwen for the categorization. "She can't lift me by herself but she's real nice. She made s'mores for dessert. They're real good. There's some left." Heath realized she was talking as if she spoke to preschoolers, toddlers, not young girls, but these battered children had slipped back in time and mind and treating them like babies felt right.

"Heath! Damn it! Answer me!" Thunder sounded in the distance underlining Gwen's shout.

"Will you stay and help my aunt put me back together again?" Heath pleaded.

"Humpty Dumpty," said the one who'd not yet spoken, and she giggled, a high uneven sound with the broken notes of hysteria beneath.

"Just like Humpty Dumpty," Heath said and smiled. "Okay. I'm going to holler for my aunt. Don't be scared, she's a nice person and a doctor. A lady doctor. Ready?

"Up here," Heath yelled. "Up the trail on the eastern side of the tent. Bring a light."

"Heath," Gwen cried again and there was the sound of feet pounding up the trail, a "*Yowch!*," a "Damn it," and Gwen stumbled up to the overturned chair. "Are you all right? My god, I heard screaming—"

"Gwen." Heath stopped her with a concrete tone. "I want you to meet some friends of mine."

Heath shined her light on her aunt's face to show the girls Gwen was truly, if not as she'd represented her, at least a kindly soul who did not apparently devour lost children. "My aunt." Introduction made, she turned her light on the girls still in the woods, still poised as if for flight. Or a blow. Gwen's light followed in natural succession and the children cowered.

"Oh my heavens, my heavens, my darlings, poor babies. Y'all come here. Whatever happened? No. Never you mind that. Whatever it is, it's over. Come on, sweethearts. Oh, look at your little feet!" Gwen started toward them, propelled by a maternal instinct that had inspired her to deliver thousands of babies and take care of their sniffles, mumps and other disasters large and small till they reached young adulthood.

The girls were mesmerized by the soft southern flow of motherly love but didn't leave their woodland darkness till Heath remembered Wiley. Or rather Wiley intruded into her world again by pushing his nose under her arm. Good sense or good training had stopped his aggression the moment Heath had identified the girls as nonthreatening.

Something—probably the arrival of Gwen, a witness to his dereliction—made him decide it was time to come back on duty.

"Bring them to me," Heath said to the dog and pointed at the shivering half-naked creatures.

Obligingly, Wiley trotted into the circle of illumination made by the two flashlights.

The dog Gwen had bought in hopes of increasing Heath's so-called independence might not have won a single show or even placed. He wasn't the best or smartest helper. What Wiley had was wit and charm. His walk was the jaunty distillation of cartoon cocksuredness, and his scruffy demeanor an example of nature mirroring art. Crooked whiskers, half-salute ears, baleful grin, raggedy fur, his maker had fashioned a Disney star. Only fate had decided he had a higher calling.

"Oooh," the girls cooed, like a movie audience when baby tigers gambol onto the screen. "A dog." Wiley sat down neatly in front of them and cocked his head as if in approval of their astute zoological perception. That pose complete, he bowed down, front legs outstretched, chin on paws.

"He's a ham," Heath said half apologetically from her bed of dirt and rock. Now that the excitement was over and Wiley had successfully taken the intruders captive, her elbows were registering complaints about supporting her body so long.

The children followed Wiley out the three or four yards from forest to path. They were in sorry shape. How sorry Heath guessed from the sharp intake of breath full view of them elicited from her aunt.

"Go ahead back to camp," Heath said. "I can get myself righted."

"No. No. I can't . . ." Gwen looked from Heath to the girls and back. The look of panic on her face as she struggled with the minuscule Sophie's choice, whether to leave her crippled niece sprawled helpless in the dirt or to get the children to safety and warmth before they bolted or collapsed, infuriated Heath.

"I can do it," she hissed, hating herself because maybe she couldn't and hating Gwen because maybe she knew it and hating the sound of her voice, peevish and beseeching at the same time.

Gwen hesitated just long enough Heath wanted to spit at her like an angry cat—or cry—then, muttering soothing nothings, she gathered the girls to her and started down the path.

Heath allowed herself to lay her head down for a moment, cushioned on her folded arms. She was exhausted in mind and body and soul, the kind of tired that gets in the bones, replacing marrow with tears. She couldn't get back in the chair. She doubted she could even set the chair back on its wheels. The fall from the ice hadn't merely taken her legs, it had taken her strength, her endurance. Her *willingness*.

Hot, none too sweet-smelling breath blew on the back of her neck. Wiley had stayed behind. He knew which side his kibble was buttered on.

"What're you looking at?" Heath growled. Wiley did his courtly bow again. "Oh yeah, like that's going to work on me." But it did. It always did.

The machinations required to return her butt to its previous place twenty-six inches up on a scrap of vinyl took considerably longer than she would have thought. Before she'd even dragged her worthless legs around the right way and got her chair up and the brakes locked, she was drenched in sweat and as filthy as a prolonged bout of wallowing in the dirt could make a woman. With the assistance of the dog, the vocabulary of a stevedore and a small pine tree, she finally regained her chair. Gwen never came thumping back up the path to see if she was all right. By turns Heath was grateful for the faith and pissed off at the indifference.

When she rolled back into camp, heralded by her wheels crunching obnoxiously on the gravel and her flashlight held in her lap like the headlight of a crotch-high train, Gwen had both girls dressed in sweat suits—one Gwen's own, the other belonging to Heath. Water was on the camp stove heating for tea, and Aunt Gwen had returned to her old persona as Dr. Littleton.

One of the girls had both her feet in Gwen's lap, allowing the doctor to bathe and dress them. The quietest one, the littlest, sat with her feet soaking in the dishpan.

The girls saw Heath, and the tranquil field hospital scene shattered. As one they cried out. Feet went flying. Dirty water and blood spattered on Gwen, hissed against the chimney of a lantern. Disregarding injuries and what had to be a lot of pain, the children scrambled free of lawn chair and picnic table.

Gwen was calling, "Wait. No. Sweetie. Your feet. No. No. Darlins, you mustn't—" Wiley, forgetting his training and his trusted position as Good Disciplined Helper, began to bark.

A litany of self-scorn poured through Heath's mind, a mind made feeble from fighting gravity and floundering helplessness. Rolling in, rocks clattering under her wheels like some sort of deformed robobeast from a *Terminator* prequel, she was more monster than human. The girls, already traumatized by god knew what— and from their state of undress, Heath could hazard a guess—were terrified, running.

They ran, not away, but toward her.

Heath stopped. The flashlight fell from her lap, rolled a few feet along the ground.

They want Wiley, the scruffy charmer, Heath realized. Then the girls were upon her—Wiley ignored, Gwen forgotten. The taller of the two hung about her neck, nearly strangling her. The quiet one crawled into her lap, knees banging the metal of the chair, elbow digging into Heath's middle, and attached herself like a limpet. Both were crying. Not the tiny whimpers of the woods but bawling like babies, gulping and sobbing. Heath could feel tears hot as embers falling on her neck and cheek.

These two battered girls saw her as their savior. Heath felt like a fraud. Wiley had found them. Gwen had rescued them. All Heath had done was writhe on the ground like a half-squashed earthworm.

"You poor little buggers," she said softly. "You must've had a real bad rap."

Gwen and Wiley shepherding, Heath blew out the last of her strength pushing her wheels through the crushed rock with her added burden. The smaller girl did not want to leave her lap and, for reasons she wasn't certain of, Heath didn't want to make her. Maybe it was just that whatever had happened to the girl, it was probably ugly. Definitely ugly. Maybe uglier than anything that had ever befallen Heath, even waking up in a hospital room and being told she'd never walk again. If sitting on a rolling lap clinging to half a middle-aged ex-climber comforted her, so be it.

And maybe Heath needed a little comforting herself.

Gwen coaxed the girls back to their former positions. The lap sitter was finally lured to the bench and allowed her feet to be returned to the dishpan but chose not to let go of Heath's hand. Wiley took up guard duty while Gwen redressed and bandaged the other child's feet.

After the tightly knit darkness beneath the lodgepole pines, the light of Coleman lanterns was shockingly bright. For the first time Heath was able to see what her dog had sniffed out and her aunt had brought home.

The limpet—the darker, smaller girl who'd flung herself into Heath's lap and still clung so tightly to her hand she wondered if she'd be able to use a knife and fork again—had jaw-length red hair and brown eyes. Shock or night or drugs had dilated her pupils till they looked as black and bottomless as deep wells. Dry wells; there was no glitter of interest or spark of life. Though she was probably in sixth or seventh grade, she had the promise of womanly beauty beneath the skin of a baby. *Deadly combination.*

Girls matured earlier every generation and Heath thought she could smell menstrual blood. In the woods she noticed both girls' legs were encrusted with a grime. How much was blood and how much dirt, she wondered. To cover the grim thoughts, Heath smiled into those empty eyes.

The girl who'd spoken first was quite tall. Heath had noticed when she'd walked next to Gwen. Gwen was five-foot-ten and this slender reed of a girl wasn't much shorter. Judging height was another thing her fall had affected. Sitting down, everyone seemed to tower. Often Heath felt like an egret among the cows.

The tall girl sat in a webbed lawn chair, her feet in Gwen's lap. The child was mostly legs and what Heath imagined, when shampooed, was blond hair—the long, pale, silky kind that most teenagers want and precious few have. Even ratty and caked with grime the hair hung to the middle of her back.

There was something utterly familiar about this girl and Heath wracked her brain trying to remember if she'd seen her around the park, in the Visitors' Center maybe, or at an eatery in town.

Then it came to her. She looked like Skipper, Barbie's little sister, right down to the preternatural long legs and stick-straight hair. Down to the blank doll-like expression on her face and the unfocused painted-on eyes.

"They aren't talking," she said to her aunt, suddenly realizing the quiet was unnatural.

"I know," Gwen said.

"Skipper can talk," Heath said. "The girl you've got. She said, 'It's a dog,' back in the woods."

"She doesn't want to talk now, do you, sweetheart?" Gwen said kindly.

Heath turned to the red-haired girl with a death-grip on her hand. "What's your name?"

The eyes seemed to grow larger, darker, till they resembled what Heath had always imagined interstellar black holes looked like: places where nothing could survive—not matter, not rock, not steel.

"Can I call you 'limpet'?" Heath took the

silence for just that, silence, and stopped prodding. She was afraid she was too heavy-handed, too inept, and would cause more damage. "Come here, Wiley."

The dog obediently trotted to between Heath's knees and those of the girl.

"You can hold onto Wiley if you want. I do it when I'm totally freaked out. It always makes me feel better." The limpet looked at the dog and reached out tentatively.

Her hand was babyish, dimples where knuckles would one day be, wrists barely defined. Her finger ends were raw and bloody. The black of dirt and old blood caked under the nails and in the tiny creases in the once-smooth skin.

"Go ahead. Pet him. He doesn't mind. I think it makes him feel important."

The small hand closed in the thick fur of the dog's ruff. Wiley sat very still and grinned.

"They can understand us at least," Heath said to her aunt, then: "Oh shit, we should call somebody," as she remembered her responsibilities.

"I already tried," Gwen said. Skipper's feet were cleaned and bound. The doctor set them gently on the ground and moved over to attend to the limpet's feet. "Cell phone won't work in this canyon. The guy camped next to us offered to drive in toward town till he could get a signal and call the rangers."

"Good." Heath should have thought of that. Since the accident, things had been dropping through the cracks in her brain. Sometimes it felt as if, in losing her legs, her independence and her mobility, she'd lost part of her mind as well. She'd wondered— but never dared to ask the doctors for fear they'd add "crazy" to the list of things wrong with her—if the much-vaunted "muscle memory" was an actual real thing, bits of knowledge stored, not in the cells of the brain, but cached in cells in other parts of the body. When her brain had lost contact with her legs, had it also lost access to information, memory and experience as well as sensation?

The sound of a truck engine vibrated out from the trees, and a boxy white ambulance came into view at the far end of the parking lot.

"Your guy must've got his signal," Heath said.

"Finish her." Gwen put the limpet's dripping feet in Heath's lap and rose to go flag down the ambulance.

Heath's little bears were in bad shape but, of the obvious injuries, those to their feet were the most serious. It was a testimony to their courage and fortitude—or their desperation and terror—that they'd kept on keeping on, putting one bloody ragged little foot down in front of the other.

And it was a testament to their peculiar attachment to her that they'd leaped up and run to her when she'd wheeled into camp. By the bright yet unilluminating glare of the Coleman lanterns, Heath could still make out the bloody prints their passage left on the crushed gravel.

She cupped the battered heels, one in each of the palms of her hands, and looked into the hopeless darkness of the limpet's eyes. Wind gusted through the trees, making the night sigh around them.

"Hey, sweetie pie, where ya been?" she whispered.

The eyes might have glimmered. Something as tiny as a minnow at the bottom of a deep night-bound pool seemed to flicker. The limpet's lips parted in an exhaled breath.

"What have you got for me?" came an alto voice, firm, authoritative and loud as a sonic boom in the fragile whisper of contact Heath had managed to establish with the child.

A woman, mid-forties or early fifties—under the brim of her flat hat, collar-length hair waved more white than brown—walked into the light. She wore the green and gray of an NPS ranger and carried a gun that was probably standard size but on her slender hips looked huge and black and in-your-face.

Heath was teetering on disliking her for a number of reasons, starting with her untimely arrival and her doing so on two good legs, when the scales tipped suddenly from casual dislike to overt hostility.

Skipper and the limpet began screaming as they'd done when she'd come upon them in the woods. The fragile calm she and Gwen had knit for them shredded. The fragment of light or life Heath had seen in the limpet's eyes dove into her internal darkness.

The ranger raised both hands as if to show she was harmless and backed away, murmuring, "It's okay. Take it easy. Nobody's going to hurt you. You're okay."

The tone and gesture might have struck Heath as commendable in another person at another time, but the girls had ceased their shrieking and began to cry silently, not the snotty gulping children's sobs they'd drenched her neck with, but the slow, unstoppable tears of old women who know nothing but despair.

Heath had great respect for the instinctive character judgement of dogs and children. True, Wiley was wagging his tail, but this time he'd been outvoted.

four

"It's okay. You're okay. My name's Anna . . ." Anna had walked into a lot of situations over the years where people weren't all that happy she'd shown up, but she couldn't remember entire parties bursting into tears at the sight of her. The rangers behind her, EMTs who'd brought the ambulance, didn't seem to reassure the children either, though Ryan, a seasonal so cute he actually had an echoing dimple on his left dimple, usually reduced girls of this age to simpering, giggling blobs of hormonal adoration without even trying.

The children weren't alone in their antipathy. A disabled woman, fiftyish and probably fairly good-looking when her face wasn't screwed up preparatory to spitting nails, sat in a wheelchair near the picnic table.

It was impossible to tell how tall she was and, briefly, Anna wondered if the question of height became moot when one was relegated to a chair. Petite probably, she was delicate-boned, her face almost a perfect oval and capped by short, very dark hair in a pixie cut. Cheekbones slashed hard lines below her eyes. Dark brows, straight as a die, ran parallel above them. On a good day her lips might have softened the effect. Tonight they were as uncompromising as brows and bones.

One of the girls had thrown herself into the woman's lap when Anna had come on scene. The kid was too big to be a lap baby and her legs stuck out over the spoked wheels like jersey-clad sticks. Dr. Littleton had run to a tall, skinny child and wrapped an arm protectively about her narrow shoulders. This girl didn't cling but sat rigid, her hands squeezed tightly between her knees, her chin tucked into her chest. Curtains of filthy, matted blond hair hung over her face like vines over the mouth of a cave.

Doing everything she could think of to make herself small and nonthreatening, Anna backed to the edge of the light, squatted on her heels and removed her Stetson. She raised a hand to keep the EMTs back. Neither girl had anything life-threatening that was readily apparent. What was apparent was that they were suffering severe emotional trauma. Anna wasn't in the mood to exacerbate it any more than she already had.

At least the camp dog seemed glad to see her. He was a scruffy excuse for a helpmate, which Anna guessed he was by the vest he wore. A lab-shepherd mix, maybe. One that had been washed with dark colors and tumbled in a too-hot dryer.

"Hey, fella," she said. Wagging his tail amiably, the dog came over.

The woman in the wheelchair shot one of them a filthy look. Anna couldn't tell if it was aimed at her for some unknown reason or at the dog for consorting with her. The pooch sat and presented his ears for scratching. For a minute Anna tended to the animal, waiting for a bit of the tension that had come with her and the two EMTs to drain out of the camp.

The weather gods were not helping. As they did most every afternoon, thunderheads had been building. Often, by nightfall, they'd dissipate. Not tonight. Lightning flickered to the southwest, startling the granite mountain peaks out of their sleep. Thunder rolled around as if auditioning for the road show of Rip Van Winkle. Anna could smell rain and taste the ozone on the back of her tongue. It was a night when, had she been a cat, she would have raced from room to room leaping at shadows. The atmosphere was charged with a wildness as much metaphysical as meteorological.

When the air felt less electric, without rising or leaving the dog, Anna addressed the older woman.

"Dr. Littleton, can you tell me what happened?"

The doctor rose, stepped into the light and spread her hands as if she were about to give a formal oration. "My niece"—she said—"this is my niece, Heath Jarrod."

"Anna Pigeon, district ranger," Anna introduced herself.

"Heath had gone for a walk—" The word *walk* clanked against the metallic reality of the wheelchair, and the doctor came to a stop.

"Which path did she take?" Anna asked, to get her over the rough patch.

"Talk to me," the disabled woman demanded. She'd been growing more restive by the moment. Something had just reached critical mass. Anna could hear the ominous quiet of nuclear fusion clicking behind her teeth.

"What path did you take?" Anna repeated neutrally. It was too late. Ms. Jarrod had apparently reached a psychic point of no return. Despite the fact she had, nominally at least, gotten what she wanted, she pushed on.

"People think a chair makes a person stupid or invisible or deaf. I can hear you. This is a wheelchair, not a fucking cone of silence."

Anna laughed before she could stop herself.

A laugh might not have endeared her to the woman, but it served to startle her out of her fit of pique.

"So you went up the path. Which one?" Anna asked.

Question by question she got what she

could of the story. It was short and simple. Ms. Jarrod wasn't inclined to be particularly helpful. The telling of the accident on the path and the discovery of the girls in their underwear was shortened to the point of haiku: "My chair, it tipped. Fell. The girls were there in the woods. Aunt Gwen fixed their feet."

The law enforcement officer in Anna was annoyed that any part of the girls that might contain trace evidence had been tampered with. The halfway decent human part of her was glad the children had been provided with some relief.

During this staccato exchange the girls grew, not calmer precisely, but less demonstrative. Anna decided to see if they could be induced to trust themselves to her, the EMTs, the ambulance: the System. She stood, her knees cracking in protest. "Girls, Dr. Littleton, Ms. Jarrod: What do you say we take a look at you, then get you a warm safe place and call your folks?"

The children shared a look, something hard and sharp. The tears continued. Anna turned from the light to one of the EMTs, Emily something, a seasonal who Anna had reason to know was twenty-six because, wondering what an apparent fifteen-year-old was doing hanging around the back-country office's computers, she'd asked. To Emily, she said, "It's them, isn't it?"

"It's them." Emily looked to Ryan, who nodded.

"It is," he confirmed. "We saw pictures. God, did we see pictures."

"Get me their names. Notify dispatch and Chief Knight. She'll want to call their folks. Tell dispatch we're going to need a child psychologist to meet us at the hospital. Tell them we'll roll as soon as we can get the kids into the ambulance."

Anna started to turn back to the sad little party around the picnic table but was stopped by Ryan's voice:

"There were three of them."

Three. Normally, even working in a park a thousand miles away, she would have known this. But there'd been the wedding. And the decision. And the move—slings and arrows she'd thought so earth-shaking. Now they seemed petty beyond belief.

"Three."

In their earnestness the rangers nodded like bobble-heads.

"I need to know who we've got and who is

still missing. Now," she added when neither of them moved.

"The little red-haired girl with the disabled woman is Beth Dwayne. She's twelve. Her folks—all the girls—live near Loveland, an hour or so east of here," Emily said.

Anna knew where Loveland, Colorado, was. She'd driven through it on her move to the park rather than take the more traveled route from Denver through Boulder and into Estes Park.

"The other one is older, thirteen. Her name is Alexis Sheppard. The one not here is Candace Watson. She's thirteen too."

"You're sure?" Anna asked. Calling the girls by the wrong names could only further any sense they had of being forgotten or unsafe.

Again the nods. Anna took them at their word. She knew from experience that the intensity of a prolonged search for missing children burned the victims' particulars into the brains of the would-be rescuers. Emily and Ryan would probably be able to rattle off this information with accuracy and in detail long after they'd forgotten their own names or the addresses of their nursing homes.

"Ryan, go on back to the ambulance—or out of earshot—and make the calls. Tell dispatch we're going to need search dogs come morning, see if we can backtrack to where the third girl is. Emily, come with me."

Anna left her hat on the ground. It went against the grain. Her dog, Taco, a three-legged but brave-hearted lab, would have made short work of the Stetson-as-chew-toy.

"Don't even think about it," she muttered to the helper dog and walked back into the light. The blonde, Alexis Sheppard, looked the sturdier of the two—if one hummingbird in a hurricane can look stronger than another. Besides, she was in the sphere of Dr. Littleton and, like the dog, the doctor seemed less likely to bite than the chair-bound Ms. Jarrod.

Anna crossed slowly to the picnic table and eased herself onto the far end of the bench opposite the girl and the doctor. All the while she talked softly, a lesson learned not from victim assistance training but from working with horses in Guadalupe Mountains National Park early in her career. If she made noise or touched them when she walked behind them, they were less likely to startle and kick her.

"Hi, Alexis," she said. The girl flinched as if Anna had flicked her with a quirt rather than used a familiar form of address. "We're so glad you and Beth are back. Everybody looked and looked. Hundreds of people. You can't imagine how much your folks love you." Anna hoped this was true. Having not participated in the search, she was flying blind, but the details didn't matter. What mattered was that children hear right away and repeatedly that they might have been lost but they'd never been forgotten, that their parents never quit hoping and looking. Even adults, lost for long periods of time, had trouble with feelings of abandonment. In children of twelve and thirteen—too young for adult rationale, too old for childish faith—these feelings could be cripplingly acute.

Half turning to include Beth in the conversation, Anna noticed the littler girl had started sucking her thumb. "Ryan—he's one of the rangers who came to help us take you to your families—has gone to call them so they can meet us at the hospital. This here is Emily. She's a ranger too. If you'll let her, she'd like to check real quick and see if you're hurt, then we'll get you out of here. How does that sound?"

Anna thought she'd made the whole thing sound pretty doggone spiffy, but both girls hung their heads. Literally let them hang from the very top vertebrae till their noses pointed at their navels. The tears fell unimpeded onto the fronts of the borrowed running suits. The Jarrod woman held the one girl in her arms like a bundle of laundry. She must be a good deal stronger than she looked, Anna thought. The kid would weigh close to eighty pounds.

Dark thoughts crowded in. These kids didn't seem thrilled to be back, just relieved to be gone from where they'd been. They didn't cry for momma and daddy. The promise of home didn't bring on renewed energy or hope but an increase in anxiety.

Maybe they hadn't been lost. This kettle of worms had been thoroughly looked into long before Anna came to Rocky. The possibilities were runaways, stranger abduction, accidental death or abduction by a family member. The lack of enthusiasm Beth and Alexis showed when the words "parents" and "home" were bandied about suggested either runaways or possible abduction by a family member.

Anna let it go for the moment. The first order of business was to get them to a medical facility. Moving emotionally damaged children was not something she'd done much. Did one drag them shrieking to the ambulance and lock them in? Force them into the cage in the patrol car at gunpoint? They needed psychiatric care. They needed nurses, mommies, the kind of succor she couldn't even begin to offer.

They needed to be moved the hell out of her park.

"Have they spoken at all?" she asked Dr. Littleton.

"One of them said something to Heath, I think. When she found them. Before I got there."

Anna turned to Heath Jarrod.

"The little limpet—Beth—said 'It's a dog.' She meant Wiley. Not me."

"Anything else?"

The woman's face lost its angry look as she sent her mind back twenty minutes and two thousand heartbeats. Anna was startled at the difference it made. She'd put her age at about that of her own, but Jarrod was probably ten years younger. Very pretty in an Edith Piaf, Gigi, apache dancer sort of way: fine and exotic. And volatile. *High maintenance*, Anna thought.

"Beth said 'Humpty Dumpty.' Me. Not the dog. Because I'd taken a great fall I suppose. Ski—Alexis—said she thought I was a bear. I don't think they've spoken since." To the child in her lap she said, "You don't have to talk till you want to."

Serious bonding had obviously taken place. Anna wasn't sure whether that was a good thing or not, but she was in favor of anything that she could use to get the kids moved.

"Mind if I ask Beth a question?" Anna asked, ceding authority to Ms. Jarrod. It might get results. Besides, she could always take it back if she had to.

"Back off if she freaks?"

"Of course."

The woman nodded. Anna came around the table and sat directly in front of the wheelchair. Knee to knee. She wondered if the woman could feel the touch, sense the warmth or if, when Anna sat, it was as if she too only existed from the chair up.

She gathered one of the girl's hands into

her own. The thumb was still damp and sticky from being recently sucked.

"Is your name Beth?"

A tiny nod.

"Did I say it right or is it pronounced *Beeth*?"

"Beth," the child said.

Anna was careful to show neither surprise nor triumph.

"You look like you've been in the woods for a while. Where have you been?"

Again a look passed between the children. Confusion? Complicity? Reassurance? Shared terror? Accusation? Surprise? Anna couldn't read it. Emotions were too high, the light too uncertain.

"I don't know," Beth whispered.

"How about you, Alexis? Do you know what happened to you?"

The blonde shook her head.

Anna turned back to Beth. "There were three of you. Candace Watson was with you. Do you know where Candace is?"

The silence was so long Anna thought the girl had clammed up again. Then Alexis said, "She stayed with Robert."

"Shit," she heard Emily whisper from the far side of the picnic table.

"Who's Robert?" Anna demanded.

"Robert Proffit," Emily replied. "He was the Christian youth group leader who got lost himself looking for them, then reported the girls missing twenty-four hours after they'd disappeared. You wouldn't believe how torn up he was about the whole thing. Ran himself into pneumonia going out with search teams. He said God had given them into his care and he loved them like his own sisters."

Emily's voice was even, professional, but her sweet young face had hardened to the point it was neither sweet nor young. Emily hated. Robert? God? Herself? If she didn't watch it, Anna knew, one day that hatred could become a way of life.

"Okay," Anna said. "Dr. Littleton, Ms. Jarrod, help me get the kids out of here. It's going to rain."

five

When the heavens finally opened up and let loose a biblical downpour, Anna was glad.

Alexis Sheppard allowed herself to be loaded into the ambulance without a fuss, without anything: she said nothing, her face was emotionless, her body moved sluggishly. The girl acted as Anna had witnessed scores of the undead—zombies, wraiths, pod people, even the occasional vampire—behave on screen. Life without life. Movement without soul. Animation without spirit.

Such was Alexis' apparent internal wasteland. Anna felt positively guilty when she found herself wishing a like fate on Beth

Dwayne. She had returned to a state of selective mutism. She remained on the disabled woman's lap. She'd returned to her thumb-sucking.

When Anna and Emily tried to remove her from the sanctuary she'd found between the spoked wheels, she'd closed her fists in the front of Jarrod's jacket, howled like a banshee and kicked out. With the poor little flayed feet, her defense probably inflicted more pain on herself and her hostess than on either ranger. Ms. Jarrod's face became an unnatural shade of gray, and sweat beaded at her hairline despite the chilly edge of the wind.

There'd never been cause for Anna to learn much about paraplegia, and she couldn't begin to guess in what kind of shape it left one's internal organs, but clearly, having four score pounds of misery flopping and thrashing about on them was not beneficial. She had to give Jarrod credit for fortitude and stamina. She never complained and never lost patience with the little girl. The same courtesy was not shown Anna. She was snapped and snarled at more than once—and not by the silly-looking dog.

The solution was obvious, but Anna hated asking. Maybe because Heath Jarrod was disabled. There was the feeling of walking on eggs, as if plain old ordinary Americans, once confined to a wheelchair, immediately became foreigners with a separate culture, different rules of etiquette, customs and taboos that, in her ignorance, Anna might break.

There was that.

And there was pity. That creeping, mealy-mouthed cousin of goodness that oozed out in a parody of empathy, leaving the perpetrator nauseated and the victim feeling worse than before. Pity was born of fear. Anna wasn't afraid to die. But to be broken so bad no one could fix it and in such a way that life and comfort became dependent on being helped by others; that thought made her blood run cold. Crippled was scary and it was hard and Anna feared she wouldn't have the strength or courage to pull it off with any shred of grace or dignity.

Making a point to speak only to Ms. Jarrod and not to her aunt, Dr. Littleton, she said, "If you could accompany us to the hospital, things might go more easily for Beth."

"Not a problem."

Anna wished she'd had the metaphorical balls to ask sooner.

"We can go in the RV. It's got a lift."

"Sure," Anna agreed easily. To Emily she said, "I'll ride with Dr. Littleton and Ms. Jarrod. You go with Ryan."

Jarrod opened her mouth to argue. Anna could feel the woman's need for a fight as a physical pressure on her brain. If the Texas clock-tower, equipped with a handicapped-accessible elevator, were instantly available, Anna didn't doubt Jarrod would be up there with an automatic rifle in the blink of an eye.

That's when the rains saved her. A flash and a boom so close as to be two facets of the same sensation rattled eardrums and retinas, then an icy torrent was loosed sufficient to cool whatever dark fires were fueling Heath Jarrod's fury.

Dr. Littleton ran ahead to the RV. Anna and Emily followed, pushing the doubly burdened chair through the streaming gravel.

The RV was new and spacious and outfitted for use by a chair-bound person. Comforts and conveniences had not been spared when the vehicle was retrofitted for a handicapped user. Somebody had money.

Heath Jarrod's hands full of Beth, Dr. Littleton locked the brakes on her wheels. Anna belted herself into a captain's chair on a swivel base. It was covered in velvet-soft butter-colored leather. She chose not to think what her soggy, metal-bristling nether parts were doing to the upholstery.

Dr. Littleton took to the driver's seat and followed the ambulance out the rain-dark road. Dispatch radioed that Lorraine Knight would meet them at the children's wing of the Estes Park hospital. Arrangements were being made for a child psychologist and a detective from the Estes Park police department to join them.

Estes Park was full of rich old retired environmentalists. The very sort to guarantee the small town had a truly excellent medical facility. That it was in one of the most beautiful places on earth didn't hurt either. Recruiting top-notch doctors and nurses, even at lower pay, proved fairly easy. Anna relaxed fractionally.

Explaining what she was doing each step of the way to reassure both Beth and Heath, she gently took the girl's vitals—blood pressure, pulse, temperature—and relayed them to the hospital via dispatch. Beth was severely dehydrated: when Anna pinched up a bit of skin on the back of her hands it remained tented far too long. Under normal circumstances she'd have been put on an IV. If Emily knew her stuff, Alexis would already be on a normal saline drip.

The cursory check over, Anna reached for a horribly green afghan on the arm of her chair. When she turned back, Beth was out like a light.

"She's asleep," Anna said, faintly surprised. Sleep had come so fast, for an instant she thought the kid had passed out. Or died.

"Poor little limpet came to the end of her rope. I've seen climbers do that—literally and figuratively—but I meant get caught on a sketchy face, go without sleep. They get to the top and, bang. Down for the count."

This was the closest thing to a normal exchange Anna had had with this woman. Instinct whispered that she was going to want Heath Jarrod on her side if for no other reason than to help unlock the secrets shut away in Beth's skull.

"You climb?" She was cursing herself for a fool as Heath Jarrod treated her to a scathing look.

"Not hardly."

Anna just nodded, not ready to risk another blunder. Besides, if her former mother-in-law had taught her anything during the years she was married to Zach, it was that there was no excuse for bad manners. Not that Anna hadn't exhibited them herself, but she'd never excused herself. She wasn't in a mood to excuse Jarrod, either.

After a couple minutes' silence the other woman either saw the error of her ways or, more likely, just wanted to talk and so chose to reattach the nose to her spited face.

"I used to climb. Ice mostly. But anything else when that melted."

Anna nodded again. She wanted to ask what happened, but by the calculating, almost triumphant look that entered Jarrod's brown eyes, it was clear she was waiting, daring her to do just that. Anna said nothing.

Another minute passed.

"I fell. Rotten ice above Frozen Lake, the Keyhole."

"Bummer," Anna said sympathetically. Frozen Lake, she knew, was in the Rocky Mountains. That was as far as her knowledge went. She'd not yet had time to do much more than study maps and fill out the reams of paperwork deemed necessary when one changed jobs. It crossed her mind to ask Heath about the Keyhole—there was no way quicker into another's heart than letting them be the expert—but something made Anna leery of exposing any weakness. Perhaps it was that Jarrod was fanatical about showing none herself. Whatever the cause, Anna sensed she would go for the jugular if it were presented.

And snarl like a wounded wolf if anyone offered help. It was that which kept Anna from pressing her with questions on her own well-being. Rain had washed the sweat away but the pallor remained, and Jarrod was exhibiting shortness of breath.

A mile or more passed in silence. When Heath Jarrod spoke again, her tone was slightly less pugnacious. "What can you tell me about the girls?" She looked down at Beth, sound asleep on her lap.

"May I take her?" Anna asked, wanting to ease Heath's stress. Fight came up in Jarrod's eyes. "She must be cramping up," Anna said. "If I move her to the sofa I can stretch her out." The appeal to Beth's comfort did what no other argument could have. Heath unlocked the clasped hands that had been keeping the girl from sliding off her splayed knees.

Gently Anna lifted the child. Half-sitting in a moving vehicle, the dead weight pulled viciously at her lower back but she remained steady until she had Beth resting on the sofa. For a moment Anna listened to her breathing, assuring herself she was truly and deeply asleep. Then she set her mind to Heath's question. Jarrod could be said to have a right to know.

During the time that had elapsed since she and the EMTs arrived on scene, much of the story of the three missing girls—read in daily snippets from the morning *Ranger Report*, a rambling collection of incidents from parks all over the country—had resurfaced and coalesced in Anna's mind. The tale of the search had been published in broken pieces as it unfolded, pieces that were mixed in with the stories of wildfires burning out of control in southern California; the badly decomposed corpse of a man wanted in the killings of two students at a boys' school in Pennsylvania, turning up on the Trace, apparent death by drinking battery acid, notes to the dead boys in his pockets; a series of rapes at Lake Mead; car lootings perpetrated by bears at Yosemite and an organized ring of humans at Yellowstone, dozens of other on-going sagas. Summers were busy in the parks. It took Anna a moment to sort out the relevant fragments pertaining to the girls and put them back together.

"A while back, six weeks I think, a church group was up at Odessa Lake on a weekend campout. A youth group. Girls. Six or seven all told. They were slated to stay two nights, Friday and Saturday. The girls were teens and preteens. If I remember right, the youngest was eleven and the oldest maybe fifteen. It was some kind of religious outing; Bible study on the rocks, or whatever."

Heath's eyes narrowed fractionally and Anna realized her cynicism was showing through the narrative. Since becoming engaged—married, she reminded herself, unconsciously turning the gold band on her ring finger—to an Episcopal priest-*cum*-county sheriff, she had worked hard to keep her ungodly thoughts from poking into others' belief systems. At times like this, when a truly heinous act sent its unholy stink to high heaven, that resolution failed her.

"Jee-zuss." Heath mimicked the traveling salvation show pronunciation with a bitterness that those raised without religion could never know. Anna wondered if the fall that took away the use of her legs had started Heath on a vendetta against her personal god.

The woman's color had improved and her breathing was less shallow. Regardless of whether it was anger at a deity or the removal of an oversized limpet from her diaphragm, Anna was glad to see it.

"Two adults accompanied the girls," she went on. "One kid's mom—I don't remember which—came as chaperone. The other was a man named Robert Proffit. He was the church's youth group leader and organized the outing."

"'She stayed with Robert.'" Heath repeated Alexis' answer when asked where the third missing girl, Candace, was. "Jesus," she said again. This time she didn't mock; she cursed.

"The backcountry ranger up at Fern Lake—it's just a half-mile or less from Odessa—"

"I know where Fern Lake is," Heath interrupted, as if Anna had insulted her.

"Okay," Anna said agreeably. "The ranger at Fern got a call from dispatch. The chaperone mom had an emergency back home. So mom hikes out with the girls who have had enough wilderness—or preaching. Candace, Alexis and Beth stayed behind to finish up their weekend with the youth group leader, Proffit."

"How old's this guy?"

"I don't know. Young, I think. Early twenties."

"They left three girls alone with him overnight?" Heath sounded accusing. Anna didn't rise to the bait. She looked at Beth curled into the fetal position, thumb in mouth. Anna, too, wanted to lay the blame on somebody with a heavy lash or, failing that, to pound hell out of a serviceable scapegoat.

"Evidently."

"Why?" The outrage in Heath's voice penetrated Beth's dreams and she whimpered.

"I don't know," Anna replied. "I didn't work here when the girls went missing."

"We're there," Dr. Littleton said from the driver's seat as she maneuvered the RV off the highway and into the Estes Park hospital parking lot.

Workers in scrubs took over the children. Despite her nap Beth wasn't ready to let go of Jarrod, and Heath was wheeled into the bowels of the hospital alongside the gurney. Alexis made no protest; she'd returned to that inner landscape where outsiders did not exist.

Anna and Gwen Littleton were left in the waiting room with Chief Ranger Lorraine Knight, the detective from the Estes Park police department, a child psychologist on call by the hospital, and a lawyer, also on call, who looked tired and mulish. His stubble-covered jaw was set in Anna's least favorite manifestation of stubbornness. Self-righteous stubbornness pushed the chin out. This man's was tucked in: the set of a man defending what he's paid to, not what he believes in. Anna was surprised when none of the three experts followed the disappearing gurneys.

"Quite a welcome to Rocky, hey, Anna?" Lorraine said.

"Quite a night," Anna agreed. Talking with Chief Ranger Knight, Anna felt a couple hundred pounds of little lost girls lifting from her shoulders. Lorraine was near Anna's age, fifty maybe, or fifty-one. Her face was aged and ageless from a lifetime of working outdoors in all weathers. Though she was tall and lean and stronger than some men her size, she'd retained a womanly roundness of body and a childlike roundness of face. When her hair wasn't sequestered in a braid coiled at the nape of her neck, it fell to her waist in gray and auburn waves, creating a strange sweet mix of mother, Magdalene and wicked child.

"There's good and bad news," the chief ranger said. "The good news is it's over. The bad news is it's over."

Anna must have looked as baffled as she felt because Lorraine explained.

"Right after I got off the phone with Beth Dwayne's mother, she called the other parents, then the lawyers." She nodded at the mulish man.

"The girls are not to be rape-tested, not to speak with a psychologist, not to be questioned by law enforcement without a parent or guardian present and only to be given life-saving medical care."

"Are they crazy or what?" This from Dr.

Gwen Littleton, who stood forgotten at Anna's elbow.

"Let's hope they are crazy," Chief Knight said. "'Or what' is too grisly to contemplate."

six

The chair might not have been a cone of silence, but it did strong duty as a cloak of invisibility. It was as if, once terminally seated, Heath had dropped below the spectrum of human sight: like the high notes on a whistle, only dogs were aware of her. Since she'd been given a life sentence to sit in it, Heath had inwardly—and sometimes outwardly—raged against the phenomenon.

This was the first time it had worked to her advantage. While the others were shut out, she'd been whisked into the room along with the limpet, parked in a corner, and promptly forgotten like a piece of portable equipment.

Heath had become accustomed to hospitals: the smell, the sounds—muted and annoying, as if bad things were happening just out of earshot—the impersonal intrusions of total strangers coldly intimate. Hospitals no longer frightened her. Though the emotion shamed her on a level too deep to question, she felt at home in them. They were the only place her disability served as a membership card; she was supposed to be there. In hospitals everyone was broken. *Too fucking pathetic*, she castigated herself and renewed a vow she made, broke and remade a thousand times a day, to be a good little cripple: strong and brave and cheerful.

Doctors and nurses came and went, muttered and poked. The limpet was attached to an intravenous tube. She cried silently but made no protest when the borrowed sweat suit was peeled off of her and her soiled underthings removed.

One nurse—or maybe she was a doctor, with gender no longer a factor and everyone wearing what amounted to medical pajamas—startled Heath by actually seeing her.

"You the mother?" she asked in a business-only tone of voice.

Heath shook her head, for once annoyed that she'd been noticed. The woman turned away and Heath again disappeared. The question launched an unpleasant train of thought. She was not the mother. She was not a mother. And now she never would be. Even at forty-one she'd always thought there'd be time. Now there was time, endless time, and nothing with which to fill it.

To derail this wretched locomotive, she concentrated on the limpet. Not praying. Praying was bullshit; she was done with that. Should she still believe in a personal benevolent god who saw each sparrow fall, she would have cursed the son-of-a-bitch for not catching them before they broke their little birdy backs on the rocks, never to fly again.

She did still believe in the power of emotional support, one lonely marooned human heart to another. Anyone who had climbed for a while did. On a cliff-face there was only the rope, the rock and the person with whom you climbed. Rope and rock were unforgiving. She'd learned the value of the person. Inching her chair closer, she took Beth's hand so the child would know she wasn't alone.

Busyness ended. The parade of people in scrubs dwindled to nothing. Time hitched by one palsied minute at a time on the classroom-sized clock on the wall. Heath began to wonder where the others were— the cops, the rangers, the shrinks—wonder if both she and the limpet had been forgotten.

Still holding Beth's hand, she laid her head down on the bed and drifted. A dream came, the same dream she always had in one of its myriad forms: ice falling away under her hand, anchors ripping out as she hurtled past. In dreams the fall was endless and, with a knowledge of the future, all the fear she'd not had the leisure to feel at the time, she now enjoyed at length and in heart-stopping detail each time she closed her eyes.

This time Sean, her climbing buddy, caught her hand and, for a moment, she believed herself saved. As always, fingers slipped and she fell. This night she was caught a second time. A fist closed tight in her short thick hair. Even while the dream had her trapped in its repetitive reality, some part of her brain registered change from the usual pattern. There on the cliff-face of nightmare she found herself muttering, "This is a new twist," as she waited for the monsters of her id to tire of mocking her with false saves, the fingers to loose, the inevitable crash, then the happy ending where she awoke in a wheelchair.

The grip in her hair tightened, pulled at her scalp. For the first time since the dreams began she was being pulled up, not down.

Tugging continued until Heath was pulled out of the dream completely. Beth had a fistful of her hair and was tweaking it.

"Are you asleep?" the girl whispered, as if afraid the sound of her voice would bring down the Mongol hordes in their dull green scrubs.

"No," Heath whispered back for the same reason. "I was, but you saved me from a bad dream."

"I had a real bad dream," Beth said. Heath didn't know if she referred to a sleeping dream or obliquely to whatever she'd been through over the last weeks.

For the first time since they'd stumbled

upon one another in the woods, Beth spoke, not in broken fragments, but in a whole and responsive sentence. Her eyes were different as well, haunted still and mostly empty, but a little person had returned behind them. She no longer looked like a child from *Village of the Damned*.

Heath was staggered by the force of the joy she felt and terrified by the sense of responsibility. This wisp of a girl, nearly lost in all that darkness, could be frightened away all too easily, maybe never to dare come forth again.

"I dreamed I was falling like I did when I broke my back. That's why I can't walk," Heath whispered. "What did you dream?"

"I dreamed Candy was with us and we were all going to Denver to shop for winter coats." This, too, was whispered. Without vocal cues Heath had a hard time reading much into it. Beth had rolled onto her side and curled down till her face was only six inches from Heath's, who still rested her cheek on her folded arms. Each of the limpet's expressions was as clear as a fish in shallow water. And as hard to pin down. Within the one short statement, it seemed Beth lived a lifetime of angst. Behind the innocuous words Heath saw conspiracy, confession, horror, shame—or thought she did. Maybe, having imagined these things, she projected them onto the smooth skin of this child.

"How come the dream was real bad?" she asked.

"Because Candy wasn't really with us. And we weren't going shopping." Her whisper trailed off to the merest distortion of air. Had Heath not been so close she wouldn't have heard it: "We were going somewhere *else*."

Heath's brain flooded with questions. Where was Candace? Where was somewhere *else*? Who was taking them "shopping"? What the hell had happened? The most pressing was where was Candace, but that had been asked and answered, though the answer had satisfied no one.

Heath decided to leave interrogation to rangers or cops or whomever. She was Beth's climbing partner. Others could worry about the rest.

"Somewhere *else* sounds like it sucks big-time," she whispered back.

Because Beth was twelve and Heath a

grown-up, the word "sucks" won Heath a ghost of a smile from her young friend.

"Sucks *big*-time," Beth said.

"You want to tell me about it?"

Heath feared she'd pushed too hard too soon. Silence flowed between them, pooling and spreading till the air in the room grew thick with it, making sounds outside unnaturally loud. The clock's second-hand's lurching progress around the dial snicked, lopping off tiny increments of life.

The clock; looking at it Heath was surprised to see her nap had lasted over an hour. It was close to midnight.

"Little animals . . . ," Beth said, her toddler's voice back.

Heath waited. This time the silence wasn't true silence. Underneath were words, stories, revelations.

A low murmur of voices crept in around the doorframe. The shuffle of feet as a hushed wave of people came down the hall.

Heath closed her eyes the better to focus, if not in prayer, then in a fervent incantation for supernatural intervention. *No, no, no. Bugger off. Not now.*

It was now. The wave broke and the door to the room swung quietly open.

Heath looked first to Beth. The connection was broken. Big-eyed and slack-jawed, the child stared at the door. Heath couldn't tell if it was terror she saw, anticipation or bone-breaking weariness.

seven

"Let's sit," Lorraine said. The lawyer and the psychologist had melted away, probably to homes and beds. Dr. Littleton had excused herself to check on Wiley. Anna and the chief ranger sat, each on her own low square sofa, the kind that ensures that those who wait also serve. The backs weren't high enough, the seats too deep, armrests lacking.

Perched at right angles, leaning forward, they talked.

"What gives?" Anna asked for starters.

"It's complicated."

Anna waited while Lorraine untangled the

complication into a coherent narrative. The chief ranger had aged in the months since Anna had last seen her. They'd worked together on a case that bore certain similarities to the one Lorraine had walked smack into when she'd transferred to Rocky Mountain: young people lost, a search. Prolonged searches, particularly where children were involved, were emotionally scarring. Two of them back-to-back had cost Lorraine.

"A couple of the girls turned up in one piece," Anna said. It wasn't her custom to barge into other people's brown studies without knocking. Maybe she hoped counting blessings would ease the harsh lines digging between the chief ranger's brows.

Maybe she was just being impatient.

"One still missing," Lorraine said.

The shepherd and the lost sheep; the parable fit Lorraine Knight to a T. Anna admired Knight for genuinely caring about each and every visitor that came to her parks. Admired but didn't emulate. Counseling herself to patience, she leaned back, giving her boss space to think.

"Okay," the chief ranger said finally. "These folks are religious. Real religious. Kids home-schooled. Social life, personal life—near as I can tell, everything—is centered around their church. They call themselves Reformed Saints.

"At one point they were Mormons but the sect broke away. The chief of police in Loveland said it was because Salt Lake City decided African Americans could hold church offices, but I have no idea if that part's true. From interacting with them during the search, I do know they think of Salt Lake City as a modern Sodom. They're a real conservative bunch. The sheriff—they don't live in Loveland proper but about twenty miles out of town in an enclave of sorts—has never had a problem with them. They're quiet. Keep to themselves.

"Sounds like every description of a serial killer," Anna said.

Lorraine laughed. "It kind of does, doesn't it? I didn't mean to paint such a sinister picture. For what it's worth, I don't think they had anything to do with the girls' disappearance. Everyone I was in contact with—one of the dads and two moms—seemed devastated by their loss. What was hard for those of us who aren't of a religious bent was that they refused to help with the search. They never walked trails, took calls, pursued family leads, put faces on milk cartons, never called the park or came up here to see how the search was going."

"They didn't do *anything*?" Anna was as appalled as she was amazed. Parents could usually be relied upon to, if nothing else, drive the search-and-rescue officer insane.

"I didn't say they did nothing," Lorraine said. She paused a beat, caught Anna's eye. "They prayed. Round-the-clock vigils. Prayed in shifts. They kept right on doing it. Their whole little community."

Anna might have thought she'd softened but with this story the old cynical edges cut sharp as ever. The closest she came to Christianity was to espouse its tenet that God helps those who help themselves. That way, if God didn't bother to show, she'd at least have done what she could. So far, that had always been enough. Not an abundance, necessarily, but sufficient to stay alive and move forward. Now that two of the girls were back, this coterie of petitioners would swear God had finally heard their prayers. Six weeks. One would think an omnipotent's hearing would be more acute.

"Alexis' mother was praying night shift when I called with the good news," Lorraine said. "She had to get a replacement before she could come."

"A replacement," Anna scoffed. "What are they praying for now?"

"Candace Watson."

Anna had forgotten. "Ah. Momma Watson must have shirked her prayers."

The chief ranger shot her a hard look. "You'll watch that kind of talk when the families are here."

Chastised, Anna was silent for a moment. Then she said, "So their religion is against medical intervention?"

"Not that so much. They were fine with the girls getting medical care. It's the psychologist and the police they balked at. During the investigation subsequent to the search, they were less than forthcoming, uncooperative even."

"Why? Are they running a meth lab out of their commune or something?"

"Who knows. A lot of these fringe sects have a deep distrust of the government, especially the law enforcement arm. It could be no more than that. Paranoias run deep."

"So we wait till the parents come."

"We wait."

They waited. Lorraine filled Anna in on the

details of the search. Anna drank two cups of pretty good coffee cadged from the nurses' station. The rain stopped in a last growling thunderous threat to return the following afternoon. An hour passed, then two. Finally the automatic doors slid open and four people came in. By the teary, anxious, joyful, tired faces, Anna knew it was family.

They were known to Lorraine and rushed over in a body, questions frothing from their lips. The chief ranger calmed the waters with the oil of normalcy. She made introductions.

Mrs. Sheppard, Alexis' mom, was a tall woman, young but looking drawn and underweight as if she'd not gotten up from her knees to eat or sleep since her daughter had gone missing. She wore no make-up and had on a loose denim jumper over a long-sleeved white T-shirt. Her long hair was pulled up severely and wound into a knot on the top of her head. Despite the unglamorous treatment it was clear where Alexis got her looks. Mrs. Sheppard's face was fine-boned, the skin pasty but unblemished, and her eyes truly remarkable, wide set and sky blue. Though she had a thirteen-year-old daughter, she didn't look much over thirty, if that.

Mr. Sheppard was considerably older than his wife, twenty or more years. He'd apparently eaten the meals his wife had missed and carried a pouch of hard fat under his belt.

Mrs. Dwayne, Beth's mother, was dressed as conservatively as Mrs. Sheppard, in an ankle-length skirt, also of denim, and a cardigan, the kind Anna had worn as a little girl, pale pink with small plastic buttons from hem to neck. She was older than Mrs. Sheppard. Like Mrs. Sheppard, she wore her hair pulled up into a bun. As a concession to fashion—albeit one that had gone out twenty years before—the front was puffed up in an exaggerated pompadour. She clutched a pair of plastic cat-eye glasses in a sweaty hand. "Beth lost her glasses, they said. I brought her old ones . . ." She held them out as if this proved she was worthy of seeing her daughter.

No hands were offered. Anna nodded politely as each introduction was made, but her eyes and mind were fixed on the fourth member of the party, a young man, early twenties at a guess, with unruly dark hair and the intense burning eyes of a zealot, a lunatic or an artist. He was an unquestionably attractive man—or at least the kind Anna had found irresistible in her youth. His body was lean and strong-looking and passion radiated from him like heat from pavement in August.

Before Lorraine put a name to him, Anna knew he had to be Robert Proffit, the youth group leader who had taken the girls into the wilderness, the one who had eschewed prayer to search tirelessly. The one Beth and Alexis had said the still missing Candace had stayed with.

Anna realized she'd not imparted this crucial bit of information to the chief ranger. Now it would have to wait. Lorraine was saying, "I know the girls will want to see you. Anna, could you show Mrs. Dwayne where Beth's room is?"

Lorraine would go with Alexis' mom and dad. All bases covered. Except Anna couldn't leave. The young Proffit was moving, ready to follow the families into the ward.

"I'll stay here with Mr. Proffit," she said.

"For this first visit it might be best to keep it to immediate family."

This assumption of authority was out of line. Lorraine bristled a little, like a dog that senses its territory is being invaded. Anna looked her plea as best she could and was relieved to see trust counter the anger in Lorraine's face.

"You're right. Mr. Proffit, stay with Ranger Pigeon. Mr. and Mrs. Sheppard, Mrs. Dwayne—" Before she could finish, the doors to the outside slid open again and a man and a female ranger came in at a jog trot. The man's hair was wet, plastered to his head, Levi's and T-shirt were drenched as if he'd been caught in the rain and hadn't had time to change.

The woman Anna recognized. Her name was Rita Perry, her call number was 202. She was one of Anna's seasonal law enforcement rangers and a park paramedic. Rita was a striking woman, close to six feet tall, with a handsome face, lustrous brown hair and a jaw that spoke of strength and determination. Or stubbornness.

Not slowing, the man ran up to the gathering, talking as he came.

"They were found? The girls? I heard it on

the radio. My god, this is great. Are they both okay? Where are they?"

Anna had no idea who he was, and for a moment it looked as if Lorraine didn't either. Then the chief ranger's face cleared. "This is Raymond Bleeker," she said. "Ray's the backcountry ranger at Fern Lake. He put in more hours on the search than anyone in the park. Ray, these are the girls' folks."

Ray, then, was also one of Anna's seasonal rangers. The name rang a bell but she'd not yet had time to get into the backcountry.

"Did you bring Ray?" Anna asked Rita, just a question to settle the two of them down.

"Yeah. He radioed from the trailhead across from Sprague. He'd heard the girls had been found and he hiked out." As if Anna might censure Ray for leaving Fern Lake without a ranger for the night, Rita added, "We all got pretty invested in these girls."

Anna had already chosen to let the matter slide. If Raymond Bleeker cared enough to hike an hour and a half in the dark and the rain, more power to him. He could hike back up to Fern come morning.

"That's fine," Anna said.

"I need to see my daughter *now*." Mrs. Dwayne cut off further pleasantries.

"Of course," Lorraine said. Then: "Ray, why don't you take Mrs. Dwayne to Beth's room? It's two-oh-six. Rita, stay with Anna and Mr. Proffit."

Ray was an NPS law enforcement ranger. Green as he might or might not be, Anna was glad he'd shown up. She hoped he was observant.

Proffit watched them go, a look of intense something on his face: longing, hope, love. Anna couldn't tell. With burning young men who had fiery responses to everything from a sunset to a Middle Eastern war, it was nearly impossible to sort and prioritize. If he noted the inherent unfairness of Lorraine and Ray going where he was denied access, he wasn't saying anything.

"Sit down, Mr. Proffit." The words sounded more like a command than an invitation. Not wanting to put him on guard if he wasn't already, Anna smiled nicely. Or thought she did. Proffit looked at her as if she'd bared pointed fangs.

He glanced once more toward the doors the others had disappeared through, then turned back toward Anna and Rita, a dazed expression on his face. "Praise the Lord," he said, and to Anna's surprise, he and her ranger ran into one another's arms. The embrace was of the chaste buddy variety, touching only shoulders, faces turned out.

"Praise the Lord," Rita echoed. Then, to Anna's consternation and annoyance, they dropped to their knees on the linoleum of the waiting room floor and commenced praying out loud.

eight

"Why don't you lie down?" Gwen said reasonably.

Heath was too tired to be reasonable, too tired to sleep, too tired to do as she was told by aunt or physician. "Later," she said. "Mind if I smoke?"

"Not if you don't mind me towing you behind the RV while you do it."

It was the answer Heath expected. The one she wanted, really. Though she smoked—until the accident only three or four a day, but more and more since—she couldn't stand the smell of cigarette smoke in upholstery, her clothes, her hair. She always smoked out-of-doors then washed and brushed her teeth.

Because she knew it for a filthy habit, it was one of her favorites. Given the emotional maelstrom that had swept out of the darkling forest and inundated the rest of the night, Heath would have broken the indoor rule just this once. The craving was strong enough she considered promising her aunt she'd hold it out the window. The very power of the addiction was why she didn't give in to it.

"I can wait," she said. "What do you think about that New Canaan invite?"

"Tell me how it came about, again."

With anyone else Heath would have thought they were stalling, begging the question. Aunt Gwen had done neither in Heath's lifelong experience of her. Heath's dad had often said of his older sister, "Gwen's not always right but she's always right there." Till Heath was in her early thirties she hadn't understood what he meant. Now she doubted she would have made it through the last half year without it. Gwen Littleton didn't evade, sidestep, lie or equivocate. She lived by what one of her patients had referred to as the Bugs Bunny philosophy of life: Wherever you popped out of the ground, you dealt with what was right in front of you.

Heath thought back as Gwen drove unchallenged through the entrance gate to Rocky Mountain National Park, the booths unmanned at this hour of the night. The account she'd given as they'd left the hospital had been rushed and garbled, as her thoughts were rushed and garbled.

Dropping a hand down to touch Wiley where he slept between the RV's front seats, she settled herself through the warmth and rightness of dog.

"I'd say it was weird," she began. "But in comparison to what? This whole thing has been gnarly. Rat shit."

"Unnecessary roughness." Gwen was a football fan as well as a fan of refined language.

"Sorry," Heath said, unoffended. "When I was left alone with the limpet we both napped a little. When we woke up she seemed better, clearer. I swear she was about to tell me what had happened."

"'Little animals,' wasn't that what she said?"

"I know. It doesn't make sense but I think it might have if she could have told her story.

Mrs. Dwayne chose that moment to bull-doze in with this guy—a ranger, I gathered, though he wasn't wearing the costume. Something is very wrong. Beth looked freaked when she saw her mother. I mean *freaked*. She wet the bed and started to cry. Her mom tried to hold her and she got hys-terical. She leaped out of bed and started darting around—not going anywhere, just banging from wall to wall like a bird trapped in a fireplace. She was babbling 'She's not my mom' and stuff. I started to get up, go to her but, hey, well, guess who remembered she was a cripple? Damn near fell on my face. Mrs. Dwayne starts crying and bab-bling. I'm flopping around trying to get my friggin' wheels unlocked.

"The guy that came in with her, I guess he'd been one of the main searchers, caught Beth in his arms, told her she was okay, her mom was there, that she didn't have to talk—that sort of thing—and she calmed right down. After that, till the nurses came running in to see what the ruckus was about, she stayed close to him and seemed okay. But the child I'd glimpsed was gone. The limpet's eyes were back to black holes with no alternate universe on the far side."

Telling the story in chronological order, without the distraction of manipulating body and chair into the RV, helped her anxiety some. Not as much as a cigarette, but some. She no longer felt like she wanted to bend steel with her bare hands or bite the heads off chickens.

"The invite," Gwen nudged.

Heath had gotten sufficiently wrapped up in her story, she'd forgotten why she'd started the tale in the first place.

"Right. New Canaan." Her left leg jumped, movement she'd at first taken as a sign of hope but which now merely embarrassed her as a tic or an attack of hiccoughs might. Yet one more indication she had no control. The spasms were worse when she was tired. Squashing the leg with her hands, she went on. "After the dust had settled a bit— the limpet came and huddled by my chair like Wiley does—" she nearly added *when I cry*, but as she had hidden her tears from her aunt along with everyone else, she chose not to confess now. "The mom, Mrs. Dwayne, started cooing about taking Beth home. The limpet grabbed my hand and put it over her face. I mean literally. She buried her nose in my palm like it was an oxygen mask. She started keening. That high, thin wail you see Middle Eastern women sometimes doing on the news when their babies are killed."

"Both girls bonded with you," Gwen said. "The little one especially. You gave her something nobody else could. She feels safe with you."

"It's Wiley or the chair," Heath said dismissively. Still, she was pleased in an odd way. Pleased to be needed. Pleased to be of help.

"I told Mrs. Dwayne how I'd come across the girls and that the limpet had sort of attached herself to me. She more or less blew it off and tried to tug Beth away. Anyway, the limpet started crying, 'No, no, she comes, Heath comes.' A nurse walked in at that point to tell us all it was time to leave. The limpet keeps my hand and keeps shrieking. The nurse gets a doctor. The doctor wants to keep Beth. Mom refuses.

"They're taking the girls home. Tonight. Can you believe that? Tonight. So the doctor suggests, if possible, I visit.

"Then the ranger searcher guy starts talking to mom and limpet, saying now that we know where she lives we'll all come visit.

The limpet calms down again. Mom splits to have a confab with Alexis' folks. The dad comes back with her. Takes a look at me and says okay, we should come."

"You must have a trustworthy face."

"Nobody can say 'no' to a cripple."

Gwen ignored the bitterness, as she always did. "I've got the time," she said. "I'm retired."

By the way her aunt vocally stomped on the word 'I've,' Heath knew she was thinking Heath didn't have the time. Or shouldn't take the time. She should return to Denver and physical therapy. Heath was done with that, done with the strapping up and dangling above treadmills, the swimming, the cheerful encouraging therapists, everybody rooting for her to transform, through tremendous amounts of work and will, her half-life into a nine-sixteenths life. The carrot of "the possibility of limited recovery" was considered sufficient to keep her going.

Gwen sighed—discreetly, but Heath heard it and it annoyed her.

"We can park the RV in their driveway and stay with Beth as long as you like," Gwen said.

"No, we can't. The dad was firm on that.

There's an RV camp about ten miles away. We're to stay there."

"Big show of gratitude," Gwen sniffed. Having traversed the dark, glorious miles into the park, Gwen maneuvered the vehicle into the circle of road at the handicamp. A ranger patrol vehicle was still parked in front of their site. Leaning against the hood, arms and ankles crossed, was the woman who'd ridden with them to the hospital.

"Ranger Pigeon," Heath said. "What the hell does she want?"

"You seem to have taken against her," Gwen said mildly.

Heath only grunted. There was something about Pigeon that set her off. Not something. One thing: Ranger Pigeon could walk. Most people could, but they didn't offend Heath in the same way. Anna Pigeon walked like a big cat—sure-footed, graceful, her feet touching the ground lightly as if ready to spring. There was nothing of hesitation. Nothing of fear. Around her Heath felt her disability more acutely, was humiliated by it. When they'd ridden together to the hospital, she'd found herself wanting—needing—to let Ms. Pigeon know that she'd been a climber, that she was in the chair by accident, not by birth, as if that made one damn bit of difference.

Gwen parked the RV. "I'll get your chair around," she said.

"No. She can come in here."

"I thought you were dying for a fag?"

Only Gwen still called them fags and the image usually brought a smile to Heath's face. Not tonight.

"I can wait," she said.

"Suit yourself."

Heath was doing it again, squirming inside. The truth was, in the swivel seat in the RV, she was like anyone else. She didn't want to lever herself out, drag her legs, cinch her straps and wheel herself in front of Ranger Pigeon. It wasn't that she was afraid of seeing sympathy—or worse, pity—in the woman's eyes. The ranger's face showed nothing but a polite business-like interest, but it was . . . She didn't know what it was but she still hated herself for it.

Ambient self-loathing. Gwen brought the ranger toward the RV. Heath swiveled her seat to face into the living space. "Get used to it," she muttered.

nine

Rain and wear had removed visible traces of the blood, but the skid marks on the asphalt and two pieces of broken headlight assured Anna she'd left Bear Lake Road at the right place. An elk carcass wasn't a subtle thing. She'd thought finding it wouldn't be a problem. But then Rita Perry was a big woman, probably strong; maybe she'd felt the need to carry it farther back into the woods where visitors wouldn't accidentally get so much as a whiff of it. Every park had a way of disposing of animal remains that was idiosyncratic to its needs and the sensibilities of the superintendent. In Glacier in northern Montana, at least in the backcountry, carcasses were let lie and, knowing grizzly bears would be coming to clean the bones, area trails were closed. On the southernmost district of Natchez Trace, when a deer was killed by an automobile, the body was taken to the Catholic orphanage in Port Gibson where good fresh meat was welcomed. In Rocky Mountain, where predators and motherless children were rare, the dead animals were simply dragged into the trees, out of sight, to return to the earth through the bellies of smaller omnivores.

Anna had chosen to view these particular remains because she was new to the park. The dead were quite informative and she wanted to see if the animal was crippled, old, flea-bitten, diseased, fat, sleek, male or female, if its coat was fine or mangy. Due to a chronic wasting disease, a freakish malady with a gruesome set of symptoms embracing the best of multiple sclerosis and Alzheimer's, Rocky's elk were some of the most closely watched ungulates in the wild. Reams of information were cached in the research center available for the asking. Eventually Anna would get around to reading them. For now, her brain worked better in fresh air with visual, tactile and olfactory show-and-tell.

It was possible Rita had taken the carcass to the dump for some reason or another. If so, Anna wasn't going to pursue it. Not only didn't she have time before she headed into the backcountry, but she wasn't that dedicated to her education.

She radioed 202. "What did you do with the dead elk?" she asked when Rita responded.

"Dragged it off the road. Standard operating procedure here."

"How far?"

A moment crackled empty between the radios, then Rita's voice, hesitant and maybe a little sarcastic: "Just far enough. You know. There's no regs on the exact distance."

Anna smiled. Any of her listening seasonals would be growing nervous thinking the new district ranger was the sort to go creeping about the woods with a tape measure to be sure dead critters were disposed of according to the book. It was good for seasonals to be frightened now and again.

"No," she said into the mike. "How far off

the road did you drag your personal dead elk? The one from last night?"

Another silence, then: "Why?"

This wasn't a "why" sort of question and they didn't have a "why" sort of relationship. Anna gave the ranger a few seconds to mend her ways. Rita was a smart woman.

"Maybe fifteen feet or so," came over the airwaves.

Anna had been up and down the road a quarter of a mile in either direction from the point of impact. On this particular stretch of the road there weren't a lot of options. The western side was a dirt cut several yards high, the eastern side a fairly thin tract of trees running down to a creek.

"Thanks." Anna let go of the mike button. Something had dragged off the elk's remains. Coyotes didn't have the strength; they just ate their fill and wandered away to sleep it off. Mountain lions sometimes cached their food. Nothing fancy like the grizzly bears, but often they'd drag it to a more easily defensible place. It would take a mighty big lion to move even a small adult elk. That left only the black bear.

People thought of black bears as cute little animals the size of Saint Bernards. They were cute but could grow to three hundred pounds. Like most species who weren't rich enough to boast obesity as their most pressing health concern, bears wouldn't turn their nose up at a bit of protein-rich carrion. From the scuttlebutt she'd gathered, Rocky had had problem black bears before. Bears, big bears, this close to the more populated frontcountry camping areas, were usually bad news. Anna looked at her watch. There was nothing she could do about it till a visitor got munched or a bear was harassed, and she had no intention of missing her date.

As always, when walking away from people, pavement and the ubiquitous golden calf Americans were determinedly sacrificing the environment to— the automobile—Anna felt her heart swell, her mind expand. Eyesight grew sharper, hearing more keen as her soul feasted on the natural world. In the years in Mississippi, she'd almost managed to forget how much the mountains meant to her, how splendid it was to run on the high octane. At sea level all one got was oxygen. At eight thousand feet one could breathe honest-to-god *air*.

With each deep breath she consciously blew out soot from the previous night's emotional conflagration. What should have been a joyous reunion between grieving parents and lost children had turned into a morass of bizarre behaviors.

Anna had had enough prayers to choke an agnostic. The frustration she suffered watching the parents risking the health of their children by eschewing modern medicine for the dubious healing powers of magic incantations had kept her blood pressure up so long her brain felt parched. When Lorraine suggested she check out the back-country in the Thompson River District, Anna had jumped at the opportunity.

Since Ray Bleeker had to hike back to Fern Lake after his impulsive dash out to see the search victims alive and well, or at least two-thirds of them, Anna had chosen to accompany him.

"How long have you been a backcountry ranger?" she asked. She hated besmirching the day with the rattle of human voices, but it behooved her to get to know her people.

Ray hiked on for a moment without speaking, as if her banal question was deserving of serious thought. That, or he'd worked in more parks than could be credited to a man of twenty-seven. Anna knew his age because she'd glanced at his employee folder before the hike. If she hadn't, she'd have put him in his early to mid-thirties. He was good-enough looking, chin a little weak perhaps, pale blue eyes a bit protuberant, but his straight brown hair was thick and his skin good. It wasn't that the years had marked his face. In fact, the skin around his eyes was remarkably unlined for a man who spent a majority of his days exposed to wind and sun. The backs of his hands, though sunbrowned, didn't look as if they'd taken the beating four or five seasons in the backcountry could dole out. And he moved as a younger man might, months on the trail making him lean and strong. He just felt older: more internal silence, less of a tendency to let every thought and emotion show.

"Not long," he said finally. "How about you?"

A human being who didn't grab at an opportunity to talk about itself; Anna found that refreshing. She gave a short answer to his question and enjoyed a quarter hour more of quiet. The trail up from Bear Lake past Odessa and to Fern was glorious. Anna doubted there was a trail in Rocky that wasn't. From wooded green canyons, glittering and chuckling with fast-running creeks, one could see granite peaks ringing the sky, bald and sharp, the cracks in these giant citadel stones visible where weather had continued the work the glaciers began. Tiny lakes bejeweled unexpected hollows and everywhere there was rock: boulders, hills, palisades of rock in gray and green and gold. Rock that took the light like seasoned actors, playing back emotions of color and shadow through the day, through the seasons.

Not many rocks in Mississippi. Mostly mud.

At length, duty roused Anna to try another foray into the realm of employee relations. "What other parks have you worked in?" That question was as standard in the NPS as "did you get all your classes" was when Anna was in college. Till now she'd never known it to fail to elicit a spate of conversation followed up by a satisfying round of "do you know so-and-so?" For all its three hundred and seventy something parks and monuments scattered across America, the

Park Service was a small world. A little digging invariably turned up mutual acquaintances.

"Mostly the upper Midwest," was the only answer Anna got from Bleeker. Perhaps he had gravitated into backcountry work for the solitude. That Anna could understand.

Duty done as far as was polite, she would have been content to walk with only the whispering of trees for companionship, but there was more than enough human interaction even without Ray. Rocky wasn't a huge park—slightly over a quarter of a million acres—yet each year it had over three and a half million visitors arriving and departing in hundreds of thousands of automobiles. At the peak of the season there was hardly a place in the park, front- or backcountry, where one was guaranteed to be alone. Summer was nearly over, the kids back in school, but there were still plenty of hikers on Bear Creek Trail leading, as it did, to two popular backcountry campsites.

Purposely, Anna had chosen not to wear her uniform. Middle-aged, female, in civilian clothes, she could fade neatly into the background each time a group of hikers met them on the trail. She was too new to the park to be of much use answering resource questions and, too, she wanted to watch Ray work. The childhood admonition to listen and learn had always stood her in good stead.

With visitors Ray Bleeker was outgoing and friendly, with just enough charm to be genuinely charming but not oily. He seemed a little weak on park knowledge. Once, Anna noticed he invented a new name for larkspur, a common enough wildflower, though nearly past its blooming season. She let it pass. Rangers had been known to make things up before.

By one-thirty the thunderheads began building. They stepped up the pace so lightning wouldn't catch them on the exposed slopes. Down a rocky defile named Tourmaline Gorge and lined winter and spring with stunning waterfalls was Odessa Lake campground, the site from which Beth, Candace and Alexis had disappeared. The name on the trail sign dragged Anna's mind from the majestic threat of the grumbling thunder cells to the darker mystery of where the girls had been during the weeks between their vanishing and reappearing.

"Tell me about the search," she said, and

accidentally stumbled upon the way to Ray's heart, or at least his language center. The man was a search-and-rescue junkie. For twenty minutes he held forth on the intricacies and thoroughness of the operation, how the area had been gridded and walked. Dogs had been brought in, helicopters, rangers on horseback and on foot, volunteers from Estes Park. He seemed almost gleeful as he told her of each dead end, of clues that came to nothing, dogs who'd followed their noses to abandoned privy holes. Because Anna had a touch of adrenaline addiction herself, and because she'd seen the depth of his concern when he'd hiked out to see the girls, she forgave him this callous enjoyment. It was the nature of the job. Contrary to popular belief, firefighters loved fires, rescuers loved to rescue, EMTs loved to stick needles in people and searchers loved the beauty of the search process.

It couldn't have hurt that Ray's cabin at Fern Lake, just half a mile from the ground zero, had been the hub of the effort. For weeks he'd had more attention than he'd probably gotten in all the other jobs he'd held combined.

At the bottom of the narrow canyon, he

gave her a tour of the Odessa campsite where the youth group had stayed. Though beautiful, it was not a place Anna would choose to spend time. Canyon walls, skirted with boulders the size of semi-truck trailers, pressed close on both sides of a tree-filled ravine. The campsites were dwarfed. This tangle of fallen pines and huge stones made Anna claustrophobic. Instead of natural order it struck her as disorder, as if the earth had become confused. Nature, rendered unnatural, cast a sinister feel over the place and she was glad when Ray had talked himself out and they climbed up to the gentler, more open views of Fern Lake.

The backcountry cabin at Fern was everything the public imagines backcountry cabins to be and seldom are. Set on a knoll above the small lake, it was made of logs and boasted two bedrooms. The park had recently refurbished it down to fire-engine red curtains in the windows. Unlike many young men, Raymond Bleeker was as tidy as Felix Unger. Anna's impromptu visit found the place in shockingly good order. Even the mullions of the many-paned windows were dust free. One of the bedrooms served as a storage room for chainsaws, ropes, sleeping bags, backboards, shovels and other necessities of the wilderness existence. Anna noted that everything was neatly hung in its place and newly labeled. Raymond had gone to the lengths of spreading a canvas tarp over the floor-boards to serve as a rug. The other bed-room had bunk beds for the cabin's human inhabitants. A spacious living room–kitchen, with a double bed and dining table set cheek by jowl, was warmed by a wood stove. Against one wall a two-by-four ladder was bolted, leading to a loft space over the bedrooms that tickled the heart of the child that still lurked within Anna. The cabin's larder was well stocked, food and other housekeeping items packed in by mules.

Raymond's personal things were on a sin-gle shelf to one side of the dining table. Clothes were folded with factory precision. A laptop and compact high-tech sound sys-tem with extra batteries were neatly covered in clear plastic. Shoes were polished and set toes out. Books, of poetry mostly, were cap-tured between two exceedingly clean rocks.

Everything painstakingly mouse-proofed.

Now that he'd opened up, Ray proved a surprisingly good companion, adept at drawing out those with whom he talked. By the time they'd consumed a fairly decent spaghetti dinner and the dishes were washed, Anna realized she'd told him just about everything but her bra size and still knew next to nothing about him; an unusual and not unpleasant state of affairs.

In the quiet aftermath of dinner she sat at the plank table and, by the light of a Coleman lantern, read through the journals. Rangers and visitors, firefighters and skiers, had been writing their thoughts down since the 1970s. Nearly thirty years of history told from hundreds of points of view, yet what caught Anna's fancy was the shared human experience, the timelessness of a life that didn't change hour by hour with the shock of the new: buildings going up next door, playgrounds razed, internet spinning its sudden cyberweb, cell phones piercing.

Along with the usual chatter of the hike and the weather, nearly every entry had two things in common: glowing reports of the landscape and scathing denunciations of the mice, some with drawings of the little creatures committing all manner of mousy depredations on the humans who intruded into their cabin.

Anna skimmed the first twenty-five years of the history more for her own enjoyment than anything else. Because of the girls who'd turned up on her professional doorstep, she was mostly interested in the entries for the previous month, those of the SAR (Search and Rescue) rangers who'd stayed at Fern.

Rita Perry, Anna's law enforcement seasonal, had written half a dozen or more times. It was no wonder she'd grown close to Robert Proffit. On at least four occasions during the search for the girls, they had bunked together. On a search-and-rescue or a wildfire, though the intensity of these activities spawned more than their share of romances, "bunked together" hadn't any sexual connotation. There was more a sense of military camaraderie, a flopping down of like-minded soldiers at the end of the day. Though with young people—any people if it came to that—sex was a powerful undercurrent, Anna had found far less gender politics when the work was hard and physical, and civilization far away.

She paged forward and read on. As the search ground down, the names of the participants grew fewer. Rangers still came but volunteers had either given up hope or run out of time. The entries became shorter, dispirited. For the last week or so, no one mentioned the search or the children. Anna stopped reading but left her eyes on the pages of the open journal, a habit so ingrained she was no longer aware she did it. Years in and out of camps and other group living conditions, she'd found if she pretended to read, fewer people felt com- pelled to talk to her when she needed to think. With Raymond Bleeker the ruse was probably unnecessary. Across the table from her, he seemed content leafing through a four-month-old *Seventeen* magazine left behind by some ranger's teenage daughter.

Taken singly, the entries illuminated frag- ments of the search, like snapshots from a roll of film shot over four weeks. There was nothing that wouldn't be covered in greater detail by reports filed in the frontcountry. Taken as a whole, the entries painted the ebb and flow of hope and strength and out- lined the players who'd dabbled, those who'd given it the old college try and those few who had stayed on till the bitter end: the rangers and Robert Proffit. The youth group leader's visits had only tapered off in the last week.

Perhaps his employers told him if he didn't stop this futile searching and join them in the real work of wearing down God with endless prayer, he was out of a job.

"Looks like you've got some days off coming to you," she said to Ray. From the varied mentions he'd gotten in the journal it looked as if he hadn't taken many lieu days since the girls went missing.

"I needed the overtime," he said, but Anna knew it was more than that. After a few weeks in the backcountry even she was ready to forgo hard cash for a hot shower and a couple hours of TV.

"I get out," he said as if reading her mind. "Lots of afternoons, sometimes overnight, to get fresh clothes, that kind of thing."

"Why don't you take a few days? Rita will be more than happy to cover. I've gotten the idea road patrol is not really her thing."

"Rita's one gnarly ranger," Ray said with a grin. Gnarly. Anna had heard that adjective before. In Rocky Mountain it seemed a compliment suggesting skill and machismo. Or, conversely, if referring to cliffs or other nonhuman objects, a reference to difficulty and obstacle.

"You can hike out with me," she said and rose. It was past ten, time for bed.

"My normal lieu days are Monday and Tuesday. Why don't I just finish up and take a long one?"

Given it was Wednesday night, Anna couldn't but admire his dedication. But then he'd had a shower and a frontcountry fix the previous night. At twenty-seven, that was enough.

"Suit yourself," she said.

The great lack in even the most adorable backcountry cabins was indoor plumbing. Small cisterns and sinks with drains into a bucket served well enough for cooking and washing dishes, but the more basic bodily needs had to be taken to an outdoor privy.

These privies were dug by hand. And they were cleaned by hand, the human waste hauled out. Rangers in the wildernesses of the national parks smelled more than the roses.

While accepting their necessity in heavy-use areas, Anna loathed the things. She couldn't hold her breath long enough and usually ended up gasping and gagging.

She'd been told many times to breathe through her mouth, and though logic told her it was impossible, imagination insisted, though she might not smell it, she could taste it.

When nature did not insist she add solid waste to the collection, she always opted for the outdoors and deposited only the paper in the privy pit. Following her flashlight beam down the well-worn path from the cabin's back door, she passed the horse paddock, now empty, and went behind the outhouse into the trees.

She was just exposing her delicate white flesh to the mosquitoes when she noticed it. Riding atop the reek emanating from the rear of the privy was the unmistakable odor of rotting flesh.

t e n

The smell of death overrode nature's other
calls. Denying the mosquitoes their hoped-
for banquet, Anna pulled up her trousers
and buckled her belt. For a moment she
stood in the crisp darkness and sniffed the
air: pine, damp needles, the odor from the
privy. Slowly she turned full circle. Faint but
unmistakable, the sweet smell of decaying
flesh was emanating from the direction of
the outhouse. With the child, Candace, still
missing, Anna's mind conjured up ghastly
images of human waste and human parts
commingling. Surely the smell of the first

would drown the smell of the second. But then maybe that was the point.

She clicked on her flashlight and pointed it toward the small wooden structure. "Jesus," she whispered. Relief and revulsion vied for predominance in her brain. Not one death but nine, eleven, thirteen she counted as she traveled the few yards to the back of the privy.

Nailed to the cedar board, one nail to each like insects on a display board, was a baker's dozen of mice. The tiny corpses were in neat rows of four. The last row, with only one little gray body, looked as hungry and expectant as an open grave. The mice had evidently been gathered over a period of time. Those in the top rows were desiccated. The last one looked to be only a week or so old: a chronology of rodent death, a miniature body farm.

Anna's eyes adjusted to the macabre and she began to see past the obvious. Beneath the mice, on the cedar, were hairline marks in dark brown. Scratching. The mice had been crucified alive, their tiny claws scrabbling in their own blood till they died.

Having seen enough, sickened and ineffably saddened, she made her way back toward the cabin. Tears stung at the corners of her eyes and she cursed the sentimentality of middle age. Mice were routinely killed in the ongoing war between humans and rodents. It wasn't so much their deaths as the cruelty that hurt her.

Ray Bleeker was at the dining table where she'd left him. Against the chill of the mountain night he'd put on a shapeless gray cardigan. Perched on his nose were reading glasses. He looked like a young Mister Rogers presiding over the suddenly unsavory neighborhood.

"Put on your shoes," Anna said. "I've something to show you."

Hands bulging in the pockets of his sweater, Ray stared at the collection of tiny corpses. "What kind of sick bastard would do this?" he asked after a moment. His voice was flat to the point of monotone and Anna guessed he held strong emotions in check.

"You tell me." It wasn't a rhetorical statement. It was an order. He was the ranger. It was his privy, his mice, nailed up with government nails.

"My fault," he said in the same featureless voice. "He wanted a live trap. Said mice were God's creatures too, that the traps we had broke his heart each time they broke a mouse's neck. What bullshit." Ray laughed then, a jolting bark. Without warmth or humor, laughter is an ugly sound.

"Robert Proffit?" Anna was remembering his entries in the journal, his stated desire to kill the mice that haunted his sleep in the cabin. Divine retribution with crucifixion to add a biblical flavor. "You're sure?"

"No. I like Robert. He seems like a sincere guy. He's a hard worker. You can't guess the hours he put in on the search. We'd have knocked off for the night and he'd go out in the dark with a flashlight to get in another hour or two. I don't want it to be Robert. I don't think more than a handful of other people—maybe Rita, Ryan, I guess—even knew about the live trap. I mean it's bullshit. Catch 'em, let 'em loose. First thing they'd do is come home."

Anna turned the light away from the mice. The sadness was coming again and she had no intention of letting it show. First thing in the morning she would take the mice down and bury them. At the moment all she wanted was to crawl into a sleeping bag and enjoy oblivion for a few hours. As they walked back over the ragged land to the cabin's back door, she sent an abrupt prayer in the direction of her husband's god that her sleep would not be filled with dreams of bloody, scrabbling little claws.

The following morning, after the one-shovel funeral, Anna hiked out. Fern Lake Trail was a loop closed on the east side by Bear Lake Road. She took the shorter, more direct route that would bring her out below Moraine Meadow, the route Ray had taken when he'd hiked out in the rain. The day was a glorious high-octane mix of sunshine and pine-scented breezes, the trail superbly maintained. Trailcrew, none of whom Anna had yet been introduced to, was to be commended. There were late wildflowers, a deer with a fawn long out of spots, gaily colored hikers sweating under packs too big for them, even an inky black Abert squirrel twitching its silly long ears, yet Anna was unable to keep dead mice from nibbling away at her inner peace. She walked fast, scarcely seeing anything but the pictures in her mind.

This noon she and Chief Ranger Knight were driving out to New Canaan to talk with Robert Proffit. Anna wanted to get on with it. Kidnapping little Christians entrusted to one's care was a bad enough crime to be suspected of. Harassing, torturing and murdering the wildlife in a national park was nigh on unforgivable.

As she showered, changed, then gobbled a hurried lunch, she wished with all her heart she'd brought her old orange tiger cat, Piedmont, with her. He alone would truly appreciate the tale of wanton waste. Piedmont was a scrupulous and ethical hunter. Sure, he played with his food, but he always ate what he killed. Ate everything but the head, feet and guts. Those he traditionally left on the back step for Anna's culinary enjoyment. She'd never told the cat she didn't eat his offerings. Piedmont's feelings were easily hurt.

In a freshly washed and detailed Crown Victoria, gussied up with the NPS shield and a tasteful shotgun rack, Lorraine Knight picked her up at eleven o'clock.

Anna told her of the mice. "I bagged the

live trap, one mouse and the nails and carried them out," she finished. "The hammer I left. Ray's been working on the horse paddock with it. He would have destroyed any prints on the handle."

"I doubt the rest will do much good either," Lorraine said.

Anna knew that. She'd gathered evidence more to be doing something than out of any real hope there'd be signs of the perpetrator. Murdering mice wasn't illegal. It was technically against park rules—mice were, after all, indigenous wildlife—but park employees did it all the time. Under normal circumstances the incident would have been reported but not followed up on, as with many after-the-fact resource depredations rangers encountered. There simply wasn't enough money or personnel to chase after small fry that would, in all probability, never be caught.

Circumstances at Rocky Mountain were not ordinary at the moment.

"I'll follow up on it anyway," Anna said. "What the hell."

"Keep me posted," was all the chief ranger said.

From Estes Park to Loveland was a drive

of a little more than an hour. Beauty robbed
Anna of impatience and she was almost
sorry when they emerged from a chasm in
the granite mountain range to find themselves suddenly facing the Great Plains. The
front range had virtually no foothills but
reared up out of the flatlands with stunning
abruptness. Driving out from the embrace of
great walls of stone at sixty miles an hour
gave Anna a brief sensation akin to that of
falling.

About halfway between Loveland and the
mountains, opposite a forlorn and treeless
RV park with a dilapidated sign reading
ROLLIN' ROOST, ROLL IN AND ROOST!, a bizarre
rock formation disrupted the land. To either
side of the road, running parallel to the front
range, reddish-brown stone thrust through
the soil like the spine of some impossibly
huge beast buried long ago, only to be
unearthed by the fierce winds of eastern
Colorado.

Lorraine turned north on a narrow dirt
road running in the shadow of the skeletal
rocks. Anna saw no sign, no name. The road
was as anonymous as an old fire road.

"I had a talk with the dispatcher at Loveland PD. She gave me directions to New

Canaan," the chief ranger explained. "Actually what she said was, 'When you're pretty sure you're going exactly nowhere, you're on the right road.'"

"We're on the right road, then," Anna said. "Rocky doesn't have a jail, where do you usually do this sort of thing?"

"Interrogate suspects?"

"Yes."

"This Proffit isn't yet an official suspect—not exactly. He's been on-again, off-again on our list, ending with a fairly firm off," Lorraine reminded her. "But usually we'd do it at the Estes Park or Loveland PD. We've got a good relationship with local law enforcement," she said with justifiable pride.

The NPS had several kinds of jurisdiction, from parks where the law was enforced completely by the federal government through the auspices of law enforcement rangers, to those that fell within the jurisdiction of the county sheriff. Territorial jealousies and disputes were not unknown.

"I opted to call on Robert at home, go out to New Canaan so we could take a look around. See why in hell these folks are so squirrelly. That sort of thing."

Anna, too, wanted to see Proffit's home

turf. Given the mouse massacre, she wanted to see if the neighbor kids were missing an unusual number of pets.

For a time they rode in silence and Anna was content watching the strange and wonderful landscape unfolding to the east, rising to the west. They'd traveled eleven miles by the odometer, passed no vehicles, homesteads or grazing animals, when New Canaan was heralded by a crude handpainted sign nailed to a fence post.

"It's not a town proper," Lorraine explained when Anna commented on it. "It's more of a commune. The New Canaanites own the land, an old ranch inherited by one of the founders of the community from what I gather."

"Why am I thinking of David Koresh and Jim Jones?" Anna said.

Lorraine laughed.

The "town" was laid out in a neat grid, as were some of the mainstream Mormon towns Anna had seen in Utah—Cedar City, St. George— but that was where the resemblance ended. This grid was laid out with an optimism that had yet to bear fruit. Like a number of the sorry "ranchette" developments carved out of Nevada's Smoke Creek

Desert never to be populated, here the graveled roads were laid down in a tic-tac-toe pattern but only the intersections at the center had been developed, eight homes total. No trees or lawns, flower beds or foundation plantings graced these graceless houses. All were more or less alike, two-story unornamented structures that looked more like miniature low-income apartment buildings than individual homes. Each had a door at either end. There were no awnings, no porches, no swing sets or jungle gyms in the yards.

There were plenty of children. The girls, like Mrs. Dwayne and Mrs. Sheppard, in long dresses. The boys wore dark trousers and long-sleeved shirts despite the eighty-degree-plus enticements of summer's end.

"I can make a pretty good guess as to why the families are no friend to law enforcement," Anna said. "I've been through towns like this on the Utah-Arizona border."

"Polygamists," Lorraine said. The investigative part of the search would have uncovered that possibility.

"Has that look about it. Too many kids, too few houses, all too big."

"Hard to prosecute," the chief ranger said. "It's not illegal to live in sin, only to actually marry more than one of your fellow sinners at a time." She pulled the car over and parked neatly parallel to a curb that didn't exist. The children stopped their play—a desultory game that seemed based on a circle of dirt undoubtedly inhabited by some unfortunate insect. They didn't run over to the car or laugh or chatter. They just stared. It gave Anna a creepy feeling.

Neither Alexis nor Beth was among them.

The tableau of stupefied children held for a moment. Curtains in the house behind them flittered. A door opened and Mr. Sheppard emerged dressed, like the male children, in dark trousers and a long-sleeved shirt. Sheppard was bearded as the prophets from the Old Testament and his hair curled at the collar of his shirt. His face was pasty for a man who lived in a state with more sunny days than not. He didn't look welcoming. As he approached the car he tried to force his stern features into a joyous cast. The effect was more alarming than the original scowl.

The clot of children broke apart to drift along in his wake. A bark, a wave of his hand, and they turned and filed back into the house as orderly as good children at a grade school fire drill.

"Any word on Candace?" he asked as Anna and Lorraine got out of the car. Whether he was astute enough to have planned it or not, the question subtly shifted the balance of power in his favor. Before they'd had time to establish themselves, he'd put them on the defensive.

"Afraid not, Mr. Sheppard," Lorraine said, ignoring the shift if she'd felt it. "We'd like to have another talk with the girls and Robert Proffit. See if anything that might help us find Candace has been overlooked."

"They're being schooled right now. We're real conscientious about that."

Anna adjusted her face into a pleasant expectant mask and leaned against the fender of the patrol car. If the girls were at their lessons they were the only children in New Canaan who were. The curtains in the house behind Sheppard were fairly dancing with peeps and pushes from those within.

A short wordless battle of wills was fought between Sheppard and the chief ranger. "I'll get Robert," he compromised after a moment.

"That's okay," Lorraine said. "Just point out his house."

Sheppard ignored her request. "Wait here." He went back into the house he'd come out of. Curtains stopped moving. Anna was suddenly aware of the silence: no people talking, no televisions murmuring behind closed doors, no phones ringing or lawn mowers buzzing, no traffic. The underlying pulse of life that is a constant where people gather together to live was missing. New Canaan felt comatose, all life locked deep within an inert body of which Mr. Sheppard was apparently the brain. Anna guessed if he wasn't the de facto bishop, he was one of the elders.

"Bet you could get a house here cheap," Lorraine said with a wry smile.

"My soul as collateral for the mortgage?"

Lorraine shook her head. "I don't understand this kind of fanaticism, trading today for an eternity elsewhere. Plain old life is the best fun I've ever had."

A door opened on the opposite end of the house from where the original activity had occurred. Mrs. Dwayne stepped out onto the packed dirt. "Why don't you come in for a cup of coffee?" she said brightly, as if they were neighbor ladies paying a call.

The room they were ushered into was about three times the size of a standard living room in a tract house, and even less appealing. No windows let in the light of day. No pictures graced the walls. The room was bare but for two rows of backless benches and a lectern. Mrs. Dwayne referred to it as the chapel but, to Anna's mind, it was the last place an omniscient being would choose to spend time. There wasn't any coffee.

Mr. Sheppard stood just to the right of the lectern, arms folded across his chest, beard thrust out pugnaciously. Robert Proffit hunched on the front bench, elbows on knees, hands buried in his hair like a proper penitent. The chief ranger took the bench behind him so he'd be forced to turn around. Anna stood to one side, her senses in a state of hyperawareness. She didn't like the space, the New Caananites or the feel of crucified rodents in her brain.

"Mr. Proffit," Lorraine said, her voice warm and motherly, "we've been told Candace stayed with you when the other two girls went for their walk."

That brought his head out of his hands. He twisted around to face her. The shock on his face looked genuine enough but, were he a manipulative psychotic, it might have been shock that one of his victims had the temerity to rat him out.

"Who told you that?" he said. Not "It's not true" or "That's absurd," but a demand for identification of his accuser.

"Who would know?" the chief countered.

In conscious or habitual drama, he reburied his head in his hands, fingers raking the long curling hair into a crazed thatch. "The girls wouldn't tell you that," he muttered to the floor between his feet. "They know I love them. They're like my own children—God's children—put into my care. I love them in a way those not followers of the Lord can never know."

"You're barking up the wrong tree." Mr. Sheppard added a dash of the prosaic to Proffit's rhapsodizing.

"What would be the right tree?" Lorraine asked.

Her question went unanswered. Proffit began to pray or converse with his knees, Anna wasn't sure which. Lorraine met her eye for a second. Time to go to work. Straddling the bench beside Proffit, her knee nudging his, Anna leaned into him and said, "Hey, Robert, what do you think of mice?"

"Mice!" he squawked and levitated at least six inches off the bench, looking around him wildly. Had he been a cartoon elephant he would have leaped atop the lectern and balanced on his four feeties. "Where?"

"Mice in general," Anna said when he'd settled a bit.

"Don't do that," he said with an odd mixture of ferocity and plaintiveness. Then: "I don't much care for mice. They're filthy things. Diseased, a lot of them."

"So you kill them to clean up the planet?"

Proffit had recovered from Anna's mouse assault. Vulnerability went underground. The gaze he turned on her was sharp, focused. For the first time it occurred to her that he might be smart; not just clever but very, very smart. That was one more "very" than she could lay claim to and she warned herself to be careful around him.

"Why are we talking about mice?" he said with the lowest wattage of intensity she'd yet seen him use, which wasn't all that low by run-of-the-mill standards. "It has something to do with my kids, with Candace, doesn't it? Mice. Rocky. My kids. Something about Fern Lake Cabin."

He'd done the equation in record-breaking time. Either he was the X factor himself or a real whiz at brainteasers.

"We found thirteen dead mice there, nailed to the back of the outhouse," Anna said. "They'd been nailed up alive." Mrs. Dwayne squeaked in a mouse-like fashion and Robert Proffit flinched. Anna was unsure whether the sudden cringing was due to mouse phobia or guilt.

"Who would do a thing like that to any one of God's creatures, however lowly?"

The words rang hollow, gutted either by revulsion at the deed or because they were the oft-repeated platitude of a hypocrite.

"That's what we were wondering," she said as she rose. Proffit had had time to school his emotions and cool his febrile thought processes; she wasn't going to get any more out of him. At least not in this interview. Time had come to shake up the variables. Mr. Sheppard, with his quelling influence, couldn't be in two places at once. Since there was no legal way to send him out of his own chapel she decided to put him on edge. To Lorraine she said, "I think I'll go outside, get some air." The chief ranger nodded her permission.

Once outdoors Anna realized how desperately she did want to get some air. The windowless room, redolent with stifled dreams and isolation, had begun to close in on her, a sense of poison pressing in through the pores of her skin. Taking off her hat she combed her fingers through her thick hair. It was grown long enough to fall in her eyes and curl at the collar of her uniform shirt. She'd let it grow because Paul liked it. After years of independence it was good to have a man worth catering to now and again, especially if there was a payoff. With Paul, so far, the payoff had been pretty good. Higher praise than that, Anna chose not to voice, even in the sound-proofed rooms of her own skull. Hope and joy were double-edged things when their fulfillment depended upon another person.

Like a horse ridding itself of flies, Anna shook off the toxins that had settled on her skin. Breathing deep of air so dry and thin it burned her lungs, she wondered why life wasn't enough for most people, why they had to hide in cathedrals, mosques and temples and rehearse human-born fictions of something yet to come, practice infinite subtleties of castigation of flesh and mind, as if by limiting pleasure and freedom in their one guaranteed existence they might earn kudos in another, one from which no explorers had ever returned alive.

"Ranger Pigeon?"

The sound was but a whisper of air, soft as the voices one hears in the murmur of fast-moving streams. Anna might have thought she'd suffered a visitation but for the fact ghosts seldom called one by one's formal title.

Turning her face from the cleansing carcinogens of the sun, she replaced her hat. Mrs. Dwayne, looking older, frumpier and more careworn in the uncompromising light of day, had followed her out.

"The girls aren't doing so good," she said in a whisper. A furtive look toward the chapel door confirmed Anna's suspicions of just who was not to overhear this tête-à-tête. "Especially Beth. She won't eat unless she eats with that crippled lady, and Mr. Sheppard doesn't like that even though I'm always with her. That other one's a woman doctor. They've not got husbands or kids, either one of them." This last was unquestionably a condemnation of Dr. Littleton's and Heath Jarrod's moral and spiritual states. "But I keep on. Beth is so thin. And the dreams. Poor child tries to stay awake. I found her asleep on her feet in the doorjamb. She'd been walking so she wouldn't fall asleep. Alexis too. But not so bad. But then she has her *dad* for comfort."

The last was said with such bitterness, Anna wondered what Mrs. Dwayne had against the ubiquitous Mr. Sheppard. Before she could finish her thought, the woman suddenly sucked her breath back into her lungs as if she would suck back the words she'd spoken with it.

Anything she wasn't supposed to know was particularly attractive to Anna. "She has her dad," she echoed neutrally.

"Mr. Sheppard. A father makes you feel safer. He's a father to all of us. But especially some of us. Blood, you know." Mrs. Dwayne was babbling, still in a whisper, overbright smile discordantly pasted on her face, hands animated; an amateur actor's rendition of "Happy Talk."

Anna let her continue this peculiar whispering monologue till it was clear she wasn't going to say anything she oughtn't, then she interrupted, to Mrs. Dwayne's obvious relief. "Have Beth or Alexis told you anything about where they were? What happened? Anything about Candace?"

"Nothing. They say they don't remember anything. I really think they don't; even Mr. Sheppard couldn't get anything out of them."

The inference was that Mr. Sheppard could pry the thoughts from a marble statue. Maybe he could, but Anna doubted the statue would have much market value after he'd done with it.

"What do you think happened to them?"

Mrs. Dwayne looked slightly startled that anyone would want her opinion on what had befallen her child. "Satan," she said without hesitation. "He likes children best because they are precious to our Lord. This world is a battleground and he will use anything he can to get at God, he hates Him so. Even here, tucked away from the world, he is at work. Ritual tortures. Sacrifices. They are especially active around Halloween and Good Friday because that was the day they killed our Lord."

Anna was half sorry she'd asked. It

crossed her mind to tell the woman that, because of persistent rumors, the FBI had done an exhaustive investigation of the satanic cults in America. The investigation was somewhat disappointing. They couldn't find any. Like razor blades in Halloween apples, satanic cults with black Sabbaths and infant sacrifices were an urban myth. In the end she didn't waste her breath. Mrs. Dwayne would not have been comforted, only alarmed that the belief system on which her world was based was being chal- lenged. A grand battle between Lucifer and God with humankind as cannon fodder was more appealing than the unglamorous responsibility of dealing on a daily basis with petty, mean human evil.

"Tell me about Beth's dreams," Anna said. She had little belief in the value of dream interpretation as a crime-solving tool—or a tool to solving the subconscious—but a scared girl might just tell things that were true as if they were only dreams, a way of communicating the forbidden.

"They're demonic," Mrs. Dwayne said unsurprisingly, given her earlier revelation. "Beth wakes screaming and crying. She wet the bed—something she hasn't done since she was three years old. Mr. Sheppard was firm about that. It's just a matter of choosing the good over the evil. Beth talked about darkness and crying things and being sorry. She asked God to forgive her over and over. She dreamed of a wolf howling. Dreams of slaughter as in the end of days."

"May I talk with Beth? I'd like to see her."

Mrs. Dwayne shook her head. "No. Mr. Sheppard thinks it would only confuse the girls further. He says they are to stay at prayers until God sends his forgiveness."

"For what?"

"We don't know," Mrs. Dwayne wailed, if wailing can be done in a whisper.

Anna truly, deeply, sincerely wanted to smack her upside her little sheep's head. Either the woman was as foolish as Robert Proffit was bright, or whatever gleam of good sense she'd once had had been sluiced away when her brain was washed.

"Why did you want to talk to me?" Anna asked sharply.

Mrs. Dwayne looked at her blankly.

"Seriously," Anna went on. "You followed me out. You are clearly agitated, afraid of being caught. It must have been important, yet you tell me nothing but ghost stories and dreams. Why did you want to talk to me?"

A moment's silence fell between them, a balm to Anna's ears and spirit. Mrs. Dwayne's eyes filled with tears. Anna was unmoved.

"I wanted you to help," she blurted out finally.

"I can't," Anna said bluntly. "Your daughter's in a living hell, another girl is missing and there's not a damn thing I can do about it. You know these girls. You talk to them. You want to keep secrets from me, fine. But without you, without being able to talk to Beth, what do you expect me to do? Arrest Beelzebub on loitering charges and interrogate him?"

Anna dropped the anger as suddenly as she had taken it up. It had done its work. Mrs. Dwayne was at least awakened from her trance of victimhood. Gently, Anna said, "Help me. Help me find out."

For the briefest moment Anna thought she'd gotten through, then the woman bleated, "Mr. Sheppard—" and feeling her way like someone in a blinding sandstorm, she turned to the house.

"What's his first name?" Anna called after her.

Stopping, she looked back in surprise. "Mr. Sheppard's?"

"Yeah. What's his first name?"

"Dwayne," the woman said.

"That would have been my best guess," Anna said.

Mrs. Dwayne fled toward the chapel door.

eleven

Solitude had changed since Heath had broken her back. Once she'd loved it, craved it, savored it. Now she craved it, but when it was given her, she found her feelings in conflict. Before, she'd not known why people were scared to be alone. She wished she could have gone to the grave in happy ignorance of this knowledge.

Still and all she was enjoying it, possibly out of sheer perverse willfulness. Gwen had taken the Cushman scooter—a retro-styled aqua and white one with matching helmet—and left the Rollin' Roost to scoot the five or so miles into Loveland. Her excuse was groceries but for that she could have taken the RV. The truth was she and Heath needed time apart, just a breather. Only in solitude could certain places in the psyche renew themselves. Or so Gwen was fond of saying, and so Heath had once believed. The other truth was that Heath's Aunt Gwen loved her scooter. On it she became the wild red-haired American girl who'd ridden madcap through the streets of Florence in her college days, the girl who'd broken hearts, drunk too much wine, studied art and medicine, gotten her own heart broken and come home to Tulane University in Louisiana to become a healer of women.

Though a seventy-one-year-old wild woman on a scooter in a herd of SUVs scared Heath witless, she never said anything.

That could change, she thought as she looked at her watch. The sun had gone behind the mountains, the sky was drifting from blue to green to the soft gray that invited the first of night's stars, and Gwen had yet to return. Refreshingly, Heath noted, she was concerned mostly with her aunt's welfare. Being self-involved was more tiring than one would think.

Sipping a mediocre but functional Merlot, she watched the purest fade of light in the east where night seeped out over the plains. A climber by inclination and trade—she'd taught at the wilderness skills training center in Colorado Springs for the past seven years—Heath had given the earth's flat places short shrift. Unless they had a deep cave one might climb down in, what possible good were they?

With wheels instead of crampons she would have to make her peace with a relatively two-dimensional world. *That or get a job as an elevator operator*, she thought wryly.

Idly wondering if there were even any elevator operators left, she drank again, then lit a cigarette. Wiley, lying half a dozen feet from her chair, chin on paws, raised an eyebrow. Like most animals of good sense, he didn't like the smell of smoke.

"Don't start," Heath said and took a drag. She was smoking a little too much, drinking a little too much, but tonight they were comparatively happy excesses. "Joyous addicts are less tiresome than morbid addicts," she said to the dog. He heaved a great and weary sigh and fell over on his side. One needn't even be an anthropomorphist to assign attitudes to Wiley. A cell phone Heath had been resisting the temptation to use to check on her aunt tootled. Gwen had it trained to play Dixieland. It was her aunt asking permission to stay an hour later to attend a premiere in Loveland's burgeoning arts district.

Worry over her aunt laid to rest, worry over herself drowned, Heath lit the kerosene lamp, poured a third glass of wine and settled into the universe. Darkness pooled in the east, bled west to the mountains. Night was complete. Heath was in a pleasant half-dreaming state, self-hypnotized by the steady fire of the lamp, when Wiley began to growl; the mean kind of growl that warns of intent to make the bite worse than the bark. At once alert, if not fully sober, Heath ordered him quiet. He'd come to stand guard near her chair and she closed her fist in the prickling fur of his ruff more to reassure herself than to restrain him.

Nothing.

"Coyotes," she said. Because a pack of these most adaptable canines would tear apart a domestic dog, even one as brave and fierce as Wiley thought he was, she took his leash from her saddlebag, clipped one end to his collar and tied the other firmly around the arm of her chair.

He didn't growl again but neither did he relax. Heath couldn't either. It was time to go in. She was leaning down to untangle her lap rug from beneath her wheels when a faint trickle of sound flowed into the campsite. High pitched, barely audible, it came from all directions and none. Voices heard from a distant playground. One at which the games were of pain and fear.

She felt the dog go rigid under her hand. "Shh," she whispered. The voices grew louder. Children's voices. "Please, please, please. No." The sound trailed off and Heath leaned forward unconsciously, trying to follow it. Again it swelled. "Please leave us alone. Please. Go away. Leave us alone." That was the limpet's voice, she was sure of it.

"Beth!" she called into the darkness, then waited.

"Leave us alone."

"Beth! Come out where I can see you." Heath squinted into the darkness that had wound tightly around her camp. Mindlessly staring into the lamp had blinded her and phantom flames followed wherever she looked.

"Leave us alone." This so small, so weak, as if the child speaking—not Beth, Heath thought but wasn't sure—was dying or fading away. Then, sudden and so clear, Heath screamed: "Leave us alone or I'll kill you. I swear I will."

The kerosene lamp on the picnic table exploded. Gobbets of fire flew into the air, rivers of fire poured over the tabletop and down onto the benches. Wiley shrieked and tried to run but he was tethered to the chair. As he hit the end of the leash, the force pulled the wheelchair over, pulled Heath into the fire running liquid beneath the table. Wiley was burning. The lap robe flamed up. The acrid bite of kerosene mixed with the smell of burning wool.

Heath could see nothing but living fire. Her eyes and the backs of her eyes and her brain were burning. Wiley was barking, high and wild and desperate.

Fear is essentially a tardy emotion, demanding the luxury of time. Apocalypse was happening too fast for it to take root. Not much giving a damn whether her worthless legs burned or not, Heath began pulling on the leash, reeling in Wiley. Her hands were on his fur, closed into fists. She pulled him to her chest and beneath her chest and smothered the flames that danced with such unholy glee along his back and left side.

A lifetime's worth of reflexes came to bear; she was kicking free of the burning lap rug. It was a shock when nothing moved. With a screamed curse, she grabbed at the blanket and threw it from her and her dog.

The end of the world didn't take as long as she'd thought it might. Within a heartbeat or two the fire was out. The kerosene had burned itself up. Neither table nor benches had caught. The world, presuming there still was one, was black and utterly silent.

"Don't make us do it," hissed from the void, was made more terrible by the children lost within it. "Don't make us do it!" Louder now. They were coming, the childish voices with their rain of fire.

Heath could not regain her chair; could not even see her chair. Had she miraculously been reseated, she hadn't the wherewithal to fiddle with ramp and sliding door. Murmuring four-letter words like panicked endearments into the ears of the dog, she unhooked the leash from his collar and, Wiley clutched to her chest, she wriggled commando-style underneath the RV. Once there, she curled herself around Wiley as best she could with no bend in her knees, no tuck in her thighs, and buried her face in his fur.

Both were whimpering.

Voices turned to laughter, unholy laughter of insane children, circling around the RV. Wiley struggled to get free. He barked to put the fear of god into whatever demons were attacking his mistress. Heath wouldn't let him go.

The laughter swelled, ebbed, drifted, cut. The sound of feet pattered around wheel to wheel. "Kill it!" a child screamed, and a stick or knife jabbed Heath in the back. "Kill it! Kill it! Make it die." Again and again the stick jabbed at her. Little girls tormenting a caged cripple and a burned dog. Footsteps raining on the hard-packed earth.

"Leave us the fuck alone!" Heath screamed.

"Leave us alone," a little girl's voice mocked.

Dust and the smell of diesel forced its way past the stench of burned hair stinging

Heath's nostrils. RVs burned like tinder, she remembered, their petroleum-based parts evaporating into toxic gases or melting into searing blobs. She hoped the fireworks, at least, were over.

The poking stopped.

Footsteps, laughter, taunts stopped. It took Heath a while—moments, minutes, she wasn't sure—before she realized quiet had returned. She listened till her skull hurt with the effort. Her eyes had readjusted from the fire and she could see a faint difference between the starlit dirt outside and the shadow in which she lay. Wiley whined. She forced herself to loosen her grip lest, in an over-abundance of fear and protectiveness, she smother him. She didn't let go of his collar. Whatever had visited the campground was too evil to be driven away by one pure-hearted dog.

Listening, staring at the crushed horizon remaining to her, she waited. Crawling out was not an option, not till the sun rose and drove all the creatures of the night back into their lairs.

This decision was a wise one. The foot-steps were coming back, coming back for her and for the dog. Heath chose not to be taken as a whimpering crippled lady. One thing Colorado had plenty of was rocks. Feeling around she found a jagged chunk of granite with a sharp edge, half again as big as her fist.

Wiley sensed the change in her. He eased from beneath her, the hair on his back running stiff and spiky beneath her hand. A killing rumble grew in his chest.

"When I say, Wiley," Heath whispered into his ear. He froze in a half-crouch as if he understood. Sly, whispering, cold as snake's scales the footsteps slithered over the sandy soil. Around the RV. Soft as moccasined feet, bare feet, cat feet, little girls' feet.

Near the front tire on the driver's side they stopped.

"Now," Heath screamed and both she and her dog struck long and low from beneath the vehicle.

twelve

Anna was having second thoughts about this visit. It was after nine. People were, if not already in bed, settled in for the night. She'd intended to come earlier but had gotten roped into an acrimonious campground dispute over a prime site and couldn't decently get away till eight. Having driven too far to give it up, she pulled into the dusty little RV camp where Dr. Littleton and her niece were reputed to be staying.

Only two of perhaps a dozen sites were occupied, one by a recreational vehicle so big a camera was mounted on the rear to facilitate backing up. The other Anna recognized as Dr. Littleton's. So they wouldn't rake rudely across the camper's windows, she switched the lights off in her 1999 Honda Accord—a wedding present from Paul. He had, and rightly so, been concerned the battered Rambler American she'd driven over two hundred thousand miles might not make one more cross-country trip.

Littleton and Jarrod's vehicle was dark. Anna would be waking them. For a moment she sat behind the steering wheel deciding whether or not to turn around and drive back to Estes Park. She was reaching for the ignition key to do just that when the peculiar sculpture between picnic table and van came into darkling focus. An overturned chair, wheel to the sky. The window in her car door was down and Anna could hear the absolute stillness of the night and nothing else. Where the hell was the helper dog? Why wasn't he announcing her in proper canine fashion? Again the crucified mice danced in her head. How much of a step from mice to dogs, dogs to women? A bad feeling crawled up her spine and tightened the skin at the back of her neck. Moving qui-

etly, she took her old Colt .357 from the
glove box and eased from the car.

Her leather-soled moccasins almost silent
on the packed earth, she walked over to the
RV. There was a smell of burning, a small
blanket thrown aside. Taking blind corners
with care, she walked around the vehicle.

At the driver's side window she stopped
to look inside. A shriek stopped her heart
and a screaming pain shot up from her foot.
Anna threw herself backward. Rolled. Belly
flat to the earth, elbows locked, she trained
the Colt on the blackness beneath the vehicle.

"Out," she yelled. "Come out now. Hands
first." A second of dark silence froze in her
ears, then:

"Ranger Pigeon?" And a dog's head
poked out of the inky shadow. The juxtapo-
sition of voice and whiskered jaws discon-
certed her. For the briefest of instants she
thought Wiley addressed her.

"Ms. Jarrod?" she returned when the
instant thawed.

"Yeah."

The dog crawled out on dog elbows and
knees. Rather than rising to all fours he continued to crawl over to her, then licked her

fingers where they curled around the butt of the gun. He smelled of singed hair and kerosene. Jarrod didn't appear, so Anna didn't put away the revolver though it was hard to maintain a killing edge with a scruffy hound slathering one's trigger finger.

"You alone under there?" Anna demanded.

"Yes, I am."

Anna waited a bit but nothing transpired. "Are you coming out?"

"Yes, I am." This, reluctantly. "Wiley's leash has me tangled up."

"You want help?"

"No."

"Suit yourself." Anna sat up and took a long and careful look around her. There was nothing but low scrubby bushes and not many of them. In a rolling countryside cut with ravines, she knew a man could hide himself even without what would normally be considered cover.

"Should I be worried about what's out here with me, or were you and Wiley just hanging out under there for the hell of it?" she said to the darkness under the RV. Now that the excitement was over, Anna's foot had begun to throb where Heath Jarrod had smashed it with whatever she'd smashed it with. Pain made her cranky.

"You should be worried," came the disembodied voice.

"What the heck are you doing under there? Don't get dressed on my account."

"Balls."

"What should I worry about?" Anna came to her knees and watched out over the undulating landscape to where it skirted the bones of rock.

"That's a little hard to say." Finally the scuffling became directional. First Jarrod's hands came out, then her head, as she dragged her weight over the ground. Wiley left off sucking up to Anna and went to his mistress. Taking her collar delicately between his teeth he began pulling, helping her move. Anna had not seen anything like it since Lassie had pulled Timmy out of everything from dry wells to abandoned mine shafts. She sat down again, the Colt held loosely in her lap, legs folded tailor fashion. With her empty hand she squeezed her injured foot. The counterpressure seemed to alleviate the throbbing from within. Anyway, it was something to do.

Eyes completely adjusted to the darkness, a bit of moon climbing in the east and more stars than God could count, Anna could see with surprising clarity. Fascinated, she watched Heath Jarrod, with the help of her faithful dog, work her way painfully out from under the chassis, inch by hard-won inch, a small berm of dirt plowed up by her chest, the dark hair sticking to her forehead in sweaty curls despite the chill of the night.

Questions piled up in Anna's mind, starting with why she and the dog were under the RV and what was worrisome but hard to speak of. With forced discipline, she held her tongue. There would be time enough when the woman was done with her extrication. Besides, Anna could see how much the work was costing. Jarrod would have little breath to spare for talking. The energetic ministrations of the dog coupled with Heath Jarrod's grunting gave the scene a cartoon quality that made Anna smile.

Jarrod caught her at it. "Enjoying yourself?" she gasped.

"Pretty much," Anna admitted. "Except for my foot. I think you might have broken some of the little bones in my toes. There's no treatment for that, you know."

"I feel your pain," Heath panted sarcastically. "Or used to."

She'd gotten herself out as far as her hips. By rolling over and using the front tire for support, she managed to sit up. From that position, and again with tug and tooth thrown in by the faithful Wiley, she was able to grab hold of her legs and drag them out in front of her.

"Shit," she sighed when she was done. She leaned back against the tire and closed her eyes. "Check Wiley. Check my dog. I think he got burned. I know he got burned. I saw the flames. There's a flashlight in my saddlebag."

Anna fetched the flashlight. Wiley stood patiently, stoically, while she checked him. Heath stroked his head. "Fur's burned but it doesn't look like it got to his skin," Anna said at last.

"I reached him pretty quick."

Anna didn't ask how. Her foot ached with the swiftness and power that still resided in this former climber's upper body. "Give him a bath and a clip to be sure, but he looks good." Anna had been a ranger and an emergency medical technician for too many years to let anyone suffer in silence—or peace. "Let me take a look at you."

"I'm fine."

"It'll just take a second." To her surprise, Heath didn't continue quarreling but held both her hands out, palms up. They were filthy, of course, but other than a bit of slight blistering along the edge of her left palm and little finger she was more roughed-up than burned. The front of her shirt was scorched over an area about the size of a dinner plate and burned through just below Heath's left breast. "Mind if I unbutton your blouse?"

Heath didn't open her eyes. "Get me my cigarettes and you can take the damn thing off," she said. "They're in the saddlebag, same side as you found the flashlight."

Anna got up and limped around the front of the truck again. "Might as well bring the chair while you're up," Heath called. "And watch out for broken glass."

Anna did as she was asked. As she was righting the chair, she could hear the other woman softly calling her dog. Fear she must have been keeping out of her voice in her exchange with Anna rattled the timbre, a creak of underlying tears trying to break through. Knotted to the arm of the chair was the dog's leash. Heath hadn't been tangled in it. She'd been scared to come out from under the RV. She was terrified and she'd kept it hidden so Anna wouldn't know.

Gutsy little woman, Anna thought approvingly. Though at five-foot-four inches she was no taller than Heath and at one hundred fifteen pounds couldn't have outweighed her by much, Anna never thought of herself as little and was usually taken aback when someone else described her that way.

She returned with chair and smokes. Wiley was tucked tight beneath Heath's arm. Seeing Anna, Heath rubbed her face in the fur on the dog's bony skull. Mopping away tears, Anna guessed.

She handed the cigarettes to Heath and took her former place. Heath lit up, took a drag and sighed the sigh Anna had heard over the phone from her sister for the past thirty years: the joyous exhalation of the confirmed nicotine addict.

Heath's bra was scorched a bit but otherwise intact.

"There's a blister about the size of a nickel on your ribcage," Anna said. "Everything else looks okay."

"Check my legs," Heath said. "The lap rug caught."

The trousers were filthy and scorched. With Heath's permission Anna cut open the legs with her pocketknife. Damage was minimal. A couple places a little bigger than postage stamps were going to blister. Regardless of what had happened—and Anna was getting more interested by the moment—Heath had gotten off easy.

Anna clicked off the flashlight and sat down tailor-fashion again.

Wiley went off a little ways to relieve himself. Heath's breathing evened out. "So what's with the playing under rolling stock with your dog at night?" Anna asked.

"I don't suppose you could bring me my wine first? My glass is on the table. You can have what's left in the bottle."

Anna shoved herself back to her feet. Though pushing fifty, she could still stand up from a cross-legged sitting position without using her hands but, with the adrenaline gone, she was too tired to perform party tricks. "Sure I can't get you a sandwich or chips and dip while I'm up?"

Heath laughed. "Just the drugs, ma'am. Just the drugs."

Anna returned with the half-full wineglass and the bottle. The table had been strewn with what looked and smelled like the remains of a shattered lamp, but the wineglass was upright and undamaged.

"Might want to feel around in this for broken glass," she suggested as she handed it to Heath. The bottle she kept. It had been offered. Sometimes Anna righteously forbore the demon of drink. Tonight she didn't.

The wine went well with the night and the circumstances and Heath's story: all three seemed unreal.

Heath spoke in the calm tones of the sane, but childish tormentors without corporeal form and sudden explosions of fire were not standard fare outside of movie theaters and mental wards. Anna asked no questions, made no interruptions, but listened quietly till Heath had said all she was going to. Unlike most people, Heath Jarrod stopped talking when she'd said her piece. Though Anna didn't jump in immediately, she let the silence lie, not filling it with unnecessary recaps, explanations or extrapolations.

Anna was both surprised and grateful. A story such as this required thought. "Wow," she said finally, summing up her thoughts and emotions.

"Do you believe me?"

There was no trace of pleading in her voice but Anna knew the question mattered. With wild tales such as the one Heath just told, lowest on the credibility scale were women, children, drunks and invalids. Heath qualified at least nominally for three out of four. There was a part of Anna that wanted to write the story off to alcohol and hysterics, maybe guilt for getting tipsy, breaking the lamp and lighting her own dog on fire. She could suggest, sotto voce, to Dr. Littleton that a couple of Xanax might not be amiss, shake her head knowingly and scoot back up to the mountains, duty done.

"I believe you," Anna said and meant it. "The chief ranger and I were up to New Canaan today. It's one disturbing town. A place where spirits are warped for the greater glory of somebody. Probably Dwayne Sheppard. They've got this whole Christian fundamentalism going, with a layer of Mormon fundamentalism to keep the sex plentiful."

"Plentiful for the aforementioned Dwayne Sheppard?"

"That's my guess. But Mrs. Dwayne, who I suspect is Mrs. Sheppard number one or two, got on about demons, Satan, Halloween. The whole ball of wax and I don't doubt for a moment that she was sincere."

"Are Mormons big on the demon thing?" Heath asked.

Anna took a swig of Merlot from the bottle, a tacit salute to the demons of the real world. "I don't think so. I think the New Canaanites' belief system is a hybrid. The worst of a number of worlds. Still it'd make sense. Using the images that scare them to try and frighten you off. Bring the girls down—maybe Proffit's version of a religious play—wait till you're alone. It's dark. You're a few glasses down. Makes for a pretty good show."

"Do you think that's all it was?"

Anna heard the fear in Heath's voice. It was too great to hide.

"I don't know," she said honestly. "But I'd hang onto that rock you smashed me with if I were you."

For a while they said nothing more. She thought. Heath smoked. Wiley lay between them, chin on Heath's ankle, feet pushing against Anna's knee, as if keeping them safe and out of trouble was his life's work. Replaying Heath's story slowly in her mind, Anna marshaled a few facts—alleged facts. According to Heath there had been three distinct childish voices: the limpet, Heath was sure of; Alexis, fairly sure; the third, not recognized. The voices taunted and threatened. Heath had heard footsteps running around the RV. This Anna had to take on faith. The other two facts were provable: the kerosene lamp had been broken and Heath had been jabbed repeatedly by a stick or some such object. There were fresh contusions on her back, forearm and neck.

The rest—who had wielded the stick, broken the lamp, organized and transported the children, why it was so important Heath leave the children alone, why Beth—the limpet, who seemed psychologically dependent on Heath—should turn on her with threats of violence, whether this incident, bizarre as it was, had anything to do with the girls' weeks' AWOL or with their reappearance in bras and panties, was up in the air.

"Before I leave, remind me to check around with a flashlight, see if anything jumps out at me," Anna said. "Tomorrow, when the sun's up, I'll come back and look again. If we're lucky, we may get a usable track or two but I doubt it. This dirt's been packed down over the years till it's almost like pavement. I hear Colorado's in a drought."

"Drought's normal," Heath said. "It was the last twenty freakishly wet years that screwed us. Zillions of people moved here. Now that the weather's back in its real pattern there's not enough water to go around."

"Ah."

"Ah."

Another piece of quiet formed between them.

"Three voices," Anna said finally, coming to the crux of the matter.

"Three. Definitely." Heath sipped her wine. By the gentle unshadowed light from the night sky, Anna watched her chin and cheeks stiffen as she held the wine in her mouth for a time before swallowing it. A trick practiced by connoisseurs for the taste and alcoholics for the anticipation. "Well, as definite as life is these days, anyway," Heath said when she'd swallowed. "The surreal is getting more real all the time. Do you know I thought I kicked off that burning lap robe? Actually felt my legs and feet kicking, felt its weight flying off, the relief of the cold air on my ankles. Then I look down and zip. Nada. Dead doornails. Lying there like wieners under the broiler. Weird."

Heath took a deep drag on her cigarette. By the sudden glow of orange light Anna saw a startled—almost comically so—look on her face, as if in sharing even that one fragmented feeling about her physical state, she'd taken herself utterly by surprise.

"Weird," Anna agreed. The glow moved as Heath reached out to tap ash. Anna would never know how Heath felt about this minor breach in the walls she'd constructed around herself. "Are you thinking the third voice was the third girl, Candace Watson?" Anna asked.

"Who else?"

"Me too."

Heath stubbed out her cigarette, worked the remaining tobacco out of the paper and tucked the filtered butt in the rolled cuff of her trouser leg. If one didn't count hunters— and Anna never did—there weren't a lot of backcountry enthusiasts who smoked, but over the years she noted the few who did tended to be scrupulously tidy about it, perhaps in hopes that when the day of reckoning rolled around, the karmic gods of nature would mark it down in their anticancer column.

"So Candace is alive and well and back in New Canaan?" Heath asked.

"Given how little Mr. Dwayne Sheppard wants strangers—particularly strangers with badges—poking their noses into his little hornet's nest, that both makes sense and doesn't. Why pretend she's lost? It only makes us pester him more."

"The limpet said Candace never went with them, that she stayed with that Robert Proffit guy. I wish he gave me the willies."

Anna knew what Heath meant: suspicious, Bible-beating, youth-group-leading, hyperpassionate young man swearing eternal fealty to God and nubile girls. A woman felt downright unintuitive not getting some sort of pervert reading off of him, but she didn't get that vibe either.

"You don't always," she said from experience.

"Weird."

"Yup." Anna drank. When she didn't, she felt so much better. When she did, she couldn't fathom why she periodically swore off the stuff.

"Maybe Candace did stay with Proffit and he's got her stashed somewhere unbeknownst to his fellow Christians."

"That works," Heath said.

"It would have to be someplace fairly close by. Daily care and feeding—"

"God, I hope so."

"—and to get her down here with the other girls tonight," Anna finished.

"You'd think Beth and Alexis wouldn't cover for him," Heath said.

"Maybe that's exactly why they do, why they have 'amnesia.' Maybe Proffit told them if they talk he'll kill their friend."

"Poor little buggers," Heath said. Her voice was full of tears and wine and anger.

"No kidding. If I had a heart it would be breaking," Anna quoted the Tin Man.

thirteen

By nine the following morning Anna had a search warrant in hand. The evidence—if it could be given such a lofty title—was a scant mention by two traumatized teens that Candace stayed with Proffit, and Heath Jarrod's unsubstantiated testimony of three childish voices chanting in the dark. Had it been anybody else, Anna doubted the judge would have been so cooperative. But the New Canaanites were strange, isolationist, standoffish. They lived differently, wor-shipped, if not different gods, then certainly a different face of the Christian god than Loveland's average church-going Presbyterian. People who are different are suspect. The judge was willing to stretch things a little where the welfare of a child might be at stake.

Anna, Lorraine Knight and three men from the local sheriff's department were at New Canaan by nine-thirty to serve the warrant. The scope of the paper was lenient: They could look anywhere a smallish thirteen-year-old could hide. The forty or so residents, at least twenty-five of whom were children or young women, watched sullenly as they searched the sprawling homes. The adult men of the town, clearly led by Sheppard, were belligerent but never stepped over the line of legality. Their threats were of civil suits and heavenly retributions rather than physical violence.

The search and the demographics of the residents ratified Anna's belief that the commune was rooted in the belief that polygamy was a religious imperative. The houses were divided into monastic cell-like rooms that housed two, three or four children each. Slightly more comfortable rooms with a single bed were evidently for the adult women. Each house had a spacious master bedroom with a queen-sized bed for the "father."

Though the judge had not been so gener-
ous as to allow the search of spaces too
small to keep a girl, Anna noted the houses
had well-organized offices. Each had a
computer with internet access and a fax
machine. From a cursory examination of the
papers in plain sight, it appeared the business of New Canaan was capitalizing on
Colorado's welfare system. With so many
"single" mothers and out-of-wedlock children, the community was doing fairly well
for itself.

Of Candace Watson, there was no sign.

Alexis and Beth were found locked in a
room in Mr. Sheppard's house. They had
been put there, Mr. Sheppard explained, to
think on their sins.

Anna, with Lorraine, insisted on speaking
with them. The weight of heavily armed law-
men and a warrant behind them, Mr. Sheppard grudgingly allowed it. The girls were up
and dressed, the room's two beds made
with military precision and what looked like
army surplus blankets. Anna had slept
under one as a kid. They were a little
scratchy but warm and serviceable. Both
the room and the children were scrupulously
clean. At a glance it was clear they weren't

hiding anything. There was no place to hide it. Blankets were tucked in, leaving the space beneath the beds visible. There were no closets and no dressers, no pictures, rugs, or curtains on the one window. Two identical sweaters hung on two of the four pegs in the wall. A single bed table with a lamp and two Bibles sat between the beds. In the corner was a stand with drinking water, an old-fashioned basin and ewer for washing and, beneath, a chamber pot with a lid. The room was Spartan and anachronistic but the children's basic needs were met. It wasn't illegal to lock children in a room with Bibles, though there were times Anna thought it should be.

To her surprise, Mr. Sheppard left them under the protective eye of his wife. Either the press of feminine flesh, nearly half of it beyond his control, was too much for him, or he was confident Mrs. Sheppard and the girls would say nothing he did not wish them to.

"Alexis," Mrs. Sheppard said, "where are your manners?"

"Won't you please sit down?" Alexis asked politely. She and Beth sat demurely on one bunk, long skirts covering their knees, ankles crossed, feet to one side in an unnatural "ladylike" pose Anna hadn't seen since thumbing through her mother's magazines in the early sixties.

Anna sat on the bunk facing them. She found herself wondering where in the hell they had found an actual honest-to-god chamber pot.

"I'm going to leave you to it," Lorraine said. "See if I can't find the elusive Mr. Proffit." She departed, closing the door behind her. Mrs. Sheppard remained standing, one hand on Alexis' shoulder. Anna's attention was caught by her long slender fingers. The woman's face was aged, not so much by wrinkles or bags, but by the careworn, almost pained, expression she habitually wore. Her hand was smooth. Young. Very young. Younger than Anna had first thought. Anna looked at her throat. It, too, was young. Mrs. Sheppard couldn't have been much more than fourteen years older than her daughter, if that. She'd been little more than a child herself when she married.

Anna left off studying her and focused on the girls, letting silence grow among the four of them. Silence worked better with adults than children. Children had not yet acquired the compulsion to fill it, but it was worth a try considering she had no better opening gambit.

Seconds oozed by, thick as mud in the small closed room. Both children sat quietly, looking at her with nervous, expectant faces. Mrs. Sheppard was equally unmoved. It occurred to Anna that mother and children had probably been trained not to speak until spoken to. To be seen and not heard. To be used as the master saw fit.

"So you're under house arrest," Anna said amiably. "What did you guys do to get locked up?"

"We lied," said Alexis.

"Lying is a sin," said Beth.

"Who did you lie to?" Anna asked.

"You. Everybody," Alexis replied.

That caught Anna off-guard. She'd been expecting something more domestic: lying about chores unfinished or cookies gone missing.

"What lie did you tell me?"

Alexis fielded this question as well. "We told you—told everybody—that Candace hadn't gone with us on the hike, that she'd stayed behind with Robert, but it wasn't true."

For a moment Anna was too stunned to speak. The one shred of evidence they had was being snatched away. If they had lied, she was back to square one. If they were lying now, she was back to square one.

"Okay," she said slowly. "Why did you say that if it wasn't true?"

This time Beth answered. "When we came back, Candace wasn't with us and we thought we'd be in trouble because we'd left her."

There was a very believable edge of despair in her voice and Anna found herself halfway believing her. "Where did you leave her?"

A look was exchanged between the girls. Nothing big, nothing flashy; Anna might not have noted it had she not seen that same look spark between them when she'd first come upon them in Heath's camp.

"We can't remember," Beth said.

"Why did you decide to tell the truth now? About Candace not staying behind with Robert?" Anna asked.

"Because we'd got him in trouble. We never meant to," Beth said earnestly. "We didn't think of it like that. We just . . ."

"Didn't want to get in trouble?" Anna finished for her.

"No."

The limpet's face was open, her needs transparent. Anna could have sworn she was telling the truth. Or what she'd been made to believe was the truth. Alexis was harder to read. She had a way of hiding emotions that was beyond her years.

"Did Robert tell you you'd gotten him in trouble?" Anna asked.

"No, Fa—Mr. Sheppard told us," Beth said. "Robert forgave us. He said it was okay and he loved us."

"When did you see Robert?" Mrs. Sheppard cut in sharply.

The limpet looked horrified. "Now you've done it," Alexis hissed.

"Alexis," Mrs. Sheppard said, and Anna could see those supple young fingers digging into her daughter's shoulder.

"Robert came by last night," Alexis confessed. "He talked to us through the window." She began to cry.

"Did you go out with Robert last night?" Anna asked.

"The door was locked," Beth answered

for her friend or half-sister or whatever the hell their convoluted family relationship was.

That wasn't a straight answer. Anna stood and stepped to the room's one window. It was an old-fashioned sash window with a hinged screen secured by a hook and eye. As a girl Anna had slipped in and out of a window very like it more times than she could remember. It would have taken little effort for them to climb out, go with Robert to the RV park for a bit of terrorizing, then slip back in with the parents none the wiser.

And Candace—or at least some third girlish voice—had been with them. For a shuddering moment Anna was put in mind of Arthur Miller's play *The Crucible*, a study of the Salem witch trials and the pack of young girls who grew wild and drunk on power till the town was strewn with corpses. Children were not inherently good. They were inherently ignorant and usually helpless. Once that helplessness was removed, the ignorance and ego of the young could be more heartless than anything adults dreamed up. It was possible they'd even done it without Robert Proffit's assistance. In the country, it wasn't unusual for twelve- and thirteen-year-olds to drive.

Earlier, while she'd waited for the warrant, Anna had returned to the RV park. The low angle of the light was superb for tracking, yet she'd found little to corroborate Heath's tale but scuff marks that could have been made anytime since the last good rain made it out of the mountains and down to the flats.

Anna turned back to the room where her captive audience watched her with an attention that would have flattered the most jaded actor. She looked at the girls' shoes. They were well-used but clean. If they'd been rampaging the previous night, they had literally and figuratively covered their tracks.

"Heath Jarrod told me you paid her a visit last night," Anna said abruptly. "Tell me about that, Beth."

The girl looked dumbfounded: eyes wide and uncomprehending, mouth slightly agape. Genuine surprise. Anna was about to consign Heath to the loony bin, then Beth's eyes filled with tears and the unlined face contorted in a spasm of guilt so heartfelt Anna felt guilty for seeing it.

"Is Heath all right?" she asked, her voice

returned to the babyish tremor it had been when she'd first walked out of the woods.

Alexis took Beth's hand. It wasn't to comfort her; Anna could see the smaller girl wince from the pressure Alexis put into the squeeze. "We were here all night. Both of us," Alexis said. "Praying and reading our Bibles. Ask my . . . my mother."

Anna wondered whom she was going to say at first. Robert Proffit? Maybe she'd concluded his nocturnal visit to the bedroom window of two underage girls had damaged his credibility in the eyes of the law.

Because she'd been invited to, Anna said, "Well, Mrs. Sheppard?"

Mrs. Sheppard was looking at her daughter in a new way. The featureless stoicism— or repressed pain—that had kept her face locked since Anna had first seen her was broken. She stared at Alexis as if she'd metamorphosed into a Kafka-esque cockroach before their very eyes.

"The window isn't nailed shut," she said flatly.

Alexis began to cry again, her face hidden in her hands. "Sharon!" Alexis cried in shock. Her mother slapped her.

Sharon. She called her mother "Sharon" and her father "Mr. Sheppard." Such a warm, fuzzy family.

The bedroom door opened. "Proffit's gone," Lorraine said without preamble. "He took some clothes and his car."

"He went to find Candace," Beth volunteered. "He told us last night when he came to say goodbye. He said he wouldn't come back without her."

"Jesus," Anna said.

"Amen," Sharon Sheppard murmured.

"May we walk the rangers out?" Alexis asked politely as Anna rose to leave with Lorraine. Mrs. Sheppard looked at her watch.

"You've seven minutes left."

"Please?"

"Don't tell Mr. Sheppard."

The girls leaped up with alacrity. Anna doubted good manners or a love for herself or her boss fomented this seven-minute revolt against the powers that be in the form of the clan's patriarch. The girls probably just wanted out. To Anna, this was completely understandable. There were studies showing the threat of prison wasn't much of a crime deterrent but it deterred her most effectively. Life in a box, as far as she was concerned, was not better than no life at all.

Mindful their early release was only on sufferance, Beth and Alexis dutifully walked down the long hall with Anna and Lorraine, through the chapel, and out toward where the Crown Vic was parked.

A ring of boys, ranging in age from seven to sixteen, had formed in the dirt yard. In another setting they would have been laughing and yelling as they pursued whatever game they were at. Here in New Canaan they muttered and snickered. Though this was probably due to the discipline of their pieced-together culture, it lent them an air of conspiracy and underhandedness.

So intent were they on their game, they didn't hear the women and girls approaching. Two of the boys knelt. Anna glanced over their heads to see what all the suppressed excitement was about.

Within the circle of knees and booted feet was a kitten, nine to twelve weeks by the look of it, but it might have been older. When an animal is half-starved, size is an unreliable indicator of age. The kitten was black, with white paws and a white ascot.

The poor thing was terrified. Each time it tried to escape, to break through the line of boys, it was thrust back with sticks, kicks, thrown stones.

Anna's blood pressure shot up thirty points. Her vision turned red at the edges. In the instant before she might have done something that would get her sentenced to life in a box, Beth, the limpet, shot by, long skirts flying, hair tumbling down. Shrieking like a demented banshee, the girl tore into the first boy she collided with, scratching and biting and kicking.

Anna waded into the melee. Under the guise of controlling Beth, she managed to send three boys sprawling and bloody the nose of the leader, a boy bigger than she was but a coward all the same.

The fracas was over almost before it started. Boys were sitting in the dirt stunned. Boys were crying. Three boys were bleeding, one from Anna's elbow in his face, two from the fierce onslaught of the diminutive Beth. Anna was not dissatisfied with the carnage. Little remained in the world that could trigger a Viking's berserker rage in her soul, but these boys had managed to stumble upon it.

She picked up the kitten. It was sitting in the wreck of boys, head low, panting like a dog. By the time an opportunity to escape had been presented, it was too exhausted or sick or weak to take advantage of it. The cat didn't fight but pushed its head down into the crook of Anna's arm to hide there.

Cat taken care of, Anna turned to Beth. Whatever had moved the girl to rush to the defense of the kitten had not receded once the battle was won. Beth was no longer violent, she was hysterical. Tears poured down her face in staggering quantities, dripping from her jaw. Snot poured from her nose. Saliva frothed at the corners of her mouth. She clawed at her face and hair as if it were she and not the boys in need of punishment. By rights she should have been wailing, screaming, but the noises she made were shut behind clenched lips and sounded like the keening of whales. Alexis and Mrs. Sheppard held her between them. Mrs. Sheppard was alternately crooning and making sharp commands to snap out of it. Alexis had her arms around her friend but that was where the show of comfort ended. The taller girl's face was as pale as her hair and utterly blank. Even in sleep the human face has emotion, an inner working that lends animation though the muscles are relaxed. The only faces Anna could remember seeing that were as empty as that of Alexis were the death masks on the marble tombs of medieval fighting men. Taking Beth's hand, Anna set it gently on the kitten's back so she could feel its warm living fur. The strangled internal whoops slowed, then ceased. Beth opened her eyes.

"See," Anna said. "You saved the kitty cat. See how he's all poked down in my arm? You saved him. He's okay. I bet he's even purring. Put your ear on him and see."

Beth mopped some of the mess off of her face with the backs of her hands and carefully laid her ear on the cat's side.

"Is he purring?" Anna asked.

"He is," Beth said with surprise.

"He's happy you saved him," Anna said. Cats not only purred when they were happy but often when they were hungry or scared, but Beth didn't need to know that.

"Are you going to be okay?" Anna asked.

Beth stopped petting the kitten and crossed her arms tightly over her chest. "Okay," she managed. The tears began again.

"What are you going to name your kitty?" Mrs. Sheppard asked kindly, relieved that a key to the child's sanity had been recovered.

"No," Beth cried. "I don't want it." She tore free of Alexis' embrace and ran for the house. Mrs. Sheppard ran after her.

Alexis never moved. Her face remained a death mask. Anna reached toward her then hesitated, overtaken by the unsettling fancy that if she touched her the girl would shatter. Or her flesh would be as cold as the morgue.

fourteen

Lying on her back on a slab of sun-warmed granite, Anna watched the afternoon thunderheads build to the southeast. Customarily her thoughts would drift to fog and reknit black and powerful as the storms, but today there wasn't a snowball's chance in hell of that happening. Civilization, so-called, had screwed around with her head so much an eight-mile hike and a few hours of Mother Nature's glamour weren't going to straighten it. Anna quit trying and let herself think about what she was going to think about even if every Zen master in the world gave her his secret mantra.

The girls. The room where they were sent to pray. The pitter-patter of little demon hooves with little children's voices around Heath's trailer. Demons poking at Heath with sticks. Demonic boys poking at a kitten with sticks. Beth saving the cat. The cat's failure to save Beth. Beth running for the house. Alexis turned to a pillar of salt as sure as if she'd looked back at Sodom and Gomorrah.

Beth. Alexis. Alexis and Beth. They'd left the camp, if the missing Proffit were to be believed, alone and under their own power. They'd reappeared near Heath's camp alone and under their own power. They both claimed complete amnesia. Both lied— maybe—about Candace. Both their voices were recognized by Heath as mocking and threatening.

As counterintuitive as it was for Anna, who had seen the cuts and bruises and battered feet, the tears and the fear and the blood, she made herself consider that these girls were in a dark drama of their own making.

Amnesia, total amnesia, amnesia not following severe trauma to the head and lasting for days, was exceedingly rare. For two people, both with skulls intact, to come down with it simultaneously was beyond the realm of the believable. Sheppard and his flock, as well as the psychotherapist who worked for the hospital, muttered about shock, denial, blocking, regression, repression but Anna didn't buy it. She'd called the only mental health professional she knew to be sane and not in deep denial about the limitations in her field's provable knowledge, her sister, Molly, an overpriced, extremely bright and ethical psychiatrist who practiced on Manhattan's Upper West Side. In over thirty years of practice, Molly had never seen a single case of long-term amnesia without severe head trauma. She mentioned that in the late eighteenth century it had been all the rage for young men of fashion to go into fugue states, vanish from London to turn up a week later in Paris or Bath having no recollection of the days in between. It was undoubtedly a handy epidemic but short-lived. Nobody much suffered from fugue states anymore.

Molly had confirmed what Anna had suspected: the girls were lying. They remembered and, for their own reasons, had decided not to tell anyone. Lying was as valid a response to handling trauma as amnesia or hysterics but it wasn't nearly as socially acceptable. People believed if one was doing something consciously then one could stop doing it on command. Not always true. What Anna needed to know was why they were lying.

Guilt and fear of consequences were common and powerful motivators. Beth and Alexis were clearly feeling desperately guilty about something. Leaving Candace? Guilty they lied about her staying with Proffit? Guilty about getting Proffit in trouble so they lied about lying?

Proffit had run, that was three days ago, and no one had heard from him since. He'd said he'd gone to find Candace. Unless the girls had lied about that, too. Law enforcement in Colorado was keeping an eye out for him as a courtesy but, so far as anyone could prove, he'd broken no laws.

Had the three girls and Proffit planned the disappearance between them and something went terribly awry? Or was the guilt Beth and Alexis suffered not because they'd left Candace behind but because they had killed her themselves in a girlish rendition of

Lord of the Flies? That would certainly account for the persistent bout of amnesia.

And why had Beth been willing to take on every boy in town to rescue a kitten, then fled in horror when it was suggested she keep it herself?

The only silver lining so far was that Anna had gotten a heck of a nice cat out of the deal. She'd named him Hector, then changed it to Hecuba when the vet informed her she'd sexed it incorrectly. When Piedmont came to Estes Park she would have some explaining to do. It was bad enough that she'd brought home Taco. But Taco, after all, was only a dog. Another cat could be viewed as serious competition.

Anna looked at her watch. Ray was late. Much as she enjoyed lounging about in glorious solitude, the thunderheads were getting ever more serious. This time of year outings in the Rockies were timed around the inevitable lightning. Today Raymond was to take Anna up to Gabletop Mountain, one of the less used climbing areas. The eastern face of it rose in a steep fractured cliff-face above Tourmaline, a jewel of a lake. The hike in was longer and rougher than that to Longs Peak and the climbing routes less varied and spectacular, so fewer people scaled it.

Gabletop was at the head of steep-sided Tourmaline Gorge, which terminated at Odessa Lake. On her earlier trip to Fern, Anna had hiked down the gorge. Today she'd crossed at midpoint and hiked up along an unimproved trail to a rendezvous point where a fallen slab of granite jutted out providing a glorious view of Gabletop in one direction and Odessa in the other. The day before, while they'd hiked to Frozen Lake, Rita had told her about the place. It was a favorite lunching spot—uncreatively dubbed "Picnic Rock"—of the backcountry rangers.

Though grateful to have a job where one's first duties were to hike through beautiful country with well-informed park rangers, Anna had suggested for today's outing Ray meet her here. It made a shorter hike for him and she got to do at least the first half of this professional adventure alone.

In the interest of looking more manager-like when Ray arrived, Anna pulled herself to a sitting position and dangled her feet over the edge of the slab. The flat chunk of granite was cantilevered over the canyon's rim a dozen feet. Below was a sheer drop of twenty feet or so to a scree and scrub slope. When heights were precipitous but not dangerous Anna loved them, loved the bird's-eye view, the rush of the nearness of empty space and the knowledge that a moment's insanity could hurl one into the winds. Perhaps it was the choice not taken that made these places so rich in life force.

As the crunching of boots on the rocky trail let her know her date had arrived, an eagle appeared in the valley below her boot soles, closer than she'd ever seen one except in the heartbreaking confines of zoo aviaries.

"My god," she whispered. It was a golden eagle, its white tail band spread and glittering in the hard noon light. The creature's wingspan was an easy six feet. Anna felt like Thumbelina; she could leave the earth and ride on its back to warm and wonderful lands.

"Ray," she whispered, not daring to look away. "See my golden eagle?"

Softly for a heavily booted man, he crept up beside her, then: "Oh my . . ." on a breath of air. He, too, was captivated by the singular beauty and the blessing of being witness to it. Though Anna expected it from fellow rangers, all the same it pleased her. More people were joining the NPS because it was a good government job rather than because they loved the parks, an unexpected downside to recent pay increases.

The eagle caught a thermal and corkscrewed out of the canyon in effortless circles. Rapt, Anna's eyes followed it till the man standing over her intruded into her view.

It wasn't Raymond Bleeker.

"Robert Proffit," she said, pretending the sight of him hadn't jolted her down to the marrow of her bones. He was standing too close. The precipitous height she'd been so enjoying became suddenly precarious.

"Step back, if you would," she said pleasantly. "It makes me nervous, you standing so close to the edge. A good gust of wind and you'd be another search-and-rescue report I'd have to write up."

Proffit backed up obediently. Not as far as Anna would have liked. Not enough she felt comfortable standing up. Once again she was hiking in civilian clothes, the better to observe her rangers interacting with the public. Once again she wasn't carrying her service weapon. She'd planned on hiking with Bleeker. Two semiautomatics seemed like overkill for an afternoon's jaunt in the woods. Now she wasn't all that sure.

The sun was directly behind Proffit's head. Anna couldn't see his face against the glare.

"We've been looking for you," she said conversationally.

"I've been around." He turned from her, looking toward Gabletop Mountain. Light caught the sharp line of jaw and cheekbone. There was no meat on him and it looked as if there once had been. His was the worn thinness of obsession or stress, not the lean wiry sort of skinny Anna often saw on people in the backcountry.

His eyes narrowed against the light. He stared up-canyon with an intensity that let Anna know he wanted to run away from her.

Given she'd stacked the deck against herself in every way possible—perched over a sheer drop, blinded by the sun, seated and unarmed—she was comforted by the idea that he was afraid of her. Scared people could be extremely dangerous but usually not unless one strayed between them and their means of escape. "Got a minute to talk?" she asked before he could act on the impulse to run.

With an obvious effort, he tore his eyes away from the mountain. "Yeah. I guess."

"Where are you headed? Gabletop?"

"Yeah. No, nowhere really."

The other times she'd had an opportunity to observe Robert Proffit, he had been anguished, ardent, passionate, theatrical, charming and confident in his righteousness. This Robert Proffit was none of those things. He shuffled. He sniffed. He avoided eye contact.

He acted guilty as hell.

"The girls recanted," Anna said, to see if that was what was giving him the fidgets. "They told us they'd lied about Candace Watson staying behind with you."

"Yeah. They told me they would. They're good kids. Just scared."

"What are they scared of, Robert?"

He looked down where she sat, extraneous movement and mental vagueness gone. "I don't know," he said earnestly. Real earnestly. Anna couldn't tell if he'd stopped acting guilty because she was on the wrong track and he felt safe with this line of conversation or because he was a born actor and the moment he trod the boards his stage fright vanished.

Or maybe he was simply an earnest young man addressing a subject he cared deeply about.

"Sit down," Anna said. "Take your pack off and rest a bit. I'm getting a crick in my neck looking up at you."

He shed his pack. By the *thunk* as it landed, Anna guessed he carried a hefty load. Having freed his water bottle from one of the side pockets, he sat down next to her, feet dangling over open space. All things now being equal, Anna felt considerably more relaxed.

Alone in the wilderness on the edge of a precipice wasn't the ideal place to interrogate a man suspected of abduction and murder, but a girl had to take what she could get. The appearance of the golden eagle and her assumption that the man behind her was Raymond Bleeker had given Proffit the perfect opportunity. Had he murder on his mind, he could have shoved her over in a trice and no one would ever have been the wiser. The fact that she still lived was a point in his favor, as far as she was concerned.

"I thought you were going to arrest me," Proffit confessed.

"Should I?"

"No. But that doesn't mean much. Many are taken in His name."

"You think this is a religious persecution?"

"Not exactly. But when Beth and Alexis said they'd left Candace with me I knew I'd be in trouble."

"So you ran?"

"No. I didn't run. I'm going to find Candace."

"Do you know where she is?"

"No. I just . . . I just have to keep looking, that's all."

"Is that what you're doing up here, looking for Candace?"

"Mostly. I . . ."

Anna waited for him to finish but he thought better of it and busied himself with his water bottle.

"The night you left New Canaan you talked with the girls at that room they were sent to."

"Yes."

"Did they climb out the window, go anywhere with you?"

"No. Why?"

The question seemed genuine enough, but then everybody in this bizarre case seemed genuine and guilty by turns, with neither rhyme nor reason separating the two states.

"Did you know Heath Jarrod was camped out on the main road?"

"The lady in the wheelchair? Yeah. Beth wanted her close. She wouldn't eat till Mr. Sheppard okayed it."

"Did you go to Miss Jarrod's camp that night?"

"No."

"Didn't take the girls out there?"

"No. What are you getting at?"

"Just asking," Anna said mildly.

For a minute, maybe two, they sat in a surprisingly companionable silence. Surprising to Anna because she'd never known Proffit to be so still. Not simply unmoving, but internally still. When Anna was a girl there'd been a woman named Loretha, a handsome black woman who came twice a week with fresh eggs. Loretha had carried such deep stillness within her that the dogs, who barked at every falling leaf and passing fancy, never barked at her. She did not disturb the ether with inner fussiness.

Robert Proffit had in no way reached the level of spiritual quiet of the egg lady but Anna sensed a lot of his internal histrionics were gone. Gone, too, was the exaggerated portrayal of them, the clutching of hair and gnashing of teeth.

"You've come to a decision," she declared, having not the foggiest notion what that decision might be about.

"I guess I have in a way." He tossed a pebble into the canyon below.

"Want to let me in on it?"

"I don't see why I should."

"Me neither."

"I'm not going back to New Canaan." Though there was a good deal about him Anna didn't trust—didn't like much—she didn't doubt that he did what he did for what he considered to be godly reasons. This softened her suspicion not one whit. Reasons touted as godly were responsible for more deaths than a whole host of deadly diseases combined.

"Why not?" Now that it had been established that neither of them thought he should confide in her, he seemed almost eager to do so.

"I got my degree at Brigham Young. A

master's in liturgical music. After that, I
worked in a couple of temples. One in Salt
Lake City and one in Provo. The hypocrisy
sickened me. The people smoking, drinking,
committing adultery and fornication like it
was going out of style and all the time keeping up this front that they're better—more
godly—than the rest of the smokers,
drinkers and adulterers. I wanted to go back
to a time when we were close to God. When
we lived as the Bible and the Book of Mormon told us to live. That's when I hooked up
with Mr. Sheppard and his flock. They were
living outside of St. George in a trailer park
then.

"At first it was like stepping back in time. I
thought my prayers had been answered."

Anna said nothing. Her views on the subject were probably too acerbic for even a
disillusioned Christian. Besides that, she
didn't much care about his spiritual journey
except as it related to the three girls.

"I guess things never were the way they'd
been. Anyway it was pretty much the same
in the Sheppard group—except for the
smoking and drinking. At first there were
more of us but most of the younger guys
split. They wanted families and all."

From this Anna surmised that Mr. Sheppard and a handful of the older men had first dibs on all the females, each of them taking multiple wives and the young men left to their own devices—or vices, as the case may be.

"Then Mr. Johanson—one of the elders—inherited the ranch and the group moved here."

"And you came with them," Anna said. "Why?"

"Partly because I had no money and no place else to go, but mostly because I'd begun working with the kids, the young teens and preteens, girls for the most part, and I'd fallen in love for the first time in my life. Not like you think. You don't know any better," he added with unselfconscious condescension. "For the first time I knew what God wanted me to do, how I was to serve Him."

"And just how was that?" Anna thought she'd kept every molecule of cynicism out of her voice but the look he shot her let her know she'd not been entirely successful.

"I was to help them to see God's grace, to feel His love for them."

Anna said nothing. Men helping girls—or

boys for that matter—to feel God's love could easily morph into precisely the kind of behavior that had gotten the Catholic Church in such hot water. Proffit might swear his love was spiritual while he was busily expressing it in corporeal terms.

"And I wanted to get them . . ." He stopped, maybe remembering with whom he spoke.

"Get them away?" Anna finished for him. He didn't respond.

"What happened to get you to abandon them now?" Anna asked.

"I haven't abandoned them," Proffit said.

"You told me you weren't returning to New Canaan."

"No, I didn't. I said I wasn't going *back*."

"You lost me there," Anna admitted.

"I have to get on," Proffit said abruptly, as if realizing that he'd either tarried too long or shared too much.

"What are you doing in Rocky? Camping?" Anna asked.

"No."

"Why the backpack?"

"I don't have to answer you," Proffit said and scrambled to his feet. Openness was gone. Whatever had him on edge before had been remembered. He wanted to get away from her. Stooping, he dragged his pack toward him, readying himself to take its weight.

The pack was leaking blood from its lower back corner. Against the gray-gold of the granite, the blood was a breathtakingly red, cartoon blood, but it never crossed Anna's mind for a second that it was anything else. Blood has a life energy that is hard to mimic with paints or dyes.

Robert Proffit, the Jesus-loving servant God had called to look after His helpless girl children, saw the blood at the same moment she did. Their eyes rose from the spreading red stain and met. For a second—less—they looked into one another's souls, or so it seemed to Anna. In, on, beyond his dark hazel eyes with their thick feminine lashes, she could have sworn this bloody Proffit pleaded with her. What he saw in hers, she didn't know.

The instant passed. Anna gathered her feet under her and began to rise as Proffit grabbed hold of the pack's shoulder straps and swung. The full weight of the pack caught her on the left shoulder. Before she could think, she was in midair, falling backward. In her field of vision was Proffit, his bloody pack clutched to his chest.

Not wanting Robert Proffit to be the last thing she saw, Anna looked to the sky. It was that which was filling her vision when she struck the ground.

fifteen

The breath slammed out of her and the world dimmed. Into this dark fog, full of holes and noise and flecks of red, came the grind and crush of rocks moving. An avalanche. Anna felt no pain but pressure on her legs. The holes closed, fog grew solid and she saw nothing.

Light returned before air. She was paralyzed, full of the unique terror only a lack of oxygen can cause and wondering if her lungs would ever work again. In scratchy sips she pulled in enough air to live. It primed the pump and she began breathing again. Air expanding her lungs sent a sheet of agony down her back. With the rapidity of a dream, where lifetimes unfold in the time it takes the second hand to make one insomniac's trek around the dial, Anna knew Heath Jarrod, mind, body and soul. Every cell in her body knew the fear and frustration of immobility, the loss of one life with no hint or promise of another. Crippled and mean with self-pity, she saw herself driving away Paul, diving into the bottle wearing nothing but her own misery and staying down till finally even Molly and Piedmont would have nothing to do with her. She would have nothing to do with herself.

That quickly, Anna was praying to a god whose image she'd recently been burning away with cynicism that her back wasn't broken, that she'd either walk out of the gorge or she would die there.

Twenty feet above, severed from its body by a granite knife-edge, a head appeared. Robert Proffit.

"Fucking will-o'-the-wisp," Anna whispered.

"Oh Jesus. Oh God. Oh shit. Are you all right?" he called down.

Anna blinked several times. She had the

air to answer, she just didn't have the answer.

The head was withdrawn.

Anna waited for it to return. She listened for the sound of him scrabbling and sliding down to where she lay. It was so still she could hear needles on the pines rubbing against one another in the sudden uncertain breezes. No sound of rescue, or even company, broke the backcountry quiet. Insects, silenced by her rude arrival on their patch of turf, began to buzz and drone again.

"Robert?" she called. The call wasn't nearly loud enough. The ache in her back kept her from taking in enough air. Putting pain aside, she filled her lungs and shouted. "Robert!" The name echoed, returning in a mutant form of itself.

Proffit had gone. Gone for help? Or just gone? Had he intended to knock her off the ledge or had he been hoping to swing his pack onto his back and make a run for it? His blood-soaked pack, Anna remembered. He must have knocked her off intentionally. Better that than jail. Or the chair. In Colorado maybe they hung people who chopped up little girls and packed them into national parks without a permit.

"Focus," Anna whispered. She forced her unraveling mind to reknit around a semblance of reality. "ABCs," she said. Airway, bleeding, circulation.

Talking was breathing. Anna got an A. Circulation at least in the vessels leading to heart, lungs and brain was functional. She'd give herself a B– in circulation. Bleeding was a tough one. She didn't feel warm wetness anywhere but she'd not yet gotten herself together enough to sit up and take a look. If she could sit. She had to settle for an "Incomplete" in bleeding.

Steeling herself to the task, she attempted to move. Her legs were paralyzed. Nightmare became real. Panic shot through, so acute her body jerked. One shin cracked against a solid object and the pain, sharper and new, momentarily eclipsed the aching of her back.

Not since the Marquis de Sade had anyone so welcomed pain. Pain was sensation, was life. The dead do not feel. Her legs weren't dead.

Having metaphorically read the obituaries and not found her name in them, Anna took stock of her greater situation. Because of the nature of her fall, her back taking the brunt of the force, it was unwise to move anymore. If her spine had been compromised but the cord not yet damaged she could do herself irreparable harm by thrashing about inopportunely.

All well and good but there were no EMTs to stabilize her neck and back, neatly package her and deliver her to the hospital for X rays. Hoping for the best, she gathered the remnants of her courage. With one great shove and a tornado of pain that ripped up her back and into her skull, she pushed herself into a sitting position.

The news was both good and bad. A pad of dense manzanita bushes growing thick and low to the ground had broken her fall and saved her bones. But for the screaming ache of traumatized soft tissues, she was relatively unhurt. On the opposite side of her survival ledger was the fact that Robert Proffit didn't appear to be coming back anytime soon and she wasn't going anywhere for a while. Her legs were immobilized, not from a failure of nerve communication, but by rocks. The mini avalanche her fall instigated had brought three boulders, one half the size of a garbage can, down upon her. Luck, or the whim of the gods, had decreed that she not be crushed. The mercy ended there. The two lesser rocks acted as side supports to the greater, creating a slot through which her booted feet were thrust. She was as securely bound as a woman put in the stocks. Beneath her legs was a slab of granite, making digging her way free impossible unless, like the Count of Monte Cristo, she had nine years and a metal spoon at her disposal. Her radio, even should it be able to broadcast out of the narrow canyon, had been flung away when she fell and lay snuggled in the shrubbery a tantalizing five or six feet out of reach. Her water bottle was in her pack up on Picnic Rock.

For a while she wriggled and struggled, scraped up both shins and worked up a sweat that went some little way toward melting away the vicious ache covering her back like a coat. Her efforts did nothing to dislodge the stone or free her feet and she was forced to face the hardest choice. She must school herself to patience and wait. Ray Bleeker was to meet her. He was half an hour late. There was nothing to do but to save her breath and strength so when he deigned to keep their appointment she could shout for help. With two people, one of whom could stand, gain purchase and fetch levers, she had no doubt the rock could be shifted. With care it could be moved in such a way her feet wouldn't be squashed in the process and she could walk out on her own. New to the park, the first female district ranger in Rocky, the thought of being the centerpiece of a carry-out was easily more frightening than lying pinned under a rock for a bit longer.

And longer.

And longer.

An hour passed, then two. Bleeker never showed. Periodically her radio bleated to life with the usual business of the park. The first couple of times the nearness of dispatch and the voices of the rangers drove her to fish for the damn thing with the stunted twiggy branches of the manzanita. Then she tried catching it with the buckle of her belt. Failing that, she secured her shirt to her belt buckle and, using it as a net, attempted to capture and drag it. Tucked down in the foliage as it was, she never managed to move it more than a quarter of an inch and nearly lost her shirt in the process.

Finally she gave up. Not from despair: the situation had come nowhere near to the place where despair waited. Not yet at any rate. She stopped because she'd begun working up a thirst and had no access to water. Intellectually she knew she could live about three days without water, especially in the cool of the high country, but her body, having lived many years in deserts, knew thirst was one of the most uncomfortable ways of suffering deprivation. Thirst put starvation to shame when it came to the miseries of the flesh. One never heard of dissidents going on thirst strikes to call attention to their causes. Maybe it was because three days wasn't long enough to get the media interested. Or maybe it was because it was just too miserable.

As the sky clouded and the breezes grew sharp and fragrant, she lay still, conserving her energies and hoping to be rescued. She missed fighting with the boulder and coaxing the radio. At least it had been something to do. It helped pass the time. Supine, bored, tired of the stress of the situation and ignoring the aching in her back, shoulders and neck, she kept falling into light dozes. The temptation to give into sleep was enormous, but the fear of being overlooked by

Ray Bleeker when he arrived kept her prodding herself awake.

By four-thirty the storms she'd watched forming from her perch on Picnic Rock reached Tourmaline Gorge and a cold rain began to fall. Anna had been expecting it and had dithered about the best use she might make of it, given that Bleeker seemed to have stood her up and might not come looking for her till she didn't show up at Fern Lake Cabin where she was to spend the night. She could either remove her shirt and spread it to catch the most rain possible in hopes she could save the water to wring out and drink, or she could shove the shirt under the small of her back to keep it dry so she wouldn't die of hypothermia should she end up spending the night trapped in the gorge.

In the end she decided hypothermia was the more imminent danger. Her shorts she shoved down beneath the boulder that held her fast. The shirt was wadded up and smashed in on top of them. For the two hours it showered, she shivered, scraped water off of her exposed flesh and into her mouth and enjoyed a brief respite from wishing to be rescued. Trapped, with her pants around her ankles, was not how she wanted to be found.

Afternoon wore away into evening. Evening faded into night. Even in dry clothing she was cold. The manzanita that had very probably saved her life was making it a misery, every branch and leaf poking into her from neck to knees. To ward off the cold she moved as much as the rocks would let her, doing isometric exercises and sit-ups. Occasionally she drifted into fitful sleep filled with dreams of butchered girls stuffed into backpacks and orchestrated by the howling of nonexistent wolves.

Three hours after dawn, when the sun finally reached down into Tourmaline Gorge, Anna was still alive. As it began to warm her she was even glad of this fact. Thirst returned. Bleeker still didn't come. The sun inched up toward noon. Thunderheads began building again. Twenty-four hours had passed. When she finally heard the sounds she had been listening for all this time, she was afraid to call out lest she be imagining them.

Thirty seconds passed and the crunch of booted feet on a rocky trail continued. Still she didn't call out. The wearer of the boots could be Robert Proffit come to see if she was dead. Playing possum seemed the best course of action. Or inaction.

But what if it wasn't Proffit? Suddenly overcome with terror that she'd waited too long and whoever it was would pass her by, she began shouting, "Down here! Help! Help. Down here. In the gorge. Help me!"

The footsteps stopped.

Anna's heart stopped.

Again she yelled; the desperation and panic she had been assiduously not feeling since she had tumbled into this bizarre death trap gave her voice the strength and range of a seasoned opera singer. Her own racket covered any sounds from above as she shrieked.

"Anna?"

The sound cut through her homemade siren song. She focused on the face hovering over the rim of Picnic Rock. "Rita?"

"I've been here awhile. I thought you'd gone nutso."

"Sorry. Didn't see you. My mouth was open so wide my eyes were shut, I guess. Welcome," Anna added for lack of anything more intelligent to say.

"What happened?"

"Come down."

Rita's face was withdrawn and Anna was overcome with a sense of déjà vu, of watching Robert Proffit vanish, and had to clench her teeth to keep from crying out, "Don't go!"

This time she was not to be abandoned. In less than five minutes—an exceedingly long five minutes—she heard the reassuring sounds of Rita making her way into the gorge from down the trail where seasonal runoff had carved a rough-and-tumble stairway of stone.

Rita was strong and she was creative. Having shored up both sides of Anna's feet and ankles with rocks of various sizes so, should the boulder roll in the wrong direction, they would not be crushed, she found two sturdy limbs and put one beneath the boulder on either side of Anna's knees. On a three count, they pried, Rita providing most of the muscle, Anna doing what she could from her awkward position to steer the boulder along the line of least collateral damage.

The plan was a complete success. Within half an hour of Rita's arrival, Anna was free. Walking was out of the question till she got the kinks worked out and the blood flowing.

Because she had shared those moments of terror with Heath Jarrod—or at least the Heath Jarrod of her imagining—Anna was grateful for the shooting pains, the tingles that verged on manic itches, all the slings and arrows of sensation letting her know she would walk home in the near future.

As she kneaded and stretched she told Rita the story of how she'd come to be found under a rock in Tourmaline Gorge. Anna had expected the satisfaction of her subordinate's righteous anger and edgy mystification at the relating of the bleeding backpack. She was disappointed. Rita let that—which Anna had considered the stellar component in the drama—pass over her as if itinerant youth ministers toting gore in the backcountry of Rocky were an everyday occurrence. The bit she reacted to with satisfying outrage was that Robert Proffit had called down to her, then left without offering aid. For a stumbling minute or two—time during which Anna remembered Rita and Proffit in the emergency room praying together like old seminary buddies—Rita tried to find excuses for Robert's abandonment of a person in need. Evidently it was hard to accept that he was a rotten Samaritan.

Anna had told her story in repayment for Rita's rescuing her from what was beginning to look like a cold, thirsty, ignoble death. That done, she asked the question that had been nagging her since she'd been able to think of anything more complex than crawling out from under her rock.

"How did you know I was here?"

Rita was probably not much good at lying because Anna could see the temptation to do it clearly on her face in the seconds before she answered.

"Robert told me," she said with reluctance.

"You've seen Robert?"

"He left me a note," Rita amended. "I found it when I came home for lunch."

Anna noted that she'd not answered precisely. She decided to let it pass. For now.

"A note."

"It said, 'I can't do this anymore. I have to go. Tell Ranger Pigeon it was an accident.'"

"That's all?"

"Yes. Just that."

Anna digested this information for a brief

moment, then again she asked, "How did you know I was here?"

Rita opened her mouth once or twice in the time-honored tradition of goldfish. After these false starts she said, "I didn't know you were here exactly. I just knew where he was hiking yesterday."

Anna waited but Rita seemed to think she'd said enough. She stood, began gathering up her daypack as if a decision had been made to decamp.

"Sit down," Anna ordered.

"It'll be dark soon," Rita said. "We should head down."

It wasn't yet three o'clock and they weren't more than two and a half hours from the Bear Lake parking lot. Anna said nothing. After a bit of shuffling, Rita took off her pack and sat down as she'd been bidden.

Anna eased herself up gingerly with the help of one of the many boulders so she could practice standing while she grilled Rita.

"This hasn't been a particularly good day for me," she said after the first wave of pain and dizziness broke and began to recede. "What with one thing and another I've pretty much run out of patience. Suffice to say I'm in a real bad mood. You rescued me. I'm grateful. But if you keep jerking me around with these bullshit half-answers, that gratitude could turn to pure meanness. Let's try this again."

Rita sat quietly through this tongue-lashing, but not docilely. Her spine straightened, her broad shoulders squared, her handsome face settled into a stoic mask. Watching this subtle transformation, Anna realized she'd not triggered sullenness, guilt, defensiveness, slyness or any of the many things she'd expected, given Rita's evasiveness. What she was seeing was the determined courage of the martyr waiting to die for the cause.

"Jesus," Anna sighed.

"Amen."

"Fuck," Anna fumed, inadvertently hitting on an expletive that Rita didn't feel the need to ratify with the god of her understanding. Using the rock for support, Anna began rotating her left foot. The movement sent shivers of a nauseating mix of sensations through her bones. "You get a note from Proffit saying to tell me 'it was an accident.' Rather than figuring he scratched my car or mowed down my lilac bush you immediately figure he's shoved me off an isolated rock on the less traveled side of Tourmaline Gorge. Tell me exactly how that worked."

Rita thought for a moment. The woman was around thirty years old, educated and smart. As a law enforcement ranger and paramedic at Rocky for seven seasons, she would have seen the darker, stupider, bloodier, more spiteful side of her fellow men and women. Despite that, she seemed to have retained an innocence—or naïveté—that rendered dissembling impossible. Her face was as easy to read as a child's.

Running under the smooth tanned skin like fishes beneath clear water, answers were trotted out, examined and then discarded. Finally Rita settled on one she liked.

"I knew Robert was up this way yesterday. I happened to be coming up here today anyway. The note hadn't made me think you were in trouble but it bothered me so I was kind of keeping my eyes and ears open more than usual. I heard somebody shouting and saw a daypack sitting on Picnic Rock—I knew you'd probably stop here because we'd talked about it. I looked over and there you were." To Anna's surprise Rita then smiled at her. It wasn't mockery or idiocy, it was pride. She was proud of herself for having managed her story so neatly, Anna suspected.

"Why was Robert hiking up this way?"

"He could have been looking for Candace."

"Why do you suppose his pack was hemorrhaging?"

"I suppose it could have been something else. A broken wine bottle, catsup, whatever."

"Why were you hiking up the gorge today? It's your day off. I'd think you'd want a change of pace."

"I hike up here a lot."

Anna had been asking the questions rapid-fire. Now she stopped. The pattern she'd been searching for—in lieu of any useful information apparently—had emerged. Rita wasn't going to lie to her, at least not yet, not over this adventure. People would often say, "I don't want to lie to you . . ." Which usually meant not only did they want to lie but, as her neighbors in Mississippi would say, were fixin' to do just that. Rita, on the other hand, was jumping through semantic hoops to avoid an untruth. Maybe she was afraid lying would get her sent to hell come the final reckoning.

Not telling the whole truth could get her there a whole lot sooner than that if Anna had any say in the matter.

"I think I'm good to go," Anna said.

"Out to Bear?" Rita asked as she let Anna set the pace on the scramble out of the gorge.

"Down to Fern. I've a couple questions for Ray." As soon as Anna had been freed, she'd retrieved her radio. In the twenty-four hours she'd lain on her prickly bed of manzanita, feet firmly clamped in a pair of Mother Nature's many jaws, there'd not been a single burble from anybody wondering where she was.

After the incarceration of the night, movement was not merely good for muscle, nerve and bone, it was a salve to Anna's spirit. Rita gave her water and granola bars, and by the time they came out at Odessa Lake and joined the main trail to Fern, Anna was feeling almost as good as new. An underlying ache in her back and a pit of fatigue beneath her frontal lobe let her know this bliss was to be short-lived and she made a point to enjoy every moment, every step of it.

She intentionally maintained radio silence. The only people that knew she had been out of commission for the past day were Robert Proffit, Rita Perry and Raymond Bleeker. He'd never kept their appointment. Anna wanted to know why. She wanted to see his face when she walked into the cabin unannounced. Even the most practiced deceivers, if caught off guard, tended to give themselves away. Maybe only for a fraction of a second, but Anna would be watching for it.

The trail curled down around Fern to a wooden footbridge that crossed over the stream fed by the tiny lake. Fern's waters, cupped in a bowl of lodgepole pine, showed emerald green even under partly clouded skies. Over the lip of the outlet where the creek ran shallow, it was crystal clear. Cutthroat trout sometimes came to sun themselves under the bridge, their blood-red throats and speckled backs enlivening an always sparkling scene.

Anna noted it only peripherally. She walked ahead of Rita, concentrating on the bits of humanity scattered around the lake.

Two boys haunted the footbridge, undoubtedly annoying the fish. A woman, trousers shoved up to let the sun warm her shins, leaned against the bole of a tree near the water reading her book. Two old people, white hair glowing from beneath the rumpled brims of cloth hats, fished from the downed logs in the water in front of the cabin. Of Ray Bleeker there was no sign. She was glad of it. It was her hope to be ensconced in his cabin when he got home, all the better for her experiment in shock.

Rita fell back, talking to somebody. Anna barely registered the defection. Rangers had a hard time getting from point A to point B without getting stopped half a dozen times by visitors with questions or stories. People like to talk to rangers. Even rangers with guns. Rangers were different from policemen—assumed to be good, nonviolent, understanding, lenient and basically on your side. Mostly that was true. Anna hoped it would never change.

Except that Rita was on her day off, out of uniform. Anna stopped.

"Hey, Anna." The words came at her from behind. She jerked around to see Raymond

Bleeker smiling at her, Rita behind his shoulder. So much for surprise.

"What are you doing here?" she snapped.

Ray, who'd been smiling in apparently genuine pleasure at seeing her, recoiled as if she'd spit at him. "Here? Fern Lake?"

"No. Here." Anna stamped her foot to indicate this chunk of trail.

For an instant he seemed alarmed. Or maybe just annoyed. "I was checking the group sites." He jerked a thumb over his shoulder toward where large groups were sequestered lest their noise or hordes infringe on the experience of others. Behind these camps was a long wall of boulders in varying sizes that extended three-quarters of a mile in either direction. At one time a lodge had been built on the flat in front of the rocky slope but that had been years before. Nothing remained of it now but a leveled area. He looked away, pulled a handkerchief from his pocket—a startling pink and yellow plaid—and wiped his face, giving her a moment to recover her manners.

"Oh," she said, feeling stupid and oddly let down.

He kindly chose to overlook her previous

hostility. "How was the big meeting?" he asked, the smile back, if not quite so genuine as before.

"What meeting?" She felt as if she'd walked in after the movie had begun and had missed a key scene.

"With the brass? Yesterday? How many fingers am I holding up?" he teased her with a standard question asked of people who'd suffered a break with reality for one reason or another.

"I had no meeting yesterday," she said slowly, trying to piece together this joking, smiling man with the crestfallen, groveling—or evasive—subordinate she'd been expecting after being stood up with such uncomfortable consequences.

Bleeker stared at her, blinked twice, then a comprehension of some kind animated the muscles of his face. "Shoot," he said. "Robert Proffit."

"We better talk about this back at the cabin."

There was no way in hell three rangers, one in uniform, were going to have an uninterrupted discussion in full view of the visiting public.

Inside the cabin, the door closed to discourage campers and hikers from dropping by to borrow a cup of sugar or conversation, Raymond made tea. Bleeker was six-foot or six-one and about one hundred seventy pounds, but he had a quiet, self-effacing way that made him seem a smaller man. With his light-toned voice—not high-pitched exactly but the sort of voice that could belong either to a man or a woman—his ratty gray cardigan and absurd handkerchief, there was something endearing about him. One wanted to trust him and Anna found herself nodding agreeably as he told his story.

At a little before one o'clock, as he was hiking up the trail to the rendezvous with her for their hike to Gabletop Mountain, he met with Robert Proffit. Proffit, he said, was sitting in the shade of a pine tree beside the trail, waiting for him.

Proffit told him he'd met Ranger Pigeon earlier and she'd asked that he give Ray a message. She'd tried to radio but couldn't get a signal. She'd been called back down to headquarters for an emergency meeting regarding deployment of rangers to the wildfires in southern California.

"Radios are fairly worthless in a lot of the

park," Ray said. Rita seconded the opinion with an unladylike snort. "I figured you'd given up and thought if I didn't get the message I'd get hold of you later from the base radio here in the cabin and we'd get ourselves straight."

Anna sipped her tea. It was excellent, neither too strong nor too weak and a good brand, English or Irish. Bleeker's story held together and made sense. A few anomalies stood out, but Anna didn't know if they mattered or were the usual vagaries of human conduct. She looked up at her companions. Ray rested easily, legs crossed, wrists on his knee. Some tension showed around his eyes and mouth aging him beyond his twenty-eight years. He had, after all, left his new boss staked out on a bed of manzanita for a day and a night. She might have been mistaken for shrimp cocktail on a lettuce leaf had a rogue black bear happened by. That could wreak havoc with a man's end-of-season evaluation.

Rita wasn't faring so well. For reasons Anna was beginning to get an inkling of, if not a handle on, she was absolutely miserable and doing a bad job of disguising the fact. Color had drained from beneath her tan, giving an unbecoming grayish cast to either side of her nose. Restless plucking and tucking had managed to drag hair out of her usually neat ponytail. The strands hung down straight and greasy-looking in front of her ears.

"Did Proffit have a pack with him when he waylaid you?" Anna asked Ray.

"Not that I saw. He could've had it stashed nearby I guess. He had his water bottle. I remember that."

"Did he hike out with you?"

"No. He said it was his last day in the park and he was going to enjoy it right there under that tree. His 'last resting place' he called it." Raymond laughed. Anna looked at him quizzically having missed the joke. "Guess you had to have been there," Ray said.

"That fits with the note he left me," Rita put in. "It sounds like he's decided to leave the area. I can't say as I blame him." This last had a bitter edge to it and Anna shot the young woman a hard look. Ray didn't know about the blood from the backpack. Anna had decided to keep that bit of grisly infor-mation under wraps till she'd had a chance to talk with Lorraine about it. Put with the other half-truths, retracted accusations, means and opportunity, it would be enough to get an arrest warrant. If nothing else, they had him on reckless endangerment and leaving the scene of an accident, if not attempted murder and assaulting a federal law enforcement officer.

Rita did know. Anna wondered why she didn't seem to hold it against Proffit. Was she in love with him? He was seven or eight years younger than she was but that meant little. Proffit was handsome in a wild boyish way and had an undeniable charm. Anna hadn't been the least surprised that he was such a hit with the teenybopper set. He possessed that ineffable magic that makes whatever one does seem cool. When Anna was in high school a boy named Steve Stricker had had it. She and her friend Paul used to sit around trying to figure out why when Steve did it—whatever it was—it was cool and when they did it it was just stupid.

Maybe the adolescent panache appealed to Rita. Maybe the intense passion with which Proffit approached life. Maybe it was the shared God and the seductive frenzy of praying together.

Anna turned her attention back to their

host. "Why did you believe him?" she asked Ray. "The mice. The live trap. The girls. I'd think twice before taking Proffit's word for anything."

Raymond thought about her question, giving it due consideration. As he gathered his thoughts, she had a few of her own. Because she'd been immersed in it up to her eyeballs, it felt as if the saga of Robert Proffit's on-again, off-again status as a suspect was headline news and had been for months. In reality, all that had transpired had happened in the last four or five days. Most of it wasn't common knowledge. Raymond would not know Beth and Alexis had said Candace stayed with Robert, then recanted. He wouldn't know about the strange visitation Heath Jarrod had endured. Seen in this light, Ray's taking the word of a man he'd come to know well, a man who'd worked hand-in-glove with the rangers during a long and heartbreaking search, didn't strike her as odd as it had a minute before.

Of course there were still Minnie and Mickey and their little friends tortured and murdered.

"I've thought a lot about the mouse thing," Ray said eventually. "There wasn't really anybody else who could have done it except maybe me or Rita. Still, it makes no sense. I kind of have to believe he did it for a reason. If he did it at all. You know, an experiment or a warning or . . . I don't know. It's just a feeling. I can't explain it any better."

"Ray's right," Rita said. "Robert would be incapable of anything like that. He's the only person I know who really wouldn't hurt a fly. He'd put it out."

Anna drank her tea, stared out the window and tried to figure out why Rita's remark, harmless enough but for a bit of hyperbole, made her uneasy.

It wasn't until supper had been eaten, the dishes done and the ache in her back fortified against by two Advil, that the answer came. Anna was making her way to the privy, an action which, forever after, would make her think of mice, when she realized what bothered her.

Rita had known what "the mouse thing" was.

sixteen

Colorado was arguably one of the most beautiful states in the Union. Probably among the most scenic areas on earth. At least parts of it were. The Rollin' Roost RV park was not one of these parts. What was gilt-edged summer ten miles west was sunbaked doldrums outside Heath's window. Another thing Heath missed about being ambulatory: now it was such a production getting in and out of anywhere, she could no longer just "run out for cigarettes" when guests threatened to bore her to death, a fate that seemed ever more probable as the woman on the couch babbled on. And on.

Gwen, who had a sixth sense about who was going to be excruciatingly tedious, made her escape early on the scooter. The limpet was, after all, Heath's pet project. She pulled her gaze back into the well-appointed recreation vehicle, grown claustrophobic from too many hours, and now too many people, inside. Had she the legs of Man O' War she knew she wouldn't have left anyway. The hungry, hurt, hopeful, hopeless face of Beth Dwayne, her very own limpet, kept her more firmly rooted to her seat than her damaged spinal cord could. This was the third "supervised visit" that had been allowed since she and her aunt moved into the Rollin' Roost four days before. The first had been with full retinue: Momma, Poppa and Alexis Sheppard filling in what space remained after the plump Mrs. Dwayne and her daughter squeezed in around Heath's wheelchair. Later it was just Sharon Sheppard and Mrs. Dwayne in attendance. Now just Mrs. Dwayne. Heath asked after Alexis but had been told only that she "hadn't been feeling well." Heath had hoped, finally, she'd have a chance to really talk with Beth, but that was not happening.

Beth's mom had grown way too comfortable. For the past hour—Heath glanced at her watch, *half-hour, just four o'clock, sixty minutes before alcohol was socially accept-able*—Mrs. Dwayne had been droning on about Mr. Sheppard, his great deeds, his love of the Lord, his special connection with heaven and with Mrs. Dwayne.

Anna Pigeon suspected Mrs. Dwayne of being another Mrs. Sheppard, and Heath agreed. Had the woman not been so god-awful boring, she might even have felt sympathy for her. She was dumpy and plain and older than the lithe, blond Mrs. Sheppard. The green-eyed monster was catholic in nature and no respecter of cults, creeds or customs. Again she looked at her watch. *Four-oh-two.* Heath was rather surprised she'd not given up and gone home to her cozy condo in Boulder. In this first great out-door adventure, she and Gwen hadn't trav-eled more than a couple hours from home. More than once—more than a hundred times were she honest with herself—she'd thought of it. Each time, the limpet's eyes stopped her. For reasons that Heath didn't understand, Beth looked to her as the capa-ble one, the strong one, the trusted one. The one who could move mountains. Not

Ranger Pigeon with her great big gun or Mr. Sheppard with his great big ego or her mother with her great big mouth. Her. Heath Jarrod. A woman broken on a pile of rock and ice. Heath knew she could not lose that look even as she felt a fraud for accepting it.

Four-oh-five. The limpet looked up from where she sat docilely by her mother. *Those eyes.* Heath had to find a way to talk with her. Necessity mothered invention: "Would you like a cherry cordial?" she intruded into Mrs. Dwayne's monologue. "It's quite good, if a little sweet."

The word "sweet" caught the woman's attention. "A cordial? Don't they have alcohol in them?"

"Not enough to matter," Heath lied easily. The cherry cordial in Gwen's private stash was a hundred and eighty proof, but Heath kept that to herself.

"Maybe a taste," Mrs. Dwayne said.

Heath poured enough over ice to take out a regiment of Cossacks and gave it to Beth's mother, then put a couple of tablespoons in a glass of ice water so she could keep her guest company.

The piously abstemious Mrs. Dwayne took to drink with a passion. Within a quarter of an hour she'd sucked down a third of the syrupy stuff. Within half an hour she was waxing rhapsodic about Heath's great kindness to her family. By twenty minutes of five she was revealing herself as a mean drunk.

"Sharon—*Mrs.* Sheppard—is no better than she should be," she confided owlishly. "When she was brought to us she was a skinny little pinch of a girl, fifteen or sixteen—I can't remember. Her folks had come down from our sister group in Canada but they didn't last long. Oh no. The desert just wasn't good enough for them. *Mr. Sheppard* wasn't good enough for them," she added, as if this proved what ungrateful malcontents they truly were. "According to the divine couple, Elijah Farmer, this *Canadian*, for heaven's sake—oh, he was an American but that wears right off after a few years if you ask me—was the prophet and Mr. Sheppard was just a big nothing. That didn't go over with Mr. Sheppard at all." She laughed a nasty little laugh. "Didn't he just send them packing! But little Miss Sharon, all baby-blue eyes and cotton-candy hair. She had her sights set, that's all I'm going to say. Had 'em set way high, snooting around like a golden virgin child. Well. I had my doubts about that and I told Mr. Sheppard as much. But you know men, even those chosen by God, have penises." This last word was whispered, hissed actually, as if the male appendage was a form of demonic possession visited upon half the human race. "It made him crazy for her. He would have her. So he did. And Alexis is no better. Little tramp. Serves Sharon right. She's getting just what she deserves. It wouldn't surprise me one little bit if Alexis took the girls up into the hills for whatever, then came traipsing back when she tired of the game."

Mrs. Dwayne had begun slurring her words. The glass was empty. Heath smiled. "Can I get you another glass? Talking is thirsty work," she offered.

"Just a wee sip," Mrs. Dwayne demurred.

By six, the woman was out cold, slumped in an untidy heap on the sofa, snoring loudly.

Heath took the glass from her hand and set it on the counter. For what seemed like a very long time Beth stared at the grumbling heap that was her mother. "Will she be all right?" she finally asked.

"She'll be fine," Heath said. "How about

you? Will you be fine?" She rolled close to the sofa. "You can talk to me, you know."

Beth looked at her mother, snoring peacefully two feet away.

"She's asleep. Nobody can hear us but Wiley, and he's good at keeping secrets."

"You won't tell anybody, will you?" She shot a significant look at the snorer lest Heath be unaware who "anybody" was.

"I won't," Heath swore. "Scout's honor."

"Like Daniel Boone?"

The question made Heath acutely aware of how little their home schooling was going to prepare them for the greater world. But that wasn't its aim. Keeping them in the fold was closer to the mark.

"Yeah," Heath said, not wanting to get sidetracked into Boy Scouts and Girl Scouts, Brownies and Bluebirds.

"Robert talked to me and Alexis," Beth told her.

"I know. Said goodbye and that he was going to find Candace. That lady ranger called and told me."

"No." Beth leaned forward till her face was scarcely a foot from Heath's, and whispered, "Since then."

"He came again?"

The girl nodded.

"What did he want?"

"He told us that Candace was alive and he knew how to find her." Given the cheery message, the sudden tears that accompanied it were incongruous. They splattered on the lenses of Beth's old-fashioned glasses, then trickled beneath the plastic frame.

Despite the tears and big eyes, she didn't sound terribly frightened. More hopeful than anything. Hopeful for what? That their friend still lived? And what did the tears indicate? Relief? Sorrow?

Several days had passed since Heath last talked with Anna Pigeon. Last she'd heard, Robert was still missing and still the prime suspect in the abduction. Not wanting to frighten Beth back into the web of secrecy and lies she'd been trapped in, Heath carefully asked, "How is it that he knows where she is?"

Clearly Beth hadn't given this much thought. She was of an age when facts, or purported facts, are shoveled at children by the truckload. Not having the experience to weigh them, all information is more or less accepted at face value, the proclamations of the sages given the same weight as those of the girl sitting one row ahead in home-room.

"I guess he found her," Beth said finally.

"And then he came back to New Canaan? When?"

"Last night. That's why I had to see you today, to tell you Candace is okay."

"You actually saw Robert last night?" Heath was trying not to sound too anything: too skeptical, too excited, too interested.

The limpet looked toward her mother but Mrs. Dwayne was down for the count. "We didn't *see* him, exactly, but he talked to us."

"How did he talk to you if you didn't see him? He came to your bedroom window or what?"

"No. Alexis and I don't sleep together. I'm still in the girls' quarters with the little kids. But every night after the evening service it's our job to take the trash out to the barrels behind the house and burn it. It's fun, lighting fires."

Heath nodded. As a girl she'd had pyromaniacal tendencies as well. She loved fire. Couldn't leave it alone. When her father found her playing with fire behind the big propane tank, it had scared him so much he changed the rules. Instead of being forbidden to ignite things she was given permission to play with fire all she wanted as long as she did it under his supervision. The apprenticeship had served her well. Regardless of weather, she could get a campfire going when others failed.

"So you were out burning the garbage," she said. "What happened then?"

"Well, it was dark and the cans are pretty far out. There's brush all around and we heard Robert's voice. He said Candace was okay."

For a while they sat in silence, Mrs. Dwayne snoring softly, Beth looking at Heath as if she expected her to pull a rabbit out of a hat or something similarly miraculous. Heath was fresh out of rabbits, out of magic of any kind. She needed help. She needed to talk to Ranger Pigeon. She needed to shift this burden of love and trust off onto a person who could deal with it. A whole person. In the end she knew she couldn't. Abled or disabled, she was the one Beth had chosen as her champion.

"What else?" she asked gently.

"Robert asked us to go with him."

That sent a shaft of ice down Heath's spine. "He did?"

"He said to follow him."

"Did you want to?"

Beth didn't choose to answer but Heath could see the indecision, temptation warring with fear in her face.

"Momma came out then, hollering for us, and we had to go in."

Thank god for Momma, Heath thought. So many questions needed answering it was a physical hardship to keep herself from riding roughshod over the child. The missing weeks, Candace, Heath sensed these were not areas Beth could go into yet.

"Why might you want to leave home?" she asked instead.

For a while she didn't think Beth was going to tell her. The girl looked to her comatose mother, to Wiley, flopped on the rug in front of the sink, out the window at the enormous RV parked next door. "We wouldn't. Not really, I guess. I mean, where would we go? We're not even old enough to drive. But Alexis wants to a lot. She says it's hard not being in the girls' quarters anymore. Maybe Robert could take care of us." She looked pleadingly up at Heath. "You know, till we're old enough to get jobs."

That was a lot more answer than Heath

had bargained for, and she felt a wave of helplessness so great it put that of merely not walking for a few decades to shame. She wanted to grab the child and hold her safe from the shadowy evils that permeated her young life but she didn't even have a firm grip on what those evils were, what menaced the limpet from without and what from within. Feeling a failure but not knowing what else to do, she changed the subject.

"What's wrong with Alexis? Your mom said she wasn't feeling well."

The disappointment in Beth's eyes stung. The declaration that followed stunned her. "Morning sickness," Beth said matter-of-factly.

"Who is the father?" Heath asked, attempting to sound as calm and accepting as her young friend.

This question brought on the embarrassment and horror that Heath had felt was missing from the original declaration.

"Oh no. Oh no." The limpet curled down into the couch reminding Heath of the girl she'd been when she'd first come out of the woods.

"Does it have to do with the time you can't remember?" Heath asked gently.

Beth looked like a small animal cornered by wolves. Heath thought to retract her question, then decided to let it lie. Whatever had happened to the children during the weeks they were missing, it would be a boon psychologically if they could talk about it.

The annoying Mrs. Dwayne chose this moment to puff and snort herself awake. Heath could happily have strangled her but Beth looked relieved.

"My goodness!" Mrs. Dwayne exclaimed. "I must have been more tired than I thought. We'd best be getting home." With a minimum of lurching and stumbling, she gathered her purse and her daughter and loaded them into the old Dodge Caravan the New Canaanites shared.

Heath felt mildly guilty allowing an inebriate behind the wheel, but consoled herself with the thought that there wasn't much to collide with between Rollin' Roost and the commune, and the rough dirt road would keep Mrs. Dwayne's speed down.

Watching them go, she realized how desperately she, too, needed to move, to be free of the aluminum box she was calling home at the moment.

Having lowered herself down on the hydraulic lift, she rolled around to the other side of the RV where she could see the mountains. Heath was as tired as if she'd scaled the highest peak in the Rockies. For the first time since the fall, she realized there were more challenging and worthwhile mountains to climb than those made of granite and ice.

seventeen

Raymond gave up his bunk and slept in the room dedicated to tools. The mattress on the bunk Anna claimed was old and flat, the metal mesh sprung, but after a night spent on granite and manzanita it felt like the Plaza Hotel on Central Park to her. She was asleep long before Rita deemed it time to turn in. Regardless of the relentless ache from nape to knees, she might have gone on sleeping through the night had it not been for Fern Lake Cabin's legacy of mice. Or what she first took to be mice.

A noise which, to a sleep-drugged mind, sounded like the squeak of a sizable rodent, forced Anna awake in the strange chill hours between midnight and dawn. Through the wall she bunked against came the sounds of mutterings and thrashings and bumpings. *Too big to be mice.* For a while Anna lay staring at the slightly darker darkness of the bunk over hers, hoping for a return to silence and, if she was lucky, the analgesic of sleep.

Having served her time in tents and other thin-walled communal living situations, she wasn't terribly surprised when the thumps settled into the rhythmic pulse of the mating dance. Knowing she would disturb no one, Anna clicked on the tiny Mag-Lite she carried as part of her standard pocket detritus. Three-forty-seven A.M. The bottom bunk opposite was unoccupied, as she'd expected it would be. At least her rest had not been broken entirely in vain. One mystery was solved: why Rita, a backcountry ranger who hiked for a living, would go hiking into Fern Lake on her day off. Anna smiled and switched off the Mag-Lite. If a Christian were hell-bent on a little fornication, Fern Lake was certainly a beautiful place for it.

Morning came as a misery. Each and

every tissue in Anna's back begged her not to move, screamed at her as she pulled on her shorts and shirt, and tried in every way possible to convince her that she'd aged forty years overnight. She winced out into the living area to find Ray and Rita drinking coffee and looking annoyingly bright-eyed and bushy-tailed. Spurred on by a temporary hatred of all good cheer, she said, "The mice were certainly restive last night."

Ray smiled enigmatically. Rita said, "I didn't hear anything. I turned in half an hour after you did and slept like a log."

Anna's crusty old soul was gratified to find the young woman was not as averse to lying as she would have people believe.

Coffee, instant oatmeal with cinnamon and raisins, and moving her muscles restored Anna to civility. She thanked Ray for his hospitality and left the two of them to linger over breakfast. Because the hike out was relatively easy and because it was her duty, Anna inspected the campground before heading down the mountain.

Like most sites in national parks, the Fern Lake camps were a ways from the lake. With increased visitation and increased awareness of the impacts on water systems, the days of campsites at the lake's edge had gone the way of cutting evergreen boughs to make a bed and digging trenches around tents to keep the rainwater out.

Campers were, for the most part, good custodians of the park, but in Rocky Mountain, an easy Friday afternoon's drive from the major urban center of Denver, visitation was relentless. It was a weekend recreation area with all that entailed: beer parties, half-assed adventures, sports people who liked to run, bike or fish in the park. The mix made campground patrol and maintenance as never-ending and important as housework.

Raymond had not been doing a damn thing. Fern Lake camp was a mess. Fire rings had been built, used and rebuilt. Tree trunks were dragged around to create benches. Each of the sites was provided with a bear-proof canister chained to a tree to provide safe food storage for visitors. One was vandalized. One was gone. Why anyone would bother packing chain-cutting tools in for the pleasure of packing out a cheap, heavy, ugly metal box was beyond Anna's comprehension. But then so was a lot of what passed for entertainment among her fellow human beings.

Bleeker had five years as a backcountry ranger. The dereliction couldn't be written off to inexperience. Laziness. Indifference. "Disrespect for the land," Anna hissed. The prolonged search gave him some small excuse but not much. Anna guessed that the search had taken up his district ranger's time and attention and, when the cat was away . . .

Mice.

At Rocky everything seemed to come back to mice.

It crossed her mind to hike back to the cabin and discuss campground responsibilities but she decided against it. Bleeker needed to be called down and addressed in the confines of the ranger station on Anna's turf and Anna's schedule.

Ray Bleeker's season ended September seventeenth. Two weeks—less, she realized as she reached into her brain to retrieve the day's date. There wasn't much point in firing him but neither would he be working at Rocky Mountain next summer, not if Anna had any say in the matter. He would be reprimanded. It was to be hoped that would be sufficient to motivate him to do his work.

Destroying and rehabilitating the fire rings would take him at least three days.

About thirty minutes down the trail she found the bear-proof food storage box. It had been tossed into a pile of broken granite when the thief realized he wasn't having as much fun with a chunk of metal alloy as he'd thought he was going to. Having retrieved it, she tied it to her daypack. Though the metal was nothing special, the construction simple and the design slightly older than that of the wheel, she was glad to have recovered it. The box might be cheap but it was not inexpensive. Nothing the federal government bought ever went on sale.

Anna radioed ahead and Emily was waiting at the trailhead to give her a ride. Knowing that once she got home a hot bath would beckon and the odds against her getting anything constructive accomplished would be significantly increased, she asked to be taken straight to the district ranger station off Bear Lake Road.

Rocky had a glitzy new Visitors' Center with administrative offices at the east entrance of the park. The offices there were carpeted, well lighted, and the Visitors' Center had all the bells and whistles, including a beautiful four-hundred-seat theater and a gift shop. The Thompson River District station was more traditional—and more to her liking. Small, old, it had been built with other purposes in mind and converted to a ranger station later in life. The place smelled of stale wood smoke and pine and, of course, mice. It reassured her that she was indeed in a national park and not a cubicle in a city somewhere.

Her office was a delight. It had been added on to the original structure, probably for use as a sunroom. Many-paned windows enclosed three sides of the small rectangular room, and pine-filtered light gave a sense of being out-of-doors. In winter it would probably be impossible to keep warm. In late summer it was a pleasure to serve there.

Her first order of business was to call the chief ranger and report on her misadventure at Picnic Rock. Lorraine would take it from there, informing Colorado law enforcement that the search for Robert Proffit was no longer a matter of mere courtesy but one of law.

Anna's next task confirmed the urgency of the appeal. A message had been left on her desk to call Heath Jarrod. Jarrod told her of Robert's visit to the girls, his attempt to lure them away from New Canaan, and Alexis' purported pregnancy. As Anna dutifully relayed this new information to Lorraine, she roundly cursed the New Canaanites for refusing to allow rape kits to be taken when the girls first reappeared. Given that the children were all they had of the crime scene—wherever the hell that was—the DNA and trace evidence on their persons might have meant the difference between solving the case and not.

After spending several hours of what was deemed by the bureaucracy to be necessary paperwork, Anna felt it was legal, moral and ethical to go home though it was only four-thirty.

Hours in a chair had undone any good gleaned from her hike down the mountain. Muscles and sinews in her back had grown stiff and ached like the dickens. As she pulled the Crown Vic under the carport of her rental house, she realized she needed emotional heat more than physical. Paul's voice, or words of love transmitted via cyberspace, loomed even larger in her vision of heaven than a long, exceedingly

hot bath and a bed without rocks and manzanita as its main structural components.

Anna had reason to regret her priorities.

There were several e-mails from Paul.
Witty, kind and beginning with the salutation that always made her go weak at the
knees and fall in love all over again: "My
darling wife." But before she was done
reveling in the knowledge that she missed
him, truly deeply missed him, missed him
even more than she was enjoying her solitude, she noticed an unfamiliar address:
goodnews@slipstream.com.

Anna had never heard of Slipstream but
that didn't concern her. The net evolved
exponentially. In moments of weakness she
could almost believe the takeover of earth
by The Machines was in the not-so-distant
future. What gave her a creepy feeling was
the "goodnews." Some repressed memory
of early Sunday school trauma suggested,
though the news might be good, it sure as
hell wasn't going to be good for *her*. For
the briefest of moments she considered
deleting it unread. For a slightly longer
period of time she toyed with the idea of

putting off reading it till she'd had her bath. Dismissing both thoughts as cowardly, she opened it.

Dear Mrs. Pigeon: I wanted you to know it was an accident. I hiked out as fast as I could and told Rita to go get you. I hope your few hours in the gorge weren't too uncomfortable. Yours in Christ, R.

Robert Proffit. Anna was getting right royally sick of that boy.

Chances were he was a kidnapper, murderer and pervert. That made him of professional interest. Pushing her over a cliff made him of personal interest. Those wishing to evade the law should never make themselves personally interesting. Proffit was not only responsible for the ache in her back, but now condemned her to postponing the longed-for panacea of a hot bath.

She re-read the short message, forwarded a copy to Chief Ranger Knight and took her creaky body back out to her patrol vehicle.

It was only as she revved the engine to scare away any cats as was her habit since

Piedmont had come to keep her company nearly a decade before, that she realized Hector—Hecuba—the little scaredy cat Beth and she had rescued from the vile boys, hadn't come to the door to greet her as Piedmont always did, hadn't made an appearance at all.

Feeling snubbed, she promised herself a pleasant evening of buying the kitten's love with bits of tuna. The way to a cat's heart is long and torturous but through the stomach was a good place to start.

The e-mail said Proffit hiked out as fast as he could and referred to Anna's sojourn in the bottom of Tourmaline Gorge as a "few hours"—about the amount of time it would take for a round trip on foot from Picnic Rock to Bear Lake and back. He said he'd told Rita. A lot of things didn't match up with Rita Perry's version of the events: told, not left a note; specificity—Rita had insisted she hadn't known precisely where Anna was or what had happened; the time frame.

If Rita Perry had left her lying in Tourmaline Gorge twenty hours longer than she had to, Anna would know the reason why. The obvious was that she waited in hopes that Anna would die. Then why come at all?

Curiosity? Remorse? Or had she become frightened Robert would tell someone and it would come out that she'd known and not responded? Any of those explanations would work except for one glaring fact. Anna was not dead. Had Rita wanted her dead, instead of levering the rock off her legs she could simply have bashed her head in. As she had not availed herself of the opportunity to crush Anna's skull, it had to be assumed Rita wanted to keep her alive. Or didn't want her dead yet. It was possible Rita had left her there overnight because she wanted Anna out of the way for twenty-four hours.

No. Rita was too sane to rely on the fact that the person she wanted out of the way was going to accidentally get knocked off a big rock and trapped under a boulder at precisely the right moment in time. The other possibility was that Robert Proffit was lying. But then so was Rita, even if only by omission.

Rita's quarters were next door to the district ranger station on Bear Lake Road. She shared a snug little two-bedroom house with one of the female research seasonals, a woman in her fifties or sixties whom Anna had met but hadn't had a chance to get to know.

The rules of search and seizure forbade Anna from breaking into Rita's quarters, but if Rita's roommate invited her in, which she was sure to do, Anna could check out the shared portions of the house where Rita could not be said to have an expectation of privacy. *Sort of like a vampire*, Anna thought. Once invited in by one dwelling there . . .

The turn into the ranger station always came as a surprise: a narrow break in the trees, a hairpin drive dropping steeply down to the left. Rita's car was parked in the gravel pull-out, but then it would be. Parking at Rocky was at a premium, particularly at Bear Lake. Rita would have bummed a ride from another ranger.

Anna knocked on the door and her half-baked theory was blasted. Rita Perry answered. She must have hiked out a few hours after Anna. Remembering the revels of the previous night, it was surprising she'd not opted to remain at Fern till her lieu days were over.

The merest flicker of joy warmed the planes of Rita's handsome face when she saw who stood on her doorstep. Immediately it was quenched as if by a sudden memory of past wrongs or planned betrayals. "You haven't even showered," she blurted out.

"Can you smell me?" Anna asked amiably.

"Not from here. I mean no. It's just I know how good it feels. You must have been busy."

"I have," Anna said. "May I come in?"

"Oh gosh, the place is a mess . . ."

From their brief acquaintance Anna knew this was an exceedingly un-Rita-like thing to say. Downright unranger-like. In her years in the parks Anna couldn't recall a single person in the green and gray uttering that phrase regardless of the domestic disaster behind them.

Before the social interaction could deteriorate further, a cheery round face appeared at Rita's elbow. Donna, her housemate, was a foot shorter than the law enforcement ranger and at least two decades older. From the ocean of new information Anna had jumped into on coming to Rocky, she miraculously fished out the woman's name and specialty. "How's the bighorn sheep census going, Donna?"

"Today we had a regular sheep jam—come in, come in. It gets cold at night. At least it keeps the mosquitoes down."

Rita stepped aside to let Anna pass. Anna smiled sweetly. Or what she hoped was sweetly and not that happy grin dogs get when they're about to catch a particularly noisome cat.

The place wasn't a candidate for a Good Housekeeping award but it was no more messy than shared and temporary quarters tended to be. The clutter was of the usual park variety: backpacks, boots, tents, water bottles and sleeping bags.

One cache of goods was of particular interest to Anna. A bag, pillow and a stuff sack of clothes were neatly pushed against the brick hearth. Beside them were a battered shaving kit, a pair of flip-flops and a Bible.

The flip-flops were too big for Rita, substantial though her feet were.

Anna crossed to the hearth and picked up the well-thumbed Bible. It was small, the cover black leather or leatherette, the kind routinely given out at confirmation.

"Nice Bible. May I?" she said, looking at Rita.

Rita nodded, defeat or acceptance hard around her mouth.

Anna flipped open the Bible and read the inscription: "For Robert. Love, Aunt Connie."

"It's Robert Proffit's."

Rita got no points for frankness. Too little and way too late.

Anna looked pointedly at the oversized flip-flops and the shaving kit.

"Oh dear," Donna muttered.

"Robert was staying with me for a few days," Rita said, her customary fire and defiance back.

"We didn't say anything because seasonals aren't allowed to have guests," Donna said all in a rush. "But he was such a nice young man—"

"Seasonals can have guests if they want," Anna interrupted, keeping her eyes on Rita. "Just not guests who are suspected of kidnap and murder."

"Oh Lord!" Donna gasped.

"Do you want to come up to the office so we can have a talk?" Anna asked Rita.

The young woman preceded her out of

the house without another word. Walking behind her, Anna couldn't help but admire her strong straight back—a back which probably was not aching like a son-of-a-bitch—and wide shoulders. At six-foot, she was a head taller than Anna and considerably younger. In a fair fight, there was no doubt she would prevail. Anna never fought fair. On the rare occasions she had resorted to the crude imperative of physical force, she'd fought to win, or at least survive. Tonight she wasn't much concerned with self-defense. Rita had had her chance.

With Rita Perry, Anna faced an obstacle significantly greater than mere brute power. The look of the martyr about to die for the faith had returned. Surely Proffit wasn't whom she was metaphorically willing to burn at the stake for, not after the hijinks Anna had been an aural witness to the previous night, but one never knew. Religion often found justification for appetite.

Rita unlocked the ranger station and went inside. Anna switched on the overhead light. The sun had gone behind the mountains and twilight in the trees came early. "Have a seat." She nodded to the Formica-topped folding table in front of a stone fireplace that looked as if it had not been used—or cleaned—since JFK was president.

Rita did as she was asked. Anna sat across from her, wincing as she lowered herself into the chair.

"Oooh, ouch! Are you hurting bad?" Rita asked sympathetically. "I can probably get you some Valium. We've got an excellent working relationship with our On Call. You're gonna seize up tonight's my bet. Second night's the worst."

The sympathy annoyed Anna. Not because she thought it was feigned; Rita—like Robert Proffit, Anna reminded herself—was ultimately quite believable. Anna believed her but she'd learned the hard way that simply because one believes they see little green men, pink elephants, gray-skinned aliens or angels does not mean these creatures are really there. Personal truth is a subjective thing and Anna had yet to discover any universal truths.

The reason the sympathy grated was because she wanted it, wanted another human being to say, "There, there, you poor dear. Here's a Valium. Let me draw you a hot bath and rub your back." Rita hadn't gone quite that far but she did offer the emotional warmth and the muscle relaxant.

Using irritation to stiffen her aching spine, Anna brushed off both sympathy and the offer of drugs. "I'm fine," she said curtly. "I'd have been better had I not lain on a rock and pointy sticks for twenty-four hours. We're going to need to go over how you came to rescue me, but first, Robert Proffit. How long has he been living with you?"

Rita looked offended. "He wasn't living with me. He was staying with me."

Anna hadn't made the distinction. It was clear Rita wanted the record set straight; she was not having sexual intercourse with Robert. *If she worried about her reputation as a good Christian girl, she should keep in mind how thin the cabin walls are*, Anna thought sourly. Maybe Rita only needed to clarify that she was not having sex with Proffit to distance herself from him now that he was a fugitive or because she didn't want that rumor reaching Ray Bleeker. Like all small, isolated communities, national parks were hotbeds of gossip.

"How long has he been staying with you?" Anna amended.

"Only a few days. He's a friend. He

needed someplace to go. He was determined to find out what happened to Candace Watson. The obvious place to start was back to the beginning, the area around Odessa Lake."

"Okay," Anna said. "Not informing me Robert was in the park when you knew I wanted to talk to him might have been rude, inconsiderate, stupid or even dangerous, but it wasn't illegal and it wasn't against NPS regulations. While I might not like it, I won't make you suffer for your decision. Now Robert Proffit is wanted for questioning. He's a suspect in the kidnap of the girls, the possible kidnap/murder of Candace Watson, and knocking me off a rock. You help him again and you are aiding and abetting a fugitive. I will come down on you with both feet. Is that understood?"

"Yes, ma'am."

A few years before, Anna might have been impressed by the "ma'am" but Mississippi had spoiled her. Everybody called her "ma'am" except the very little kids and they called her "Miss Anna," which delighted her no end.

"You are a federal law enforcement officer. Your responsibility goes deeper than that of an ordinary citizen. If Proffit calls you, you tell me. If he comes by for his stuff, you tell me. If he writes, sends e-mail or smoke signals, you tell me."

"Yes, ma'am."

"Good." Anna relaxed the hard-nosed boss persona and let the crackle of anger drain from the room. The discovery that Proffit had been living twenty yards from where she parked her patrol car every morning irked her more than she cared to admit. Nobody liked being made a fool of.

When her rattled nerves settled and Rita Perry recovered from the lecture, Anna began again.

Rita stuck to her story. Robert hadn't seen her. He'd left a note. The note said only to tell Anna it was an accident and that he was leaving. No, she didn't still have the note; she'd thrown it in the trash. Yes, the trash had been taken to the dump.

Asked the same questions for the second time, Rita acted more affronted than guilty until Anna brought up the bloody backpack.

Again Anna was struck by the lengths Rita went not to tell an outright lie. Sexual misconduct was evidently the only transgression she felt heinous enough to warrant true dissembling.

"All I can tell you is that I love this park. I've worked here every year since college. This is my park. I wait tables and coach girls' basketball in Jackson the six months I'm not here, just marking time till my season starts again. I would never ever do anything that might hurt the park. And I would do anything—almost anything—for the park's welfare."

Not an answer to Anna's question but a good enough little speech, delivered with just the right touch of fanaticism. The environment needed zealots. Anna's concern was that what Rita might deem to be in the park's best interest and what truly was might be entirely different things. Maybe Rita thought finding the sliced and diced remains of a local teenager within NPS boundaries would reflect badly on the park and had decided to keep it her little secret.

Rita was right, of course. It would look bad. Anna sighed. "Think about it. We'll talk again." She pushed herself to her feet, careful not to wince or groan lest it elicit another outpouring of debilitating kindness.

"By the way, do you have Robert's e-mail address?" she asked.

"Yeah. Goodnews dot something—not one of the biggies. Not AOL or Yahoo! Slip or slippery. I can get it for you." Rita was anxious to be of help now that she had been so assiduously of no help for the past hour.

"Tomorrow's soon enough."

Anna entered her house calling, "Here, kitty, kitty." Guilt over having forgotten about her new ward when she'd come home the first time, coupled with the need to feel warmth and hear purring, made her anxious to see Hecuba.

The kitten wasn't downstairs. Her food and water bowls were still full. Bedroom and bath were on the second floor and the bath was calling her nearly as forcefully as the need to reconnect with feline kind. Nearly. Shucking clothes as she went upstairs, Anna talked kitty-cat nonsense to lure the little beast out from wherever she'd hidden. Entering the bedroom, she switched on the overhead light.

Her bed was a charnel house. Burns and blood and bile were smeared over half the coverlet. In the middle of the mess were the charred remains of a kitten-sized corpse, bits of black fur in pathetic patches between burns so deep, bone showed through.

Sorrow so heavy she could not stand under the weight of it settled on Anna. Keeping her back to the carnage, she sat on the corner of the bed and buried her face in her hands. She didn't cry. The misery of knowing anyone could destroy so perfect a life was too great for the release of tears. A part of her knew she should be afraid. This taker of beauty and lives might still be in the house. Fear did not move her. Surely cruelty that great would leave a palpable miasma of evil behind.

She might have stayed paralyzed on the edge of the defiled coverlet for some time had not something reached out from beneath the bed and grabbed her ankle.

eighteen

Gwen wasn't happy, Heath could tell, but her aunt had steeled herself to say nothing, and she appreciated it. Gwen had wanted her to find a new interest in life. She simply hadn't bargained on that interest being a damaged child who brought with her ghosts with sharp sticks and a commune lorded over by a patriarch who was far from reassuring.

Though retired, Dr. Littleton still delivered babies for a chosen few. Many of the babies she'd delivered were now having babies of their own and wanted no one but her to preside over their introduction to the world.

She'd been called back to Boulder to attend just such an event and she had to go.

Heath had to stay. She'd dropped her aunt off at her condominium in the center of the small booming city and driven the RV back to the glamorous outpost of Rollin' Roost.

When she'd told Gwen she planned to stay on at the RV park for a while, her aunt had asked her what good she thought she could do. Heath hadn't been able to articulate an answer. She just had to be here. Rather like her grandfather, who attended all weddings, funerals, bar mitzvahs and ball games, she believed in the value of showing up, of being there, being seen to support, to celebrate, to participate in the events of other peoples' lives. Heath had chosen to show up. The limpet knew she was here. For the moment that was good enough.

But for bits and scraps of time, Heath hadn't been alone since she'd fallen. Always there were nurses, therapists, her aunt— someone within call who would be coming by to prod, poke or check on her. Sitting outside the RV, beside the scarred picnic table, watching the light fade over the eastern plains, no help, hindrance, company or annoyance near but for Wiley, who was more entranced by the possibility of a crepuscular jackrabbit than the needs of his mistress, she wasn't sure how she felt about it.

Good, she decided. Good, and good and scared.

Sitting outside alone had taken an act of courage. The frightened woman who'd come to replace the valiant climber when Heath lost the use of her legs, urged her to cower indoors behind locks. Anger rather than courage lent her the impetus to come out. She was damned if she would let one visitation by voices armed with rocks and sticks rob her of this peculiar joy.

Sticks and stones. She better than most knew they might break bones.

Like a badly cut film, the memory of the night she'd been attacked played through her mind. The fire. The crawling on her belly like a reptile. Hiding under the RV. Smashing Ranger Pigeon's foot with a rock.

The last image made her laugh out loud. Despite herself, Anna Pigeon was growing on her. Pigeon was a flinty sort, not given to warm fuzzies. Heath wasn't used to that; she had grown up with a mother and an aunt from the South. Still and all, she had come to rather like the fact that Anna treated her without deference. Around the feisty ranger, Heath had come to feel like a perfectly good specimen of humanity who happened to travel by chair rather than a vague embarrassment to the belegged and ambulatory race of bipeds.

The sound of tires leaving the hum of the pavement for the crunch of gravel brought her out of her musings. Wiley went on alert, rabbits forgotten in the promise of bigger game. The car, lights blinding Heath to make and model, drove past the one other occupant of the scabrous camp and came toward her site. Wiley took up his position at her right knee.

"Good boy," Heath whispered. And swallowed the urge to roll quickly to the RV and, raising the hydraulic lift behind her like a drawbridge, hide within.

The car stopped. Heath exhaled, realizing a part of her had expected to be run down. Fear was insidious. Once it settled into the soul, even the most preposterous threats seemed real and imminent.

Headlights switched off. A car door creaked open, slammed shut. Heath squinted through the thick dusk trying to ascertain whether her caller was a Bible salesman or the Grim Reaper.

It was neither. The slightly ethereal form of Mrs. Sheppard materialized out of the gloom and dust.

"Please can we go inside?" were her first words.

Heath was glad to comply. If it was somebody else's idea, she could retreat with dignity.

Mrs. Sheppard sat on the couch without waiting to be asked. Heath was unoffended. Now that she was perpetually seated, she preferred that to having people loom about. The woman was distraught. The times Heath had seen her before, she'd been . . . not aloof, aloof was a choice . . . she seemed distanced, disconnected, as if there was a part of her she held safe—or prisoner—in a place others could not go.

Mrs. Sheppard was dressed in her usual denim jumper and cheap flat shoes. Sitting with her feet together, knees clamped tightly, she smoothed the fabric over her thighs again and again, palms pressing out invisible wrinkles.

"I feel like a fool coming to you," she said

without looking up. "But we're not from here and there is nobody else."

"I'm flattered," Heath said dryly, then immediately felt guilty for being a smartass.

She got a bye. Sharon Sheppard was so caught up in her own misery, if she heard the remark, it didn't register. "Alexis is pregnant," she said abruptly.

Beth had told her as much, but since it was privileged information she was not supposed to know, Heath said, "Ah," for lack of anything more insightful. Then: "How far along is she?"

"Three months. Or four."

That took Heath aback. She'd assumed the pregnancy was a result of whatever had transpired while the girls were missing. Maybe Proffit, if he was the perpetrator, had gotten to the girls before their disappearance. Obviously somebody had.

"Does she know who the father is?"

Mrs. Sheppard looked up for the first time. "Of course!" she snapped and Heath realized her question might have suggested Alexis was a tramp.

"I just thought it might have happened while she was gone. A stranger," Heath explained.

"Oh." Eyes down, Mrs. Sheppard went back to her smoothing. "No. We know. The father is her husband, Mr. Sheppard. Alexis is my little sister."

"Man, that's gotta suck," Heath blurted out.

Without a smile Mrs. Sheppard said, "If 'sucks' means what it sounds like, that's just what it does. Suck. Suck."

Heath thought the woman would start crying, but she didn't. She just sat there pressing and pressing her skirt over her knees. It put Heath in mind of the rocking she'd seen people in the hospital do, people who didn't want to—or couldn't—think. On impulse she reached out and took Sharon Sheppard's hands in hers. For reasons of obstinacy or rebelliousness, Heath hadn't fastened her seat belt. The sudden movement shifted her new center of gravity and she half fell into the younger woman's lap.

"Oh my goodness. Are you okay?" Sharon was holding, helping, making those maternal mutterings that usually brought on a fit of foul language from Heath. Instead, she found herself laughing at her clumsiness. It was grand not to mind toppling. That thought made her laugh harder.

Sharon did not join her but neither did she return to her infernal pressing and she managed a smile, albeit a shaky one.

When Heath had done enjoying the miracle of finding her physical faux pas funny, she said, "What do you need me to do?"

At this unlikely juncture Sharon Sheppard did start crying. "You've been so good to Beth—both girls. I thought maybe you would help. Thought it but didn't believe it. Now I believe. Oh Lord. I have been . . ."

Sharon laughed. There was a hysterical edge to it but it was a sign of life and strength in what Heath had hitherto thought was a Stepford wife.

"I was hoping you could take us somewhere, somewhere we might stay till we can get home."

"Back to the commune in Canada?" Heath was remembering Mrs. Dwayne's drunken diatribe. Surely that would be jumping out of the frying pan and into an old familiar fire.

"No. We wouldn't be welcome there. We'd just be made to come back. Or maybe given to somebody else as wives. I'm old but Alexis is of an age to be sought after."

"How old are you?"

"Twenty. Twenty-one in November."

For a moment Heath said nothing. Sharon easily looked fifteen years older than she was. "How long have you been 'married' to Mr. Sheppard?" Being married to Dwayne Sheppard would be like dog years, aging a woman seven for one.

"Since I was fifteen."

"And Alexis?"

"Six months for her."

"Why do you want to go now? I mean, after all these years and after Alexis has been . . . is pregnant?"

"Because there are three of us. Patty is nine and it's already starting."

"Fucking goat," Heath muttered.

"What did you say?"

"Nothing. Go on. If not Canada, where?"

"Our dad—our real dad—used to live in Lewiston, Idaho. Momma left him years ago and took us girls with her. Maybe he's still there. Maybe he'd take us."

"You haven't seen him in all that time?"

"It wasn't allowed."

"What Mr. Sheppard is doing is massively illegal," Heath said. "Why don't you go to the police?" As soon as the question was out, she was sorry she'd asked. Sharon looked both frightened and scornful, a bizarre combination. She'd evidently been raised to think anything to do with the government—federal, state or local—was both evil and stupid. The authorities were the last people she would turn to for help. Sharon bestirred herself as if to make a dash for the door.

There was no way Heath could undo a lifetime's indoctrination in an evening. "I see your point," she said quickly, though Sharon hadn't made one.

Sharon settled back. Heath tried to come up with a reassuring thought or word. If the three girls could get away, she supposed she could drive them to Lewiston. The trip would tax her physically. The damage to her back was new, outraged nerves and tissues had yet to settle into their final mode. And maybe the father was no longer there. Momma splits, taking the kids. Maybe Poppa Whatever had run from bad memories.

"What's your dad's name?" Heath could at least make a few calls, find out whether the guy was still around, still alive.

"Rupert Evan Dennis," Sharon replied in a measured voice that made Heath think she'd said her father's name many times, repeated it over and over like a mantra.

n i n e t e e n

After the initial jolt of terror, when her heart had started beating once again, Anna was down on all fours, eyes near floor level and filled with tears of joy, relief and other emotions she couldn't begin to name.

She'd been raised with cats. Lots of cats. When she was a baby there'd been little money and a tarpaper shack that had been impossible to keep warm on bitter winter nights. Cats had been allowed—encouraged—to sleep in her crib to keep her warm. Like a little duckling, she'd been imprinted. Enough cat fur and dander had made its way into her body that she would not have been surprised to find she had feline DNA floating about her chromosomes. Anna knew a cat's paw when she felt it grab her ankle.

Hecuba, the little scaredy cat, had learned survival skills under the rough tutelage of wicked boys. She had hidden under the bed and probably saved herself from a painful death. A bit of coaxing and the kitten came out. Dropping tears and kisses indiscriminately on the little creature's head, Anna carried her down to the kitchen and a belated supper out of a can that promised chicken, vegetables and a healthy urinary tract.

Like a lot of kittens, especially those snatched away from their mothers too soon, this little cat purred while she ate. Anna sat on the floor, her back against the cupboard doors, and listened to her favorite music. Why, with all the trauma that had been visited, and continued to be visited, on her new duty station, the life and well-being of one little black-and-white cat should give her such comfort, she didn't know but she recognized a gift horse when it crawled out from beneath her bed. For a time, she was content to enjoy it without even a temptation to look in its mouth.

After Hecuba had gobbled and rattled her dinner down and curled up to sleep, Anna made her a bed of dish towels and nestled her warm soft body into it. Past the knee-weakening first wave of relief and fortified by exposure to one exquisite fur-coated life, she felt able to climb the stairs to the abattoir a psychopath had made of her bedroom.

The carnage was no less horrifying for being expected. Knowing her cat to be safe, Anna was better able to see it in all its ghastly glory. Touching nothing, she examined the animal remains. The burning went deep but she could tell it had been a squirrel, an Abert she assumed from the bits of black fur remaining. The Aberts were particular favorites of hers. She'd never seen them anywhere but the middle West, from Grand Canyon to Rocky. These squirrels were coal black with exceedingly long white-tufted ears. While glad it wasn't Hecuba, Anna grieved for the loss of the small life and, because of the wanton cruelty of it, suffered a cold desire to surgically remove the perpetrator from the land of the living.

Through the sharp odors of burned flesh,

fur and scorched fabric, she could smell an accelerant. Most of it had been consumed but several drops had fallen on the down comforter. Lighter fluid was her guess: cheap, efficient, easy to come by. Also easy to detect, but this crime was committed with detection in mind. The squirrel had been soaked but not the coverlet. The intent was not arson but terror, terror painted in blood and bone, choreographed, as if the perpetrator fancied himself an artist of cruelty.

Or herself.

A woman could as easily ignite a caged squirrel as a man, though Anna had significantly more trouble picturing it. Women could be as brutal as their male counterparts, as unfeeling and possibly even more vicious. Women were also more practical. Evil was done to get, avoid or control. This was done partly to frighten Anna but, from the care taken to stage it, she guessed it had been done mostly for fun.

What remained of the squirrel was beginning to stiffen. The incident had happened several hours earlier, between noon and four or five. Plenty of time for Robert Proffit—or a long-legged woman—to hike out and arrange this nasty surprise. But time to plan it? Aberts weren't common—not rare, but not common. The animal had to be trapped and transported before it was sacrificed. Did the doer of the deed know Anna had adopted a black-and-white kitten? Proffit knew. Maybe. They hadn't found him at the enclave but that didn't mean he hadn't been around, or returned and heard the story from Alexis or Beth. Anna doubted the plan had been that intricate. Had that been the case it would be logical that the wretch— whoever he or she might be—wouldn't have brought the squirrel at all but would have expected to find and kill Hecuba. *All the better to terrorize you, my dear . . .*

Anna tried to picture the handsome, competent Miss Perry in the act of insane evil that had resulted in the ruin of her bedroom, the Abert and her peace of mind. Rita didn't give off those vibes but then neither, it was said, did Ted Bundy. Rita had proven alarmingly unconcerned over Anna's report of the blood-dripping backpack. With her passion for an as yet undiscovered greater good, Rita could probably bring herself to slaughter a squirrel for the cause, whatever it was. Slaughter maybe, but Anna could not see her torturing it or nailing thirteen living mice to an outhouse wall.

The individual she could easily picture tormenting small helpless creatures was Mr. Sheppard. What he might hope to gain from such a theatrical display of wanton cruelty wasn't readily apparent. The crime, though aimed at frightening Anna, was anonymous. There wasn't much that was more personal than butchering an animal in one's bed; anyone who'd seen *The Godfather* knew that. She was being warned away. Away from what was unspecified. Given the only case she'd been in Rocky long enough to be associated with was the kidnap of the girls, she had to make certain assumptions.

Had Sheppard, for reasons of his own, spirited the girls away? Was that why Alexis and Beth were less than anxious to be reunited with their families when they'd finally reappeared? Why they would not say where they had been, where Candace still was? Had Candace been killed or had she chosen to stay gone, taken a bus or hitchhiked out of the clutches of Sheppard?

Speculation was giving Anna a headache, or, rather, adding to the ache that locked back, shoulder and neck in an unkind embrace. The hot bath, like the Holy Grail, seemed a chimera leading her onward, yet never letting her get any closer.

With a sense of doing her duty, yet without much hope that duty would pay off, she called the chief ranger to report the breaking and entering. In truth no actual breakage had occurred. Anna hadn't bothered to lock her doors, a situation that would change until this butcher of squirrels, abductor of teenage girls and disembodied taunter of disabled rock climbers was behind bars.

While she waited for Lorraine and whomever else she deemed necessary to arrive, Anna photographed the grisly bedspread and Abert remains with her 35 mm camera. One day the NPS would graduate to digital. Maybe after patrol rangers were issued cell phones.

The rangers came. Rita Perry wasn't with them. Due to the renewed search for Candace Watson, ranger schedules had been scrambled. Rita was on six ten-hour days, off four. She still had two lieu days coming this rotation.

The crime scene investigation was carried out with diligence, if not optimism. Nothing so delicious as a dusty footprint on the hardwood floors or a hair follicle with DNA was found. The furnishings in Anna's room had been used in Mississippi, packed by broad-shouldered strangers, moved by the kind auspices of half a dozen park employees. Fingerprinting and trace evidence was a complex nightmare that there wasn't time, money or expertise to unravel. The incident, after all, was merely a gruesome prank involving only the death of a squirrel.

Possible motives were bandied about: resentment of Anna as the first female district ranger hired, hostility from family members of the former owners of the house who'd taken umbrage when their widowed mother sold out to the NPS to rent to government employees and moved to Florida with a man half her age. The search. Mr. Sheppard. Robert Proffit.

Anna didn't bring up Rita Perry's name. She had too little to go on and the new kid on the block wasn't going to earn any points accusing a beloved seasonal who was both younger and prettier than she was.

After an excessively long interval during which the rangers surmised, speculated and fumed, Anna resisted the urge to scream and throw herself on the floor in a tantrum of fatigue and muscle rebellion. Finally the party broke up. Anna gathered the four corners of her comforter together and deposited the ruined Abert in his oversized goose-down shroud in the garbage can outside.

Having locked every door, checked the closets, even those too small to harbor a criminal over the age of six, and carried Hecuba up the stairs for company, she at long last lowered her stinking raging body into a bath so hot it stung the skin. Her deep groan of relief brought an answering chirp from the kitten, who sat on the edge of the tub the better to witness this disgusting immersion ritual.

Hecuba was still young enough her brain wasn't yet aware her tail was part of the same cat. She allowed it to fall over the edge, the last two inches in the water. Anna smiled. Smiling was about the only movement that didn't hurt. She wished she had not blown off Rita's offer of Valium. Not that she'd feel particularly comfortable at the moment ingesting any drug provided by her frontcountry ranger.

It crossed her mind to drag Molly or Paul into the tub with her by way of the cell phone. Fearing the sound of a loving voice would be the undoing of her, she settled into the heat with only the cat for company. As she slid down in the niggardly prefab tub, sacrificing her knees to the chill air that she might soak both spine and skull in the hot water, she set about ordering this unconscionably long week in her mind.

Mice. Unkempt campsites. Bleeding pack. Twenty-four hours on the manzanita. The note from Proffit. Rita's lying about it. Proffit's voice luring children. Alexis pregnant. Candace and the other girls, unseen but laughing, prodding at Heath under the RV. Proffit bunking at Rita's, a stone's throw from the Thompson River District ranger station. The butchered Abert.

Working at Rocky Mountain National Park was way more exciting than Anna had bargained for. The days just flew by when others were having fun at one's expense.

Hoping the hot water heater was a big one, she nudged the left knob with her big toe. Her fragmented thoughts floated on the sound of the running water. She didn't examine them too closely, just allowed them to brush by each other, seeing if any connections could be made.

Two things formed out of the mental mist. One that was there too often, and one conspicuous by its absence. Nowhere could she detect money or personal gain. The cases she'd worked in the parks—other than those of spontaneous combustion: a fistfight over a campsite, domestic violence—were fueled by greed. Lust for money, power, prestige. Mostly money. Money could buy the other two. Lesser crimes had been fomented by lesser demons: jealousy, revenge, spite.

In Rocky's mess of mice and squirrels, battered girls and bloody Christians, there didn't seem to be anything to gain. At least nothing a sane person would find alluring.

That brought Anna to the other thing, the thing that appeared too often. The through line, the consistent theme. Murder of the mice was psychotic. Burning the squirrel: psychotic. Disembodied voices, poking at a paraplegic with pointy sticks: psychotic. Battered girls in panties. Psychotic. Stuffing bleeding flesh into backpacks. Major psychotic. A sudden chill took her, despite the steaming water. The winter before, in the high country of Yosemite National Park, she'd dealt with an individual she felt to be genuinely evil, the kind of evil that suffers such a cold indifference to the wants and needs—the very lives—of those around it that to kill a busload of rabbis on their way to temple, simply to obtain an olive for one's martini, wouldn't give the monster pause.

Though she found it unsettling on several levels, Anna could understand that sort of criminal. Dormant, comatose, she told herself with more fervency than an innocent woman would have required, that evil dwelt within her. In the snow of the Sierra it had been called forth. Perhaps it had saved her life. Still, she never wanted to feel its icy grip again.

Whatever—whoever—was torturing rodents and children and bloodying innocent backpacks in the Rockies was different. True evil had logic, desire, goals and a sense of self-preservation. The miasma poisoning Rocky was not so much evil as sickness. A deep festering so putrid and toxic that, in a way, Anna was relieved she could not understand it. A busload of holy men versus an olive . . . well, if one were starving for a bit of pimiento . . . but to *understand* why one would torture the helpless for no other reason than personal enjoyment would be a glimpse into a part of one's mind better left unknown.

One or more persons in or around Rocky was a serial killer of small animals. This person might or might not be one and the same as the abductor of girls—if the girls had indeed been abducted and weren't using the story to cover up running away.

Most of what Anna knew of psychopaths, she had gleaned from movies and books— fiction, not documentary or texts. In America there was a great and fluctuating sea of common knowledge dispersed and ratified by the popular media's echoing what they gleaned from other popular media sources. A lot was inaccurate. Not all of it. That would be too easy. But a lot of it.

Anna "knew" that psychopaths—or was it sociopaths, she really must call Molly—who wanted to grow up to be serial killers customarily started out, often at a heart-stoppingly young age, with the destruction of lesser lives. Like Bram Stoker's Renfield, hoping to work his way up from flies to spiders to mice, then asking in one of the most frightening lines in a truly scary book: "May I have a kitten?"

Given this was true—and where Homo

sapiens were involved, nothing was consis-
tently true—Rocky's own personal psycho
might yet be immature, still in the caterpillar
state where small, legal murders, murders
which, without the torture, were even considered admirable in pest removal circles,
were sufficient to slake the need for pain
and death. Again according to the movies
and paperback thrillers, baby psychos
could be from five years old to teens or possibly early twenties. Then there seemed to
come a decade where they disappeared
into cocoons. A sort of awkward age, too
old to slaughter the family pet, too young to
kill the girl next door.

At age thirty they emerged to meet the
profile: thirties, white, male, often intelligent,
tends to be a loner, could live with Mom.

Robert Proffit was a bit old—and a bit
young—for the overt part of the predatory
pattern, but perhaps he was slower than
others to mature and continued to amuse
himself with small game.

Sheppard was older than the template
and struck Anna more as an abuser, a
tyrant, than a killer. Far more satisfying to
lord it over one's victims for a lifetime than
snuff them out in a moment. No, Sheppard

didn't strike her as a man to break his toys past all mending.

But then no person had been killed, or at least no body found. The saga of Beth, Alexis and the still missing Candace could be one of crime and punishment. The crime: running away. Maybe the punishment, whatever it was, was what Anna was being warned away from sticking her nose in.

Rita Perry resurfaced in Anna's mind. Rita knew of the live mousetrap, the bleeding pack. Rita harbored Robert Proffit. Rita was sleeping with—euphemistically speaking— the Fern Lake ranger, Raymond Bleeker.

Having been handed much guiltier-looking prospects, Anna would have preferred to overlook Bleeker. He had proximity to the mouse incident, the live trap, Odessa Lake and Picnic Rock. The New Canaan enclave and Rollin' Roost were a bit of a stretch, but he was young, strong, owned a car and, judging by the look of the Fern Lake campground, hadn't been spending a whole lot of time doing his job.

As with all law enforcement personnel, Bleeker had undergone a thorough background check prior to being hired. Anna had read it. Nothing popped up in the way of red flags. The man had never been arrested or accused of so much as shoplifting or vandalism. Neither the high school nor the college he attended had anything to say against him but remarked on a tendency to tardiness. His reviews from previous parks were uniformly glowing. In a litigious, feel-good, politically correct world where victimhood was claimed and lauded by many, the rating system for seasonals had become as inflated as the grades in most schools, but managers found ways of cluing in one another: things not said, damning with faint praise. In retrospect the good reports surprised Anna. Maybe Ray had done a better job in other parks than he was doing at Fern Lake. Rita might be proving a distraction. Backcountry/frontcountry romances required a lot of hours on the trail.

Sheppard would have been checked out by both the NPS and local law enforcement during the search. Such was the cynical nature of the law, when children went missing, moms and dads were front and center on the list of suspected kidnappers. Same for Robert Proffit. A handsome young man who went out of his way to work with seventh- and eighth-grade girls would not go unnoticed. If there'd been anything unto-ward in either of their records, Lorraine would have told her.

Anna would recheck the background reports, see what she could find by way of alibis for the time the squirrel was killed, but first on her list in the morning, when it came, would be finding out why Rita happened to be passing Picnic Rock at such an auspi-cious moment in Anna's life.

Tired as she was, Anna was not sorry when her alarm woke her at 4:30 A.M. The hot bath and Advil had done her back a world of good, but lying in one place for so long had brought back the ache. Movement was what was needed, warm blood flowing through the damaged soft tissues.

Her days as an iron woman of thirty-five were long gone. Strength and endurance had waned a bit. What took their place served her better: the stubbornness of keeping on keeping on. Perhaps it was only an increased ability to suffer discomfort. Whatever it was, it had carried her up steeper trails than the one she would tackle today.

Having locked the house, she loaded Hecuba, her litter box, food and water into the Crown Vic. The little cat would spend her day at the Thompson River District office. Anna did not want to waste time wondering if there would be bleeding cat parts festooning her house when she got home.

This being the third of Rita Perry's four days off, Anna hoped she might again make the hike to Fern Lake or the Tourmaline Gorge area to do whatever it was she did up there other than pry boulders off the legs of the girl rangers and have wild unhallowed sex with the boy rangers.

The kitten settled in, she grabbed a flashlight she'd found in the bottom drawer of her desk. The sun would be up in half an hour. To the east she could have seen the faint hope of dawn had she not been down in tall pines. Beneath the lodgepoles it was as chilly and dark as a November midnight in Mississippi. Anna was pleased. What she was doing wasn't illegal, or particularly unethical; still, she didn't want any witnesses.

Rita's Crown Vic—or rather the patrol vehicle Rita shared with Thompson River

District's two other law enforcement seasonals—was parked on the gravel between
the ranger station and Rita's quarters. In a
shared government vehicle there can be no
expectation of privacy. Anna was well within
her rights to search it to her heart's content.

Had Anna been required to tell a judge
specifically what she sought for the purposes for warrant, she wouldn't have been
able to do it. Anna was fishing, hoping to
snag any bit of information that might illuminate the enigma that was Rita. She was definitely a woman with secrets. Anna could
smell them on her like a man's cologne after
a long embrace. At the best of times Anna
had trouble resisting a secret. When that
secret might pertain to budding psychos
and destruction of park wildlife—and her
best comforter—she didn't even try.

The vehicle yielded nothing but a weakness for Hershey's Kisses on the part of one
of the seasonals. The ranger with the sweet
tooth had not been so rude as to leave
wadded up pieces of foil littering the seat or
cluttering up the ashtray, but several of the
candies' thin strips of paper reading "KISS
KISS KISS" had escaped, blown under the
seat, worked their way into crevices. One

had wended or wafted through the cage to settle on the floor of the back seat. That one Anna left in place, a cheery message for the next person arrested.

The trunk contained the customary patrol paraphernalia: flares, first aid pack, accident investigation kit, field drug-testing kit— pretty much a waste of space but somewhere along the line it became part of the gear—Breathalyzer, a couple of traffic cones, tow chain. The only thing unexpected was the tidiness with which these items had been stowed and the cleanliness of the carpeted area beneath them.

Rangers' trunks were occasionally tidy but seldom clean. They suffered too much use. Items used in rain, mud, sand and forest duff were routinely chucked in. This carpet looked freshly vacuumed.

No law forbade employees from detailing their patrol vehicles even unto the inside of the trunk. Under most circumstances, Anna would have found it commendable. Given the hellacious schedules the rangers were working at the tail end of the tourist season while burdened with search-and-rescue assignments and out-of-park fire details, Anna found it suspicious.

Working quickly and quietly she removed the gear, then played her light carefully over the exposed carpeting. Clean. Vacuumed. But not shampooed. On the right rear side near the wheel well there was a dark stain, two sides of it ruler-straight where a tarp or canvas had been laid down, the other edge irregular as if liquid had spilled over. Pinching up a bit of the dried substance, Anna spit on her fingers and rubbed them together, a quick and dirty field test. The brownish particles reconstituted to blood red. Finding yet one more use for her battered Swiss Army Knife, she neatly cut out a two-by-two inch square of the carpeting and slipped it into a small manila evidence envelope. That done, she pocketed it and restored the items to the trunk in the same order in which she had found them.

By the time she finished, dawn had made it over the mountains and was reaching fog-colored fingers down into the trees. Time to go.

She ascended the shorter, if no less steep, route to Fern Lake that began at the Bierstat Lake trailhead. The trip up was more time-consuming than the trek down had been. She reached the campground near eight o'clock. Most sites were full. Campers were stirring about in a sleepy chill, metal and plastic cups of hot beverages clasped between their hands. Anna liked campgrounds best in the early hours. Removed from their safe houses and comfortable routines, human beings showed a vulnerable, more benevolent aspect of themselves. People hiked without alarm clocks, and those who were sensible enough to experience the natural rhythms of the earth maintained elastic itineraries. Around a morning camp at a vacation spot there was none of the mindless hurrying of a workday morning. There was also the heady smell of campfire smoke. The perfume calmed Anna the way lavender was purported to soothe agitated Victorian ladies, until she remembered fires were banned in all but a few of the frontcountry sites.

For the next half an hour or so, she played her least favorite role required by her job, that of wet blanket. The campers made the usual excuses. A woman said they were unaware of the regulation, never saw any of the multitude of signs or read any of the brochures or the regulations printed on the backcountry permit. A man, gruff at first but growing more amenable when he found Anna was going to give him a warning rather than a citation, went for the classic excuse: "The *other* ranger said I could." Though Anna had heard that more times than she could count and under practically every illegal circumstance she could think of, this time it was the reason she issued only warnings. After the conditions she'd noted on her previous visit—conditions that had not been rectified in her short absence—if not actually giving visitors permission to have fires, Ray was certainly turning a blind eye to it.

Bleeker was up and dressed. *As he damn well better be*, Anna thought sourly, having spent the last three-quarters of an hour doing his job for him. Sitting in the morning sun on the cabin's front steps, he greeted her with a smile. "Coffee's on," he said, as if he were expecting her. Probably he was. While she was fiddling about with her firebugs, fisherpersons making the early commute from camp to lake would likely have told him. People liked to tell rangers things they didn't already know.

"You changed your hair!" Anna said. His sandy brown baby-fine hair had been dyed a dramatic dark brown, almost black.

"You like?" He tilted his head and struck a pose in such a perfect mimicry of a fashion model that Anna laughed.

"Hair's a renewable resource," she said equitably. "Might as well amuse yourself with it."

"If I take after my dad, mine's an endangered species. Figured I might as well enjoy it while it lasts."

Anna followed him into the cabin, once more struck by how immaculate he kept it. Too bad his housekeeping skills didn't bleed over into campground maintenance. Over excellent coffee, she talked with him about this professional shortcoming.

When she first broached the subject what she took to be startlingly cold fury froze his eyes and she braced herself for a long and ugly bout of justifications, shifting blame and counteraccusations.

Apparently the look had not been fury but chagrin. He readily admitted that he'd let the campground chores slide. Apologizing profusely, he promised to be vigilant in the future. Anna hoped he was telling the truth. His ready acceptance of blame put her in mind of a landlord she'd had in college. Complaints on the part of his tenants were handled with the same mix of "Sorry" and "I'll get right on it." He never did. Moving the man was like trying to move a warm wall of mud with nothing but one's bare hands.

Anna moved on. Proffit, Rita and Ray were the only people she knew for certain could have been in place for both the murder of the mice and the Abert squirrel in her bedroom. Of the three, only Proffit seemed to have a motive—if psychosis could be called a motive. Rita had the ghost of one, her association with Proffit. Ray might have had reasons of his own. Unlike the Shadow, Anna didn't know what evil lurked in the hearts of men. Ray could have hiked out the previous afternoon. He assured her he'd been in the high country all that day but could think of no way to prove it.

Anna wasn't surprised. Fern Lake was not isolated. Campers came and went, knocked on the door for shelter when it rained, sugar if they'd forgotten it, or simply because the cabin was cute and they wanted a peek inside. In the nonpark world this would have provided a plethora of witnesses to a person's whereabouts on a given afternoon. Here, people were mostly nameless vacation nomads.

For a minute or so, a long and not uncomfortable silence, they sipped their coffee.

"I led a nature walk from two till maybe three-thirty," he volunteered. "Then sat around with a couple from Missouri, I think. Or Mississippi. Minnesota. One of those 'M' states till around five, if that helps."

"They still here?" Anna asked.

"I doubt it."

"Don't worry about it."

"This about that squirrel business at your house?"

Anna was startled. She'd not mentioned the nature of her disturbance over the radio. Then she remembered cell phones. She'd been warned the reception was nil at Fern Lake, but a mile up the Bear Lake Trail, one could call Istanbul if necessary.

"Yeah."

"Checking alibis?"

"Yeah."

"Why do you have to check mine?" He seemed merely interested, not defensive or angry. Anna was relieved at the professionalism.

"The mice on the outhouse."

"Ahh. Weirdness personified. Makes sense."

"No. It doesn't. That's the problem."

"It must make sense to somebody."

Anna knew that to be true, but it wasn't a somebody she'd care to meet in a dark alley. Or let cat-sit.

"I wish I had a video of me someplace else at the crucial time," Ray said.

"Me, too," Anna said sincerely, then again: "Don't worry about it."

Ray excused himself and vanished into the room where the gear was stored, saying he had something to show her. Listening to him crash around for what seemed a phenomenally long time, she helped herself to another cup of his fine coffee. Finally he emerged empty-handed.

"Couldn't find it," he said with a grin that indicated he wasn't heartbroken over the failure.

"What was it?"

"Nothing much. If it turns up, I'll show it to you next time you drop by."

Not in a mood to aid and abet the mysteriousness her seasonal was so obviously enjoying, Anna said nothing. She had someplace else she wanted to be anyway.

Getting away was delayed for thirty minutes. Bleeker was in a chatty mood and kept

up a steady stream of conversation, jumping from one subject to another. Throughout
the chitchat ran a subtle line of justification
for his letting the campground go to hell. He
would have her believe all of his time was
taken up with nature walks and evening programs. These weren't scheduled at the
backcountry camp but neither were they
discouraged. Anna commended him for his
edifying the visitors, then reminded him
none too gently that that was only a small
part of his job. At the end of the half-hour,
Bleeker looked at his watch, stopped talking
and abruptly announced it was time to get
to work on putting the campground in order.

Thus was Anna dismissed.

The Odessa Lake campground was on
her chosen route. Because Ray had failed
so spectacularly at Fern, she stopped to
inspect it on her way through. Two of the
sites were occupied, the tents nestled like
bright and poisonous mushrooms among
the spectacularly huge boulders that had
fallen into the narrow neck of Tourmaline
Gorge. Both camps had been abandoned
for the day, their residents hiking or fishing
or annoying the natural resources in one

way or another, but for one rather woebe-
gone vacationer.

Perched on a rock like a Goth version of
the White Rock fairy was a girl of ten or
eleven. Her hair was coal black and cut in a
spiky punked-out style that made her look
younger and ageless at the same time. She
was gaunt to the point Anna wondered if
she suffered the early stages of anorexia,
and dressed in the uniform of a boy emulat-
ing gang chic: oversized shorts with the
crotch nearly to her knees and a man-sized
football jersey with the number 1 in white on
a red background.

"Hey," she said listlessly as Anna walked
into her camp.

"Hey your own self. Where is everybody?"

"Fishing."

Anna couldn't tell if the girl was sullen or
just hadn't had enough to eat in her short life
to give her the energy for enthusiasm.

"They leave you behind to guard the
camp?"

"I don't like to kill things," she said with a
vehemence Anna couldn't but admire.

"A girl after my own heart." Anna was in a
hurry but there was something about this
champion of fishes that touched her. "What

do you like?" she asked, to prove another human being cared on at least a rudimentary level.

The girl looked away, toward Odessa and Fern lakes, and spoke as if to the killers of fish who'd left her to her own devices for the day. "The ranger from the other lake leads nature walks and does evening programs," she said in the flat voice with which she'd hailed Anna. "Yesterday afternoon he took us all around the lake in the afternoon and told us about the plants and the animals for a couple hours."

Receiving an education about the fishes didn't spark in her the same passion that the thought of killing them had. Perhaps she was more about rejection than acceptance. Not unusual in a preteen female.

"Sounds interesting," Anna said. "Tell me what you saw." She didn't give a damn what the kid saw but she wanted to keep her talking. She sensed something off about the girl.

The ploy was unsuccessful.

"I've got to go," the scrawny Goth announced and slid down from the rock, hiking the baggy shorts up over her skinny thighs. Without a goodbye or a wave of the hand she walked toward Odessa Lake and the murderers of fishes.

Mildly unsettling as the interview had been it had settled one question. Ray Bleeker was telling the truth. Having led a two-hour nature walk the previous afternoon, there was no way he could have been Anna's squirrel butcher.

By ten o'clock she'd reached Picnic Rock. Rather than try and follow Rita unseen, she'd gambled that pulling her out from under a rock wasn't the only reason Rita had hiked up Tourmaline Gorge, just as shoving her off one hadn't been Robert Proffit's goal. Both, she believed, were fortuitous accidents. The first lucky for her, the second for Mr. Proffit.

Waiting when there was an action to be taken drove Anna nuts. Waiting when waiting was all she could do, she rather enjoyed. A time of forced indolence for the body and necessary alertness for the mind.

She watched through the quiet of the morning as the sun's warmth worked its golden stillness down the ragged granite and into the trees. By one o'clock, even the birds and insects seemed to drowse. The golden eagle never returned, but she imagined him close and twice saw shadows glide across the sparkling gray of the granite slab. At two o'clock, the first white cloud appeared. Soon it was joined by others, and their subtle grumbling suggested there was lightning within and they were not averse to loosing it on the unwary hiker who dared climb too near their heaven.

At two-forty-three the crunch of boots on dirt and gravel grated on Anna's ears, so long attuned to the more euphonious whisperings of the real world.

Pay dirt, she thought. Waiting rather than trailing had been a gamble. Far more satisfying to win on a long shot. It was in her mind to spring silently to her feet to await the younger ranger's passing. Damaged muscles and sinews rebelled and she did little more than flinch and fold. Bowing to necessity, she eased up slowly, pushing off the rock and wondering if this was what one felt like all the time when one was very old.

First you must live that long, she told herself reassuringly. Like many a wild child of the sixties and seventies, she'd figured she'd die young. The idea had never bothered her much till she'd met Paul.

The owner of the crunching boots was

Rita Perry. Anna let her pass, then quietly fell in behind her.

Following her was not terribly difficult. People not expecting a stalker travel in blind cocoons of thought. A phenomenon muggers count on to further their predatory ends. Anna had taken the rudimentary precaution of wearing pine- and dirt-hued shorts and shirt. There was no shortage of this unexciting palette in her wardrobe. It was as if, wearing the national park uniform for so many years, she'd come to think of variations on the green and gray as the only suitable color for clothing.

For a couple of miles, maybe less, Rita followed the trail up toward Gabletop Mountain. Since Gabletop was not a terribly popular destination in the park, the trail was not maintained with the assiduity of those to Longs Peak or Frozen Lake or a dozen other heavily visited destinations. This was not only a practical choice on the part of the Park Service, but an aesthetic one. Visitors willing to push farther and harder into the wilderness enjoyed a sense of newness, of being one of the few to discover this world. A wide, well-maintained trail with water bars and rock steps up the tricky bits spoiled the fantasy.

Rather than walk steadily as was her habit when covering ground, Anna walked in fits and starts, pausing often to listen for Rita's boots on the trail. With no crowds for cover and Rita's easy recognition of her, Anna couldn't risk keeping her in sight. On the few occasions she misjudged and rounded a bend in the trail to see Rita's retreating form, she backed off and waited. Given her weakened condition, the difference in their ages, Rita's long-legged stride and the fact the woman hiked like an all-terrain vehicle running on premium fuel, Anna's greatest concern was that gasping for breath would give her away. Two years at near sea level, her days spent sitting in offices and patrol cars, hadn't served her well for a return to mountain duty.

After ninety minutes of this forced march, tree line was reached and Anna was afforded a clear view of a sketchy trail winding up to the barren rocky heights. No Rita. Backtracking, her attention on the minutiae to either side of the trail, Anna found where she had turned off. Again uphill. Had she not been fighting for breath, Anna would have noticed it when first she passed. The cut-off had been used many times. This must have been where Proffit was headed when he and Anna had met up at Picnic Rock, where Rita was going when she stopped to rescue her.

Anna took out her topographical map of the area. It looked as if Rita was cutting up to the backside of Loomis, a small lake, scarcely more than a pond. Ignoring the burning in her lungs and the plaints of her back muscles, Anna picked up the pace. No mean feat in country grown so steep she slid on the downed needles and clung to trees to help herself along.

The burst of speed paid off. Twenty minutes of hard climbing and she caught a glimpse of Rita. Another hour and the woman, who Anna had come to believe was a machine, her heart a nine-pound hammer, her legs pistons of titanium, crested the butte above Loomis, dropped down several hundred yards and came to a stop.

Lest she lose her again, Anna waited till Rita had removed her pack before she, too, set hers aside and sat down with her back to a tree, her binoculars in her lap.

Rita's destination was a small clearing several hundred yards above Loomis Lake.

Another trail, far easier than the cross-country route they had followed, ran from Fern Lake to Loomis' eastern shore. Rita hadn't wanted to be seen, hadn't wanted anyone to know where she was headed. That was reassuring. Anna hated to think she'd pushed her aching body over hill and dale to observe her seasonal law enforcement ranger bird-watching or sketching the wonders of nature.

The clearing where Rita had stopped was rich in one of the park's most abundant resources: rocks. Boulders formed a truncated Stonehenge, a natural wall on three sides. The fourth Anna couldn't see but surmised was open by the fact Perry appeared and disappeared as if she entered and exited a small box canyon. This bizarre exercise was repeated six times. Each time Rita brought in something she'd had cached in the trees out of sight from Anna's binoculars. Twice the young ranger went down to the lake and returned with a bucket of water. The bucket was presumably stored with whatever else she had hidden away beneath the evergreens. Occasionally Perry's lips moved as if she spoke or sang to whatever it was she tended in the corral of granite.

After these six trips, her work, whatever the hell it was, evidently done, Rita sat down with her pack and a paperback book and ate lunch.

Curious what Christian prison wardens read in the backcountry, Anna trained her binoculars on the book in Rita's hands. John Sanford's *Evil: The Shadow Side of Reality*.

Out of a sense of duty to the body that had served her so well—if not without complaint—Anna tried to eat but excitement robbed her of her appetite. That Rita watered and spoke to whatever was incarcerated in the rocks suggested it was alive.

Candace Watson.

Unbidden, half a dozen Dean Koontz novels flittered piecemeal through Anna's brain. Mr. Koontz's unique and terrifying visions combined with no respect to publication dates. The one that could not be eradicated by bites of peanut butter and cloudberry jelly or washed away by draughts of water was from a novel where the villain created grim and intricate sculptures from murdered victims whom he carefully arranged in his gallery beneath an abandoned amusement park.

The mice.

The Abert.

Perhaps Rita didn't need her victims alive to feed, water and converse with them.

twenty

Thunderheads formed. Temperature dropped. Sudden hectic breezes ruffled the tops of the pines. Anna waited and she watched. Rita finished her lunch, set aside her book on the rock she used as a table, talked to the enclosure of stones, fetched another bucket of water. When nearly two hours of this had passed, the lanky ranger finally hefted her pack and started back up toward Anna's hiding place. She passed within twenty feet of where Anna sat but never looked right or left. Her eyes were fixed on the tops of her boots, her mind god knew where. Most people walked through life seeing only the movies they played in their head. A majority of the reels Anna had accumulated over half a lifetime weren't the sort she wished to view a second time. This outward focus allowed her to see without being seen more times than she could remember.

She listened without moving until she could no longer hear the crinkling thump of Rita's boots on the needle-strewn earth. When the living silence of the high country returned, a silence made deeper by the grumble of thunder and the rare call of a bird, Anna waited another ten minutes just to be sure. Then, with an adolescent mix of dread and excited anticipation, shouldered her daypack and started down to the ring of boulders in the clearing. From habit and caution she walked quietly. There was no guarantee that whatever Rita held captive would be glad to see her.

The rocks were more than head-high. The cluster appeared to have grown there, no nearby escarpment to give a clue from whence they had fallen. As Anna reached this tumble of granite, she stopped and listened. The first drops of cold rain had begun to fall and the stamp of tiny wet feet on pine needles and stone masked any sounds from within. If anything was alive in this natural enclosure to make sounds.

After half a minute her patience was rewarded. A thin whine, like that of a small creature enraged, cut through the dull patter of the wind-driven rain.

"Shit," Anna whispered and, with visions of lacerated children dancing in her head, she walked around to the lakeside of the rocks, the side on which Rita had lunched and talked and delivered water. There the boulders almost completed their ring. An opening two feet wide at most had been closed off with a waist-high gate made of pine branches lashed together with twine. The gate was not sturdy enough to keep anything in or out that was not already in a crippled or weakened state.

The stick gate was held in place by two rocks the size of bowling balls. The whine came again, sharper this time. Anna moved the rocks, lifted the gate away and squeezed between the boulders. Within the rough circle, the granite chunks leaned together, nearly meeting at the top, forming dark alcoves beneath. The area they protected wasn't more than six by eight feet. With the overcast sky, light was at a premium. What Anna could see appeared to be empty. The air was tainted with the smell of rotting flesh.

Movement, faint and furtive, from the dark crevice to her left caught her eye. Then a whine and the flash of eyes. Anna crouched and shined her Mag-Lite under the over-hang of rock.

Puppies.

"What in hell . . ." She held out her hand and was rewarded by a fierce growl from a beast slightly bigger than a breadbox. She couldn't but admire its courage.

Seasonals were not allowed pets and anyone who lived inside the park wasn't allowed pets that went outside of a fenced yard. During her years in the parks Anna had had to deal with the occasional unautho-rized cat or dog. As handmaiden to a cat— now two cats—and a three-legged dog, she understood the need to have one's com-panions near. This was the first time she'd known someone to go to such absurd lengths to make it so.

She lay down on her belly the better to study Rita's little family. There were four of them: one nearly black, two silvery gray and, the littlest one, gray with tawny ears.

Wolves.

Rita had wolf puppies. A snippet of a ranger report Anna had read came back to her. A wolf bitch had been shot by a rancher near Jackson, Wyoming. The local vet said it appeared she'd recently had a litter of pups. The pups were never found, they'd said.

If Anna remembered correctly, Rita coached high school girl's basketball in Jackson. She must have found the pups and brought them to Rocky, where there was an overabundance of elk for them to feast upon when they grew up. It wouldn't be the first time park policy was given a wee boost from an enterprising ranger.

Much as she wanted to, Anna didn't try to lure the pups out, pet them or play with them. Though Rita conversed with the little wolves, she'd very rightly not tried to domesticate them. It was even bad form for Anna to remain in the pen. A wolf desensitized to human beings is destined to have a very short life span.

"Don't touch them," came a voice above and behind her.

Rita had come back and Anna, so recently proud of her powers of observation and stealth, was so engrossed in the delight of wolf pups that she'd heard and sensed nothing. It took all of her self-control not to squawk.

"I'm not," she said calmly. "But it's not easy."

Regretfully she shoved herself to her knees, her back still denying her her usual grace and ease of movement. Part of the problem was she was tensed up, waiting for a blow or a kick. Instead Rita crouched down beside her.

"I know." She was gazing intently at the hostile little faces beneath the rock. The rain was coming down harder now but neither woman seemed to notice. "I've had them since they were two weeks old."

"The wolf bitch that was in the news?"

"The same," Rita said. "It took me nearly forty hours searching but I found the den. The poor little guys were half starved. I guess when they're so young it doesn't take all that long. A good thing really. It's not like they can count on Health and Human Services finding foster homes for them when Mom is murdered."

"You bottle-fed them?" Anna asked. She

wasn't quite successful in keeping the envy out of her voice. Rita heard it and smiled.

"For as short a time as possible. I was afraid of making pets out of them. Soon as I could, I got them on meat. I haven't touched them since and I throw the meat in."

"You feed them elk meat," Anna said, the bloody truth of the backpack dawning on her.

"The resource manager, Ellen, told me they should be habituated to their natural food source. Ellen knows nothing about this," Rita added quickly. "She thought we were just talking 'what ifs.'"

"Road-kill elk," Anna said, remembering the vanished elk carcass on Bear Lake Road and the bloodied bit of carpet she'd excised from the trunk of Rita's patrol vehicle.

Rita nodded. "I froze what I could fit in our weensy freezer and packed it in."

"Robert Proffit was carrying food for the pups when he knocked me off the rock."

"It was an accident." Rita rose.

For a long moment they stood there in the rain staring at the rock overhang that hid the little wolves from view.

"What's going to happen to the pups?" Rita asked finally.

That was the question Anna was pondering. Rocky Mountain was in dire need of an effective predator to keep the elk herd healthy. Though these four carnivores might not live, might not find any way to reproduce, might never form a viable and sustaining pack, they were a start. Once it was established that wolves had returned to these mountains of their own volition—Rita's abducting and reintroducing them remaining a secret—the endangered species protections would kick in. A wolf program would be instituted, maybe animals from another pack introduced, a mating program begun.

Maybe.

If.

Possibly.

Too many stumbling blocks. But it could happen and the idea thrilled Anna. Suddenly she laughed.

"What?" Rita said.

"The night I spent in Tourmaline Gorge I thought I heard wolves howling."

"They do howl," Rita said. "Puppy howls. I love it. I'm surprised you could hear it on the other side of the gorge."

"Sound does funny things in the mountains," Anna said. "It was a still night and, Lord knows, I wasn't sleeping all that soundly."

"It was an accident."

"Yeah."

"Come on," Rita said. "I usually don't come into the pen. I don't want them associating people with lunch."

Anna looked at her watch. "More like high tea," she said.

Rita disappeared through the narrow entrance to the pen. The pups, seeming to sense that these intruders were departing, began to scuffle and growl happy little puppy growls. Knowing she'd probably only see them again in cages, Anna squatted down for a last look at these predators in the making.

The little guys were in a three-way tug-of-war over what must have been a particularly tasty morsel. The fourth pup, the smallest one, sat at the edge of the fray watching intently. An opening presented itself and the runt was in quick as a cat and out again with the prize. So intent were the wolves on the hunt, they had forgotten Anna's existence.

In a tumble of downy soft fur—or so Anna imagined, she dared not move lest they remember her and end their game—they rolled out from beneath the lip of granite, tiny teeth clamped on stubby tails, cushion-fat ears laid back. The runt was rolled by a tremendous pounce from a fatter sibling and the coveted morsel fell from its jaws half a yard from Anna's knee. Most of the flesh was eaten away but Anna knew that ingenious articulated arrangement of bones existed nowhere in the body of an elk.

It was a finger. A small human finger.

Venison wasn't the only thing Rita and Robert Proffit had been feeding their little friends.

twenty-one

Mrs. Sheppard—Mrs. Sharon Sheppard, as opposed to her pregnant fourteen-year-old sister, Mrs. Alexis Sheppard, and the dumpy middle-aged Mrs. Dwayne Sheppard—had left Heath's RV home in a panicked fluster of "I've got to get back. He'll wonder where . . ." eighteen hours before. During those hours Heath had not been idle. Nor had she been noticeably productive, though that was not for want of trying. She'd made a dozen calls to Idaho, starting with Lewiston, in an attempt to track down Alexis and Sharon's father, Rupert Evan Dennis. The closest she'd gotten was a vague suggestion from a Robert Dennis—no relation, or admitting to none—that he thought there were some Dennises in Pocatello.

Several times Heath had called Anna's cell phone number and cursed the ranger each time the message beep answered. Cell phones had done a good deal of damage not only to the viability of the callee's excuses but the patience of the caller. In a few short years it was as if it had become de rigueur for everyone to be instantly available to everyone else.

Anna Pigeon was unavailable to most people whether she answered her phone or not, Heath guessed. Still, it pissed her off. Weren't park rangers public servants? *So give me some fucking service*, Heath thought uncharitably.

The only two calls that had proved satisfactory were those she'd placed to her Aunt Gwen. Having been in the business of caring for women and children for nearly fifty years, Dr. Littleton knew most everybody in Colorado similarly engaged. She'd promised to find what could be done for the three Dennis sisters in the way of services and inalienable rights.

Gwen cautioned Heath not to be overly

optimistic, particularly for Beth. Because Mrs. Dwayne was the oldest of Sheppard's known "wives," it was a possibility that she was legally wed to Mr. Sheppard. Short of proving abuse—which wasn't easy to do in a community as closed as that of New Canaan, even when one knew for a fact it was occurring—there was no reason the daughter could be removed.

Indeed, Heath didn't know if Beth wished to be removed. Perhaps Mr. Sheppard drew the line at incest—or incest with blood relations.

Alexis was a good bet for proving abuse because she was carrying proof that Sheppard had had sexual intercourse with a minor. Even if neither she nor her elder sister would testify to that to a legal system they'd been brought up to demonize, the threat of it might be enough to twist Sheppard's arm into letting them make their own choice whether to stay or go. A choice Heath wasn't convinced they had the strength to make. Both had been trained to helplessness before their God and their husband who, like as not, they were encouraged to regard as two parts of the same being.

If only I weren't trapped in this goddamn

chair, Heath thought, and not for the first time. This time a second thought followed on the heels of the much-used lament. If she were again a functioning biped, what could she do that she wasn't already doing? Storm New Canaan commando-style and abduct the Dennis sisters and Beth? Arm wrestle Mr. Sheppard for dominance over their minds and hearts? There was nothing. Most of life's battles in the modern world weren't fought with legs and feet, muscle and sinew, but with the mind. Since she'd lost the ability to climb, Heath had been forced to refocus. In the past she'd used her considerable intellect to find climbs, prepare for climbs, strategize climbs, remember and discuss and critique climbs, boast and hob-nob about climbs old and prospective.

Now she concentrated on finding that easy chute, that safe traverse for a woman and three girls who needed to get off a ledge on which circumstances had marooned them. In a sudden insight that was as unpleasant as it was unsettling, she felt the absolute self-centeredness of her former pursuit and, other than the joy and athleticism, the ultimate futility of scaling peaks where there was nothing to be had at the top but a fleeting sense of glory and a self-serving memory.

In truth, had she been free of her chair, she wouldn't have made time for Beth and the Dennis girls. She wouldn't have had the patience to pursue the tedious business of tracking down people by phone, of waiting in a tacky RV park for a communication from Sharon.

Before the woman had skittered away like a terrified creature who knows it inhabits a low link on the food chain, she had promised Heath she'd e-mail the following day. Phoning was out of the question. New Canaan had service, several lines in fact, but the only telephone proper resided in Mr. Sheppard's office, the door to which was kept locked when he wasn't in.

The internet was nearly as rigidly controlled but Sharon was one of the community's several clerks. She had been sent to a training course at a junior college when she was eighteen so she might be of greater service to the commune. Mr. Sheppard would have been appalled had he known how much she had built on this rudimentary training in computer skills. Both she and

Alexis had e-mail to keep in touch with friends in Canada.

Eighteen hours and seven minutes and Heath had yet to hear from her. She glared at the laptop on the kitchen counter. Computers had never captured her imagination. As a consequence she used them when necessary but had never become fast friends with the things. The cell phone and laptop set up in the RV struck her as the ultimate in Buck Rogers, George Jetson magic but she knew it worked. She and her aunt e-mailed several times each day.

As if its ears were burning, the laptop emitted a suitable here-comes-Tinkerbell strumming sound.

"Come *on*," Heath said as she pivoted her chair toward the counter. "Hallelujah." The sender's address was "ssdennis." The message was short and to the point.

"Come get us." No salutation, no "Love, Sharon."

Though Heath had been awaiting a communication for so many hours her anticipation muscles—and she swore such anatomical oddities existed, she could feel them at the base of her skull and between her shoulder blades—fairly ached with the burden, her hand shot out and closed the laptop, shutting it down. She should never have gotten tangled up in these crazy people's twisted schemes. While cursing herself for a sucker and a coward and a fool, her mind raced after plausible, or even merely possible, excuses she could use to get herself off the hook: never got the e-mail, computer down, cell phone not working, batteries dead. Crippled.

The last smacked her upside the head as smartly as her dad's second wife had been in the habit of doing when she'd had too much cheap wine.

How very handy this being paraplegic could become if she let it. How easy to blame character flaws, spiritual emptiness or sloth on the fact that she no longer walked. Seductive not to be challenged, differently abled or disabled—appellations she'd earlier scorned as mere semantics—but to be *crippled* as in broken, less than, excused from having to compete, cope and strive like everybody else.

"Damn," Heath whispered. This epiphany didn't leave her feeling any less cowardly, suckered or foolish. It merely spoiled the escape plans she was busily hatching.

Quickly, before she could change her mind and choose to be a victim and the abdication of responsibility that road offered, she opened the laptop and sent off two quick e-mails. The first was to her aunt informing her she was leaving for New Canaan. The second to "ssdennis": "I'm on my way."

twenty-two

Before Anna could recover and snatch up this macabre trophy, a pup pounced on it with a ferocious growl, snatched the bones up and ran back beneath the rock overhang, the other three little wolves in plump and gangly pursuit. *No wonder they were so fat*, Anna thought. Elk and Homo sapiens. She couldn't but hope they preferred elk as she lay on the wet ground, Mag-Lite in one hand, and reached into the furry fracas to retrieve what might be the only evidence of a girl's murder.

The struggle was quick and fierce. Anna got one painful nip on the heel of her hand but emerged the victor. If one couldn't take candy from babies, taking fingers from puppies had to be the next best thing. From a habit of many years in law enforcement, she always carried a couple of small evidence bags in her shirt pocket. If used for nothing else, during the long idyllic spells when the parks were quiescent, the bags were handy for storing cigarette butts found along the trails.

"Sorry, guys," she whispered as she dropped her gory acquisition into one and sealed it up. "Have a hoof." By way of restitution she tossed a well-chewed elk's foot gently into the growling darkness.

The gnawed finger she stowed in a side pocket of her pack. She was rising to her feet when Rita reappeared in the narrow gateway flanked by the rocks.

"We really can't be getting the pups used to human—" Rita began in that half-exasperated, half-apologetic voice people adopt when admonishing a superior officer. She stopped when she noticed Anna's bedraggled, mud-soaked clothes, needles from elbows to boot heels.

"What happened?"

"I fell."

"We'll walk out slow," Rita promised. Anna could sense that, had Rita been a Boy Scout, she would have harassed perfectly good old ladies in her zeal to help them across streets.

Anna said nothing, just followed her out. When she had passed the homemade wicket gate, she picked it up and turned to Rita. "Do me a favor," she said. "Hold this for a second."

Dutifully Rita took the gate in both hands. Anna reached under her rain jacket and drew her service weapon from its pancake holder on her belt.

"Get mud in your gun?" Rita asked.

For a perpetrator of murder and dismemberment, she was breathtakingly unconcerned. Either she was innocent, a psychopath or a fine actress. Anna wasn't sure which of the three was the most dangerous and was in no position to gamble.

"Back up a tad," she said.

Rita did. When there were a couple of yards between them, Anna moved out from the tight embrace of the granite and leveled the gun at Rita's middle.

"What are—"

"You can go ahead and put the gate in

place," Anna said. "Keep the pups from getting away. Carefully. Hands where I can see
them. Roll the rocks in place with your foot.
Good."

"This isn't necessary," Rita said, somewhere between shock and righteousness. "I
doubt it's a felony. You'd shoot me for doing
something that the park needs so desperately?"

"Take your weapon off. You know the drill.
Carefully. Don't scare me into pulling the
trigger."

With a "Humph!" that struck Anna more
as that of a snotty teenager than a raging
homicidal maniac, Rita complied.

Anna then had Rita hug a good-sized pine
and cuffed her wrists together. Cuffing suspects to inanimate objects was against regulations, but no other solution came to
mind. With every minute of delay, evidence
was being devoured by wolves. *Dogs eating
my homework*, Anna thought.

"Where do you keep your handcuff key?"
Anna demanded.

"Watch pocket."

Anna took it. "Where's your spare?"

Rita said nothing.

"Bugger all," Anna muttered and began

searching her seasonal. The spare was in her right breast pocket. Anna took it as well.

The sun was close to setting and the sky overcast, making it difficult to pick and choose between one lump of meat and the next, but it appeared as though, had more of the finger's original owner ever been in the enclosure, it was now transformed by the alchemy of digestion into sharp teeth and warm fur coats. *Not a bad end*, Anna couldn't help thinking. Burial was barbaric and cremation struck her as clean but wasteful.

To be on the safe side, she bagged every gruesome bite that wasn't clearly elk meat, then returned to her prisoner, unlocked her from her forced romance with the tree and recuffed her hands in front so she could steady herself on the hike out and so the cuffs would be hidden in the sleeves of her rain parka. It wouldn't do to have the public see a ranger marched out of the wilderness in chains, so to speak. During the process Rita complained with scathing bitterness that she should be treated like a common criminal, ready to tear out Anna's throat merely because she fed an already dead elk to a few needy puppies. Throughout this diatribe Anna didn't catch so much as a whiff of remorse or guilty knowledge that she was being arrested, not for a resource violation, but for murder.

Rita once again secure in bracelets, Anna told her to lead the way out. Not cross-country the way they'd come, but down around Loomis Lake on the improved trail.

The younger ranger refused to budge. "Take the cuffs off me. This is stupid. I only did what somebody had to for the park. I won't be made to go in in handcuffs when all I did was feed wolf pups."

Anna lifted the first evidence bag she'd taken from the man-made den. "You're not cuffed because you fed them but because you fed them this." She held the clear plastic bag out so Rita could see the contents.

Removed from mud and puppy jaws, the finger looked more pathetically human than it had when it first came to Anna's attention. The bones were crooked slightly from the remaining knuckle joints, giving it the aspect of a spectral and rotting hand beckoning one to the unspeakable.

"Jesus H. Christ," Rita murmured.

Anna was pretty sure that qualified as taking the Lord's name in vain.

"It's a finger," Rita said.

"Your pet wolf pups were chewing on it."

Rita didn't answer. Turning she stumbled, righted herself, and led the way down the trail.

She hadn't gone more than a dozen yards before she suddenly sat down with a thump.

Thinking she had slipped, Anna stopped and waited for her to get up. She didn't so much as try. "You okay?"

"Other than being under arrest for murder?" Rita said without turning to look at Anna.

"Other than that," Anna replied with more patience than she felt. Floundering about in the wolves' den, fighting for scraps of human flesh, had gotten her wet. With the closing of the day she was getting cold and cranky.

"Yeah. Fit as a fiddle." Still Rita didn't look back.

"Get up. We're losing the light."

"No."

"What do you mean 'no'?"

"No. I won't get up. I won't hike out. I didn't kill anybody and I won't do it. No."

Damn, Anna thought. She'd always dreaded this moment, waited for it. By some miracle she'd managed to avoid it for a long time. She remembered when she'd first gone to seasonal law enforcement training in an abandoned women's prison in Santa Rosa, California, asking one of her teachers, a strapping park policeman from the Presidio in San Francisco, "What do you do if people don't do what you say?"

"They'll do what you tell them to," he'd said smugly. "You've just got to tell 'em the right way." There'd been a titter of masculine laughter as the men in the class pretended they weren't worried about the same thing.

From that Anna learned two things: not to admit weakness in front of the boys and that the big park policeman hadn't the faintest idea what to do in the face of a refusal that couldn't be met with brute force.

It was the secret of passive resistance.

Rita was too big to drag or carry. Much as she was tempted to at the moment, Anna couldn't shoot her and Rita knew it.

"Damn," Anna voiced her thought. "Just sit here all night freezing half to death?"

"I don't mind."

Rita never once looked over her shoulder at the captor she was effectively taking captive. Anna didn't need to see her face, she could hear the calm finality in the words. Nothing better to do, she sat as well, her back against a kindly tree, and ran through her options. Once again she could cuff Rita to a tree, hike out and bring back help. That wasn't only against park regulations but was dangerous. A stunt like that would get her fired.

She could try and radio to request backup, backup which wouldn't arrive till way after dark, in which case they could all spend the night by Loomis Lake. Carrying out a good-sized woman at night was too risky to try if it wasn't life or death. Not to mention that nasty part where Anna would have to broadcast over the airwaves that her prisoner—her *seasonal employee*, for heaven's sake—wouldn't obey her and could some big strong somebody please come make her.

This being the twenty-first century, it might be expected that a helicopter could be called on to swoop down and carry them both to civilization, but Anna knew that wasn't the case. Night landing, no lights, roving storm cells wreaking havoc with the air currents: pilots weren't willing to risk their lives nor owners their machinery under such conditions. Possibly not even if it were a life and death situation.

"How about just down to Fern Lake?" Anna compromised. There was no sense in blustering or playing at heavy-handed authority. Being rational was the lesser of evils. "At least we'd be warm and dry and fed."

"No."

"I'll just call for backup and first thing in the morning you'll be hauled ignominiously out, a spectacle for all your friends. Wouldn't it be better to walk out quietly? Who knows, maybe you'll get off easy. A slap on the wrist. Hailed as a hero. Restoring the natural order and what not."

"What about the finger?"

"That's going to be a problem," Anna admitted. They sat in silence for a while. Soon Anna would have to radio dispatch and report the situation. Not yet, though. She still had hopes of getting Rita back on her feet and moving. Silences were usually easy for Anna, a boon in an overly noisy world. This one was not. It was full of the racket of questions she wanted to ask about the finger, the pups, the girls, Proffit. As

soon as the cuffs went on and Rita was offi-
cially under arrest as in no longer free to
come and go as she pleased, Anna didn't
choose to ask a single one. Rita had yet to
request a lawyer but judges tended to look
on interrogation post arrest with a jaundiced
eye. Law enforcement had become a good
deal more complicated since Matt Dillon
first rode into Dodge.

"What do you hope to gain by sitting here
all night? Other than a cold butt and a lousy
end-of-season review?" That question
seemed safe enough.

Rita said nothing for a while. Then: "I
haven't thought it through. I just know I'm
not going out like this. I don't know where
that finger came from. If it's even a finger."

The last rang hollow. They both knew it
was a finger.

"ROMO, Two-oh-one," Anna radioed dispatch. There wasn't light to drag Rita out
but someone could hike in with a flashlight
to bring food, sleeping bags and the comfort of backup. "ROMO, Two-oh-one."

"Can't get out from here," Rita said with
weary satisfaction. "You'll have to hike back
up the way we came. On the ridge you can
get a signal."

Anna had been afraid of that. In a world of soaring granite peaks and deep stone canyons, radio accessibility was spotty at best.

"Don't suppose you'd come with me?"

"Nope."

More time passed. Dusk became dark. Anna got colder, achier. Her thoughts grew more sinister. She had found blood in Rita's patrol vehicle, followed her, caught her flagrantly breaking park regulations, discovered a human finger amid the scraps of meat Rita fed to her pups, arrested the woman and yet, through all that, she'd not seen Rita as a threat. Not really.

Why would Rita plop down on a trail, putting herself and Anna through a long cold night for nothing? The confusion of innocence? The stubbornness of righteousness?

Or because she expected a friend to come along and help her even the odds?

Again Anna considered her options. It was a good twenty-minute hike to the ridge where she could establish radio communications. Forty minutes there and back. During that time the annoying Miss Perry would have to be tethered to a tree.

In Rocky's backcountry there were a few remaining predators—not counting the four Rita had imported from Wyoming—black bears, cougars. There was little chance that one would come upon one particular ranger tied to one particular tree. If this did transpire, chances were the beast would run away rather than attack.

The chances of whomever or whatever Rita waited for coming by and freeing her, then waiting in ambush for Anna to return in the dark, were incalculable.

"You're a royal pain in the patootie, you know that?" Anna said irritably.

"Uncuff me and we'll walk out."

Anna levered herself up from the cold damp earth and unlocked the cuff from Rita's left wrist.

"Thank—"

Before the woman could finish, Anna clamped her thumb and elbow in a pain compliance hold, forced her to the nearest tree and recuffed her with the trunk in her embrace.

"I'll be back as soon as I can," Anna said. "Don't feed the wildlife."

twenty-three

Heath hadn't degenerated into a total idiot. Before she dashed into the coming night for a rendezvous with destiny in the guise of the New Canaanites, she put in one call to her Aunt Gwen and left a message and another to Anna Pigeon. Again she left a message. It would have given her greater courage to have talked to a real live person but she could think of no one else to call. Certainly not the Loveland police. They were probably fine fellows all in all, but she wasn't a hundred percent sure what she was doing was legal and she was damn sure the cops, like most authority figures, had been trained to believe citizen action was a bad idea; that it smacked of anarchy and vigilantism at best and made them look bad at worst. Citizen action by a middle-aged, female paraplegic? She'd be head-patted and kid-gloved and pooh-poohed right out of her mind.

Part of her knew it would be a relief to be put on the shelf. Part of her knew it would be another little death. She pushed fear aside and drove. The RV rattled and shuddered down the dirt road, the headlights catching the dust, and Heath felt as if she moved through a fog idiosyncratic to her mind rather than to the outside world. This blurring of mental and ocular vision deepened a sense of unreality that had been growing since she'd returned Sharon's e-mail. Surely she was out of her head.

Commuting through the world in a wheelchair brought with it a host of concerns she was not yet accustomed to addressing. Would the girls be waiting outside? If she were expected to go in, help them pack or unchain them from their prayer benches, would the compound be wheelchair friendly? Did her enemies have handicapped-accessible dwellings?

Panic began to rise, a welling up of liquid terror so cold it tightened her scalp and blurred her already impaired vision. Then Heath suddenly laughed. Grumbling down a one-lane road to nowhere in a vehicle half the size of Rhode Island to rescue three sisters from an old goat of a patriarch bent on bedding them all: a sense of unreality was the sanest reaction she could have. Discovering herself to be sane did nothing to alleviate the fear.

The hand-scrawled New Canaan sign loomed up like a signpost on a dream road to hell. Just past it a ghostly apparition, the American equivalent of Wilkie Collins' woman in white, drifted into the road.

Heath was almost relieved to see her too-real sense of unreality made manifest by the appearance of occult phenomena.

Not a ghost of course. Perhaps on England's moors ectoplasmic beings could wander with impunity for centuries. On the front range of the Rockies, the poor specters would be burnt or frozen or blown away before they could get a good haunt going.

Heath tapped the brake. She'd been going too fast. The RV was too heavy, the road surface bad. The great lumbering vehicle slid on the gravel for a stomach-churning second before lurching to a stop. Her ghost vanished in a cloud of dust then reappeared, coughing, tapping on the driver's side window.

Heath pushed the magic button and the glass hummed discreetly into the door. "Where are the others?" she asked.

"Wait." Sharon quickly ran to the bushes and returned with a gray-blue hard-sided suitcase, the kind all the girls wanted when Heath was fifteen, the kind that came with a square overnight case with a mirror in the lid.

"Where are the others?" Heath repeated and felt a stab of guilt as she realized she was thinking only of Beth, her limpet, and not of Sharon's sisters.

"We've got to go back. Patty told Mr. Sheppard we were going. About two hours ago, I guess. He's locked her in the chapel. I couldn't find Alexis or Beth. They're probably locked there too," she said as she climbed into the passenger seat.

"Buckle your seatbelt," Heath said automatically. The anxiety she'd felt earlier couldn't be said to have returned because it had never left. It did change, and not for the better. Her hands went numb on the wheel and her adrenaline-drugged mind whispered of creeping paralysis from a new complication in her spine. Though she could see, it was as if she looked through a tunnel, and Sharon's words reached her ears a fraction later than normal. Her voice sounded tinny and far away as if a tiny person whined from deep inside her skull.

"What are we supposed to do?" she asked.

"I can't run off and leave them. I can't," Sharon said unhelpfully.

"I have to go there to turn around anyway," Heath said numbly. "This thing's like driving a semi."

She shoved the gearshift into drive and the RV crept ahead. The speedometer read seven miles an hour. All of a sudden she wasn't in a hurry. During her aborted time in physical therapy the medical staff had attempted to teach her, among other things, relaxation techniques. She wished she'd paid more attention. The out-of-body experience—numbness, altered vision, audio distortions—were growing worse. Heath looked at Sharon, wondering if she could tell her that her driver, her hero, was melting, dissolving, right down to her functionless feet of base clay.

Sharon, white-faced, eyes as glassy and gray as the window beyond her, was caught in the faint green glow from the dashboard lights. Written in the younger woman's profile was the alphabet of Heath's fear: jaw muscle rigid, lips pressed too tightly together, corners of the mouth pulled down. In her lap, the delicate-boned rough-skinned fingers flexed and stretched as if she readied herself to play a difficult concerto. Or strangle a man.

Heath might lose her dignity. Fall on the ground. Flop around a bit perhaps. Boys could laugh at her. Mr. Sheppard or one of his disciples could come after her with a shotgun or, worst case scenario, she might soil herself.

Sharon, carrying only one old-fashioned suitcase, was leaving behind the only life she'd known since she was a little girl. Wretched though it might be, a warm bed, three meals a day and a roof to keep off the rain were not to be taken lightly. And she had two sisters at risk, sisters she might lose forever tonight though all three went on living.

The stakes were hardly comparable. Heath felt the panic recede—not much but enough she could unclench her jaw, enough she could loose the death grip she had on the steering wheel, reach over and take Sharon's hand.

"It'll be okay," she said, and felt better for saying it. "Mr. Sheppard can't lock us all up. My aunt and that ranger, Anna Pigeon, know what we're doing. They'll come if we don't call."

"Patty and Alexis, we have to get them out," Sharon said. "I don't care about me. I'm over."

Heath gave Sharon a startled glance, not because the sentiment was unique, but because it was one she shared. To hear it from a woman twenty years younger than she, a woman with two good legs for walking through the long life that presumably lay ahead, jolted her into the realization that giving up was the saddest disability of them all.

"You're not over till it's over," she said harshly. The condemnation in her tone was for herself, not Sharon, but she didn't apologize.

In front of the building housing the Sheppard clan, Heath stopped the RV. Only a single light showed. No dogs barked. No one came out to greet or banish them. She put the vehicle in park, the engine idling. They might be leaving in a hurry.

"The cars are gone," Sharon said. "We have two—all of us, two cars. He's taken the girls somewhere."

"Maybe not," Heath said and was ashamed at the part of her that hoped it was true, hoped to avoid a confrontation.

"You said he locked them in the chapel?"

"Patty. Yes."

"We'd better check it out," Heath said before she could chicken out and change her mind.

"You'll come with me?"

Sharon's voice had gone thin and wispy. Being back in New Canaan robbed her of what was left of her courage. Heath knew if she didn't go, Sharon wouldn't leave the van.

"I'll come as far as I can," she promised.

The process of swiveling the driver's seat, transferring herself to her chair and engaging the hydraulic lift went without a hitch. Knowing she might be driving the getaway car, Heath had rehearsed it a dozen times during the hours she'd awaited word from New Canaan.

"Stay, Wiley. Guard the fort." The dog wasn't pleased but, being a professional, dutifully trotted to the driver's seat, leaped up and settled in to keep watch. Or nap.

Pressed as close to the side of the RV as she could get without actually melding with the metal and fiberglass, Sharon waited as the lift descended.

"The kitchen door has no steps. Do you need me to push you?"

Heath started to snarl no, as had become her habit when being offered help, but she didn't. Sharon needed something to do, something to think about besides her own fear. If Heath's infirmity could give her a fleeting sense of strength and control, a little humility was a small price to pay.

"I'd appreciate it," she said with a graciousness she'd not known she still possessed.

So quiet was the compound, Heath's wheels on the rocky soil seemed excessively loud. In her mind, if not in actuality, the noise echoed like the approach of a tank battalion. She wished she felt as formidable.

Sharon came around the chair and opened the door on the side of the building. Heath wheeled herself through, the wide tread of her rubber tires moving easily over the doorsill. The kitchen, of industrial size as it would have to be for a family with at least three wives and heaven knew how many children, was dark and deserted. Dinner hour had come and gone, yet a kitchen, the heart of a house, should still be bustling.

"Where is everyone?" Heath whispered.

"Lockdown," Sharon whispered back. "Mr. Sheppard must have ordered it after I got away."

Not left; got away.

"When things are some way he doesn't like, everybody is confined to quarters until he says they can come out again. I was ordered to my room after he locked Patty in the chapel. I don't think he believed I would leave without my sisters. I went out the window and waited for you. He must have figured I'd gone."

"And gone out looking for you," Heath said, thinking of the missing cars. "I didn't pass anybody on the road."

"There's lots of dirt roads. Old ranch

roads. He might have thought I'd gone out one and hid."

During this whispered exchange, Sharon had again taken the driver's position and pushed Heath through the oversized kitchen and into a long hallway that ran from the kitchen at one end to the chapel at the other. Closed doors lined either side like a dormitory after lights out.

"We have to hurry." Sharon leaned down so close Heath felt the warm breath stir her hair. "Mr. Sheppard won't have gone far." Urgency could not counteract the fear that had entered her bones; she continued to push Heath at a lame snail's pace.

Fear had settled in Heath's bones as well, though of precisely what, she wasn't sure. Not death. Fear of something worse than life—worse than life in a wheelchair. Though she couldn't think what that might be at this moment, over the last week she'd come to know it existed. Grabbing the wheels, she rolled herself forward. The handles of her chair slipped from Sharon's grasp, the tires squealed on the linoleum. Moving fast, Heath could hear Sharon's Keds snuffling on the hard floor in her wake. Ahead was the door to the chapel. Heath wished she carried a lance or a battering ram. She wanted to hit something. Hard. And she was afraid if she stopped she'd never find the courage to start again.

One of the side doors opened abruptly. Heath was going too fast to swerve. Her left wheel clipped it, then she struck the opposite wall. The hall, the darkness, the miasma of twisting emotions oozing under closed doors, conspired with this sudden violence and Heath exploded in a battery of language so foul it was a wonder the walls didn't melt and the flooring curl.

Not a door opened. No voice called out to ask what was happening. Lockdown was a serious matter in New Canaan.

Mrs. Dwayne stepped into the hall between them and the chapel door. Light from her room—or the room she'd come out of—lit half of her face and cast long shadows over the other. The usually innocuous dumpling visage was ugly, frightening.

"Filth," she hissed. "You're nothing but filth. The both of you. Get out before I call Mr. Sheppard." Her hands were fisted on lumpy hips. Jowls quivered at her jaw line. Spittle flew, obvious as moths in the unilateral light. Mrs. Dwayne was a caricature of the harridan but Heath had no desire to laugh. A face like that could countenance murder and never suffer a moment's remorse.

The fear that had been shuddering through Heath's frame since Sharon had called for help was suddenly gone. She didn't feel brave, just unafraid. All the ugly and crippled in the world was embodied in the woman standing before her. None was left over for Heath. She felt free.

"Mr. Sheppard's not here," she said, marveling at how reasonable she sounded—and felt.

"Oh," Mrs. Dwayne said. Then: "I don't believe you."

But she did, Heath could tell. She didn't want to admit that her beloved kept her as much in the dark as he did his other wives. For a long moment neither moved, caught in the tension of the dark hallway, tethered by the rope of yellow light coming from Mrs. Dwayne's doorway.

"You've come for that little slut, Patty," Mrs. Dwayne said finally.

Heath felt her chair shiver as a spider might feel a helpless thing twitching in its web. Sharon had come up behind her and taken hold of the handles.

"That's right." Quiet authority reverberated in her words. The voice of command;
the voice that had talked terrified climbers
off ledges and calmed panicked neophytes
on icy crags; a voice Heath had never
thought to hear again.

Mrs. Dwayne came to a decision. The
venom that had been frothing behind her
eyes, spewing from her lips, solidified till she
looked old and mean and hard. "You can
have her," she snapped. "And good rid-
dance. The little whore is no better than her
sisters. Casting sideways eyes at my husband, tempting my husband to sin, coveting
my husband's attentions."

"My husband" was stressed each time it
was uttered, as if Mrs. Dwayne were a
priestess calling on the name of her god.

"Stay," she commanded. Pushing by
Heath's left wheel, she trotted down the
hallway in the direction of the kitchen.

"Where's she going?" The voice of command was gone. Heath was back to whispering, intimidated by a silence only
sharpened on the squeaky thumps of Mrs.
Dwayne's determined march.

Sharon looked over her shoulder. Mrs.
Dwayne had taken keys from her pocket

and was unlocking the last door to the right before the kitchen. "Mr. Sheppard's room," Sharon said. "She's the only one besides him that's got a key and doesn't she let the rest of us know it. She acts as if that room is her private sanctuary, like she's the priestess of a temple. It's not like she sleeps there much," Sharon finished bitterly. "Nobody but Mr. Sheppard actually *sleeps* there. Me and Alexis are just called in, then dismissed."

Before Heath had to respond to this unwelcome peek into the lives of the Dennis girls, Mrs. Dwayne reemerged, carefully relocked the door, then steamed back down the hall.

"Come on," she puffed as she passed. Sharon pushing and Heath letting her, they followed toward the door to the chapel. Selecting a key from the jingling bunch she'd fetched, Mrs. Dwayne unlocked the chapel door and shoved it open. "Get your dirty baggage and get out," she said viciously.

Sharon wheeled Heath past her. Mrs. Dwayne didn't give an inch. Though Heath pulled in her elbow, her wheel and shoulder pressed the soft belly. It was not a pleasant sensation.

The chapel was dark, no windows to let in what feeble light the night sky might offer. Heaven forfend any of the natural world He was purported to have created with miraculous love be allowed into the man-made box where Mr. Sheppard held forth.

"Turn on the lights," Heath said to Mrs. Dwayne.

"There are no lights in the chapel."

"There are lights," Sharon said and switched on the overheads. There were three naked bulbs hanging from the low ceiling by electric cords.

A little girl, blond like her sisters, long-legged and reed-thin like her sisters, was kneeling between two of the benches facing the altar. She was dressed in an odd mixture of turn-of-the-century fashions and twenty-first-century workout clothes. A ruffled dress came down past her knees and up to her chin. Beneath the hem were running shoes. Over the bodice was a pink hooded sweatshirt.

"Sharon," she breathed when she saw who'd come for her. Bursting into a storm of tears, she jumped to her feet and ran to her sister.

"He told me you'd gone. Taken Alexis and

left me behind." Sharon met the little girl halfway and folded her in her arms.

"Where is Beth?" Mrs. Dwayne asked. "What have you done with my daughter?" she screamed just as Sharon was crying, "Alexis!"

The shouts canceled each other out. Much as they hated one another, there was no doubt that both were genuinely ignorant of the older girls' whereabouts. Not knowing where the limpet was opened a pit inside Heath. She felt the falling sensation she suffered each night in her nightmares.

"Mr. Sheppard, he's taken them," Sharon accused.

"So what if he has," Mrs. Dwayne shot back. "They are his to do with as he will."

It looked as if Sharon would launch herself at her co-wife. Heath would have genuinely enjoyed seeing the harridan taken down, but time was at a premium. Besides, Sharon would come out the loser. Probably she'd never been strong and the time with Mr. Sheppard and his flock had worn away what resilience youth might once have lent her.

"Sharon, she doesn't know he took them," Heath said firmly as she wheeled herself between the two Mrs. Sheppards. "Hell, she didn't even know *her husband* was gone. She's as much in the dark as we are. Let's get Patty someplace safe. Then we'll worry about—"

The sound of an automobile approaching stopped Heath mid-sentence. Heads cocked, eyes wary, the three women and the girl listened as rabbits might listen to the coyotes howling.

"Out the back," Mrs. Dwayne said quickly. Heath didn't for an instant believe she had decided to help them from empathy or altruism, but she trusted her all the same. They shared a common goal: to get the Dennis girls out of Mr. Sheppard's bed.

Leading Patty by the hand, Sharon ran to a door left of the lectern that opened to the rear of the building. "Hurry," she urged as Mrs. Dwayne fumbled with the keys. Mr. Sheppard had outfitted the compound like a prison. Outer doors needed keys to open from both the inside and out. Heath was willing to bet that the doors of the women's and girls' quarters could only be locked from the outside.

Men's voices broke through the enforced

stillness of New Canaan. The kitchen door slammed shut.

"Hurry," Heath repeated Sharon's plea.

"Out," hissed Mrs. Dwayne as she got the key turned and jerked the door open. Sharon and Patty didn't hesitate but bolted down the steps.

Steps.

From the bottom, the sisters looked back. Light from the overhead bulbs in the chapel touched only the planes of their faces and their eyes, giving them the soulful disembodied stare of the cheap velvet paintings Heath remembered from the mid-seventies.

"We could help you down," Sharon offered faintly.

They couldn't. It would have been a struggle for the two of them to lift a pudgy dachshund, let alone a woman. A woman and a chair.

Mr. Sheppard would figure out where they were in a moment, if he hadn't already.

"Go," Heath said. "Get in the RV, lock the doors. If anybody bothers you, drive off. Don't go to the park. Someplace else. I'll be okay. Sheppard won't dare touch me. I've got my cell phone," she finished as if a cell phone were a magic talisman. In a way it was. According to the tales, magic was a whimsical thing working least when needed most. Cell phones were much like that.

Maybe the Dennis girls trusted her. Maybe they didn't give a damn about her. Either way, they ran into the darkness without another word. Mrs. Dwayne did, too, but turned left toward the long end of the building rather than right, around the corner of the chapel. Probably she hoped to return her husband's keys and secret herself back in her room so she wouldn't be blamed for letting his chattel escape.

Heath closed the exit door, hearing the lock snick into place, then moved soundlessly across the chapel, her rubber wheels silent on the hard floor. Having switched off the lights, she rolled into the hallway and shut the chapel door behind her.

"I hope the son-of-a-bitch draws the line at hitting cripples," she muttered, and set the brakes on her chair.

twenty - four

The Mag-Lite was tiny, more for peeping at locks and finding keyholes than any true illumination, and its batteries were small. Anna didn't want to waste her only source of light and so she ran, chasing the last gray mirage of light to the top of the ridge.

At least she ran as much as her middle-aged body and flatlander's lungs would allow. It was a good half-hour and full dark by the time she reached the elevation from which it was purported her radio would work. Drenched in sweat and panting, she threw herself down on the nearest rock to recover before calling dispatch.

Purported to work: it was Rita, her felonious seasonal ranger, now handcuffed to a pine tree, who had told her where the best place to call out was.

Sitting in the duff, Anna wondered why she had believed her so readily. The bottom line was she trusted Rita even while arresting her for importing endangered species into a protected area, the massacre of mice, the slaughter of a squirrel and the murder of a teenage girl. Sitting there, Anna realized she believed Rita innocent of all but the care and feeding of illicit puppies.

Regardless of woman's intuition or its more manly cousin, gut feelings, Anna called dispatch as soon as she recovered her breath. Experience had taught her that she was not the best judge of character. More than once she'd been dead wrong—or nearly dead wrong—about her fellow humans. She would not bet her life that this time she was right.

The chief ranger was out of pocket, the dispatcher informed Anna. She'd gone to the Denver Resource Center and wouldn't be back in the park till the following afternoon. Lorraine would have grasped the gist of things without a lengthy explanation.

Anyone else would require chapter and verse. Anna's situation was complicated— baby wolves, a ranger flaunting park regulations and state laws, suspected of murder—she didn't want to broadcast details to the entire park as well as anyone else who might choose to listen in. In the end she merely asked that the Fall River District Ranger be contacted and asked to send a couple rangers up in the morning to assist in walking out a prisoner in a routine arrest.

Her next call was to Fern Lake and Raymond Bleeker. He'd been monitoring the radio. "Hang tight," he said. "I'll get together food, water and sleeping bags and head your way. I should be there in an hour or so."

Having done all she could, Anna started back down the hill. The descent was slower than the climb. No longer was she headed into the light, however feeble it had been, but into the greater darkness of the forest.

As she picked her way down the ragged slope, she reviewed the plans she had set in motion. There was nothing she could do that hadn't been done. Within an hour or two she'd have backup and enough in the way of worldly goods to pass the night in relative comfort. Tomorrow she'd have hot and cold running rangers to ease the hike and/or carry out, depending on Rita's mood. Yet she didn't feel relieved. If anything, she suffered a deepening disquiet, a sense that somewhere she'd left a fire burning and that fire was going to blaze out of control.

In the not-too-distant past Anna had had bad experiences in the woods at night. "Little Red Riding Hood syndrome," she muttered as she literally and figuratively tried to shake off the willies. She smiled at the image. This time there were real live wolves in the woods, four of them. "And you're not to pet them," she reminded herself.

Using the Mag-Lite more than she wanted to, she arrived at the ring of boulders holding the nascent wolf pack. Here the slope she'd been following leveled out down toward the shores of Loomis Lake. Within a hundred yards and one hundred eighty degrees was her prisoner. With neither light nor trail, Anna couldn't be sure of the exact route the two of them had been following when Rita staged her sit-in. Leaning against a chunk of granite, Anna waited and listened. The alarm that had been jangling her nerves all the way down the mountainside warned her not to walk blindly back into the woods in search of that one particular tree to which she'd manacled Ms. Perry.

"That you, Anna?"

Apparently Anna wasn't the only one keeping an ear out for nonnative species. Anna didn't reply.

"If it's you, I've got to pee."

Listen as she might, Anna could hear no subterfuge in Rita's announcement.

"It's me," she called back. "I got turned around in the dark. Keep talking so I can find you." Anna had placed Rita when first she'd spoken. She wanted Rita's chatter to cover the sounds of her passage as she circled to come upon the prison tree from what she hoped would be an unsuspected direction. The sense of impending danger had entered into her body on a cellular level. Her nerves were stretched till each rustle of needles or breath of air brought forth an answering reverberation within her. It wasn't Rita Anna was afraid of exactly, but she was most definitely afraid.

While Rita sang "Frère Jacques" in a rich alto voice, Anna slipped around to the lake side of the tree, then closed in on her singing captive. Eyes adjusted to the dark as much as they could, lacking the cones and rods of a cat's eyes, she could just make out Rita's shape melding into that of the pine's trunk. Moving as little as possible and not using her light at all, Anna assured herself there was no accomplice lurking nearby. Nothing. Nothing she could see, hear or smell at any rate. The feeling of something sick and mean lurking nearby didn't abate one jot.

Rita's singing broke off.

"Where the heck are you?" she shouted. "A woman's bladder can only take so much."

"Here," Anna said and Rita squawked satisfyingly. It was good not to be the only one scared.

"You're a creepy, sneaky little thing," Rita said.

"Thank you."

Anna uncuffed Rita from the tree, then drew her service weapon and held it and the Mag-Lite on the young woman while she relieved herself. Keeping Rita Perry at gunpoint till she'd buttoned her trousers and recuffed herself didn't make Anna feel any safer. It made her feel foolish. Rita's vocal disdain for these precautions didn't help matters.

Calls of nature answered, Anna reholstered the 9 mm and they sat again beneath the pine to which Rita had been so recently cuffed. The rain had stopped or, as was more likely with the storm cells that built every afternoon in the mountains, moved on. The sweat Anna had worked up during her dash up the ridge cooled, leaving her damp and chilled.

"What now?" Rita asked. "The cavalry coming to help you bring in your dangerous fugitive?"

"Something like that."

Rita was also in a foul mood and for a long time neither spoke. Anna dug through her pack and shared her granola bar with Rita. The pack she tossed a couple yards away, out of lunging or footsie distance should Rita take it into her head to try and retrieve her service weapon. Inspired by generosity, or just still hungry, Rita volunteered to split her remaining bologna and cheese sandwich if Anna would retrieve it from her daypack.

Having broken bread together as well as

taken the edge off their hunger, they began to feel more kindly toward one another.

"Tell me about your wolf project," Anna said, both because she was interested and to pass the time. There would be no sleep tonight, at least not for her.

Rita liked talking about the pups and told Anna how, once the little family had fallen into her hands, she had researched reintroduction techniques that had been used successfully in other parks, put together a pen and a plan, then smuggled the pups in. It would be a couple months before they would be ready to release but Rita hoped by then they'd be old enough and strong enough to make it through the winter.

Anna did, too, but she didn't say as much. These pups would be put in a zoo, destroyed or introduced into another wolf program by the time the first snows fell in Rocky. The thought saddened her. Reports filtered in occasionally of grizzlies, sharks and, increasingly, mountain lions attacking humans as their territory and food sources were reduced by encroaching development. To keep herself out of hot water, Anna pretended to be on the side of the people attacked. She did feel sympathy of a sort for the fear and pain they endured. When they were killed, she managed genuine compassion for the friends and relatives who mourned them.

Inside though, down deep, she was really pleased the critters got lunch. She always hoped—usually in vain—that the beasts would get away with it, not be hunted down and killed like . . . like *animals*.

Personally, she relished hiking and camping where there were predators greater than herself. It kept her on her toes, alive and alert. In Glacier/ Waterton National Peace Park, where the great grizzly bears were a real threat, Anna had found the blessings of being alive—breathing, seeing in color, the taste of glacier milk and the smell of burnt earth and new grass—to be more piquant than anywhere else she'd been.

"How did Robert Proffit figure in?" Anna asked.

For a long time Rita didn't respond. The storm cells had spent themselves. A quarter moon rose above the mountain to the east, rendering the darkness beneath the trees incomplete. The faint silvery light caught rain drops on the needles, creating a pale nimbus that allowed Anna to distinguish the pines from sky and Rita from the pines. Weak as this illumination was, it raised Anna's spirits. Time lost in Lechuguilla Cavern and a bloody black night in the high country of Yosemite had engendered in her a fear of the dark, the real dark, the kind that settled into the pores and clogged the lungs.

At length Rita raised her head. Light caught on her strong chin and the flat high planes of cheekbones, hard beneath the skin. "You've got Robert all wrong," she said. "He's a good man. He loves the Lord. And he loves those kids. When they went missing, he was crazy with worry and eaten up by guilt. He thought if he'd not gone looking for them, not gotten lost, gone straight to Ray to report it, they might have been found. I thought Robert might do something awful. Might kill himself even. He almost did, in a way. He worked himself harder than anybody on the search: hiking sixteen, eighteen hours a day, going without sleep, forgetting to eat. He looked like a scarecrow—a zombie. Even after the park had given up, he kept on. The people at New Canaan tried to stop him. They'd more or less decided the loss of the girls was

God's will. Robert never bought it. I think he came to think it was a judgement against him. A test of some kind."

"That sounds egocentric to me. Thinking it was all about him," Anna commented.

"It wasn't like that," Rita said. "He wasn't thinking of himself. Not the way you mean it. Robert didn't think God's will was focused on Robert Proffit and everybody else was just pawns in a cosmic game. It was more the God within him, his own faith. When the girls went missing he felt himself losing it. Every day we'd all come back tired and depressed and nothing to show for it. I could tell he felt that God turned away from him. Or that he was turning away from God. After a while he no longer believed that God would look after his lost lambs. He quit the prayer vigils the New Canaanites held and spent all of his time searching, thinking God was gone and there was only him left in a godless world to find Beth and Alexis and Candace. He found my wolves. He was the only one who did. There wasn't anyplace up here he didn't cover more than once. We got to know each other then. He started helping me out when I couldn't get up to take care of the little guys. He'd've been up here searching anyway. I think when Beth and Alexis came back he got his soul back. Most of it anyway."

"Never gave up? Candace doesn't count? According to you, he knocked me over a cliff, fed the puppies, left you a note and split."

"I don't know why he left," Rita said simply. "I only know he had a good—and honorable reason. You can't understand a man like him."

Anna wasn't sure whether she understood or not, she was only sure that she wanted to. Keeping Rita talking, keeping her stirred up and on the defensive, was a way she might achieve that. This was the one plan that might actually be helped by isolation, discomfort and darkness. That in itself made it worth trying.

"Oh, I understand perfectly," Anna said. "Proffit puts himself in a position where he is in the company of, and has control over, young girls. Circumstances call away the chaperone. He sees his chance and takes it. Two of the girls run away, traumatized by his advances. The third isn't so lucky. He kills her to shut her up, then works his tail off trying to find the two witnesses before they're found by anyone else. He fails. The girls turn up too freaked out to talk. He starts trying to get next to them to kill them, keep them quiet, whatever."

Anna spun the theory to provoke Rita, but having put it together, found she rather liked it.

"It wasn't like that," Rita snapped.

"Sure it was. You just don't want to admit he grabbed onto you using God as his handle so he could keep an eye and ear on how the search was progressing. Not to mention a connection to get him in good with the Park Service so he could base himself out of the cabin at Fern Lake. You can't stand the thought that you've been used."

"That's not true," Rita spat. "Robert loves me."

The trite phrase and the vehemence with which Rita uttered it took Anna aback. Admittedly she'd been fishing in dark waters with improvised bait, still her catch surprised her. Usually with a man and a woman and a secret, sex or love would have been the first thing that came to mind. Part of this oversight was because of the disparity in their ages. Robert was twenty-two, Rita eight or nine years older. The one time she'd seen them together there'd been hugging and praying but the heat had seemed more for their adventure and their God than one another. Other vibes coming off them had struck her as platonic. The reddest of herrings, however, had been Rita's night of passionate disporting with Raymond Bleeker.

Annoyed at herself for being fooled by a woman who used piety to cover both promiscuity and dishonesty, Anna said with more of a sneer than was necessary to keep the pot boiling, "What does good old Ray think of all this?"

Dead silence met her query. Anna was attuned to the language of silence. Lack of noise had many notes: hostile, uneasy, comfortable, dead. Till now, she'd believed the sense of a silence was transmitted by the eye. Not so. The darkness, though not perfect, was sufficient to hide the nuances of facial expressions and still she knew. Apparently silences had a tone, a timbre that didn't require sight. This one played the dull blank symphony of confusion.

So rapidly was her brain working, she scarcely heard Rita when she put voice to her silent music: "Why would Ray think anything about it?"

Pictures were held up in Anna's brain like flashcards in the hands of a manic tutor: Ray in funny reading glasses, Ray with an odd pink-flowered handkerchief. Ray with punk-dark hair. Ray disappearing to fetch something to show her, something he seemed pleased not to have found.

"You and Ray didn't have sex half the night when you and I stayed at Fern?" Anna interrupted her own thoughts.

"No. Ish. *No.* I came to bed right after you. I told you that."

"I woke up in the middle of the night. Thumping. Grunting. Voices from the storage room. I shined my light. You weren't in the bunk. Where were you?" Anna didn't succeed in keeping the pleading out of her voice. She wanted Rita to be lying.

"I was on the top bunk. The bottom one on that side is too sprung. Ask anybody."

More flash cards. Beth in her old replacement glasses. The underweight girl on the rock at Odessa, a girl with punk-dark hair inexpertly cut, a girl who verified Bleeker's alibi in such a timely fashion.

Anna pressed the tiny button on her watch and the face lit up. Over an hour had passed since she'd radioed Fern Lake.

"Give me your hands," she demanded of Rita. Working by feel she unlocked the cuffs.

"What—" Rita began.

Anna cut her off. "We've got to get the hell out of here."

twenty-five

The door to the kitchen banged open with such force that when it struck the wall, the hallway reverberated. Lights had been turned on in the kitchen, throwing Mr. Sheppard into stark silhouette. He looked huge, black and menacing. Heath remembered him as a stocky man but of no more than middling height, five-nine tops.

Stomping on legs like pistons, his short, thick arms pumping, he came down the hall like a juggernaut. He struck each door he passed with a fist, calling, "Out! Out! Out! Where are they? Anyone hiding or helping them will answer to me." Knobs rattled in desperate, futile attempts to obey but the doors were all locked from the outside.

Recovering from her initial shock at the wrath of the clan's patriarch, Heath realized he had not seen her. Parked sedately below eye level, in a dark chair, dark clothing and an unlit hall, she was invisible. Literally this time, rather than figuratively.

Reaching to the walls on either side of her, Heath felt for the switches. Most halls had them at both ends. This one was no exception. Putting her palm over the three toggles, she waited. When he was five or six feet away from plowing into her, she switched on the overhead lights. The effect was gratifying. Sheppard stopped so suddenly the soles of his shoes screeched on the floor and he blinked at her as if she had appeared in a puff of magician's smoke. From the tangle of his beard, his mouth formed a neat "O." Heath was put in mind of other orifices.

"Hello," she said with what, given the circumstances, was a miraculous impression of calm. "I was hoping you'd get back. I need the keys to the chapel. I've come to pick up Patty Dennis."

Her feigned innocence or her sheer

effrontery held Sheppard motionless for a moment. With a peculiar sense of detachment, she studied him as she'd once studied the ice, looking for flaws, rotten places, handholds, traverses. Sheppard was overweight and over sixty. He would have lost speed, endurance and agility but looked to be at the height of his strength. His mouth, partially hidden by facial hair, showed more of rigid fanaticism than outright cruelty. The lips were pulled thin by determination, no sensuality to soften the corners or warm the eyes. It proved nothing, but Heath had a strong sense that he'd never admit to being a hedonist or a run-of-the-mill pervert who impregnated thirteen-year-olds and kept women locked in their rooms and their narrow lives. He'd believe he did it because it was his duty as a more exalted being. Because he was personally told to by God.

Hearing voices.

Was one any less crazy when they were purported to come from God rather than the fillings in one's teeth or the family dog?

The other facet of Sheppard's face was hatred. Whether a strength or weakness or both, Heath guessed it ruled his life and the lives of those around him. Hatred was an outgrowth of fear. Suddenly Heath knew that too well. With a clarity that dropped her jaw she knew she didn't hate this new way of living, moving, relating. She was scared to death of it. She didn't hate the words "disabled," "other abled," "physically challenged." She was terrified of what they meant. It wasn't even never being able to climb again that she hated. Though she would miss it terribly, mostly she was frightened she wouldn't find something else that made her feel so alive, as powerful.

Looking up at Sheppard she knew the man lived in fear of nearly everything: the government, the church, women, foreigners, the past, the future, his god.

Fear paralyzed in its early stages. Turned to hate, it became dangerous. And right now it was focused on her. The moment of insight and contemplation shattered.

"Move," Sheppard ordered in a cold, flat voice. Fists were balled at his sides, knuckles knobbed and sprouting black hairs. Heath was certain only the fact she sat in a wheelchair stopped him from striking her, and it wouldn't stop him long.

"I can't," she said reasonably, hoping he would overlook the fact that she was facing in a direction that attested to where she'd come from. "There's not room to get by you. Hand me the keys and I'll just unlock the door and back in." She nodded to the over-sized ring of keys he sported at his belt in the time-honored tradition of jailers.

Sheppard didn't respond. Behind his eyes things began to move. His beard rippled as he clenched and unclenched his jaws. Either he was thinking hard or about to suffer a psychotic break.

Into this strange standoff came the sound of an engine revving, gravel being thrown by tires too quickly started in motion. Sharon and Patty had gotten to the RV. They were getting away. That unacceptable truth dawned in Sheppard's eyes.

"Filthy bitch," he snarled. Heath didn't know if he referred to her or Sharon. She was given no time to figure it out. Holding to the wheel of her chair for balance, Sheppard drove his heel past her shoulder, kicking open the door behind her.

"Goddamn filthy bitch," he reiterated and backhanded Heath to one side as he pushed by her.

The blow caught her on her ear. Pain was sudden and paralyzing. Her head snapped toward the wall. Her thoughts exploded into red fragments. Sheppard pushed. She could smell his sweat and feel the repulsive softness of his belly against her hand and arm. Maybe if he hadn't hit her she wouldn't have found the courage to do what she did. Face burning from the blow, too furious to be sensibly scared, she lifted the hook that held the keys on his belt.

Stench and softness were gone. Sheppard was in the chapel. Heath heard the heavy fall of his feet as he charged toward the outer door, then a bestial roar when he found it locked. She tried to move but the chair seemed rooted to the ground.

The brakes; she'd set the brakes.

A crash resounded behind her: Sheppard kicking at another door. The chapel doors opened inward and wouldn't give. Frustration brought another guttural burst of sound from the man's considerable lungs.

Heath released the brake and spun her wheels. Pounding thundered behind her. Too much adrenaline coursed through Heath's veins to coordinate fine motor control. Careening down the hall, weaving like a drunkard, the chair veered left, the wheel scraping the wall.

Sheppard was upon her. Meaty hands grabbed at her chair. During the past week a metamorphosis she'd been told of had occurred. The wheelchair ceased to be The Other, a vile contraption in which she was imprisoned, and had become an extension of her body. The pressure of his blunt fingers on the chair's handles felt like a violation of her person.

"Keys," he yelled. His breath, smelling sweetly of cinnamon and mint, was hot on her cheek. The odor jarred her. It should have reeked of the grave, the corruption of flesh.

Snatching the keys from where she'd dropped them in her lap, she turned as far as she could and hurled them back down the hall toward the chapel.

"Filthy bitch." Sheppard growled. It was apparently his only description of females who were not under his control. Heath covered her ears with her hands and tensed for another blow, but he had more pressing abuses to mete out. He raced after the keys.

Doors banged opened, slammed shut. Muffled shouts came faintly from outside. Adrenaline's strength and courage deserted Heath, leaving behind only a quaking fatigue. It was all she could do to breathe, to not cry. Noises from out-of-doors abated. Noise behind the closed doors began murmuring out through keyholes. The kitchen light was switched off, as was the hallway light, by a hand Heath never saw. Somewhere along the line she stopped gasping like a landed fish. Time proved its relativity: she couldn't have testified as to whether she sat in the hall for three minutes or thirty.

Apparently Mr. Sheppard wasn't returning to wring her neck but neither was the local sheriff's department coming to rescue her. Not that she'd expected the latter. Sharon's terror of the United States government in all its many guises was too deeply engrained to allow her to dial 911.

Heath roused herself from this post-traumatic torpor and began to move slowly toward the kitchen. As she rolled past each door on silent rubber wheels, she could feel the lives behind, waiting, scared, excited, frustrated, bored. This sensitivity was so pronounced she wondered if loss of the use of her legs, coupled with her recent adventures, had rendered her psychic or just made her crazy.

Besieged by the real or imagined emotions of others, she traversed the length of the hallway and entered the darkened kitchen. At the threshold, she experienced a twinge—not of anxiety precisely, but of expectation—a waiting for a corporeal life form to manifest so that she might know she herself was real and this bizarre night wasn't a dream brought on by too much wine, too many cigarettes.

Cigarettes.

At the thought came an overpowering craving. Alone in the deserted kitchen, she fumbled in her saddlebags, retrieved a pack and lighter. The first drag was heaven, comfort in a toxic cloud, and Heath savored it. Again flicking the lighter to life, she held it above her head. Nothing, no one lurked in the shadows.

Oddly at peace—or at a loss, at the moment they felt one and the same—she sat quietly in the darkness and enjoyed her smoke. When she finished, in an act of supreme disrespect, she dropped the butt on the kitchen floor and ground it out with two careful passes of a wheel.

Revived by nicotine and minor vandalism, she bumped over the doorsill and onto the gravel outside. After the confines of the hall with its locked doors and muffled lives, the Colorado night, black of mountains walling off the west, the impossible distances of the prairie beckoning to the east, blasted into Heath's consciousness, cleansing the muck of humanity's sty from mind and soul. Stilling her thoughts and her wheels, she absorbed the immensity and beauty of the real, the eternal, cosmic reality.

Unfortunately, the wee human intellect cannot encompass the divine for more than an instant or two. Following a rush of grati-tude so intense she felt as if she might levi-tate, the sense of wonder vanished, leaving her in the middle of nowhere with people who did not wish her well.

The instinct for self-preservation re-asserted itself. Heath took stock of her sur-roundings. No lights shone from any of the buildings. Lockdown must encompass more than the securing of entrances and exits. A flashlight beam poked under the hood of an old Chevy van, the only vehicle in evidence. By its sporadic movements, Heath counted three men, Dwayne Shep-pard and two others, likewise bearded, star-ing intently at the engine. The sedan Mrs.

Dwayne, then Sharon, had driven to the RV park was not in evidence.

Mr. Sheppard would have taken it to pursue Sharon and Patty if it had been available, of that Heath was certain. The fact he was still here indicated the car had been gone when he erupted out of the chapel. Possibly before that. Sitting unnoticed in the dark, no attractive course of action open to her, Heath thought about what that might mean.

It had been clear Mrs. Dwayne did not know where her daughter was. She had fully expected to find Beth and Alexis incarcerated in the chapel with Patty. From Mr. Sheppard's reactions, Heath didn't believe he had taken the two older girls. She doubted he knew where they had gone.

Either someone else had taken them or they had run—or been lured away. Had they been taken, the kidnapper would have spirited them away in his own car. Neither girl was old enough to drive legally but Heath knew what it was like to grow up on a ranch in rural Colorado. As soon as kids' legs were long enough to reach the pedals they were carrying feed to cattle, fetching fence posts from one side of the property to another. At least one of the girls, and probably both, would know how to drive a car.

Heath badly wanted to think they'd stolen the car and run away, but she couldn't. Where would they run? They'd have run to her and she hadn't seen them.

They had been lured. The voices that called to them from the brush had called them again. This time they'd followed.

"Shit," Heath whispered. Regardless of Sharon's sensibilities she was calling the sheriff's department. Having dug her cell phone out of her saddlebag, she flipped it open. No signal.

"Shit."

She couldn't—and wouldn't—stay where she was. Heath grasped her wheels and began moving over the gravel, her passage making an unseemly noise in the stillness of the night. The men stopped staring into the van's engine compartment and turned as one to stare at her. In what seemed an unreal eternity of outer silence and inner cacophony, Heath rolled through the dirt yard and onto what passed for a road. From there she turned south, propelling herself past the disabled van and the hostile wall of bearded men. No one spoke; not to her, not to one another. Finally they were behind her. Feeling their eyes on her back, an odd visceral pressure to either side of her spine, she pushed on. It was ten minutes before that pressure eased and she dared stop and look back.

A low rise in the road and the darkness erased New Canaan. Already her arms were tired and she was sweating. Scrub brush lined either side of the road. To the west the Rockies blotted out the sky. To the east the low jagged ridge of rock cut into the eastern horizon. Though the moon was far from full, the sandy soil picked up the light and the roadway shone clear, stretching away for miles.

And miles.

For the first time Heath wished she'd gotten a motorized chair. When she'd been choosing a conveyance, the motorized version was strongly recommended for those who could afford it. Heath had opted for the hand propelled model, the cheapest one they had. At the time, she'd not wanted to think, to spend, to commit. She'd believed she chose the inexpensive one for reasons of frugality and to retain at least some of her independence. Sitting in the middle of the dirt track, flexing fingers cramped from grasping and pushing, she realized she'd picked the cheapest chair because she didn't believe she'd be using it long. It wasn't that she thought she'd be up and walking soon, climbing rock and ice just like old times. She'd believed she would die. Suicide was never a conscious thought. There'd been too many times she'd literally clung to life by her fingernails for her mind to work that way. But sitting in that room sur-rounded by the shiny unkind-looking para-phernalia of the disabled, a part of her had decided to let go, to fall again. This time she would not survive.

Heath grabbed the wheels and pushed on. As soon as she was near a credit card she was getting the high-end machinery. Not for everyday—she didn't want to lose the strength of her arms and upper body— but for special occasions.

Like touring the western plains of Col-orado at night.

twenty-six

Heath's palms were blistered and her arms felt as if she'd free-climbed Everest. At a guess, she'd traveled two miles, maybe three. It felt like thirty. With a grunt and an effort that tore more skin from the palms of her hands, she rolled over a small rise; a small rise for a recreational vehicle, a veritable mountain for a tired woman in a wheelchair.

Before her, hideous black and bloated on the iridescent sand, was a huge spider. A tarantula. Bigger, much bigger than a tarantula. A tarantula whose parents had immigrated to Colorado from Three Mile Island.

"Jumpin' Jehosephat!" Heath panted, wondering even as she said it from whence the ridiculous oath had sprung. She came to a halt and lifted her ravaged hands from the tires. Unbraked, the chair began rolling toward the oversized arachnid, oversized in a Chihuahua-eating sort of a way.

"Fuck," she screamed, finding a more satisfying way of expressing her alarm. She stopped the chair then wiped her eyes. Sweat ran in rivulets from her scalp, dripping off her nose and jawline, soaking through her shirt between her breasts.

Eyes clear and mind under control, she saw the monstrosity for what it was: a distributor cap. The mystery of the broken-down van at New Canaan cleared up. Sharon had sabotaged their vehicle. Heath was proud of her. Because she'd always been strong, liberated and fiercely independent, it had been hard at first to feel sisterhood with women who lived under the thumb of a man. Like most people, she took her upbringing for granted, but lots of girls didn't have nice daddies, mothers who worked for a living, aunts who became doctors.

Looking at the leggy bit of rubber with

images from the Sheppard household still reeking in her mind, Heath glimpsed the determination and courage Sharon must have had to open His van and rip the guts from His engine that she might steal her sister—and herself—from Him.

"Good girl," Heath whispered.

Free of the worry that the van would be made operational and come roaring up the road in pursuit at any moment, Heath allowed herself to rest for a while, just sit and breathe and let the cool of the night soothe her palms and take the burn out of her lungs.

Despite the fact she was exhausted, alone, aching and had hands resembling cheap hamburger, Heath realized she was experiencing a sensation of well-being. She'd not felt just plain old good in such a long time, at first she couldn't grasp what was happening and wondered if she verged on hysteria, denial or some other mentally unbalanced event.

It was runner's high. *Roller's high*, she amended, and shook her head in awe of her discovery of the patently obvious. Because she could not do what she wanted, Heath had chosen to do nothing—nothing but smoke and drink and feel sorry for herself. As her heart rate returned to normal, she promised herself as soon as she got the okay from the medical world she would join a gym or whatever paraplegics joined to stay fit.

Energized, she grabbed her wheels. The jolt of pain from her ruined palms took the edge off her good cheer but didn't manage to eradicate it. That took two more miles of rough road.

Finally Heath stopped. Not stopped to rest but quit, ceased, gave up, threw in the towel.

You didn't give up, she corrected herself. And she hadn't, she'd just given out. There were no more reserves to draw on. She wanted a cigarette but was unsure if she had enough strength in her arms to lift it to her mouth; enough grip left to flick the lighter.

A large part of her still-functioning brain urged her to make comparisons of the woman in the chair who'd covered five miles in four and a half hours and the woman who'd run eight miles every day before breakfast. Heath ignored it. Only once, on a hellacious climb in Canada, had she pushed herself so hard she hit the wall. Tonight she'd done it again. Regardless of the goal, there is a pride in giving one's all.

Heath only had enough strength remaining to let her head fall back that she might better scream the way a child does when it is too tired to sleep, like Charlie Brown does in the cartoons, *"Aaargh."*

Heath laughed. She'd always wondered how that sounded aloud. Now she knew.

Something else knew, too. The brush at the edge of the road twenty or so yards ahead of her clattered, its bone-dry sticks hitting against one another, as a body of considerable size shifted within. The rattling came again, moving away maybe. Then the pound of feet or hooves on hard dry ground.

Heath expected to be afraid. Hadn't it been only recently she'd had to screw her courage to the sticking place just to sit outside the RV alone of an evening? Here she was in the night, in, if not the middle, then certainly the back forty of nowhere, too spent to swat away small mosquitoes, and yet footsteps in the bush didn't move her.

Another good thing about holding nothing back: self-pity, grief, loss, even fear had been ground up, used for fuel to push her chair a couple more feet, another quarter of a mile.

"Hello," she shouted. If it was a mountain lion with the sense it was born with, it would run from the sound of a human voice. If it was a person, maybe they'd kill her. Or, more likely, offer her a ride back to civilization.

No answer. Then an animal moving low and fast, with the sleek outlines of a wolf or coyote, sneaked from the underbrush running straight for her. Unable to do much else, Heath watched it come. In an instant it was upon her, paws on her chest, tongue up her nose.

"Wiley," she cried. Literally cried. Tears she'd thought long paid out in the form of sweat now poured down her face at the earth-shaking joy she felt seeing her friend. Wiley was never, ever to leap on her without an express invitation to do so. This was written in stone somewhere in the companion-dog manifesto. Heath let it pass. In her heart, in the depths of her soul where only angels and dogs can look, the invitation had been writ large and Wiley, being the best dog in the known and unknown universes, had seen this.

Lights cut across the dirt at a right angle to the road, and over the smacky attentions of her dog, Heath heard an engine fire up. Shortly thereafter the boxy silhouette of her aunt's recreational vehicle crept from behind an arm of the rocky crest to the east. The first fleeing footsteps would have been little Patty, hiding and keeping watch with Wiley, running back to tell her sister Heath had come.

They didn't return to Rollin' Roost RV park. Though the New Canaanites had been effectively stranded, it wouldn't last. Mr. Sheppard had contacts in the neighborhood of Loveland. A new distributor cap would be brought out. Or a sympathizer or convert sent to find Patty and Sharon and bring them home.

Sharon drove till the mountains opened a crack to let them in, then followed Highway 34 along the winding Thompson River. When a pull-out with enough depth and trees to screen a vehicle of immoderate size presented itself, she pulled in and parked out of sight from the road.

Rescue was nearly the undoing of Heath. What with the unconditional love lathered on her by Wiley, the warmth of the RV and the knowledge these wheels had a powerful diesel engine to turn them, fatigue caught up to her. Muscles turned to jelly. Brain fogged. Concentration flagged. Her heart's desire was to sit and do as she was told. Like in the hospital in Denver, just abdicate and give the world over to those who cared. The problem was now Heath was one of those who cared, and looking at her impromptu nurse, she realized Sharon was on the ragged edge. She had energy but it was that of raw nerve. Heath doubted she was capable of much in the way of rational decisions.

Though the shades were closed and snapped down, Sharon tended to Heath's hands by the light of a single votive candle. She'd not had the cathartic cleansing of physical exertion. Sitting, hiding, waiting, unsure whether to go or stay, to search for Alexis and Beth or go back to New Canaan for Heath, to leave Patty hidden in the brush or take her with her, had worn away at her till Heath believed half her nervous system lay exposed on the surface of her slender body. A slightly raised voice, an accidental brush of fingers against her arm, and she would jerk as if an electrical current had been sent through her.

Patty, all eyes and elbows, was anxious to help: run errands, make sandwiches. The child even lit Heath's cigarette when her own hands were too stiff and sore to work the lighter's magic. But Patty was only a little girl.

Heath shook herself, much as Wiley was wont to do after his hated baths, and forced her mind to focus. When a cup of hot strong coffee and a cigarette pulled her back together sufficiently, she could ask: "You guys waited for me the whole time?" Not a particularly brilliant opening to a campaign to rescue lost girls but it was a start.

"We didn't know what else to do. We didn't know where the girls had gone. We didn't know if you were all right." Sharon's voice rose in pitch, the words coming hard upon one another. She was fast reaching a breaking point.

"That's good. Of course you didn't. And I'm grateful," Heath cut in with a flood of her own to divert the rising tide of panic. "Now. Let's sit a bit. Patty, pour your sister a glass of wine. There, inside the refrigerator door."

"We don't use alcohol—" Sharon began.

She was doing that smoothing-pulling thing with her skirt again, flattening it over her knees as if her life depended on it being wrinkle-free.

"It's not alcohol. It's medicine."

Patty handed Heath the glass. In the way of children, she'd filled it to the brim. "Do I need medicine, Miss Jarrod?"

"No," Heath said. "Children are stronger than grown-ups." She passed it to Sharon and watched while she dutifully swallowed a good slug of the stuff. Aunt Gwen—and Heath when she was drinking for pleasure and not for pain—had a connoisseur's taste in wine up to their self-imposed twenty-dollar-a-bottle limit. It hurt to see Sharon choking down an excellent Pinot Grigio as if it truly were vile-tasting medicine.

Heath accepted a glass Patty poured for her unasked. She wanted another cigarette but having a kid both serve up the booze and light the fags struck her as too decadent. In California it was probably a felony. Even in Boulder, citizens had become so politically correct it was as much as one's life was worth to light up within three feet of a building. Heath made a mental note to try it from the vantage point of a wheelchair, a sociological experiment to see if, to the PC police, deference to the disabled won out over death to all smokers.

Sharon calmed down fractionally. At least holding the wineglass kept her hands from their infernal pressing.

"There's not a lot of ways I can think of to try and find the limpet and Alexis, short of bringing in the police," Heath said neutrally. She'd reverted to her pet name for Beth. It passed unremarked. If there was a favorite with Heath, so there was with Sharon: her sister.

"No. No police!" Sharon said. Fear, honed sharp by nerves and fatigue, warped the words. "The internet. Remember? Robert was sending them e-mails, trying to get them to come away somewhere. They took the car. He must have e-mailed them or they wouldn't know where to go except to you."

Heath chose to let the issue of the police rest a moment. Sharon had worried herself till she wasn't rational; she needed time to accept the inevitable.

The internet. Pushing the lovely Pinot Grigio to the farther side of the counter lest any more of it accidentally fall down her throat and further dull her intellect, she said, "Did you check their messages?"

"No connection. I was afraid to leave you. I couldn't find your cell—"

The hysteria was beginning to shriek through again.

"Right. Right. Right. Of course. Of course," Heath repeated till the danger passed. "Let's do it now, shall we?"

Granite walls blocked the signal. Sharon again driving, they returned to the flatter lands toward Loveland. In a turnout, Patty keeping a lookout for suspicious vehicles— a category they'd made too broad considering she set off her alarm at every passing car—Heath got on the internet then turned the laptop over to Sharon. Within a minute Sharon was downloading her sister's e-mail. Over fifty messages, all purportedly from Robert Proffit. They ran the gamut from threat, to promise, to seduction and back again. The last seven had hooks baited with Candace Watson.

"'You didn't kill Candace. But only you can save her. Come back. Your loving friend, Robert,'" Sharon read aloud. "What does he mean 'You didn't kill Candace'? Of course they didn't."

Like most Americans, Heath knew alto-
gether too much about crime. After all, it
was the entertainment media's—and so the
public's—obsession.

"Beth and Alexis said they didn't remember anything. Aunt Gwen told me that kind
of amnesia is rare to the point of being virtually fictional." It had actually been Ranger
Pigeon who had told Heath, but an auntie
would be more acceptable at the moment
than a cop, even a tree cop. "She thought
the girls remembered but chose not to tell.
Either because they were frightened into
silence by threats—Robert knew where they
lived, who they cared about—or because
they felt guilty. Maybe they were forced to
participate in the torture or killing of Candace."

"Oh God. Oh Lord." Sharon shrunk, inter-
nalizing the pain both of the death of a child
and the belief one was responsible for that
death. "Candace is dead?"

"Not necessarily," Heath said overloud.
The kid probably was dead but she could
tell Sharon needed to deny that a while
longer. "E-mails," she urged.

Sharon forced her eyes back to the computer screen.

"'Candace...only you...alive...come... come save her...we're here still...come back...he's dead...I need you...he's gone...we need you...come back...'" Sharon skimmed the remaining messages, her voice cracking wet with tears. When she'd done, the three of them stared at the gray wasteland, the face of cyberspace.

For a minute no one said anything. Not even the faint comforting sound of Wiley licking hypnotically at some part of his anatomy could kill the echo of the unvoiced siren's song Proffit had been singing via e-mail.

"'*He's* gone' . . . ?" Sharon looked over at Heath.

"Get the light, would you, Patty?" Heath had had enough of this ghost gray computer glow. Then, remembering they were hiding, said, "Never mind. Thanks anyway." The little girl waited by the switch, wanting to be on hand to help should Heath change her mind again.

"*He*, from the context of the messages"— Heath put the thoughts together as she spoke—"must be the kidnapper. A man the girls have reason to be afraid of. '*He's* gone.

He's dead.' That looks to be said by way of reassurance."

"Robert telling the girls that he's killed or gotten rid of their kidnapper? That doesn't seem right."

"My guess is it's the other way around, the kidnapper's pretending to be Robert to lure the girls back. He's hooking them with their faith in Robert Proffit. The bait is Candace. Saving Candace. He's playing on their goodness. Or their guilt."

"'Only you . . . we need you . . . save her. Come back, we're here,'" Sharon repeated the highlights of the litany.

"Where the hell is *here*?"

"The park."

Heath said nothing. The girls had been found—or rather, had found her—in the park after who knew how many days walking, wandering, running, maybe much of that time lost. Even half-naked and unshod they could have covered a lot of country.

Heath had covered a lot of country herself. There were few places in Rocky she'd not been. A place where a man could keep three girls. A place with access to computer and internet. Within walking distance to the handicamp. The west side of the park was out—too far. Two girls without gear, food or water couldn't make it that far. And it meant a climb up and over the great divide. The frontcountry was a possibility. It was densely populated but often there's more anonymity in crowds than in solitary climes. They'd been missing too long for them to have been kept in a camp, tent or RV. At the height of the season permits weren't that long and compliance was rigorously enforced.

This place: "back," "here," was still extant six or seven weeks after the initial disappearance. An employee, then. Dorm and shared housing were out. Most of the permanent employees lived in Estes Park.

"Fern Lake Cabin," Heath said with certainty. She'd not thought of it before because no one really knew if the girls had been kidnapped or run away, whether any accomplices or perpetrators remained in the area or had long since departed. Besides, Fern Lake Cabin was occupied during the summer months by a law enforcement ranger. A ranger who was by now dead, or if he wasn't, would be if Heath got her hands on him.

twenty-seven

Either Rita heard the urgency in Anna's command or she was too glad to be free to push her luck. Without a word of protest or a single question she shrugged into her day-pack.

Anna was already on her feet. "Quietly," she whispered. In the darkness beside her, Rita rose effortlessly. Strong and young, knees didn't crack, hands didn't grab at the tree for support or balance. Jealousy was the furthest thing from Anna's mind. At the moment she needed all the strong and young she could get.

"He's had time. More than enough. Rita,

you'll need your sidearm." She dropped to one knee and reached for her daypack. Nothing. Eyes were useless. Filtered moonlight was sufficient for the big stuff, not for this. On all fours, she dragged her hands lightly over the duff, feeling for it.

"My pack's gone."

"It's not gone," Rita said reasonably. "You must have shoved it farther back than you thought."

"It's gone. Shut up. Listen."

He'd been there, close enough to take the pack with Rita's gun, and Anna had heard nothing. Rita safely under lock and key, she'd let down her guard, happily interrogating a woman whose greatest crime was saving the lives of four wolf pups, then transporting them to a place that needed their pointed teeth and predatory minds to bring nature back into balance.

The thought that a monster—an honest-to-god, raise the hair on the back of the neck monster, the likes of which kept entire cities in terror—had slept in the room next to her, poured her coffee and lied to her about mice made Anna feel vulnerable. Worse: a fool, a mark, a victim. That the same monster could walk lightly enough to sneak up on her in the night woods scared her half to death.

In the sane world, criminals could be negotiated with, threatened, bought off. For the most part they were rational folks just suffering from poor impulse control, arrogance or lack of moral rectitude. In an insane world, what was negotiable, threatening, legal tender? Where monsters be, monsters' rules are law and only the monster knows what they are.

He'd been so close, unseen, armed. It would have been easy to put a bullet in their heads and drag them off somewhere the bodies would never be found. Or feed them piecemeal to the wolf pups. Why hadn't he?

The answer that came to Anna was not reassuring. He hadn't killed them because that wouldn't be any *fun*. Piedmont, her beloved yellow tomcat, loved to play with mice, birds, butterflies, cockroaches. Once he broke his toys, and they would no longer peep or flutter or run, he lost interest.

This man didn't want to break his toys. Not right away. Not quickly.

For the count of maybe ten breaths Anna and Rita stood stone-still, ears trying to pry into the night and the forest. Anna could see, but only enough not to bash into trees if she moved slowly. Down by the lake there would be more open space, more light. With their backs to the water there'd be only half as many directions from which an attack could come. A fifty percent improvement in survival odds, providing they could find cover. Anna was about to catch Rita's hand, move her toward the water, when she heard what she'd been listening for. More than she'd been listening for.

From the darkness came an eerie cackle. The sound mimicked the maniac's merriment heard in grade-B horror movies. In another setting Anna would have smiled. Stranded in the woods at night, it wasn't even remotely funny. The laughter whirled around them, crackling liquid as directionless as poison gas, then drifted away into the night.

"Jesus."

"Shh."

Silence. Then Robert Proffit's voice: "God forgive me, but I hate mice."

"Robert?" Rita called.

"Shh." The sound seemed to be coming from uphill, from the direction of the makeshift wolf den. Anna pulled Rita back till their shoulders touched the bulk of the pine tree that had been prison and home for the past few hours.

A muffled click, then: "I love those girls like they were my own flesh." Another click.

"Robert?" Rita whispered.

"No. It's a recording," Anna said with sudden realization. She'd seen the equipment at Fern Lake Cabin but, at the time, had thought nothing of it. "He's used it before on Heath Jarrod and I'm pretty sure he used it to try and lure Alexis and Beth back. Quiet now."

Snippets of information gleaned from conversations with Molly, her psychiatrist sister, floated haphazardly through Anna's mind. Challenging a psychotic's delusion could produce violence in the subject. A symptom of attachment disorder is the inability to care about anything or anyone except as it relates to the subject's own needs or desires. Sociopaths are incapable of feeling compassion for others.

None of it helped. Anna went with her instincts. "Cut the crap, Ray," she said into the darkness. *Ray*. His name wasn't Raymond Bleeker. He wasn't a ranger. Anna felt an idiotic rush of relief as if a stain had been removed from her people. Before she'd come to Rocky there'd been a rotted corpse found on the northern end of the Natchez Trace in Tennessee. Battery acid had burned hands and face and been poured in the mouth. Evidence of the murders of two boys in Pennsylvania and notes to the dead boys had been found on the body. The suspect in the Pennsylvania killings had jumped bail and run, the notes were in the suspect's handwriting. Descriptions of the suspect and the measurements of the corpse were a match. Lacking any indication to the contrary, the official theory of the Federal Bureau of Investigation was that the murderer had either killed himself in a gruesome manner or gotten his just reward from an outraged accomplice.

No one fitting the corpse's general description had been reported missing. But then a seasonal backcountry ranger wouldn't be. Family and friends were accustomed to them dropping off the face of the earth for months at a time.

Raymond Bleeker was undoubtedly lying in an FBI morgue somewhere in Tennessee, rotted beyond recognition, dental work and fingertips destroyed by battery acid.

"You took Ray Bleeker's identity," Anna said more to herself and Rita than to the killer in the woods. "How'd you do it? Befriended him, then killed him? What?" Only silence came back. For once, Anna hated silence. Feared it. "You couldn't hope to fool people very long. You were too piss-poor a ranger for that," she goaded.

Rita started to move. Anna sensed rather than heard or felt it—maybe Rita only thought about moving. Anna put a hand on her arm to keep her still.

There was a stirring in the duff to the left and slightly uphill.

"I fooled you," came a high-pitched singsong, the tune of quintessential derision recognizable on any playground from Miami to Nome.

"You fooled me all right, buddy," Anna admitted. What had inspired her to call him "buddy" she had no idea but it got a reaction.

"Don't fucking call me Buddy, you pushy faggot whore," exploded through the still damp air, followed by what sounded like the whimper of a child. It might have been one of the wolf pups frightened by the uncharacteristic noise.

A hand clutched Anna's wrist and she almost screamed. It was Rita. "It's okay," Anna breathed. It wasn't. She knew it. Rita knew it. But it had to be said for some reason. Maybe to see if God—or the fates—would laugh out loud.

"What should I call you?" she asked in the direction from which the fury had come, knowing Ray, Buddy—whoever—was probably no longer there. For a man who had lived most of his life in cities—according to the news reports the school where the boys' killer had done his hunting was in Philadelphia—he moved through the dark forest with remarkable stealth.

Maybe he isn't human, Anna heard a whisper in her brain and suffered a terror so ancient it could not be stilled with logic. Navajo skinwalkers, vampires, werewolves: nothing but the rising of the sun could banish them. With a mental jerk so pronounced her head shook like a comic doing a double-take, she ridded herself of the thought before it could take root and blossom into panic.

"What's your name?" she asked, to keep him engaged. Like she had to amuse him to keep herself and Rita alive until a better plan presented itself. Once they weren't *fun* anymore, their life expectancy would shorten considerably.

"Buddy. My name's Buddy."

Maybe his name was Buddy. Maybe she'd hit on it by pure dumb luck. Whether good or bad remained to be seen.

"Yeah. Old Buddy boy," he added. "I'll be your pal. We'll have such fun."

The voice moved. Now Anna could hear boots or, more likely, sneakers shushing over the duff. As he talked she unsnapped the keeper on her pancake holster and eased out her semiauto. Straight-armed, both hands supporting the weapon, she aimed at the sound, pivoting slowly as the words trailed down to the right.

"I'll be your friend. Like Mister Rogers. Okay, everybody, take your buddy's hand!" A few bars of the television theme song were hummed, then a scream: "Are you out of your fucking mind?" and Anna went blind. The beam of a powerful flashlight was trained in her eyes. She'd been spotlighted as sure as a hapless doe by an illegal hunter.

"Put the gun down like a good little ranger." The voice had gone back to singsong. Anna found the screaming less disturbing.

"What's in it for me?" She squinted past the glare.

He pulled the trigger. The report hurt her eardrums. Rita cried out and fell. Anna squeezed off three shots in quick succession. One at the light. One just left of it and one to the right. The beam went wild as the flashlight fell, then rolled. Rita was panting. A child cried piteously. In the spill of the fallen flashlight Anna could see what she'd shot. Not a monster but a little girl. Buddy had been too clever to make a target of himself. The underweight girl with the punked-out hair who'd alibi'd him had been holding the light.

"Sweet Jesus," Rita said, as Anna said:

"Candace."

"What's in it for you is you get to live a lee-tle teensy-weensy scoche of a bit longer." Buddy was to Anna's left. By the time she turned and aimed she'd be dead. Dead she was no good to anyone. And she had shot a child. Anna let go of the gun.

"I'm going to check Rita and Candace," she said.

"Leave them."

"Not happening."

"Move and I'll shoot you."

"Then fucking shoot me. I'm getting the flashlight." Moving unhurriedly, she stepped to the light, crouched and retrieved it.

The bullet she expected to plow into her back didn't come. Buddy Bleeker wasn't an altruist; he didn't give a damn about any life other than his own. Sure he might want them alive to play with, but only so long as they weren't a nuisance. Anna had been a definite pain in the neck. That he didn't kill her maybe meant she was useful to him. The thought gave her courage.

Careful not to do anything sudden and to stay away from the gun that lay temptingly close, she shined the light on Rita. The ranger was curled down over her left foot, both hands a gaudy red, shockingly cele- bratory in this night landscape. Blood dripped from beneath her fingers.

"Are you going to live?" Anna asked.

Silence.

"Rita?"

"I guess. It's my ankle. God but it hurts."

"You'll live," Anna said firmly. "Remember that. Don't go shocky on me." Following the light, she went to where Candace lay. The girl had not made a sound. She did not move. The light picked up a crimson banner of blood down the right side of her T-shirt. The horror of the law enforcement officer's nightmare—to cause the death of an inno-cent—was visited upon Anna. Her knees grew weak. Her insides heaved.

Falling more than kneeling, she collapsed by the child's side. "Candace?" she mur-mured as she played the light over the small head and flat-chested torso, trying to see where the bullet had entered. Candace's dark eye was open but staring blind. Anna's heart made a palpable lurch, as if a dying fish lay trapped beneath her ribcage. She'd killed Candace.

"Holy Mary Mother of God, pray for us sinners now and at the hour of our death," she whispered, wondering as she did so from which antique Catholic school closet those long-forgotten words had come.

The eye blinked.

Not dead.

"Hallelujah."

"Cut the fucking revival meeting. Leave her," said the man who'd stolen Ray Bleeker's life. Indifference flattened the high notes. He might have been talking about a pebble fallen from a gravel truck, a nothing.

Quickly Anna searched the child's neck and shoulder. When she'd fired into the dark she'd been aiming for the body mass of a six-foot-tall man. Candace, small for her age, was scarcely five feet. Anna's bullet had caught her across the top of her left shoulder, cutting a groove an eighth of an inch deep and two long. Six inches to the right and it would have ripped out her throat. While Anna pulled at clothing, poked at wounds and felt the girl all over for any peripheral damage from the fall or, as unlikely as it seemed, the other two shots, Candace lay as one dead: limp, quiet, eyes open but not in focus.

At first Anna was afraid she'd gone into shock. Shock could kill just as surely as a chunk of lead. The quick examination revealed an answer even more unsettling. Candace had learned to lie still, keep silent, retreat within herself while being handled, hurt, dressed and undressed. Given that after weeks in the hands of a man who possibly had tortured and murdered at least three other people, Candace still survived, Anna knew she'd learned her lessons well.

What kind of life she would be able to make for herself should this streak of luck continue through the night, Anna couldn't hazard a guess.

"You crazy bastard," Anna said, not because she thought it would do any good but because she couldn't help herself. Having eased Candace into a sitting position she grabbed Rita's pack. The first-aid kit rangers were required to carry on duty had accompanied Rita on her off hours, as Anna had figured it might.

Pretending Buddy Boy Bleeker wasn't standing in the darkness, his sick mind deciding whether they were to live or to die, she put a commercial Band-Aid over Candace's wound. Then turned her attention to Rita. During the brief time she'd worked on the girl, Rita had recovered somewhat. As Anna trained the flashlight on her leg, she began reporting, "Near as I can tell by feel, the bullet hit square in the ankle and passed through. It's probably lodged in the tree or dirt behind where I was standing. Bones are broken. More than one. Bleeding can be controlled. It missed the main artery."

Anna looked up from the mess Rita cradled in her hands. The ankle would never be as strong as it once was, as supple. There was a good possibility it would cripple Rita, take away her job as a park ranger in summers and a basketball coach in winter. Yet Rita's eyes were clear and dry, her gaze steady, if a little too fixed.

"You're a rock," Anna said sincerely.

"Leave this shit," Buddy warned. Indifference had become irritation.

"Soon as I dress Rita's ankle."

Quick as a snake, a running shoe flashed into the tiny operating theater illuminated by the flashlight and struck Anna's hand. The light went spinning. Rita screamed as the shoe smashed into her injured ankle. Metal collided with the side of Anna's head. She went down on her side in the blood and the dirt. Before the world quit heaving, the light was in her face.

"We'll go now." The same flat voice, almost bored sounding. "Put these on. Hands behind your back." He threw his handcuffs at Anna.

"We" clearly didn't mean Rita. There was no way she could so much as hobble, let alone walk. The ankle was shattered. It was hard to tell about Candace. Buddy neither spoke nor looked at the child. If she could stand, she would probably follow like a beaten dog follows her master: mindlessly, hopelessly. Should she falter, slow them down or simply clog Buddy's vision at an inopportune moment, Anna knew he would shoot her and never give it a second thought.

Rita he would shoot the instant Anna put on the handcuffs. Buddy was a tidy fellow. That was evident in the way he kept Fern Lake Cabin. He wouldn't be a man to leave witnesses scattered about.

She held up the cuffs. "I put them on; Rita lives."

"Sure."

"At the lake. I'll put them on when we get to the lake."

"Now." Buddy put the pistol to Candace's temple.

"The lake, or not at all." Inside of Anna, bits and pieces were shaking. Quivering viscera sent waves of weakness out to her extremities. She held tight to the cuffs so he'd not see her hands shaking and locked her knees to keep them from buckling. What did Buddy-the-psycho need a ranger for? How much did he need her? If she were of greater cost than value, she wouldn't outlive the equation.

The two women and the child watched him decide whether they were to live or to die. How often, Anna wondered, were such choices made, the victim never knowing her life turned on the idle whim of an unseen predator.

Buddy was thinking it over too long.

"Rita's crippled. She's not going any-where." Anna tried sweetening the deal. "And she can't radio out from here. You know that."

The moment the words left her lips and entered the Ray creature's ear, she knew how big a mistake she'd made. In the spill of light she saw it on his bland face: he hadn't thought of the radios.

"Take yours off," he said, and again held the gun to Candace's temple. Little girls were his victims of choice. He was careful never to get that close to her or Rita. This was wise.

Initially Anna had been swept away on the tide of emotions, the first and foremost being staggering, mind-numbing guilt. Not at shooting the girl, though that hadn't helped matters, but because through her blind dim-wittedness she'd gotten them in this mess. A little self-incrimination is a good thing. It spurs one onward, inoculates against the stupidity of arrogance. A lot of self-incrimination was deadly, causing paralysis so all-encompassing the only course of action is no action: abdication of responsibility. Anna hadn't sunk that low, but the sense of inadequacy, of failing others, had made her mind sluggish.

Now that it had passed she nearly glowed with the need to do something, and that something was get her hands on Buddy. When his foot flashed in and struck Rita's ankle, it had taken every drop of her self-control not to grab it, wrench it upward, lay into it with tooth and claw. The SIG Sauer pointed at Candace's head was all that had dissuaded her.

"The radio," Buddy said. "Give it to me."

"By the lake," Anna promised. "Everything. I'll do it by the lake. That or kill us all and be done with it." She was kind of sorry she'd added the last. It was the second time in as many minutes she'd suggested he shoot her. Even in the feeble glow of the flashlight's backwash she could see how much the idea appealed to him. His face took on the happy perky look dogs get when their masters walk toward the treat cupboard. Anna made a mental note not to tempt him further.

"By the lake," she said and moved slowly away from Rita toward the western shore of tiny Loomis Lake.

"Can she walk?" he asked indifferently.

Anna stopped, looked back. Buddy aimed the flashlight beam at Candace. Like a doll, played with then abandoned, she sat exactly as Anna had arranged her when bandaging her shoulder. Not even her eyes had moved.

In Anna's peripheral vision, light flashed; the shine of the pistol barrel. Buddy was waving it, conducting a macabre symphony in his head, composing a death sonata for Candace, Rita and her. He was a man in need of a fix; a vampire jonesing for a blood meal.

"Candace can walk," Anna said matter-of-factly. She used the girl's name to remind Candace that she was a person, deserved life. Maybe it would shift Buddy a degree closer to that view as well, make killing her a little less appealing, but Anna doubted it.

Buddy was too far gone into monster. He might have been born too far gone.

Grasping Candace's upper arm, Anna pulled her to her feet. The child's skin was cool to the touch and she weighed next to nothing, eighty pounds at most. During her weeks in captivity Buddy must have fed her only enough to keep her alive. This cruelty was probably done for the entertainment of the perpetrator. That it weakened the victim in mind, body and spirit was just a bonus. With a gentle shove, Anna got Candace walking and put herself between the child and the gun.

"I'm taking off my jacket," she said as she tried to walk over uneven ground in dancing light without stumbling.

Buddy made no reply. Taking that to mean he wouldn't kill her for disrobing, she took off her rain jacket and draped it around the girl's shoulders. Candace showed no sign of noticing. Oddly sure-footed in the dark, she followed the erratic jerk and twitch of the flashlight, a mindless moth-child. This wasn't the first time she'd been forced into this mode of night travel with her captor.

A quarter of an hour in which Anna tried to think and could not, tried not to feel the bullet rip into her spine and could, crackled away beneath her boots.

Her insistence on complying only at the lake shore had nothing to do with a plan for escape by water. Her motive was to get Buddy away from Rita Perry before she handed him all the cards. Had Anna done as he asked up in the forest, she believed he would have broken his promise not to kill Rita as soon as she'd obligingly cuffed herself. One of the mysteries Anna had pondered over half a lifetime of dealing with victims was why they put faith in the promises of bad people: rapists who promised not to hurt them if they didn't scream, kidnappers who promised not to kill them if they didn't struggle. To her it was obvious a man who'd kidnap, kill or torture probably wouldn't balk at telling a lie.

Her hope was that after getting Buddy to the lakefront he wouldn't bother to walk back uphill for a quarter of an hour just to spill a little blood.

Trees began to separate from the black of a wall into individual trunks and branches silhouetted against the reflective water of Loomis Lake. Candace walked straight to the water's edge and might have kept going had Anna not told her to stop. The girl stopped. She didn't turn or ask questions. Buddy had taught her to do as she was told. Exactly as she was told. Anna had always thought she preferred obedient children. Watching Candace, she realized a bit of sass is an indicator of life and well-being in the adolescent spirit.

"Throw your radio in the lake." Buddy was bored, testy, like a jaded child. Anna could think of little more frightening than a crabby psychopath made to stay up past his bedtime.

She threw the radio in the lake.

"Cuff her."

Buddy indicated Candace. Anna took the cuffs from her belt and gently turned the girl from the lake.

"I've got to put the handcuffs on you. It won't hurt."

Candace held her hands out obediently and Anna loosely fastened the cuffs around them.

"Cuff key," Buddy said.

Anna took the handcuff key from her watch pocket.

"Toss it to me." She did, watching the small silver key flash like a minnow through the starlight. It fell several feet short of where Buddy stood. "Now your spare."

"You've picked up quite a bit about this rangering business, haven't you?" Anna remarked dryly.

"Anybody can do it," he said. "You think you're something. You're nothing. All of you. Just nothing. Running around like a bunch of puffed-up pigeons pecking here, pecking there, scratching in the dirt, finding nothing. My things were there all the time. Right at Fern Lake Cabin. Right under the nothing noses of the nothing rangers. Toss it," he finished.

Again Anna threw a key. Again it fell into the wiry grass at his feet.

"Now your cuffs. There on your belt. Put your arm through her arms and cuff your wrists."

Anna did as she was told, manacling herself to the child in a parody of a square-dance promenade pose.

Buddy picked up the keys, then said, "Make your widdle selfs comfy. I'll be back in two shakes of a lamb's tail."

The change from bored monotone to baby talk jarred Anna disproportionately till she realized what it augured. Buddy Ray

Bleeker was happy. He was happy because he was about to do something he really enjoyed.

That couldn't be good.

Putting the flashlight under his chin in the tradition of children playing at hobgoblins, he fixed a horrific caricature of a stare on Anna. Never before had she seen the light trick work so well. The bland oval of his face became a vicious triangle of white, his short unremarkable nose grew, the nares cavernous. The eyes were what turned Halloween into hell. The whites fairly glowed and the brown of the irises was black as pitch. Flat black. The light seemed to have no power to illuminate the windows of this soul. Perhaps because there was none.

"Don't you move, Annie Fannie. Don't you move one little inch," he said, then loped back in the direction of Rita's tree. Anna's ploy had failed. Buddy was going to kill the young ranger and there was nothing she could do about it. Yelling "But wait! You *promised*!" at his retreating back probably wasn't going to turn the tide.

Rita's death could justifiably be laid at Anna's door, but she didn't think about that. Self-recrimination had long since been set aside in the interest of survival. Either she'd have the rest of her life to atone, or she'd be joining Rita before the night was out.

Buddy moved quickly, easily, a creature of the night. In a heartbeat his light was cut up, then consumed by tree line. If he was going to Rita, moving fast, he'd be at least seven minutes up and about that returning. For her own sake and that of the girl, Anna hoped he'd take his time over his murderous treat, give them an extra few minutes. Since this was out of her control and merely a practical thought, she felt no disloyalty to Rita thinking it.

Leaving her and Candace unattended was the act of a madman. *What else?* Anna thought.

A trap.

So? It wasn't like she could make the situation any worse.

"Come on, Candace. We've got to hide," she whispered.

"He said not to move. Not one little inch," Candace said, as if she spoke not of an order, or in favor of obedience, but was stating an irrefutable law of physics. When Buddy said she couldn't move an inch she became incapable of moving that inch.

Anna considered dragging her but the going would be too slow, too noisy. Buddy might postpone his deadly recreation to come back early. "It was a game," she said. "He told *me* I couldn't move. He didn't say *you* couldn't. He wants you to move. That's why he only said it to me."

By dint of great necessity Anna managed to keep the desperation and fury—not at Candace but at her tormentor—out of her voice. The child was probably inured to violence. That, or any more, could break anything left of her as yet unbroken.

Games, Candace understood. In the past weeks there must have been many games where a wrong choice meant punishment and a right one a bit of food or simply the reward of not being hurt for that moment.

"He wants me to move?" The fear and confusion in the question raked at Anna's heart.

"That's what I think."

"Move where?"

"I'll show you."

"You can't move."

"Let the son-of-a-bitch try and stop me," Anna said with more heat than she'd intended.

"He will." Another law of physics: Buddy always won.

Anna walked two steps, her manacled wrists tugging at Candace's. Candace took two steps toward her. The spell was broken. Anna let out a breath she hadn't realized she was holding.

"We better be quick or we'll lose the game." Whether Candace responded because of the clever psychological maneuvering or because she no longer had a will of her own didn't matter. Just doing something was raising Anna's hopes.

The light she'd welcomed when first they'd reached Loomis was now the enemy. She headed toward the trees at an angle to the path Buddy had taken. Without light they couldn't get far. Shackled to a frail and battered child, Anna had no hope of staging any sort of assault. The best they could do was to go to ground and hope the night and luck would keep Buddy from finding them. They only needed to last the night. In the morning, Buddy knew rangers would be on their way up.

Unless he canceled them.

"Shit," Anna whispered as she stumbled

on a root and she and Candace collided in an aborted do-si-do.

In the trees it was beast-belly dark. Hands cuffed together, they couldn't even hold up their arms to protect their faces from low branches. Above nine thousand feet there was little in the way of undergrowth to hide small human animals from a predator. Running might not have been such a great idea, but since it was the only idea, Anna had no regrets.

Blind, they would not find the ideal hiding place. Had a cave been a yard ahead it would have availed them nothing in its cloak of invisibility. Shoulders banging into trees, toes catching on stones, Anna pressed on, gaining as much distance as she could. Every minute or so she stopped, listening for the sound that would signal Buddy's imminent return to the shore of the lake.

When the sound did come, it hurt more than she'd expected. A shot rang out and she flinched as if the bullet struck her own flesh. Another, and weakness washed over her as though her own life blood was pouring out along with Rita's.

"Get over it," she whispered, but it was a moment before her body remembered it

was alive and would again obey her commands.

"He'll be coming back now," Anna said
softly. "We've got to hide."

"Yes. That woman has gone home. That's
good."

Anna brought up her hands and found the
girl's face. Because she needed to make
contact she ran her fingertips over the gaunt
cheeks and small girlish nose. Candace
didn't jump at the unexpected familiarity,
didn't move away or protest. Her hands,
manacled together through the circle of
Anna's arms, slid down, the cuff chain heavy
against the inner side of Anna's elbow joint.
Like a rag doll, Candace let herself be done
to, handled. Buddy had killed the child then
left her in an emaciated little body to wander
the earth, a mockery of the life that was to
have been.

Feeling through the dark, Anna located a
good-sized pine and pulled the girl down to
her knees at its base. "Put your feet out,"
she ordered and proceeded to arrange the
child till the two of them were sitting hip to
hip, legs straight out in the way of dolls on a
bedroom floor. "Stay still." This last wasn't
necessary. Candace stayed where she was

put until such time as she was ordered to move. Bending and scraping awkwardly, first on one side of their legs then the other, Anna scooped enough needles over them that, though not completely covered, their extremities were at least camouflaged.

"Lie down and see if you can't kind of wriggle down into that heap of needles beside you. I'll do the same and we'll be hidden."

Candace did as she was told but with so little energy Anna doubted much in the way of torso coverage had been attained. Within a few minutes they lay quietly side by side, arms mechanically linked, breathing in the dust from the pine needles and staring up into the boughs of their tree.

"Now wasn't that fun?" Anna said because fear and absurdity goaded her into it. She didn't expect a response. She was shackled to a ghost. But for the occasional rattle of chains, the child specter scarcely seemed to be there at all.

Silence joined the darkness, making it more peaceful. Through the imperfect cover of the pine's branches Anna could see two stars. The minute pinpricks of white were comforting, reassuring her she'd not gone

blind, that the Buddies had not yet managed to snuff all the light from the world.

The quiet continued to deepen, unre-
lieved by the slightest rustle of movement
from the girl pressed to her side. Night's
usual music was absent, the small creatures, sensing a great ravening beast in their
midst, had silenced themselves.

Listening with nothing to hear wears hard
on ears and nerves. Anna's head began to
ache. The sound of Buddy's return to
Loomis came almost as a relief. Their flight
into the woods, though an arduous trek, had
only put forty or fifty yards between them
and the water. They were close enough that
the crunch of his feet on the rocky shore
carried clearly in the breathless chill of the
air. Given that Buddy had no way of knowing which direction they'd taken, it might
suffice.

It had to suffice.

"Fucking, fucking, fucking, fucking girls."
An angry muttered mantra. Anna was surprised. He'd wanted them to run, she was
sure of it, wanted the game he knew he
couldn't lose. And she'd thought the thrill of
butchering a crippled ranger would have
lifted his spirits.

"Quiet as a mouse," Anna breathed into Candace's ear.

A thump. Rocks pelting to earth. A curse. Buddy had kicked at something and banged his foot. "Game over," he yelled, then he whistled, the staccato bursts of sound rising in tone, the way one whistles for a dog. The sharp sounds cut through the thin air like knives, killing the quiet.

With an abruptness that jarred Anna on a cellular level, Candace began barking wildly.

twenty-eight

"Shh. Jesus. Fuck. Shh." Anna scrabbled in the dark trying to drag her hands up to where she would get them over Candace's mouth. Cuffed together as they were, she couldn't get a grip on the child's head, her face, to cut off the maniacal barking.

"Arf, arf! Arf!" Candace's high-pitched parody of Orphan Annie's dog was bringing Buddy through the woods. His eerie chortle tittered into the chinks between the mechanical barking.

"Shut up shut up shut up please God shut up," Anna muttered as she sat up, found Candace's shoulder and maneuvered her hands around the girl from behind. Candace pressed tightly to her chest, Anna brought her left arm up, closed it around the soft throat and, left wrist clamped in her right hand, the crook of her elbow just out from Candace's larynx, she squeezed.

The sleeper hold. Professional wrestling had made it famous. Law enforcement had used it for a while, though in recent years it was considered right up there with deadly force. The bones of the arm pressed into the carotid arteries on either side of the victim's neck, cutting off the flow of venous blood from the brain. Within seconds the victim was "asleep." Within a couple of minutes she was brain-damaged. Too long and she was dead.

Anna kept the pressure on only till she felt the girl, rigid in her mad-dog manifestation, go limp, then she loosed her hold. The freakish barking silenced, she could again think. The sudden onslaught of aural insanity had done more than threaten her life and assault her ears. It was as if each shrill "Arf!" had dimension and neon glare as well as sound. Freed of it, Anna could feel the space around her expanding.

Maybe fifty yards away, maybe a hundred

and fifty—trees and adrenaline played tricks with the eye—was Buddy's light poking here and there like a Star Wars light saber but more deadly. The chortling had stopped.

Soon Candace would come to. Anna pulled the girl's head back hard against her sternum and, as she felt the little body begin to move, she clamped her hand tightly over Candace's mouth, the other on her forehead, holding her close.

"Bad dog," Buddy called, his light stabbing between trees. Erratic, halting, he was coming toward them. "Bad dogs get punished," he called.

Candace's eyes flew open. Anna could feel the delicate brush of lashes against her wrist.

"You know what the alpha does to the bitch," Buddy called. He sounded apologetic, as if he was sorry in a way for what bad-dog-girl-child Candace was going to force him to do to her. He whistled again.

Beneath her hand Anna could feel the girl's jaw working as she tried to bark for her master, sit up, beg. Hot drops fell on Anna's thumb. Tears far hotter than the 98.6 allowed for human beings.

Crushing Candace to her, so tightly she

could feel the cut of the girl's shoulder blades against her stomach and the bird-boned fragility of her ribcage and arms, Anna breathed reassurance into her captive's ear.

"It's okay. Shh. Shh. We'll be all right. Stay with me. Hush. Hush. I'm here. You're safe. Shh. Shh."

Candace began to relax. Anna could feel the rigor leaking away, the bundle of sticks she clung to becoming a girl. The bones of the jaw Anna held stopped trying to unloose. There was a chance now, just a chance.

"Good girl," Anna whispered.

Candace spasmed. Too late Anna realized she uttered magic words, black magic. Dog words. Fighting as if her life depended on it, as it had for so many weeks, Candace tried to bark. Muffled noises, reminiscent of the bark of seals, broke into the night. Candace kicked her heels into the duff. Her fisted hands pounded Anna's face and skull.

"Good doggie," crowed from the dark. The single great star that sought them turned toward where they hid, wending and winking through the trees.

Anna slid her arms into position,

squeezed, choking the blood from Candace's brain. The pummeling fists fell away. Struggling and sound ceased. The girl melted against her.

The light that was no light at all but a harbinger of a darkness so great the sane mind could not comprehend it, slowed, stopped. Knife-sharp feelers went out, ripping orange life from dead needles and green from boughs, then killing them with its passing.

Whistling resumed: short, sharp, demanding.

Anna hadn't loosed the vise her arm made around Candace's throat. Candace's brain was sleeping. Soon it would start to shut down. Then it would die. If she let up, the child would awake. There would be noise. They both would die. Was it so bad after all that Anna helped Candace from this place? Should the child wake, and Buddy find them, would her death be easier? Would he let her drift quietly to sleep and then to oblivion? Or would he fill her last moments with terrors as great or greater than she'd already experienced? If, by some miracle beyond Anna's ability to devise, Candace should live out the night, survive Buddy, would she truly be alive? Already he had killed her childhood, her sense of herself as a person. The scars he had carved on soul and psyche would be there forever. Wasn't it better that she slip peacefully away in the arms of someone who loved her?

Anna did love her, she realized with a jolt. An incomprehensible alchemy born of proximity, shared humanity and nearness to death connected them as surely as the steel cuffs entwining their arms. Anna loved the sweet warmth of Candace's body against hers. She loved the dusky smell of her unwashed hair and the memory of tears too hot to the touch. She loved that she had learned to bark rather than to die.

Anna loved the girl with an intensity that took her breath away; she loved her enough to kill her. But not now. Not till she had to. Not till the next death, guaranteed, would be her own.

Her arm fell away from the slender throat. Her cheek dropped to rest against Candace's.

The girl swam to consciousness on a scream.

Then Buddy was upon them.

Abruptly Candace went silent, her body stony in the circle of Anna's arms, a rabbit frozen under the coyote's eye hoping beyond hope it would be passed over. This time.

Fierce glare from a six-cell flashlight a yard from her face robbed Anna of everything but a harsh vision of the afterlife. This was fine; she had no wish to see Buddy's face.

Candace had gone away inside herself.

Buddy was cloaked in the absence of light.

Anna was alone under the spotlight. "So. What now?"

"I have made time for you now." The words came from the black beyond the field of Anna's vision. Buddy didn't speak. Nor did the ersatz Raymond Bleeker. This was a new entity. One Anna wasn't crazy about getting to know.

"You must be taught your place."

In a time warp that took Anna off guard, she was suddenly in a darkened theater—a black box, really, on the Lower West Side in Manhattan. Zach, her husband, slouched beside her, his bony knees wedged against the seat back in front of him, his shoulders about on a level with the armrests. Rehearsal for *The Boys in the Band*. The salad monologue.

"No. Pace! Pace! I could drive a truck between lines," boomed down from overhead. Actors, blinded by the kliegs, stared up at the light booth where the director sat behind the mike.

"God," Zach had explained.

"God," Anna said staring into the light masking Buddy.

"You learn quick."

From the white-hot glare of the cold dead night emerged a gray cylinder. Two cylinders, one melded into the other, the barrel of an efficient, German-made semiautomatic weapon. Close. Closer, till it stopped four inches from the tip of Anna's nose. Her eyes crossed and two pistol barrels crossed, swam away from one another. She made herself look away, turn her eyes to the kinder shadows on the ground.

Buddy had come nearer. His sneakers rested either side of Candace's thighs. Anna sat on her heels, the position she'd adopted the better to asphyxiate children. This was the closest to her he'd come. Buddy was confident. Not confident, realistic. There was nothing she could do with the dead weight of a girl in her arms, their fates linked by bonds of Bethlehem steel.

"Open your mouth."

Against Anna's will her eyes fixed again on the gun barrel.

"What?" she asked stupidly.

"Open your mouth."

Anna might have complied had she not been paralyzed by the thought that she was about to die. Her body was locked but her mind was racing. If she took the barrel in her mouth and Buddy blew her brains out through the back of her head, could he make it look like suicide? Get away with it? Anna did not intend to go to hell alone.

"Suck it," he said sweetly. "Suck it like it is St. Peter's cock and you're paying your way through the pearly gates."

The obscenity shocked and appalled her and she was amazed that she could be shocked and appalled by anything new a monster who tortured children might come up with.

"Open, open, open. Suck, suck, suck." Buddy was back with the playground singsong.

The barrel of the SIG Sauer twitched slightly up and down as an erect penis might twitch as its owner tensed with excitement and anticipation.

"Suck it like you love me or I'll jam it in our little doggie here and make it go off." Playground pervert was gone. It was the empty place within the shell that spoke.

Anna tried to look away from the gun and failed. Molly, her sister, came into her mind, as did Paul, her brand-new husband, Taco and Piedmont and the newly acquired kitten. People and animals who loved her, who would grieve if she were gone from their lives. She thought of her husband's god who, real or not, had imbued half the world with the concept of sacrificing one's self for the good of others.

Those who loved her and those who depended upon her, like the warm still child in her arms, would be better off if she stayed alive, regardless of what it took to do so.

She leaned in toward the pistol barrel.

"Oh baby," Buddy moaned, as if he truly expected a blowjob. Maybe he did. Maybe this violence was his sexuality.

Those who needed her to live lined up across Anna's brain. It surprised her how many had come, how many cared.

But she'd been raised to worship John

Wayne, not Jesus of Nazareth. Smiling an apology, she launched herself forward and rammed the thickest part of her skull into Buddy's left kneecap.

twenty-nine

Buddy twisted away screaming. Anna hoped she'd managed to dislocate the joint or break the kneecap. Hands entangled with the girl's, arms around the narrow shoulders, she could do nothing to check her forward motion and fell, Candace jackknifed beneath her.

Constrained by child and chains, the blow hadn't struck squarely and Buddy cried out as much from rage as pain. Before she could draw breath, he was on her back, riding her. The pistol whipped hard across the side of her face, the back of her head, her shoulders.

The speed of the battery shattered conscious thought. Arms pinned, center of
gravity upended over a crushed girl, she
could not defend herself, could not roll
away, could not separate pain from shock.
Maybe he hit her half a dozen times, maybe
twenty.

Then it was over. The whipping was fren-
zied, vicious but not deadly. His weight lifted
and she rolled to the side lest Candace suf-
focate beneath her.

Buddy retreated out of reach. She could
hear him panting, out of breath from the
exertion or sexually excited. Candace didn't
move. Dragging their manacled hands up,
Anna pressed her knuckle under the girl's
nose. Warm air blew reassuringly across her
skin. Candace still breathed.

A shoe slammed into Anna's back. Word-
lessly, Buddy kicked and, using the six-cell
flashlight, flogged her to her feet. Standing,
she was able to lift her arms from the killing
embrace she'd maintained around her
fellow captive's neck and pull Candace up
from the ground.

A kick hard enough to momentarily para-
lyze the big muscle landed on Anna's left
thigh. It would have brought her to the

ground again had it not been immediately followed by Buddy grasping the waistband of her shorts and jerking her up. Still breathing audibly, he whipped and kicked them back through the woods. Grunts and gasping and blows took the place of conversation.

Had she had time to think as she and her young chain-gang sister were driven down the dark trail, she might have been reassured. Clearly one or both of them were still of use to Buddy. Candace, she suspected, was kept on in the role of albatross. With a brainwashed girl shackled to her, Anna was effectively neutralized as a threat. How Anna herself might be expected to serve, she couldn't guess.

For the next eternity, they fell, were kicked to their feet, beaten onward to stumble and fall again. Gravel and needles and dirt packed into bloodied knees and elbows. Unable to break falls with her hands Anna's face was scraped.

When she could breathe she tried to draw Buddy out, tried to rally an echo of life from Candace. She cursed, threatened, promised, spat, speculated and reviled. Nothing worked. Buddy panted and herded them with blows and pokes from a broken branch he'd picked up. Candace had hidden so deep within herself she didn't cry out when she fell or when the skin was raked from her shins, made no sound when her lip split open against a stone. Anna believed she would go on like an abused beast of burden till there came a time when dying held no more terrors than living. At that point she would stop and be beaten to death.

After what seemed a lifetime, they descended the trail to the little bridge over the outlet of Fern Lake. Up on its stony rise the cabin was dark. Though Anna had the feeling it would be the end of the line for her, she felt a stab of gratitude. The forced march was over. The ground would stop rushing up from the flash-cut darkness to crack kneecaps and elbows, peel the skin from bare legs. Maybe the rough point of Buddy's stick would stop castigating the flesh of their backs, cutting at shoulder and neck.

Maybe that was too much to hope for.

It was also too much to hope that Jean Claude Van Damme and Jet Li would be doing a bit of night fishing and hear calls for help. The lake was deserted, the surface calm and mirror-bright. It was considerably past midnight and the air had turned cold. What campers remained following the exodus after Labor Day weekend would be snug in their down sleeping bags.

Anna would not have called out to any camping group less formidable than the 10th Mountain Division anyway. It would only be inviting them to step into an early grave.

As she and Candace staggered in tandem toward the wooden steps up to Fern Lake Cabin's door, Buddy uttered his first words since the pistol whipping a couple of hours earlier.

"Home again, home again, jiggity-jig." He had cheered up since Loomis Lake. Perhaps some more fun was in the offing.

The narrow window of opportunity Anna was hoping for when he uncuffed them was never opened. In a move so sudden she never saw it coming, he smashed her on the temple with the butt of his gun. The next thing she knew he had uncuffed Candace and locked her wrist bracelets together around a head-high rung of the ladder that was bolted to the cabin wall to provide access to the small loft space. Chainlooped through Candace's linked cuffs, Anna could bring her hands no lower than her chin.

Chatting and bustling like a happy home-maker, Buddy began to lay a fire in the cast-iron stove. "I'd been hoping for company," he said conversationally. "They hadn't arrived yet when your radio call came through. Bad timing that. At first it looked like it would be bad for me—heavy-footed Neanderthals clomping around being heroes in my clean house. I shall miss this place. If it had a flush toilet I could live here. But now I have fixed things—I am a great fixer of things—and so it will be bad timing for you."

Candace, though freed, had remained standing in the middle of the floor, an automaton whose batteries had gone dead. The sound of water dripping caught Anna's ear and she shifted her attention from Buddy. Urine poured unchecked from the wide leg of the men's cut-offs to spatter on the wooden floor. The expression on Candace's face didn't change. Buddy's did. The Mister Rogers mask he'd donned so abruptly outside the cabin dropped away.

Beneath it he wore that of an angry nun from a Catholic schoolboy's hell.

"Disgusting," he snapped. "Like a pig. Decent people live here. Clean it up. Now."

The dialogue was stilted and hit the ear as awkwardly as a poorly written play. At first, unsettled by Buddy's rapid change of personas, Anna wondered if he suffered from multiple personality disorder. It was rare but occurred often enough to be taught in med school during the psychiatry rotation. Watching him, ice cold and authoritarian as he threw his words at the child soiling herself, she realized that he knew exactly who he was. The masks, the play-acting, were a game, an exercise in power, an entertainment.

"I have to go to the bathroom, too," Anna said before he could do anything to Candace, if that was what was on his mind.

"Be my guest," he said pleasantly. "Clean it up," he ordered Candace in the nasty nun voice.

Candace got down on her hands and knees and began to lick at the puddle. Anna was grateful it had almost immediately been absorbed by the tinder-dry wood on the floor.

"That's attractive," Anna said acidly. "What's the point of it?"

"Discipline. And it amuses me." He turned from lighting the kindling in the stove. Masks were gone. Instinctively, Anna knew she was seeing the real man beneath the poses.

The most terrifying thing about the look of him was the sanity. Eyes were clear, muscles relaxed, humor of a hard and edgy sort played around lips neither too niggardly nor too lush. He had dropped the aura of a flesh-eating Jeffrey Dahmer and doused that inner burn that ate away at the jailed remnants of Charlie Manson. Not that Anna had had any personal contact with either of these men, or others of that ilk, but even through the diffusing effects of the television screen their dysfunction was visible. At least in retrospect.

This guy, this new Buddy, was the old pseudonymous Ray Bleeker. He was comfortable. He felt like people.

Without any more thought than a man batting aside a crumpled-up bit of newspaper, he kicked Candace out of the way with the side of his sneakered foot. She crawled from the urine stain to sit in a narrow space

between the rope-sprung bed and the dining table. Anna could see nothing of her but
the toes of her shoes, then they, too, were
drawn from sight.

Buddy stepped carefully around the wet
spot on the boards and looked squarely at
Anna.

"I doubt you'd take well to discipline and
you don't amuse me," he said. "I need you
to assist me in a housekeeping chore. Man's
best friend there isn't strong enough."

"Maybe because she's half-starved."

"There is that," he said with his razor-
sharp smile.

"Had my other guests arrived, you would
have been saved a walk down the hill. As it
is, my departure from this little Eden won't
be as tidy as I hoped, but it will have to do.
After we've had our tea—the royal 'we' mind
you, you would have trouble holding the cup
in your present position—you and I will go
fetch Brother Robert."

Of the many things Anna expected, this
was not one of them. When Candace
showed up with all ten digits accounted for,
Anna had assumed the bone in her evidence envelope, the finger bone rescued
from the wolf pups, had once carried the

flesh of the vanished Robert Proffit's pinky finger.

But Robert was here.

Robert was in on it.

Psycho meets psycho in the beautiful mountains of Colorado, a marriage made in hell.

No.

She was to help fetch Robert because Candace hadn't the strength. "You killed him and kept the body."

"Don't make it sound so dramatic," he said peevishly and turned from her to answer the call of the kettle murmuring on the stove. "It's not as if I intended to eat it or make Christmas tree ornaments from the viscera. It's a prop I need for the last act. My disappearing act. Besides, I didn't keep it all."

"You threw a handful of fingers to Rita's wolves."

"I was curious. They seemed to like human flesh just fine." He poured water over his tea bag, then set the alarm on his watch before leaving it to steep.

Her hands had been held higher than her heart for so long, the blood was draining from them. She began clenching and unclenching her fingers in an attempt to pump some back uphill. Why she might need them was not immediately apparent, but she wasn't anywhere near ready to lie down and die, literally or metaphorically.

A tiny beep sounded. Buddy's tea was steeped. Having removed the bag, he wrung it out against the spoon, then held it up by the string. "Remind you of anything?"

Anna drew a blank.

"I'm disappointed," he said as he tossed it into the fire. "A dead mouse maybe? Nailed to a wall?"

He sat down in one of the ladder-backed chairs by the dining table and blew gently on his tea. There was a skittering sound that might have been Candace moving deeper into her own darkness or the little feet of Fern Lake Cabin's mouse population.

"I think you just reminded them why they hate you."

"I have evened the odds somewhat," he said amiably. "My three pets were quite good mousers. We made a game of it."

In her mind's eye Anna saw the thirteen mice nailed alive to the outhouse wall, the charred and bloodied remains of the Abert squirrel burned alive in her bedroom.

Beth, when she had rescued the kitten that was to become Anna's, had gone berserk at the sight of boys torturing it, yet had run screaming at the suggestion it be entrusted to her care. The ritual torture and murder of small animals must have been part of the package.

As he sat at apparent ease studying her, Anna studied him. At this moment he looked sane. Mostly he *felt* sane. Yet, knowing what she did, he could not be defined as sane by anyone's tenets. *Not true*, she realized. The world was full of killers, they simply didn't make Lifetime's movie-of-the-week lineup if they did it on a grand scale. If they weren't white males between the ages of twenty and forty who kept to themselves. Idi Amin, Saddam Hussein, most of the boy soldiers surviving in the armies of Africa and Asia, despots from Nero to Stalin, all behaved far worse than Buddy.

According to the rules of his kind, Buddy was perfectly sane, reserved even.

To take some of the weight off her feet, Anna rested her butt on the third rung of the ladder. Her hands were cuffed above and behind her head and she realized she was posed like a sadist's vision of a forties pinup girl.

"So," she said. "You killed those two boys—students in your freshman sociology class weren't they? At that school in the East."

"Pennsylvania." Buddy sipped his tea. The temperature was to his liking and he took a longer drink. Anna realized how terribly thirsty she was. Not wanting to give him the pleasure of refusing, she didn't ask for water.

"Your name is Steve Whittfield, Steve D. Whittfield," she said, suddenly remembering. An all-points bulletin had gone out to every state in the lower forty-eight when the suspect wanted for questioning had disappeared.

"Stephen. Not Steve. And 'E' not 'D.' The 'E' is for Eisner, my grandfather on my mother's side. Gunter Eisner. He was a guard at Buchenwald during World War Two. They moved to the United States when Mother was three."

"You're a chip off the old block, is that it?"

"Grandfather was a gentle soul who did his best for the unfortunates in his care. He was the soul of kindness. At our house even cockroaches were merely banished."

"Who else have you killed?" Anna interrupted the questionable eulogy.

He smiled at her. "Other than Raymond Bleeker and that insufferable preacher boy? I'm not a serial killer stitching dresses out of women's skin or eating livers with a nice Chianti, if that's what you're getting at."

"What are you?"

There was genuine interest in her voice. It got a surprising reaction. He set down his teacup, leaned forward and looked at her as if, for the first time, he genuinely saw her.

"I'm a sociologist."

"You killed two little boys as a sociological experiment," she managed after a moment.

"Not per se, no. And they weren't little boys. Jason—they are all named Jason, are they not—was nearly as tall as I am and fifteen pounds heavier. Chad was somewhat smaller but not by a great deal. Jason was spineless. He actually killed himself, which, I admit, was handy. Chad showed promise but it was early in my new venture and I couldn't trust him not to revert, so I had to put him down. Then things got a bit out of control. I had to . . ." He smiled ruefully. "Leave town in a hurry, as they say."

Anna's hands were definitely going numb, as was her butt. She stood again, stomped, shifted, stretched. Muscles she didn't want to spasm, did; muscles she would have been grateful to have the use of were too tired to so much as cramp.

"I'd let you go but you can't be trusted," Buddy said. Anna found she could not think of him as Stephen the sociologist. He would always be Buddy the psycho-sociopath. "I'll have to kill you. Killing. Now that's inconvenient, did you know that? Bodies! Try and get rid of one sometime. I honestly believe Hitler would have won World War Two if he hadn't wasted so much time, energy, manpower and money on killing gypsies, Jews and cripples and whatnot. Think of the *bodies* he got rid of. It's monumental. I'm having a heck of a time with the preacher boy. And now you."

Anna refused to apologize for creating a nuisance though he seemed to expect her to. "So why go to all the trouble? I mean what with the corpses and all?" she asked.

"Trying to keep me talking to put off the inevitable?" He smiled. "Better rethink the old Scheherazade strategy. Wouldn't it be smarter to hustle me along? Surely you'll have a better chance of escape—or at least evening the odds—as we lumber through the dark fetching the preacher boy's mortal coil."

He was right. Anna gave him the satisfaction of letting him see that she realized it.

"Fine then. Let's go."

"I haven't finished my tea." He sat again, crossed his legs neatly and picked up his cup, sipping, watching her over the brim.

He was bright, educated. Anna guessed he believed himself to be even smarter than he was, believed himself to be almost a breed apart from ordinary human beings, an intellectual Titan. Maybe he was, but he was only half right about the wisdom of keeping him talking. She would have a greater chance for action uncuffed from the ladder, but once Proffit was in place, Buddy would kill her. Since leaving Bleeker's body behind as a red herring had been so successful, he was probably going to try it again with Robert Proffit. Proffit was the prime suspect. With a bit of stage-managing, it might be made to look like a murder-suicide. Like as not, a hunt would commence for Raymond

Bleeker's body. Even if it were guessed "Bleeker" lived, it was an identity Buddy could shed as easily as his NPS uniform.

He would need transportation that couldn't be readily traced. She guessed he would take her patrol car and drive quietly out of the park. With blue light and a uniform, he could simply pick the kind of vehicle he wanted and pull it over. One with out-of-state plates would be best. Chances were, no one would even know it was missing till long after he'd abandoned it for another make and model.

The longer Anna put off all of the above, the less night he would have remaining to clean up the evidence and pull his disappearing act, the sooner the rangers she'd requested to assist with her prisoner would be headed up the trail.

"So, what makes you so darling damn different than your basic, scratch-and-grunt, run-of-the-mill mass murderer?" she asked equitably. "Didn't you grow up torturing little animals like the other boys? Momma didn't molest you? From where I stand, I see absolutely no difference between you and John Wayne Gacy."

Buddy was stung. He hid it well but

nowhere near quickly enough, and Anna's senses were preternaturally tuned in to his moods. Like many a battered wife, her survival hinged on seeing and understanding every nuance of her batterer's emotional repertoire.

"All right, if you insist. We've got time to get to know one another." He poured himself another cup of tea. Anna could smell the crisp enticing aroma. *Dry enough to spit cotton*, the old cliché came to mind, freed from some memory trunk by its stunning accuracy. What saliva she could muster was gathering in puff balls at the top of her throat and the corners of her mouth. Before pride had time to interfere, she heard herself saying, "I could use a drink."

"Certainly," Buddy replied. "Tea, water, wine? All you had to do was ask."

"Water," Anna replied, careful to keep the gratitude from her voice. After all, she'd not yet gotten it. *After all, he's fucking chained you to a wall*, she reminded herself. Even when one was aware of the Stockholm syndrome, it was hard to remain utterly free of it.

"Get our guest a cup of water."

Far quieter than the mice she shared the

cabin with, Candace brought a cup of water and held it to Anna's lips while she drank. Such was her incredible relief, she nearly missed Buddy's first few words.

"What makes me different from Gacy? You might at least have chosen Bundy. He was mentally ill but he didn't let it ruin his fashion sense."

"Thank you, Candace," Anna whispered when the water was gone. The girl didn't acknowledge her. The phenomenon of prisoners siding with their abductors in the front of her mind, Anna believed she sensed more than just empty nothing coming from Candace. Was there an underlying sullenness, anger or resentment? There had to be. Anna hoped it would be enough so she could use it to break through to her at some point.

"I'm not interested in killing for its own sake," Buddy went on. "A waste of time, really. Oh, I'm not averse to it, but it should have a point, don't you think?" Anna chose not to answer. He expected none. "I'm not a sexual predator, though I use it as a learning tool. It's not the best, frankly. Pain and reward remain the most powerful. Not much has changed since Pavlov and his dog.

"When you were grasping at degenerates

with whom to compare me, Charlie Manson would have been your best bet. The man's a mess. Crazy as a bedbug. But his use of psychedelic drugs to break down the minds and wills of his followers, then the rebuilding of them to his own ends was an interesting study."

"Could I be uncuffed? Or at least recuffed so my hands aren't over my head?" Anna asked. Why not? Asking had worked with the water.

"No. I am a scholar, you know. My interest stems from my grandfather. He killed himself when I was five. Guilt over what he'd done during the war, or so my mother said. I expect that's what first interested me in sociology, then later, in socialization. I got rather fascinated by the idea that anyone could be turned into a monster, a sociopath with no sense of right or wrong. This isn't an original thought, but I've taken it to the next step. My contention is not only can anyone be made into a killer but can be taught to enjoy it, can be made into a serial killer so to speak, a human being, who once was like others, turned into a creature that feasts on the pain of living things."

He stopped then, seemingly to admire the lingering resonance of his verbal résumé.

Anna's pains and fatigue were banished with the eruption of the fury one feels when made a complete fool of. "Then what the fuck was all the singsong, suck-my-gun bullshit?" she demanded.

Buddy's smile wavered for half a beat, then it was back. "You seemed to expect it. I didn't want your first serial killer experience to be a disappointment."

Anna met his eyes mostly because she was too pissed off to do the smart thing and be submissive. To her surprise he looked away to keep her from seeing . . . what? Shame? Fear? With cringing detail, the gun-as-phallus scene replayed in her mind. She doubted all—or even most—of it was an act, and that frightened him. Buddy wasn't so far removed from Gacy, Dahmer and the gang as he wanted to believe. This didn't strike her as a good time to point that out.

"A Modest Proposal," she said after a while.

His brows lifted in polite inquiry. Evidently it hadn't been required reading when he took his college English courses. There was no point in enlightening him. Anna had only thought of the story because, like its author, Jonathan Swift, Buddy had managed to make the unthinkable seem like an interesting proposition.

Mesmerized by the telling of his own story, Buddy drifted off into the contemplation of the bottom of his teacup. Anna wanted to think, to plot, plan, fight and ultimately live out the night, but her brain acted as blood-starved as her hands.

Punctuated by the occasional creaks inherent to old wooden buildings and the skritch of unseen mouse feet, quiet settled. Anna found herself wasting precious moments drifting into a Willard-like fantasy of hordes of mice pouring down the walls, devouring her captor.

"Besides," he said, rousing himself and sending Anna's mental sea of vengeance-bent rodents scattering, "You cannot imagine how boring teaching ninth-grade sociology can be. But enough of this, there's work to be done."

As he rose to do whatever was next on his list, a timid knock came at the door.

Moving as silently, and with the same linear grace, as a snake through clear water, Buddy slipped his service weapon from its holster, stepped across the room to the cabin door and pressed his eye close to the narrow gap between the faded red curtain and the window glass.

He snapped his fingers. Candace came instantly to heel. Buddy whispered to her, then leaned back against the wall and nodded. Anna thought to scream, "Save me!" but in the end she didn't. Shouting would not win her relief and it would most certainly cost some late-arriving or panicked camper his life.

Candace unlocked the door and opened it so neither Anna nor Buddy could be seen.

"Come in," she said. "Robert will be back any minute."

Too late Anna realized who had come tapping at the door in the middle of the night. Raging against her manacles she screamed, "Run! Run! Run away!"

Beth and Alexis had already started through the door. Showing surprising strength, Candace grabbed them and pulled them the rest of the way in. Buddy kicked the door shut.

There was none of the crying and wailing Anna might have expected from normal thirteen-year-old girls in a like situation. Beth went dead still, replicating the way Candace behaved most of the time. Alexis whispered, "You really are alive," and reached out to embrace the smaller girl.

Candace batted away her arms. Her thin face contorted, lips pulled back from teeth, chin jutted forward, fury unleashed.

"Enough," Buddy snapped. Candace retreated toward the stove, still glaring at the others. It was the most life Anna had seen her exhibit.

"It's about time," Buddy said pleasantly to the girls. "Better late than never. I'm glad you could make it." He smashed his fist into Beth's temple, then Alexis' belly. Anna thought of the unborn child, but its life was of less interest to her than that of its mother. Both children collapsed. Buddy kicked them each several times: breasts, bellies, backs.

Looking at his handiwork, he said, "Well, hey, looks like I've got hostages to burn. Let's make a call to dispatch, shall we? Let them know we're A-okay and have no need for backup?" Buddy grabbed Beth by the upper arm in a grip so hard even in the cabin's uncertain light Anna could see the flesh turning white. The girl squeaked inadvertently, then clamped her lips closed on the sound. Teaching them not to make noise would have been one of the first lessons in Buddy's School for Psychopaths.

He led her to the stove. To Candace he said, "Get the mike on the base radio. Pull it out as far toward her"—he jerked his chin at Anna—"as you can. When I tell you to push the Send button, you do it."

Candace did as she was told, each action executed with the careful precision of one who knows the least infraction can have dire consequences. When she was in place and the curling wire stretched till the mike was only a few feet from Anna's face, Buddy gathered Beth's hair at the nape of her neck and forced her head down till her nose was an inch from the hot cast-iron of the wood-stove.

"You will say exactly what I tell you. Word for word. No more, no less. Any deviation, any weird inflection or pronunciation, anything I even think is funky and we cook this pretty girl's face off. Understand me?"

Anna understood perfectly. The text was short and she memorized it with the intensity of desperation. Within two minutes, backup was canceled.

"Get a knife and cut the mike wire."

Candace did, then on his instruction, threw the mike into the fire. For half a minute Buddy continued to hold Beth's face near the stovetop, his eyes boring into Anna's. Anna did not breathe or blink, swallow or sweat, terrified anything, any change, would send the child's face onto the hot metal.

Buddy had her where he wanted her, paralyzed. He was good at his craft.

As if he'd seen the defeat in her gaze, he let Beth go.

"You two proved a disappointment and caused me a great deal of work," he said to Alexis and Beth. "But, out of the kindness of my heart, I'm going to give you an opportunity to atone. We're going to fetch Robert Proffit. It was him you came to see, was it not?"

The girls showed no relief at the sound of their beloved youth leader's name, and Anna wondered if they'd come to blame him, either for letting them be taken in the first place or failing to find them, to save them. The wariness in Alexis' pale blue eyes as, using the edge of the table, she pulled herself to her feet told Anna otherwise. The girls had learned to trust nothing, to expect nothing good.

"Robert is dead," Anna told them. Knowledge was power of a sort. If nothing else, it might reduce the number of mind games between the cabin door and wherever the body was stashed. It also served to get the girls to look at her. The room was not brightly lit and they'd been given little time for sightseeing.

When their eyes met hers Anna saw hope spark there; an adult to keep them safe. Then the shift that cut Anna so deeply she had to fight not to turn her face away in shame: resignation. Seeing her chained up, they accepted that, in the face of Buddy, everyone was helpless. Watching the young faces harden, the eyes dull, Anna could almost hear the faint cracking as they crumbled.

"We'll not need you," Buddy said to Anna and she felt another crack, this time within herself. On his way out the door he picked up her service weapon, removed the magazine, shoved it in his gun belt and dropped the pistol back on the bed. "Enjoy yourself," he told Candace and left. Beth and Alexis followed meekly.

When the door had closed, Anna looked to Candace, only to find the girl who had studiously avoided eye contact since their unfortunate introduction over the sights of Anna's SIG Sauer, staring fixatedly at her.

thirty

Small and emaciated, in the hard light of the single lamp, Candace's eyes seemed to take up half her face. Despite weeks of abuse, Goth hair and ill-fitting men's clothes, she was gamine pretty. The triangular face and flawless skin added an otherworldly touch.

Instinct warned Anna to treat this elfin child as a cornered animal.

"Hey," Anna said softly. "How're you doing?"

Candace stared. The noise of the Coleman lantern filled the cabin with the hiss of a thousand snakes.

"Could I have a bit more water?" Anna asked in the same soothing voice. Though a drink would be welcome, she wouldn't have wasted precious time just to procure it. By requesting help she hoped to establish a bond; one in which Candace felt she had the power for good, the ability to help, first Anna then herself.

"Don't you want something pointed to unlock the handcuffs? I know how they work." Candace sounded so kind, so intelligent, so . . . so *okay*, that Anna was momentarily stunned to silence. The unutterable delight she should be experiencing at this unexpected deus ex machina, turning tragedy into triumph in an instant, was not forthcoming.

"That would be nice," she said carefully.

Candace went to the bed and peeled back the mattress. When she returned she had a bit of wire about six inches long and about half the diameter of that used to make coat hangers: ideal for opening handcuffs.

"Is that what you used to get free when Buddy handcuffed you? You're a clever girl."

"His name isn't Buddy."

"Stephen, then."

"Ray."

"Okay." Why the name was important, Anna couldn't guess, but what Candace chose to call the son-of-a-bitch was all the same to her.

Holding the wire up in front of her the way the priest holds the communion wafer at Mass, Candace stayed where she was.

The delay was driving Anna nuts but she didn't want to do or say anything that might shut the child down. "Ray won't be gone long unless he's put the . . . it someplace far away," she hinted gently.

"Robert's body. I saw it. It's not far. We put it in the lake wrapped in plastic bags and held down with big rocks. The cold keeps it fresh, just like meat in the refrigerator."

Elfin-faced abused waif or not, the kid was beginning to give Anna a bad feeling.

"Could you give me the wire?" she said, abandoning psychology.

"Yes." Candace dropped the weird chalice pose, walked over to the ladder and drove an inch of the wire into Anna's thigh. The pain and shock made her scream.

"Shh, shh," Candace whispered, her index finger in front of her lips. "Quiet as a mouse." The wire was jerked out and plunged in again.

This time Anna didn't scream. It wasn't that she didn't want to or had the iron control to resist. There simply wasn't enough air remaining in her world to do more than grunt. Arching her back against the ladder, she jammed her knee into Candace's midsection and pushed. The girl flew back, landing on her butt. The piece of wire was still sticking out of Anna's thigh. A thin trickle of blood oozed from the first puncture wound and was quickly lost in the dirt and abrasions from their march down from Loomis.

"Why did you do that?" Anna demanded. "Jeez. What a little creep."

Candace remained on the floor for a second, looking neither pleased nor displeased with her handiwork and completely unmoved by having been sent sprawling.

Recovering from the anger brought on by the unexpected attack, Anna said in a kinder, if less honest tone, "I'm not here to hurt you, Candace. I'm here to help. I've seen how Buddy . . . how Ray treats you. Look at your legs. You fell down as many times as me. You were cuffed just like me. Us girls have to stick together."

Up until the last bit, Anna could have sworn Candace was listening, if in a disinterested brain-dead sort of way, the way seventh graders listen through English class. As soon as the "us girls" plea was uttered Candace's mouth curled in on itself. In the strong sideways light from the lantern it looked like a flower wilting on fast-forward. The pixie face grew red. Spittle sparked the air in the light of the Coleman. Candace looked like a demon child.

"They knew where I was. They were here, too. They knew and they didn't care. Not even to tell anybody. They left and went home and told people I was dead and that they didn't know. They told everybody I was the one that got everybody lost. That I stole their food and was a whore and dirt."

This diatribe from the heretofore mostly silent girl poured over Anna like hot ashes. For the blink of an eye she had no idea what Candace was talking about, then she realized: "us girls"—Beth, Alexis and Candace. To her knowledge, neither Beth nor Alexis had called Candace a thief, a whore, a corpse or dirt, but Anna didn't waste time arguing details. They did know where Candace was and what she was enduring and they didn't tell law enforcement or their parents or even Robert Proffit. They'd sworn repeatedly that they remembered nothing: not where they'd been or whom they'd been with.

Anna could guess reasons for this alleged amnesia. Fear that Buddy, a ranger, would be believed and they would not. Fear he would find them and kill them if they spoke. Looking back, Anna remembered his promises when they were in the hospital, telling them repeatedly he knew where they lived and would keep an eye on them. At the time she had mistaken it for concern. As she had mistaken his sudden appearance in the frontcountry, tired and rain-soaked, as a zeal for the finding of children so long lost.

It was. He was zealously covering his tracks, keeping them under his control. He probably hadn't had a moment's comfort between the time they escaped and tonight when he'd successfully gotten them back.

Perhaps he had threatened their families.

Perhaps he had told them Candace was dead.

Perhaps he had told them, should they speak, he would kill Candace.

Reasons.

But they had known the hell Candace was living in and they had left her there. In the face of that, ameliorating circumstances didn't amount to a hill of beans.

"I don't know why those things happened," Anna said truthfully. "I know they care about you. I know nobody ever quit looking for you. I know you've been hurt, hurt real bad." Like she had seen Heath Jarrod do when Alexis and Beth first came out of the woods, Anna spoke as if to a much younger child. There was that about trauma that either aged victims or stripped away the meager defenses age provided.

Candace had been starved, beaten, humiliated and raped till she had abandoned even the pretense of being an adult, being in control. Anna saw her as a little kid, scarcely more than a toddler, and with a toddler's inability to grasp another's reality.

The Charlie Manson school, Anna remembered Buddy describing it. Buddy had torn Candace down, ripped away every defense, every hope, every innocence, every belief she had, then he'd begun rebuilding her in the image of a serial killer. In his own image, whether he chose to admit it or not.

Anna was the final exam. Probably it was meant to be Beth and Alexis. What better triumph than to see one's monster kill those of her own kind, those she once loved and who still loved her?

"You don't have to be who Buddy wants you to be," Anna said, carefully using "Buddy" instead of "Ray" in the small hope it would help Candace disengage.

"This is who I want to be," Candace hissed. "I let them do those things to me. I *let* them. Ray's made me strong. Now I won't *let* them hurt me. I won't let you hurt me."

Candace pushed up from the floor, coltish and shaky on too-thin arms and legs. From the counter in the shadowy kitchen side of the room she gathered a paring knife, then disappeared into the short ell that led to the cabin's back door. The sound of rummaging triggered hideous visions in Anna's brain of the torture potential of household implements. When Candace returned, in addition to the knife, she carried a broom and a roll of duct tape.

She seated herself at the dining table where the light was best and began taping the knife to the broom handle, making herself a spear. The collapsed face of the feral girl was gone. Back was the expressionlessness. Of the two, it was the more frightening. The other was angry, twisted but very much alive. This was the face of the dead, the kind that walk out of the night woods carrying torches to slaughter and eat the people of the village.

During the brief tool-making exercise, Anna tried to engage Candace with her, with the living. She questioned, pleaded, flattered and cajoled, but Candace had gone deaf again, incapable of hearing or responding to anything but her master's voice.

In not too many minutes the spear was completed. Candace examined it for workmanship, banged it on the floor several times to make sure the blade would stay fixed to the shaft under pressure. This done, she held it in front of her and came for Anna.

thirty-one

Heath was so angry she was having trouble staying in her own skin. At least that's how it felt: as if she could dig her nails into her sternum, pull her flesh apart and release a monster that would do justice to anything in the Book of Revelations.

She had been flouted, tricked, robbed, hijacked and kidnapped, all within the space of thirty minutes and all by two skinny young blondes earnestly repeating, "I'm sorry, I'm sorry, I'm sorry." The burst of self-worth she'd earned from rolling herself miles through the dark of night had been canceled out by a wave of helplessness that might have left her whimpering had she not known how upsetting that would be to Wiley.

Aunt Gwen did keep a can of pepper spray in the drawer next to the sink. In such close quarters she'd probably have ended up peppering them all, including herself and the dog. Had she not been so fond of her abductors, she'd have done it anyway.

This course of action closed to her, she sulked.

Sharon drove. Heath fumed in the passenger seat. Patty hung over their shoulders and flitted in and out of sight doing whatever it was nine- or ten-year-old girls do with such enthusiasm.

"There's nothing they can do till sunrise anyway," Sharon said as she conned the RV through the deep canyon between Loveland and Estes Park.

She was convincing herself, not Heath. Even sequestered on a ranch with the modern conveniences doled out by a man sporting a Luddite streak—at least where his women were concerned—Sharon had to know that was absurd. The trails were wide, well maintained; rangers could hike to Fern with lanterns, flashlights, floodlights run on portable generators. Heath didn't bother to make the argument. She'd already tried and run smack into an impenetrable wall of paranoia and prejudice, both exacerbated by the emotional stress Sharon was suffering. *Emotional breakdown*, Heath thought, but was too mad to feel much sympathy. The law terrified Sharon. Outsiders. Them. They. The Other. She was as scared of falling into the hands of the authorities as she was those of the criminals. To her they were one and the same.

"An hour or so won't make any difference," Sharon said after a moment of following sinuous curving of road and headlights. Her voice was brittle and over-bright. "Then you can have your cell phone back. You can call anyone you want. I promise. The FBI, CIA, UFO, the cavalry. I won't make a peep. The girls may not even have got there. Or they might still be at the parking lot. I bet they're still at the parking lot. They'd be way too scared to hike so far in the dark."

Again Heath said nothing. An hour could make all the difference in the world; freedom and capture, success and failure, life and death. They'd been over that as well.

"They'll still be at Bear Lake. Candace's

dead. They know that. They won't go to the cabin."

"He may come down to Bear."

"Nobody can really do anything till sunrise anyway."

Heath gave up and stared at her reflection in the side window. Patty had, for reasons known only to herself, decided that the small light over the galley sink should be on. It effectively blanked Heath's window. For the sake of her aunt's investment in the RV, she hoped Sharon was not likewise impeded.

As deeply betrayed as Heath felt, as helpless and as worried about Alexis and the limpet, as willingly as she would have spanked, demoted or fined both Sharon and her relatively innocent younger sister, Heath couldn't find it in herself to genuinely hate them or wish them ill. That Sharon was making a decision out of fear and indoctrination that might cause Alexis' death only added to Heath's burden of angry compassion. Should that happen, the guilt would ride Sharon like a rabid monkey for the rest of her days.

Heath knew about that, about regrets. There was no way to calculate the number of times she'd relived the decision to sink her anchor in ice that struck her as a shade rotten, the color a hair off, the texture not quite what it should have been. Part of her knew. Part of her didn't. Part of her was cautious. Part of her wanted to set a record time for the climb. In retrospect the parts of caution seemed so clear. Never had she been reckless. Never had she been careless. Still and all . . .

What if it had not been she who'd paid that price? How could she have lived with it then? Furious as she was with Sharon, mostly she feared for her. She was as trapped in her belief system as Heath once felt in her wheelchair. Even Mr. Sheppard, whom she purported to detest, when she said his name there was . . . something. Not love or respect. Not merely fear or awe. But something. Mr. Sheppard was the embodiment of all that Sharon had been taught God would be. Mr. Sheppard was God's representative on earth. Sharon could never be able to be party to bringing him down.

According to the scriptures, Peter turned his face away three times, yet he was the rock upon which the church was built, became the saint who, legend would have it, stood at the pearly gates deciding who should be let in and who turned away.

Judas, on the other hand, the man who actively had a hand in bringing Jesus down, Judas despaired, took his own life and, again as legend would have it, suffered on one of the lowest levels a creative mind such as Dante Alighieri could envision.

Sharon could turn away. Asking more of her would not only be unprofitable but cruel.

Given the mood Heath was in, she wouldn't have hesitated being cruel for a nanosecond had she thought it would get her back her cell phone so she could call 911. Since it would serve no purpose but to bring a bit more bitterness into the world, she said nothing.

As they entered the park the sky was graying in the east. Heath, Sharon, even little Patty, too wired to sleep, had been up nearly twenty-four hours. The dull nausea brought on by seeing sunrise from the wrong side of the day curled low in Heath's middle, adding to weariness deep enough it ached.

Sharon turned left onto Bear Lake Road. There was a ranger station part way up,

Heath knew, with employee housing near by.

This last chance at good sense spurred her to try one more time.

"What can we do?" Heath asked. "Seriously? A paraplegic, a scared woman and an exhausted child: what do you propose to do when we get there? There's a ranger station in a few miles. Let's stop and get help. Please."

In this narrow forested canyon it was still nearly full dark, but in the faint glow of the dashboard lights Heath could see a ripple of pain cross Sharon's face, deepening her premature crow's feet and hardening her mouth.

"The girls won't have gone in. Not in the dark. They'll still be at Bear Lake. Probably in the parking lot," Sharon insisted.

The turnoff for the ranger station came and went. Heath waved. They'd be at the Bear Lake parking area shortly. Hours the rangers could have used to reach Fern Lake had been already sacrificed to Sharon's learned paranoia. Heath doubted a few more minutes would make any difference. She promised herself if Alexis and the limpet weren't in the parking lot she would try more drastic measures. Just what form that might take she hadn't a clue.

So late in the season, kids back in school, the number of visitors dropped off radically. It was a weekday as well and the Bear Lake parking area was nearly deserted. In August there would have been bumper-to-bumper traffic. A few weeks later and the lot boasted eight cars.

"There," Patty squeaked, leaning between Heath's and Sharon's seats to point. The aged New Canaanite sedan was parked crookedly half a dozen spaces from the trailhead leading to the Bear Lake campground and on to Fern Lake.

"They aren't here," Heath said.

Sharon rolled down her window as if that might be what was obstructing her view of the missing girls. "They could be asleep on the seats." She parked the RV in the slot next to the sedan. From her raised vantage point Heath could see down into the car.

"They're not there. Give me my cell phone."

"Wait. They're here," Sharon said desperately. "Probably in the bathroom. Let me go check. I'll be quick like a bunny."

Before Heath could manage anything

more coherent than, "Oh for Christ's sake," Sharon had jumped from the vehicle.

The keys were in the ignition.

For half a second Heath eyed them, then heaved her weight up on arms still rubbery from her rolling sojourn, to maneuver herself into the other seat.

Sharon's head appeared in the driver's side window with the alarming suddenness of a Jack-in-the-box.

"Patty! Keys. Keep 'em till I get back."

The little girl grabbed the keys from the ignition and retreated back behind the seats.

"You might be killing your sister," Heath shouted, too angry to care whether she was motivated by a belief that honesty would change things or just wanton cruelty.

The honesty didn't work. The cruelty did. Sharon looked as if she'd been slapped.

"I won't be a minute," she whispered and staggered off, trying to run on feet too long unused.

Heath pivoted her seat so she could see Patty. The little girl, looking like a lost member of Bob Cratchit's brood in her mismatched old-fashioned clothes, sat on the edge of the sofa opposite the tiny kitchen area.

"Give me the keys," Heath said none too gently.

"She'll only be a minute. She promised," Patty replied miserably.

"Wiley is a trained attack dog," Heath said. "Give me the keys or I'll sic him on you."

"No sir. Wiley's not mean like you."

Heath gave up. She just wasn't cut out for terrorizing children. And Sharon would only be a minute.

She promised.

thirty-two

Being terrorized by a child was more unsettling than Anna would have thought. Had it ever entered her mind to envision such a thing. The utter wrongness of it jarred the brain, like being devoured by butterflies. If Candace had taken joy in her cruelty, even of the maniacal sort, it would have been easier. Then there would have been the visible specter of mental illness to stand between Anna's eyes and the ruinous child.

Candace showed neither anger nor glee but jabbed Anna with the fierce concentration of a novice 4-H'er working on her first apron hem. The jab was experimental, tentative. Anna kicked it aside.

The next was not so amateurish. With her hands tethered above her head, Anna's soft white underbelly was exposed. No way could she curl down, take cuts with shoulders, back or upper arms. Any lucky hit could pierce an organ. Candace came two steps closer, not close enough Anna could reach her, but close enough she could do some real damage. Feet planted firmly, one a bit behind the other, she thrust her spear hard at Anna's gut. Bracing spine and buttocks against the ladder, Anna swung a sideways kick with her right leg, connecting hard with the spear's shaft.

The makeshift weapon flew from Candace's hands, clattering across the worn plank flooring.

For a moment the girl stared at Anna, the muscles of her face tensing as thoughts came and went, and Anna dared hope the violence had broken through her robot-like state.

"You could have killed me," Anna said gently. Words were a risk when their context and denotations had been so radically altered for one of the parties. This risk did not pay off.

"Right. Could have killed it. Too soon," Candace muttered, a child at her lessons. With no change of expression, the wisp of a girl retrieved the homemade weapon, returned to position and planted her feet as before. This time she gripped the spear more tightly.

Before she set about her work, Anna had just time enough to wonder how long the thirteen mice had lived before succumbing to their final crucifixion on the outhouse wall.

Not wanting to kill "it" too soon, Candace concentrated jagged thrusts at Anna's legs and feet. The paring knife was sharp, but short of a direct stab, couldn't cut through the heavy canvas and leather of Anna's hiking boots, and she focused on catching the knife with the soles and sides of her feet. Twice the narrow blade slipped above the boots. Blood began to flow. Anna was glad for her cordovan-colored socks. She had no desire to know how much damage she was taking.

Each kick grew more difficult. Her legs and back were already tired from the push down from Loomis. Fortunately Candace had taken that same road. On top of that, the girl had been starved and tortured till she had scarcely any strength left. The spear thrusts weakened rapidly as her pencil-thin arms tired. To compensate she began taking little runs at Anna, spear held fast to her side. These were easier to gauge and so avoid. Once, she got close enough Anna managed to land a bloody boot on her shoulder and knock her down.

The macabre scene wore on Anna as much as the sheer physical force required to keep lifting and swinging legs grown heavy and unresponsive as wooden prosthetics. Sweat she could not wipe away blinded her, yet she dared not blink too long because child-of-Satan would be coming at her again.

Candace did not sweat—probably too dehydrated and malnourished to spare so much as a drop of water or a pinch of salt— but she gasped for breath. Anna began to lose track of who Candace was torturing, the ranger cuffed to the ladder or the abused child holding the spear.

After a couple minutes, she didn't care. The two of them, like Prometheus and the vultures, seemed locked together in an eternity of misery.

So engrossed was Anna in this hellish *pas de deux* that when the front door banged open it took her completely by surprise.

Alexis and Beth were soaked from head to toe, hair streaming water down their backs and faces. Buddy was wet from the chest down. His duty belt had been slung around his neck to keep it dry. Fern was a fishing lake—too cold for swimming—but the waters were clear. The package with the body would have had to be stored out a ways in deeper water.

"Buddy," she cried, never before so glad to see a corpse-bearing serial killer. In her moment of distraction, Candace rushed in. Pain so deep it encompassed the marrow of her bones, and the fillings of her teeth screamed through her. It wasn't a cry, it was the shriek of an enraged and hurting animal.

Candace fell back. Buddy and the other two girls dumped the dripping body bag they carried between them.

Candace's spear stuck out from Anna's leg where the tip of the paring knife was embedded in her shin bone. Anna tried resting the shaft on the floor but it only brought another tide of pain so rapacious it nearly took her consciousness.

"My, my," Buddy said. "How fast they grow up. Before you know it they are off killing people of their own. Interesting, isn't it? How there is no baseline of decency, honor, compassion—God, if you like—sugar and spice grows up with a knife."

Anna could barely hear him through the clamor inside her head. His smug self-satisfied smirk conjured up a rage so intense, for the briefest of moments, it anesthetized her to the knife embedded in her bone.

"Let me give you a hand," Buddy said solicitously, enjoying the role of sane, kind man every bit as much as he did that of giggling monster. With him, they were one and the same. He stepped in front of Anna and leaned down to pull the spear from her leg.

This was it, the one chance. Slim as it was, she took it. Calling on what reserves she had, Anna wrapped her legs around him and locked her ankles. No time to find the perfect position, she held him around his waist and his left arm in an awkward scissor grip. With a twist of hips and back she levered him off of his feet. Luck, so long conspicuous by her absence, threw Anna a bone: the gun belt flew from his neck and slid into the relative darkness at the kitchen end of the room. Setting her jaw, she squeezed with the strength of someone who has no need to save anything for later.

He bellowed with surprise and began hammering at her. She ignored the blows from his free right arm. They were of no significance at the moment. She couldn't hold him more than fifteen or twenty seconds. Half a minute at most.

"Kill him," she screamed at the girls. "Do it. Do it. Kill him. Fucking kill him." Candace stood motionless, the robot switched off. Alexis and Beth looked first to one another then the cabin door. "Now. Quick. Chairs. Logs. Kill him," Anna begged. "I can't hold him much longer."

Her legs were weakening. Buddy was moving, squirming. He had his feet back under him.

"Run," she yelled at Beth and Alexis. "Run away!"

For some reason they both looked at the corpse of Robert Proffit on the cabin floor. The sight of the black plastic, running with water, black and shiny and elemental in the ugly light from the Coleman lamp, threw a psychic switch. As one they ran at Buddy, screaming and clawing. They kicked and bit. Beth grabbed the fire poker and, two-handed like a baseball player at bat, laid into his back and legs. Several of the blows struck Anna and he fell from her scissor grip to the floor. Alexis took up a cast-iron frying pan. Again and again she brought it down on his hands, head, arms.

Buddy curled up in a ball. The girls were crying, weeping, shrieking, uttering visceral grunts that, before this night, Anna would not have believed could come from the throats of twelve- and thirteen-year-old girls. Then Buddy was still.

The pounding didn't stop.

"Enough," she yelled, perhaps a bit later than an upstanding law enforcement officer should have. Beth and Alexis were past hearing.

Candace reappeared from the edges of Anna's vision and snatched up the home-made spear that had fallen from her shin in the struggle.

Whether Candace intended to dispatch or defend her master, Anna hadn't a clue. "Look out," she yelled at no one in particu-lar.

The paring knife poked Alexis' thigh, then Beth's shoulder. The beating stopped and the three children—schoolmates, playfellows, confidantes— stared at one another over the curled-up body of their tormentor.

Blood seeped from Beth's and Alexis' wounds. Candace was spattered with Anna's blood and that which she'd shed in the long fall from Loomis Lake to Fern Lake Cabin.

Anna saw not children but maenads, the women from Greek mythology said to go mad on the day they worshipped the god Dionysus. They'd run wild in the woods. Any man they caught was torn to pieces, the gobbets of flesh used to festoon their dresses and hair. The myth of the intoxication of revenge and violence must have had its roots in the same bottomless well of hatred Anna had witnessed.

"Candy," Beth whispered. The first human sound in what seemed a very long time.

The ersatz spear fell to the floor. Candace ran for the cabin's back door, then was gone into the thinning darkness at the ass end of the night.

thirty-three

Frying pan held at ready, hatred narrowing her wide blue eyes, Alexis stood guard over the unconscious Buddy while Beth fished his spare handcuff key from his shirt pocket and freed Anna from the ladder.

The temptation to fall in a heap was sufficiently powerful in both body and mind that for several long breaths before she dared move, Anna had to hang on to one of the rungs she had come to loathe. The bits of her that weren't numb, hurt. Both categories suffered exhaustion. She believed her lifetime's supply of adrenaline to have been used up till Buddy groaned.

Before he could move an eyelash she was upon him, rolling him to his stomach, one knee in the small of his back, one on the nape of his neck. Using the cuffs she'd worn most of the night, she secured his hands behind his back. In haste and fear she ratcheted them down too tightly. The steel cut into the flesh of his wrists. They'd cause him a good deal of pain.

She didn't care. It was because she didn't, because she would have *enjoyed* his pain, that she loosened them. Evil wasn't the thought; it was the deed. She chose not to identify with his acts, chose not to let the girls see her doing so.

The first order of business was to get help. The base radio was of no use. Rising with difficulty from the prone person of Buddy Ray Stephen, she backed into the darker kitchen area to retrieve his weapon and portable radio.

The floor was bare. In a small space with nothing to slide under or behind, the fact, unpleasant as it was, couldn't be denied. Candace had taken them. She was a frightened child, a brainwashed serial-killer-in-training, and she had a 9 mm semiautomatic handgun, three magazines of ammunition and a radio.

"We can't stay here," Anna said. "We're hiking out."

Alexis and Beth had hiked in from Bear Lake. They'd been half drowned, terrorized, beaten and kicked, but they said not a word of protest. They wanted out of the cabin and away from Fern Lake as much as Anna did. More.

Anna doused Buddy with water. He came to with a theatrical sputtering that led Anna to believe he'd been conscious for a while. Playing possum. Lying in wait for an opportunity.

She wasn't going to give him one.

In an act that, though not strictly by the book, was imminently sensible, she chose to hobble him. As she searched for a light, strong, cotton rope in the tool room, Beth watched her.

Through the doorway Anna kept an eye on Alexis and Buddy. Alexis straddled a chair behind and out of reach of their prone captive. She held Anna's service weapon trained at his head. The pistol wasn't all bluff. A single round remained in the chamber when Buddy took the magazine.

Buddy, chin on the floor, neck at an uncomfortable angle, stared at Anna. He'd said nothing since reviving. Said nothing and missed nothing.

Beth folded back the clean canvas tarp Buddy had kept over the spotless, dustless floor. A square of flooring about eighteen inches on a side had been rough-cut from the planks with a chainsaw. A long hinge, the kind used on big cabinet doors, ran along one side. Opposite that was a heavy dead-bolt. Strips of rubber were nailed onto the door overlapping the cuts. Why Buddy had needed to seal cracks so narrow nothing larger than a cockroach could escape through them, Anna couldn't guess.

Beth squatted, staring at the crude trap-door. "This was the sky."

"Don't open it!" Alexis cried, as if once the trap were opened all the light and life of the world would be sucked down it.

Beth shot the bolt. It moved quietly, effortlessly. She seemed surprised by this.

"No!" Alexis wailed. Buddy never moved, never blinked. Beth raised the door, using the bolt as a handle.

The smell of a cesspit poured upward, that uniquely foul odor of human degradation masquerading as human waste. The stink was so thick Anna half believed she could see it, a black fog threatening to poison them all. In a swift move she kicked the trap shut. The rubber gaskets snapped in place. Hell was once again trapped below.

"That's where you were kept," she said flatly. It must have given Buddy such joy to know the children being so desperately sought were under the feet of the searchers the whole time, that while two armed rangers slept in the next room he could bring out one of his victims, rape her and put her back. That must have been especially piquant. How smart he must have felt, how powerful, how superior.

Rage burned the stench from Anna's nostrils and for a moment she saw red. Literally. The room filled with a mist the color of fresh blood and a sound like that of a winter sea. What she'd assumed all her life was a metaphor was instead a rare phenomenon.

Till it passed she stood perfectly still, afraid, should she move, she would spontaneously combust and burn down this filthy cabin and the man who'd made it so. The psychic fire died, leaving cold ash. Vision cleared, then super-cleared, the edges of objects hyperdefined, human features thrown into high relief.

The piece of rope she'd sought had found its way into her hand. She returned to the main room and squatted in front of Buddy, close enough he had to crank his neck to look up at her.

"There's a theory in psychology circles that people tend to manifest their internal lives in the external world. Those whose minds are dark and chaotic live in lightless messy houses. You. This cabin. Neat as a pin for the public. A festering sewer beneath."

Having delivered this clinical observation, she continued to look down at him for a few beats of her heart. His cheek was on the worn planking, his neck twisted and kinked as he stared up at her with one eye. He resembled nothing in nature, not a snake or a toad or a wounded bird. Not a person. He didn't look human to Anna, but like a soulless alien from a sci-fi movie who'd taken on human form.

It was easy to kill things like that. Was this how he saw her, the girls, the boys he'd killed back East, how he saw everyone but himself?

The loneliness of it struck her with sufficient force a teaspoon's worth of the cold ash within her soul stirred, an ember of humanity glowed. Not enough to pity him but enough to let him live.

Buddy said nothing, just watched as she hobbled him and pulled him to his feet. In the predawn chill the four of them began the long walk out. Anna sent Buddy first, hands cuffed behind his back, steps limited by the eighteen-inch hobble rope, the tail of which she carried that she might trip him should he run. Unorthodox, possibly against park regulations, but with three adolescents, all traumatized, one armed and missing, she chose to err on the side of caution. Alexis and Beth followed her with instructions to stay close; instructions they obeyed with such zeal they trod on her heels more than once. She didn't complain. In arranging their order of egress from the backcountry, Anna had felt she was back in the fourth grade with the story problem of how to get the fox, the goose and the bag of corn across the river in a boat that could only carry one of them at a time, without somebody eating somebody or something. If she put the girls first they would be vulnerable to Buddy behind them. She didn't want them between her and the prisoner, yet if they trailed, they would be vulnerable to Candace should she be stalking them. Close on her heels was the best of the bad choices.

Anna kept the pace slow both for the girls and to minimize the number of times the prisoner tripped and fell, but she didn't make any rest stops. The girls needed to get out. Buddy needed to be put behind bars. Rita's body needed to be recovered before the scavengers did too much damage. Rangers needed to be sent in to find Candace, a task Anna dreaded. She'd already shot the child once; she was craven enough to hope her generally beat-up condition would get her excluded from the search.

They met no one on the trail, which was a blessing. By the time they reached the final descent to Bear Lake, the sun was rising over the hills to the east. Another blessing. The end of the journey and the coming of the light gave new energy. Anna heard Alexis and Beth talking quietly behind her. Even Buddy, though he'd yet to say a single word, seemed to be standing a little straighter, tripping less often.

Maybe monsters did want to get caught,

Anna thought wearily. *Maybe he's feeling the same relief at the end of it as the rest of us.*

Not so.

"Ah," he said and stopped.

Anna's mind, already in the parking lot stuffing him into the cage of her patrol car, took half a second to register what was happening. Because she'd been expecting it for two hours, when a childish voice addressed them from behind her left shoulder, she wasn't the least bit surprised. There was nothing she could have done to guard against it and she wasted no time in self-recrimination. She'd gambled Candace hadn't the strength or speed to make it down the Bear Lake trail ahead of them. She'd gambled the girl hadn't the mental clarity or emotional stability to stage an effective ambush.

Both had been good bets. On both counts she'd lost.

"I'm going to shoot everybody," Candace said. "We can't go out. I'm going to shoot you all now." Her voice was toneless and tight.

"Not right now," Anna said gently. "You

can shoot everybody in a minute, okay? No hurry. We're not going anywhere."

Candace would be standing behind the information sign where the trail forked, Anna guessed. Ideal cover, the sign was eight feet high and at least that long, built like the fake walls police and rangers sometimes used in training.

"Can I turn around?" she asked politely.

"I guess."

"No." This was Buddy. He turned slowly, smiling.

"No," Candace echoed.

"You don't want to shoot everybody," Buddy said past Anna's shoulder. "You want to shoot who I tell you to shoot. You shoot everybody, then you're alone. They lock you up. You've been locked up. Do you want to have to do it again?"

Candace didn't answer. It wasn't a question, it was a threat. Though she had the gun and the cover and he was cuffed and hobbled, Buddy was still the figure of absolute authority: omniscient, omnipotent.

He shifted his gaze to meet Anna's. "You're never as smart as you think you are, isn't that right? How that must have blighted your life." The smile flickered but didn't go out. "Drop the rope and hobble and give the short girl the cuff keys."

"Not on your life."

"My life? *My* life? How about their lives? Shoot the tall one," he ordered. Without hesitation Candace pulled the trigger. Spinning, Anna fell to her knees and pulled her weapon, training it on the northern edge of the wooden sign.

Candace wasn't visible. Freedom, escape, safety so close, Beth and Alexis had fallen several yards behind. When the gun went off they'd not had the sense to drop for cover if the bullet had missed them, or fall down if they'd been shot. Leaning together for support, they hid their eyes on one another's shoulders.

Another report gutted the stillness of morning. This shot was wild but not by much; Anna saw bark splinter from a pine four feet from where Alexis' pancreas was located. Anna could have shot back. Her bullet would easily penetrate the wood of the sign and anyone standing behind it. But she wasn't sure where Candace stood or if she were standing.

"All right!" she yelled. "All right. Stop her."

"Stop," Buddy nearly whispered into the

bleeding silence, enjoying his power, show-ing off. "Now you drop the rope."

Anna let go of the line connected to his hobble.

"Give a girl the cuff key and the gun."

"Why? You took the magazine. I can't use it to bluff you."

"Because you didn't look like you were bluffing. Hand it over or she kills you all." He said each word distinctly, as if he spoke to an idiot.

"You're going to kill us all anyway," Anna said.

"Not all. Just you. And not right away. I wish the pleasure of your company till we leave the park. You'll be sacrificing yourself to save the lives of three innocent children. Well, two damaged children and one bud-ding psychopath, but the idea's the same. And who knows what clever escapes you'll come up with given that much time, that many more minutes of life? I can practically smell you salivating from here."

Anna hesitated. If she'd been by herself she would have tried taking Buddy down, using him as a shield as he was so fond of doing with others. Or she'd have run into the trees. A weak and shaken girl, even as close as she was, wasn't much of a marksman. Anna might get shot but probably not killed.

But she wasn't alone and, in a crunch, Anna suspected Beth and Alexis would follow Buddy's orders rather than hers. She wasn't the one who would kill them for disobeying. So much for sparing the rod.

Buddy's eyes slid to where Candace hid with a pistol and nearly forty rounds of ammunition. He'd give the order. He had nothing to win by bluffing and time was running out. He would be as aware as she that two gunshots this close to a campground in a national park would not go unremarked. Now that most tents housed two or three cell phones, the shots would be reported the moment a signal could be found.

"Fine," Anna said, and unsnapped the keeper on her holster.

"No. The short girl will get it. And the key."

For a moment Anna empathized with the docility of the girls. For a moment it seemed right, wise even. This man, this creature, could not be beaten. The fates themselves had decreed his darkness unstoppable, that he be placed on earth to try men's souls, to force one to make increasingly hideous and futile choices till the only choice left was death.

Beth took Anna's gun, fished the tiny handcuff key from her pocket and walked them to Buddy. As she reached him Candace stepped from behind the sign. She had moved from one side to the other. Before, she'd been behind Anna; now, she was in front of her at Buddy's elbow. He ordered Beth to give Candace Anna's gun. For a moment Anna dared hope the frail girl wouldn't have the strength to hold them both, but she found it somehow. While Beth unlocked Buddy's handcuffs, Candace held the barrel to the temple of the girl she'd grown up playing dolls with, held it just as Buddy had held it to her temple at Loomis Lake.

Anna grieved for the seconds while Candace was moving from one end of the sign to the other, moments Anna could have put her one bullet to good use, but the girl's sneakers made no sound on the asphalt. Anna had never known she'd moved till she reappeared by Buddy.

Every cloud, Anna thought as she realized that she was now between Alexis and both pistols. There was one choice for life left.

"Alexis," she said softly. "Run into the trees now. *Now.*" Anna didn't choose to call attention to herself by turning and she didn't hear any movement. "Run or die," she hissed.

Alexis ran. Cuffs still dangling from one wrist, Buddy snatched a pistol from Candace, grabbed a handful of Beth's hair and jerked her to her knees, the barrel rammed into the soft cheek.

His mask—masks—were disintegrating. It was becoming possible to read his face as desperation ate away layer upon layer of deception. Anna watched his narrowing options flicker through his mind as his eyes flickered from Beth to Anna to the woods where Alexis had disappeared.

Time was short. Campers would soon be wandering to the trailhead or returning to their cars. More shots fired would raise the level of alarm, hasten the process. He dropped the idea of trying to coerce Alexis out of hiding.

"Car keys?" he snarled at Anna.

"Top of the left front tire."

"Get the car," he ordered Candace. "The patrol car." There weren't many visitors and Anna's NPS patrol vehicle was easy enough to spot. Candace, the gun with its single chambered round dangling at her side like a forgotten toy, moved toward the car with a robot's measured pace.

"Walk ahead," Buddy told Anna. To convince her to do as she was told, he jammed the barrel of his 9 mm into Beth's cheek so hard Anna heard the crepitus of broken teeth through the soft tissue. The girl made no sound. Her four weeks of "training" was coming back to her. Eight or ten steps into the parking lot, Anna was told to stop.

The sound of the car starting let them know Candace had found the keys. The Crown Vic backed up awkwardly, then described an uncertain path across the tarmac to lurch to a standstill behind an oversized recreation vehicle and a VW bug twenty or thirty feet away.

"Stay," Buddy ordered Anna.

Careful to keep Beth between himself and her, he went toward the car, turning so he would not lose sight of Anna. Beth's head was held at the level of his waist, the gun hard in her cheek. Hair hid her face. Blood and saliva trailed down in shining lines on the black pavement.

Candace had left the Crown Vic, walking

around the rear of the car back toward her master. Soon Beth would be in the car's cage, Candace or Anna with her. Buddy would drive them out of the park. Then he would kill them. The only reason they'd survived these last minutes was his reluctance to make more noise than he had to, leave telltale corpses that would inspire 911 calls to the rangers who would send out an all-points bulletin for an NPS vehicle.

Anna wasn't getting in that car. If she had to be a corpse she intended to be an inconvenient corpse.

Buddy and his captive drew level with her. Keeping his eyes battened on hers, he began crabbing back toward the Crown Vic. When he was five or six feet past her, Anna raised her hands over her head, gently waggling her fingers. "If I might make a suggestion . . . ," she said, taking a firm step forward.

"Don't," Buddy retorted and jumped back quickly to maintain the distance between them. It was what Anna had been hoping for. When she'd come forward, she'd stepped on the tether trailing from the rope hobbling his ankles.

Sudden stoppage unbalanced him and he

fell. Startled, his grip loosened on Beth's hair. Bent double, blinded, she half fell, half walked on.

"Run, Beth," Anna yelled as she snatched up the rope. Buddy was taking aim. At point-blank range he could scarcely miss. Anna jerked the rope hard and he fell onto his back, the gun still in his hands.

"Go home, Candace. Go home," he screamed as he rolled over, fighting for position.

The command took Anna off guard and she glanced quickly to where the ruined child stood behind the Crown Vic. With no more emotion than she had shown when torturing Anna, Candace was calmly putting the barrel of the SIG Sauer with its single bullet into her mouth.

thirty-four

Till a noise, a car backfiring or the hard slamming of a door, woke her, Heath hadn't known she'd been sleeping. Forehead against the window, she'd drifted seamlessly from consciousness to unconsciousness. Judging by the quality of the light, she'd not been out long. Fifteen minutes maybe. Sharon was not yet back. Not finding the girls in the bathrooms, she must have gone up the trail a little ways to the campsites.

Wasting time. Heath turned as far as she could in the RV's passenger seat. Patty, too, had succumbed to Morpheus' charms.

Curled up on her side like a kitten, she slept on the padded bench in the breakfast nook. The ignition keys Sharon had entrusted to her for safekeeping had dropped from her fingers to the carpet beneath the table.

"Wiley," Heath whispered. The rangy dog stretched, front paws out, hind quarters high in what could have been mistaken for obsequious homage if one did not know Wiley, then ambled over to put his chin on his mistress' knee. Heath scratched behind his ears because she loved the way he loved it, then gave him his first command of the day.

"Get keys," she said and pointed to where Patty had dropped them. He looked at her as if he'd hoped for something a bit more challenging, then fetched the keys, holding them delicately with his front teeth.

"Good boy." Heath dropped them into a cup holder in the central console, one of approximately two hundred cup holders standard with this model, then pushed up to maneuver her nether half from the passenger side to the driver's side. Her elbows buckled and she fell back into her seat, surprising a comic book "Oof!" out of her. She'd forgotten her marathon roll the previous night. Muscles in arms, shoulders and upper back had been worked to exhaustion. They didn't ache much—she could look forward to that in eighteen hours or so—but they'd effectively been turned to jelly.

Changing tactics, she used the dashboard and the high seatback and swung rather than lifted herself from one seat to the other.

Patty never stirred. At nine she still retained the sleeping skills of the innocents.

Heath hated to abandon Sharon, but there was no help for it. An emotionally damaged young woman, a child and a paraplegic weren't anybody's dream team when it came to rescuing damsels in distress. Heath wanted as many armed law enforcement types as could be raised.

She readjusted the side mirror. A reflection from behind the RV appeared like the fairy-tale granting of a wish. In the glass an NPS patrol vehicle moved at a snail's pace across the lot.

In another instant she would have begun honking and hollering to catch the driver's attention, but the sun broke between the trees and spotlighted the front seat of the Crown Vic. It was being driven by a child, a kid whose head barely topped the steering wheel. Reality shifted. For an instant Heath didn't know if she'd awakened and taken the driver's seat or still slept in the passenger seat and was dreaming.

"Shit," she whispered. This crude reaction of lips, tongue and bad manners reassured her she was awake. More to the point, she was now alert. Adrenaline had cleared the tunnel vision of ignition keys and fanny transfers.

Turning the mirror she saw three people: Anna Pigeon, the limpet and another park ranger. Anna Pigeon looked like she'd been through the wringer. Alexis was nowhere to be seen, nor was Sharon. The limpet was safe in the male ranger's embrace but bent nearly double as if she suffered from a stomach ailment. Stance, spacing, expressions: something was terribly wrong. The male ranger backed away from Anna Pigeon and Heath saw the gun he held to the limpet's head and his fist in her hair.

The dark-haired child climbed from behind the wheel of the Crown Vic and walked around the rear of the car. She, too, carried a gun. In her hand it looked oversized, macho, like Clint Eastwood's weapon in a Dirty Harry movie. The girl didn't point it at anyone but held it cradled in her arms as if it were a baby.

Anna Pigeon was standing stock-still. Arms, legs, face, uniform were filthy, caked with mud, muck and dirt. Her hands hung limply at her sides. She was the only one who appeared unarmed.

As Heath watched, the ranger holding Beth sidled past Anna. Anna raised her hands in surrender, said something, then stepped forward.

With a rapidity that was hard to follow, the scene began to unravel. The male ranger sat down abruptly on the pavement. Pigeon snatched something off the ground and began jerking and shouting like a lunatic. Beth broke free and began to run. The ranger who'd fallen to the asphalt was struggling to sit up, to take aim. Each time, Pigeon jerked him like a fish on a line. Three bullets were fired. Heath heard glass breaking but had no idea what had been hit.

Suddenly Anna Pigeon screamed, "No, no!"

Heath looked to where the dark-haired girl stood, watched her put the barrel of a gun into her mouth.

Then Pigeon was running toward the sui-
cidal child. As her boots left the ground in a
flying tackle Heath saw the ranger on the
ground roll over, plant his elbows on the tarmac, and take aim at Anna Pigeon or the
fleeing form of Beth.

"Goddamnmotherfuckingsonofabitch,"
she let out on one long breath. The intensity
of her anger could find no adequate words
to express itself. Fury boiled up from within
her with the terrifying and unstoppable force
of magma erupting from the center of the
earth.

She turned the ignition key, dropped the
RV into reverse and squeezed the gas lever
to the steering wheel.

thirty-five

There was no time. Candace was beyond the reach of anything but force. She was "going home," taking the one ticket out of Hades that Buddy had allowed her to keep, to believe in. In her usually expressionless face was the first thread of what might have been joy Anna had ever seen there.

"No! No!" she screamed, more in hopes of distracting Candace than convincing her, and threw herself at the underweight girl in a flying tackle.

As she smashed into Candace, a gunshot rang out. The two of them struck the ground with such force Anna's brain was knocked loose in her skull. One of them cried out. A good sign. Somebody was still alive. Anna was base enough to be glad it was her. Candace was in her arms. The gun fired again. An engine roared to life. Anna looked up to see a wall of metal and rubber descending fast.

A thump and the immense vehicle jarred to a stop. Beneath the double wheel on the right side was Buddy. The RV had not run completely over him and the wheels pinned him to the ground.

Amazingly, terrifyingly, he was still alive. Slowly, he turned his head and looked at Anna. His eyes—sclera, iris, everything but the pupil—were red, blood forced into them. Blood leaked from his nose and mouth, from his ears.

The SIG Sauer was still in his right hand. Bit by bit he began forcing it around, toward Anna and the girl she held.

Candace wriggled and Anna saw she was dragging the pistol with its single bullet from beneath them. Whether she meant to kill herself, Anna or Buddy, Anna didn't choose to find out.

"Here, honey, let me," she said. She took the semiautomatic from Candace's nerveless fingers, stretched her arm along the pavement and squeezed the trigger, sending a bit of lead into Buddy Ray Stephen's brain. A neat small hole appeared between and just above his brows, the place the third and all-seeing eye was said to dwell. Then the strangest thing happened.

Anna had seen people die before, not a lot but more than most women her age, more than she would have chosen to. She'd seen them die in peace, by violence and, a time or two, at her own hand. Cats, dogs and, once, a wild deer had died in her arms. She had seen life go out of the eyes, the quick become the dead, the windows of the soul close.

Nothing happened in Buddy's eyes. Nothing. They looked precisely the same dead as they had alive. It unnerved her so completely, had she had the ammunition, she would have shot him a few more times. To be sure. To make him blink. To be safe. To end him.

With a physical jerk of her head she broke the gaze his eyes had trapped her into and looked to Candace. She had to be miserably uncomfortable. One arm was trapped beneath her chest, her cheek was mashed into the asphalt; Anna lay across her back, but she didn't squirm or complain. She, too, was staring at the blood-red and black of Buddy's eye.

The fragile thread of joy that had softened her face as she put the gun barrel in her mouth was gone, replaced by what looked like envy. Candace stared at the bloody broken corpse of her captor, her torturer, her rapist, and felt envy.

Buddy had gotten to go home.

The world was full of high places, sharp objects, fast cars. Candace was going to be exceedingly difficult to keep alive. Buddy hadn't ended. Buddy was still going to kill her.

"Beth! Beth!"

It was Heath Jarrod shouting. Anna was pulled back from that place where death was the greatest good. She pushed to her feet. "Don't look at him," she ordered, but Candace could not look away.

Anna grabbed her upper arm in the same hard pincer grip her maternal grandmother had used to propel her and Molly from place to place, the kind of grip that left no bruise but poked painfully into the hollow between muscle and bone. "Let's go. Up."

Candace peeled herself from the asphalt, her eyes on Buddy's till elevation caused the rear bumper to block him from sight. When the last of him, the final staring ruby eye, slipped beneath the hulk of RV, Candace was freed from the trance. Her head wobbled like that of a foolish dashboard doll and she turned, finally, to look at Anna.

She'd been freed of the trance, not of the spell. No gratitude and little recognition were reflected in her face. Only a sense of waiting.

"So wait here," Anna said, answering her own thoughts. Taking a deep breath as if for a forty-foot free-dive, she squatted down. For the briefest of moments she did not look under the vehicle. She was afraid Buddy would be gone. Or not gone. Afraid he'd reach out like a nightmare beast beneath the bed and drag her under by her ankles. "Damn you," she whispered, and lunged beneath the chassis, snatched the loaded SIG Sauer from where it had fallen from his hand, and backed out quickly.

Buddy was the only dead person she'd ever met that Anna didn't trust.

Candace waited.

All this had taken less than half a minute,

the time between Heath's last "Beth!" and now her demand: "Find Beth." Along with this shout came the low drone of hydraulics and the scrabble and leap of Wiley jumping off the lowering chair lift.

"Hey," Anna said.

"Hey," Heath replied. "Beth?"

Anna turned and pointed. Beth had been running past Candace as she put the gun in her mouth. With a startlingly focused part of her eye-to-brain circuitry, as Anna had knocked Candace to the ground she'd noted Beth ducking behind a hunter green Chevy minivan.

Heath didn't even glance toward the RV's undercarriage where her wheels rested on the spine of Buddy but, with a push that elicited a grunt and left what looked in the harsh light of the morning sun to be traces of blood on the wheel of her chair, rolled in the direction Anna pointed, calling Beth's name.

Decency, sanity, life began to return to the parking lot. Beth ran to Heath. Wiley looked on with canine delight. Sharon and Alexis, having found one another, returned warily from the protective cover of the woods and reunited with Patty. Anna, feeling a heel but doing it for the child's own safety, locked Candace in the back of her patrol car, then radioed dispatch.

Ambulances, rangers, both the useful and the curious, arrived: the superintendent, the assistant superintendent, Lorraine Knight, one of the other district rangers. A team was sent to Fern Lake Cabin to collect evidence, though between them, Heath and Anna had mitigated the necessity for a trial.

Responsibilities lifted, shifted. From a lead actor in the play, Anna became a prop that more important characters moved around according to their own requirements. She answered questions, described routes, detailed injuries.

As the only truck with toilet, refrigerator, beds and running water, the RV became the de facto convalescent hospital and interview room.

Before this benevolent incarnation, the RV, in its *Christine* aspect, had been carefully driven off the corpse. Buddy Ray Stephen. Anna had watched him being zipped into a black body bag. Before the plastic closed over his face he'd given her one last dead-alive glare. Anna had winked. They would meet again in one guise or another. When that came to pass, she again intended to be the last one standing.

Freed from the paralyzing influence of Buddy Ray Stephen, the girls poured their stories out in a torrent. Not the gory details—for which Anna, in her cowardice, was grateful—but the main points.

Ranger Ray lured them to Fern Lake Cabin by telling them he was doing a survey on park use by young campers and would they help by filling out questionnaires. Of course they would, being good girls. On the pretense of giving each private space, he put one in each room. Starting with Alexis, he bound and gagged them with duct tape.

For the first week or more he kept them in a hole formed by piled boulders a quarter mile from the group campsite on the far side of the lake. When he moved them to or from this prison they were blindfolded. He led them up and down hills, in circles, then told them they were miles into the wilderness, no one would hear them shout or whimper or cry. No one but him. He said he'd sneak back at different times and listen; if he heard a peep it would be a very bad thing.

Buddy had been as good as his word.

They remained bound and gagged except when they ate or he was with them. The entrance to their hole he kept sealed with what sounded to Anna to be a three-quarter-inch piece of plywood cut into a couple feet on a side and wedged in place by the trunk of a downed pine cut to length for the purpose.

He told them if any one of them tried to escape he'd kill the others and their deaths would be the fault of she who disobeyed. He told them the police would arrest the survivor for murder. The cops would believe whatever he said. He was a ranger. Then, he told them, he would murder their families.

After a while he said he'd made them a new home and he moved them, again blindfolded, to beneath Fern Lake Cabin. During the height of the search, the three of them had been moved back to their boulder prison. The last time, for reasons of his own, Buddy had moved only Beth and Alexis, keeping Candace with him at the cabin. It had rained hard that night and the wind had blown in fierce gusts. The log wedge shifted and the plywood fell away.

Alexis said it was an hour or two before

they had the courage to crawl out. Once they'd put some distance between themselves and Fern Lake it was an easy matter to rub tears in the duct tape and free their hands and mouths. Even in their stone prison it could have been done but the knowledge that Buddy could return at any moment, that no one would hear if they yelled, that the door was sealed and there was no other way out, that any damage to the tape would bring swift and brutal retribution, kept them from the attempt.

The hike out took that night and all the next day. Afraid Buddy would find them on the trails, they walked cross-country, shoeless, in their underwear. A lot of the time they were lost. Near the end they reached Bear Lake Road. Fearful Buddy would look for them on a road, they crossed it and hid in the woods, following the creek till Wiley found them above the handicamp.

There'd been plenty of time for the two of them to plan the survival strategy. They'd disobeyed. Candace was dead, they'd killed her. Nothing would be gained by telling what had happened to them. No one would believe them. They'd be sent to prison.

Buddy would take Sharon, Patty, Beth's mom and he would hurt them, kill them.

Beth had nearly broken the agreement and told Heath. Heath, she said in a way that cut Anna to the heart, would have believed. But then Buddy Ray came to the hospital. He'd seen Heath in the wheelchair. He told Beth what he could do to a crippled woman, what he would do after he made her torture and kill her dog, if Beth talked.

The tale was quick to tell. Much as Anna appreciated having the gaps filled in, she was relieved when it was over. Beth and Alexis weren't done talking—and for that she was glad if the words gushing out cleansed them of any small part of the poisons they would carry with them as long as they lived—but they'd exhausted what remaining strength they had in the telling. Anna had been nearly as worn in the listening. The evil Buddy had done was living after him. If it was true, and the good was interred with his bones, she doubted the undertaker would need to dig any bigger a hole.

Arms around one another, the girls fell asleep on Gwen's bed with the suddenness of infants.

Sharon poured both Anna and Heath hefty doses of medicine, dry and red and welcome even before breakfast.

Heath sat outside in her chair beside the partially raised hydraulic lift. Anna sat on the lift itself, her feet swinging free of the ground.

"Wiley's on the bed with the girls," Heath said. "You're not supposed to let work dogs sleep on the bed but it seemed important to the limpet."

Anna nodded, wishing Taco was here, wishing she had a dog to sleep with. Remembering the new kitten, she felt better. It wasn't good to sleep alone when death was still on your skin, in your hair.

"Thanks for saving my life," Anna said. Vehicular homicide was more common than people might think, and one of the hardest murders to solve. Anna doubted this one would ever make it to trial. No prosecutor would want to try and convince a jury that a paraplegic woman— who'd saved the lives of two, possibly three, children and a federal law enforcement officer from the likes of Buddy Ray Stephen—should be put behind bars.

"You're most welcome," Heath said

politely. A minute ticked by. The two of them sat in the full glory of the morning sun watching the efficient bustle of park personnel and the eager curiosity of the visitors vying for space. Emily and Ryan, two of Anna's rangers, had finished with Candace. They closed up their orange bags and came toward the RV.

"I thought he was aiming at the limpet," Heath admitted while the emergency medical technicians were still out of earshot. "It was her I was saving. I'm sorry."

"I'm still grateful. Being *lagniappe* isn't a bad thing."

"Lan-yap?"

"A word they use in the South. A little something extra for free.

"How is she?" Anna asked as Ryan set his bag on the lift beside her.

"Sedated. On an IV of normal saline. She needs to get to a psychiatrist, a doctor and a McDonald's. Kid's a mess, all skin and bone. Janet's sitting with her." Seeing Anna's ignorance, he filled in: "Janet's in admin but she used to be a psych nurse. Dispatch asked her to come when they heard what you had here."

Despite their pervasiveness and ugliness,

both Heath's and Anna's wounds were superficial: scratches, bruises, abrasions, blisters. The gouges from the wire Candace had stabbed her with and the cuts from the paring knife were the worst Anna had suffered. Four of them were deep enough, cleaning them was a seriously unpleasant experience; but all were closeable with butterfly bandages, though Emily warned they'd leave scars if Anna didn't get them sutured in the next few hours.

At quarter till eight, Chief Ranger Knight made her way to where they sat, bandaged and wrapped in warm blankets.

"You have wine," she accused, sniffing the air.

"We are important people," Anna said.

"I'll pour you a cup," Sharon offered from within the RV.

"Coffee," Lorraine pleaded and rested one buttock on the lift. "You two have been busy little bees," she said.

"It's been a long night," Anna admitted.

"Long," Heath echoed.

"We're about done with you. You can both go home and sleep a couple days. Lord knows you've earned it." Lorraine looked across the parking lot, her blue eyes squinting against the early sun, her long hair afire with it. There was more gray in the red than Anna remembered from Yosemite. Both of them had had way too many adventures in too short a time. Two days sleeping sounded inviting.

Soon, Anna promised herself.

"What a mess." Lorraine watched the ambulance with the body roll away. The second ambulance, the park's old standby, called the Ghost Buster for reasons lost in antiquity, was just loading up. It would carry two law enforcement EMTs and Candace Watson. Buddy had done his work well. The child had been made a danger to herself and others. Anna wished she could nail her into a crate and mail her to Molly's Park Avenue clinic. If anyone could mend her, her sister could. Maybe something could be worked out. Molly did some pro bono work. Anna made a mental note to speak with Mr. and Mrs. Watson. A sudden thought startled her.

"Is there a Mr. and Mrs. Watson? Does the kid have folks? I've seen neither hide nor hair of them."

"She has a brother, much older," Lorraine said. "He's apprenticing or going to seminary or being indoctrinated or whatever these guys do in their sister compound in Canada. We looked at him for the disappearance but nothing came of it."

"He never came down?"

"He sent his prayers," Lorraine said noncommittally.

A snort came from the direction of Heath's chair. "Who looks after her?"

"The community, I guess. Everyone. No one."

Efficiently tending to business, the green-and-gray at its best was soothing, and for a bit the three women watched in silence.

Heath broke it first. "What now?"

"In cases like these that's a bitch of a question," Lorraine admitted. "If you two hadn't . . . If the perpetrator hadn't died, we could satisfy ourselves with crime and punishment. As it is we're left with only victims, pain that may never heal and dysfunction that might not be illegal. If Alexis sticks to her promise to testify, Dwayne Sheppard will be tried and probably convicted by the baby's DNA on the charge of having illegal sex with a minor. They'll charge him with child molestation, obstruction of justice, littering—whatever the DA can get to stick.

My guess is the rest of the 'patriarchs' and their harems will melt away, form another enclave or join a sister group somewhere, before the investigation spills over onto them. They may already be packing. Sheppard might be too. Cut his losses and disappear with what he's still got."

"Sharon's old enough to get legal custody of her sisters," Anna said. "Whether that's a job she's psychologically prepared to take on is anybody's guess."

"She's stronger than you'd think," Heath put in. "And there's a dad."

Both rangers looked at her in surprise. "I've had a lot of time on my hands," Heath said. "Or maybe I should say on my butt."

"Good work," Lorraine said. "You going to follow up with those three?" The chief ranger wasn't being lazy, it was that park jurisdiction ended when the girls were found. Human services took over from there. Or Colorado law enforcement. Apparently Lorraine had more confidence in the compassion and free time at Heath Jarrod's disposal.

"Yeah," Heath replied. "Yeah, I guess I am. What about the limpet? Beth? What happens to her?"

Anna could tell this was the question closest to Heath's heart. That was probably why
she saved it for last, waited as long as she
could that she might keep her hopes up
even if only for a few moments longer.

Enjoying the luxury of emotional cowardice, Anna let Lorraine answer.

"She goes home. We've got nothing on
Mrs. Dwayne, no signs of abuse that would
justify removing her to foster care. Nothing.
Whatever happens to Beth is between her
and her parents."

"I'm pretty sure Mrs. Dwayne was the first
Mrs. Sheppard," Heath said. "I'm guessing
it's the one legal marriage and Sheppard is
legally Beth's father."

Anna was relieved to hear rock-bottom
reality in Jarrod's tone. She'd known the
answer to her question before she'd asked
it, prepared herself for the inevitable. Out of
respect for Heath's grief, Anna said nothing.
Once again she had underestimated the
woman. Heath was not so much mourning
her loss as plotting to avert it.

"Should Sheppard get sent to prison,
would it be locally?"

Lorraine thought a bit. "I'd guess so," she

said at last. "This is going to be state, not federal."

"Mrs. Dwayne thinks her husband is God's testicles," Heath mused. "She'll stick close. From what I've seen of her, she's lazy and greedy. Dollars to doughnuts we can work something out that'll give me time with my limpet."

Anna raised her eyebrows in an unspoken question.

"There's Jarrod family money," Heath explained.

"Ah." Heath was undoubtedly right. Mrs. Dwayne could be bought, and probably fairly cheaply.

"What will you do?" Anna asked, because she'd genuinely come to care about the woman.

"Physical therapy first," Heath replied. "I sort of let that slide. I have a feeling I'm going to need all the strength I can get for this little adventure. You?"

"Same old, same old."

The hard-edged chuff of air being cut swelled over the trees and a neat dragonfly-like helicopter set down in the middle of the parking lot.

"My ride," Lorraine said. "Take a week off. Go home to your new husband."

"Wait." Anna pushed herself off the chair lift. Each and every aggravated cell in her corpus had stiffened during the long sit. Now they seized, ached, cramped or screamed. Anna let none of it show in her stance or taint her voice. "Let me go with you to recover Rita's body." She hadn't meant to plead but had been less successful at keeping it out of her voice than she had keeping out the pain.

Lorraine looked her up and down, a trainer viewing a spavined swaybacked nag. "You're a wreck," she said not unkindly.

Anna said nothing. She suspected she had that begging-dog look on her face, but there wasn't much she could do about it.

"Come on then." Lorraine turned and walked swiftly toward the waiting helicopter, as if challenging Anna to prove she could keep up.

thirty-six

The flight was short, minutes only, and Anna was amazed such a great deal of human drama, the sort that warps, changes and ends human beings, could have unfolded in this relatively tiny space. An emotional epic altering forever the lives of so many should have required more acreage.

On the brief hop she contemplated telling Lorraine about Rita's unauthorized wolf reintroduction program. In the end she didn't. The flight was too short, and the wolf pups would explain themselves far better than Anna could.

The nonstop entertainment Buddy had

provided since she'd met up with him at Loomis Lake had crowded Rita Perry from her mind. What with one thing and another, she'd scarcely given her a thought. Till now. Tears prickled in the corners of her eyes. Anna shoved them back with thumbs. Rita had been a good ranger, a first-rate paramedic. Had Anna been thirty years old and orphaned wolf pups appeared near a park overrun with dying elk, she, too, might have made an effort to restore the health of the food chain. True, Rita was a fairly heavy-duty Christian, but so was Pope John XXIII and Anna had always thought well of him.

Sorrow at the loss of Perry's idiosyncratic flame of selfhood in an occasionally dark human landscape melded with fatigue and grim images of Buddy Ray and Candace Watson's empty eyes. Feeling a weight like unto that suffered by Giles Corey in Arthur Miller's *The Crucible*, Anna slumped against the side of the aircraft and stared out the window, totally blind to some of the most beautiful landscape on earth.

The helicopter set down on the shore of Loomis so gently that, until the pilot cut power and the sound of the rotors changed, Anna was unaware they'd landed. Snapping out of her self-induced trance, she realized, though she'd begged Lorraine to be allowed to come, she didn't want to be here. Didn't want to see another corpse. Didn't want to feed the wolf pups into the bureaucratic mill.

Doors were opening. Lorraine, the pilot and Ryan, the delightfully baby-faced paramedic, were deplaning. Anna followed suit. For a moment they all looked at her as she got her bearings.

"This way." She walked toward tree line in the direction the wolves' den was located. Rita had been killed between the lake and the stone pen.

By night, shackled to a child, a gun at her back, she had thought the trek endless. By day, with armed rangers for company, Anna found herself only a few minutes' walk from where she had cuffed Rita to the tree, where she'd shot Candace, where Buddy Ray had shattered Rita's ankle with a bullet. There was no mistaking it. Brown-black and fly-covered blood soaked the needles.

Rita's blood. But no Rita.

"He moved the body," Ryan said.

There'd been a shot, Anna had heard it, then Buddy had reappeared in record time and in a foul mood. "No. *She* moved the body. She knew he'd be back. Clever woman. Rita!" Anna shouted. She was half wild, like a tired kid strung out on cotton candy at a late-night amusement park, but she couldn't help herself. "Rita!" she screamed again.

"Track," she ordered herself, ignoring her boss and her fellows. Tracking was a bit of an overstatement; following the designated trail was closer to the truth. Dragging herself, Rita had plowed a two-foot-wide furrow through the deep forest litter. Anna could see where she had tried to sweep the needles back with her hands as she went, but the differences in color and surface contour from the surrounding duff were obvious. That would not have been true at night; in the dark her track would have been close to invisible. Anna leading, they walked into the trees ten or fifteen yards. Just beyond a tangle of fallen logs the track ended. Needles had been heaped. It was here Rita had covered herself and hidden till Buddy Ray left. Given the state of her ankle, she should still have been here.

"Where is she?" Anna asked stupidly. Then yelled, "Rita!"

"You did say her ankle was shattered?"

Ryan asked respectfully, much too consid-
erate a young man to imply Anna had been
wrong or, god forbid, actually lying.

"I said that." Anna moved off along the
new drag trail, this one Rita had not bothered to try and cover. Every couple yards
there was a wider spot where she'd stopped
to rest—or passed out. The pain must have
been bitter. The track changed slightly after
the second of these stops, a smoother
groove ran along the right side of the drag.

"Smart," Anna said.

"What?" This from Lorraine, her first word
since they'd begun. The chief ranger had
risen to the top of a highly competitive
man's world, yet kept her intuition intact.
When others worked she could psychically
withdraw, giving them space.

"Rita rigged a travois for her injured leg, a
piece of bark is my guess, so it wouldn't be
jarred so much as she pulled herself backward." Because to her it was obvious, Anna
didn't mention that Rita was moving backward in a sitting position, her legs trailing.

"Rita!" Lorraine, Anna and Ryan hollered
in unison.

A tiny "here" trickled weakly through the
trees. Anna began to run. The sound had

seemed directionless but she knew where Rita would be; she would be with her wolves.

They found her lying near the granite to the right of the makeshift gate. Both feet were elevated on a sloping stone to ward off shock and reduce the bleeding in her injured ankle. In her rattled and shattered trek from where she'd been shot, she'd even had the presence of mind to bring her daypack. It served as a pillow and source of water. Despite pain and horrifying circumstances, she'd found sufficient strength to save her own life. Still she was a ghastly shade of taupe, that peculiarly unattractive color tanned skin takes on when the blood beneath it retreats.

Why she'd felt the need to put herself through what had to be a brutal form of torture, moving from her first hiding place uphill to the den, was a question for the psychiatrists, not Anna. Maybe if Rita thought she was going to die, she wanted to be with friends.

Rita waved weakly, smiled. Anna fell to her knees and started to cry. It was crushingly embarrassing, yet she was relieved she had the strength of mind not to give into another uncharacteristic urge and gather the younger woman in her arms murmuring, "Oh my poor dear."

Rubbing her face with the flat of her hands, Anna managed to smear the outburst of emotion around a little. "Whew boy!" she breathed. "Tireder than I thought. How are you doing?"

In this short chunk of time Anna had been gently nudged to one side. Ryan and the chief ranger, orange pack open between them, were beginning emergency care, getting an IV in to rehydrate Rita, cutting away sock and boot to assess and stabilize the ankle.

Anna allowed herself one sop to whatever maternal demon had chosen to possess her and held Rita's hand. Rita acted as if kindness and compassion were normal human interactions and squeezed Anna's fingers gratefully.

Not wanting to look at people during this bizarre interlude, Anna let her gaze wander: signs of scuffling, duff torn, moved. A lot of it and in a different direction from that of hiding place number one. For reasons she was not privy to, her backcountry ranger had been dragging her battered body hither and yon a good bit in the last twelve hours.

The pilot arrived with the stretcher and Anna let go of Rita's hand. The time had come. "Do you want to show the chief what's in this western Stonehenge of yours or do I do it?" Anna asked.

"You do it." The pilot and Ryan started to lift the stretcher. "Wait," Rita said. "Just one minute."

Anna figured if pictures were worth a thousand words, the item itself should be worth even more than that. "There's something you need to see," she told Lorraine, and held open the stick-and-twine gate into the den. Lorraine wasn't crazy about going first into this unknown, but pride or trust in Anna moved her gracefully between the boulders.

"Ah!" A cry of delight. This was good. It wouldn't earn the wolves a place in Rocky, that was out of park hands, but it would ensure they were well placed. "A wolf pup," Lorraine exclaimed.

"*A* wolf pup?"

Rita nodded.

Why one? Then it came to Anna. Had she told anyone about the wolves, it could be argued she was mistaken about how many. It would not be possible to argue they'd never been there at all. Too much wolfy activity had taken place to clean up in a single crippled night.

Anna looked to the wide-ranging tracks in the duff. What had it cost in pain and blood for Rita to move the other three to a new secure hiding place? No wonder her skin was the color of old parchment and lines of agony radiated out from her eyes and hacked downward from the corners of her mouth.

"Yeah," Anna raised her voice to be heard by the chief ranger. "Rita smuggled it in in hopes of normalizing the elk situation."

Lorraine emerged through the gate and closed it behind her. "One wolf wouldn't do much good. Still, I'm kind of sorry we found it. Let's go," she said to the stretcher bearers. "I'll send resource management up with a kennel for the pup." To Rita she said, "My agreeing with you in principle won't do you one damn bit of good."

Anna hoped that wasn't true. She personally was going to lobby her little heart out to keep Rita on the payroll. It was that or she hiked up here every other day for the next couple of months to feed the little buggers.

Thanks, Rita mouthed when no one was looking.

Anna returned a stare so blank even the most socially challenged could not mistake it. This would never be mentioned again.

"You'll come out next trip," Lorraine told Anna. "Your seat's been removed to make room for the stretcher."

In half a minute more than the time it took to tell it, the rear seat had been excised, the stretcher locked into place and the doors were slamming shut. Anna watched until the helicopter was gone from sight. A moment later the echo of its engine and blades faded as well. The carnage was being air-lifted from the park. It came to Anna that one of the many things she loved about her job was its immediacy. Law enforcement seldom had to deal with the aftermath of crime. That was for survivors, psychiatrists, social workers, prison guards, lawyers. For the officer it was me or them. When it was over only one remained on the field.

Me, Anna thought, and standing in the quiet, the sun on her face, she realized the world was new again. Or ancient once more.

Loomis Lake, the fragrant pines, the edged breezes, none were touched with cruelty, pain, sickness. People—humanity—were blessedly short-lived, blessedly unimportant, truly nonevents floundering about in paradise.

She sat down on the marooned aircraft seat, tilted her face to catch the sun and opened her eyes the barest of slits that she might watch the silver dance on the wind-ruffled surface of the lake.